PLAYING

FOR

THRILLS

WANG SHUO

PLAYING FOR THRILLS

A MYSTERY

Translated by Howard Goldblatt

NO EXIT PRESS

First published in Great Britain by No Exit Press, 1997.

This edition published in 1997 by No Exit Press, 18 Coleswood
Road, Harpenden, Herts, AL5 1EQ, England.

FIRST BRITISH PUBLICATION

A CIP catalogue record for this book is available from the
British Library.

ISBN 1874061-92-0   Playing for Thrills

9 8 7 6 5 4 3 2 1

Acknowledgments

The translator acknowledges the generous assistance of Shelley Chan, Howard Choy, Xu Xiaobin, and Zhang Dongming for various suggestions and clarifications, and especially Li Li, who read the entire manuscript and whose recommendations markedly improved the translation. Volume 2 of *Wang Shuo wenji* (Huayi 1992) was used as the authoritative text.

PLAYING

FOR

THRILLS

1

I stayed up all night playing poker with some friends. The first half of the night I was on a roll, I couldn't lose. Then my luck dried up. No matter how good a hand I was dealt, somebody else wound up with a better one. By morning, I was cleaned out, so I got up from the table to take a quick nap, but my mind was so fried that I was wide awake and spaced-out at the same time. I no sooner closed my eyes than poker hands began popping into my head, and sleep was out of the question. Then the phone rang. It was the mailroom; I had a telegram. Too lazy to go downstairs, I had them read it to me. It was from someplace down south: "My friend so-and-so his wife so-and-so arrive on such-and-such date by train such-and-such on honeymoon please meet and treat as you would me." Signed "Mingsong."

I slammed down the receiver and grumbled to Fat Man Wu, who sat there with a pat hand, slurping his tea and trying to get the banker to call instead of fold, "This must be your handiwork. You're always giving my address to your out-of-town pickups. It's great for you, but what am I supposed to do with them when they show up on my doorstep?"

"Don't pin this one on me," Fat Man said after learning who the telegram was from. "What makes you think I know anyone who has the nerve to call himself Mingsong? You're barely out

{ 1 }

the door before you start setting traps, and anyone, human or otherwise, who takes the bait gets your address. You thump your chest and say, 'Look me up next time you're in Beijing.' Well, somebody took you up on your offer, so don't act so surprised."

I asked if anybody recalled this Mingsong. They didn't. "What kind of person would call himself 'bright pine'?" Liu Huiyuan asked as he shuffled the cards. "I know a 'bright snatch' or two, but no 'bright pines.'"

We had a good laugh over that.

"Who cares who it is? I say to hell with them."

"*You* say?" I replied. "I won't send anyone to hell before I see what she looks like."

"Cold!" they said. "Predator . . ."

Now that my spirits had revived, I scrounged up a timetable to see when the train was due. I only had an hour, barely enough time to change.

"If anyone calls for me, tell them I'm at a meeting at Headquarters. That's where they can find me."

"Are you wearing your leather uniform pants? You don't want the gate guard stopping you."

"If it's a guy he can fuck off, if it's a girl I'll take her into custody."

After scribbling "I'm Fang Yan" on a shoebox lid, I stood at the exit holding it up for arriving passengers. They and the people there to meet them must have thought I was some kind of idiot. Which wasn't far from the truth, since I stood in the bone-chilling wind for two solid hours without anyone coming up to me. The station was a lot more chaotic than I'd expected. Late-arriving morning trains were just now pulling into the station, along with midday trains that were more or less on time. Passengers flowed through the exit in waves, and since I couldn't tell who was from which train, I had to be constantly vigilant, thrusting my shoebox sign in the faces of every decent-looking couple, then gazing with fervent anticipation. Eventually, it stopped mattering what they looked like; even if the girl was ugly, I confronted her and her companion anyway. But nothing came of it, and by the time I bumped into some guy I knew who was there to meet his girl-friend, my spirits were flagging badly. He advised me to check the station timetable for arrivals and departures, which is when I discovered that I'd been using an old schedule, and that my train wasn't due for another two hours.

Two hours, shit! If I went home, I'd barely have time to catch my breath before turning around and heading back; but if I stuck around, the wait would kill me. At first I thought I'd dressed warmly enough, but the cold was working its way through my clothes and had turned my toes numb. Time to find a warm cor-ner someplace and get something to eat. But now that it was lunchtime, the local eateries were packed with noisy diners intent on only one thing—stuffing their faces. Tables were piled high with dirty, greasy plates, scraps of food, and puddles of spilled soup. The smell alone was enough to make me gag. So I took the subway one stop to try my luck at bustling Chongwen Gate. There, at least, the crowds were more civilized, the cafés and the food they served a lot cleaner. Sure, they were more expensive, but I could look at them without puking or feeling like my brain was being smoked. At a cozy, well-lighted fast-food joint, I fin-ished off a plate of so-called Italian spaghetti and a bowl of so-called American soup, then bought a can of real Chinese beer and sat down by the window to kill some time. A guy having a lei-surely beer with friends at the next table nodded to me, I nodded back, and when he pulled out a chair for me to join them, I got up and walked over, beer in hand and a smile on my face, then sat down after nodding to his companions.

"What've you been up to lately?" he asked with a laugh.

"Me? Not much." I laughed back. "How about you?"

"Not much," he replied. "Haven't seen you around. I hear you were down south somewhere."

"Um," I mumbled ambiguously, my attention caught by a real beauty across from me who was flirting with some bearded guy.

"I hear you made a pile of money."

"Not me, no way." I glanced at the second girl at the table. Nothing special.

"No need to be modest. What's wrong with that?"

"You heard wrong. A pile of money is the last thing I'd be modest about. I only wish you'd heard right. I sure wouldn't be hanging out here." The third girl at the table had pale skin with a touch of pink showing through, like a frozen persimmon.

"Anyone who won't tell his pals the truth sucks."

"Honest, I mean it." I turned back to him.

"Someone saw you renting a room in Guangzhou with a satchel full of money. Just last month, wasn't it, Tan Li?" he asked the good-looking girl.

She glanced over at me. "So you're Fang Yan."

"Well, someone finally got something right," I said with a laugh.

But she remained deadpan. "Do you know Sha Qing?" she asked.

"Yeah, I think I know him."

"Well, aren't you a wise guy?" Now she was smiling. "How can I talk to someone who calls a girl 'him'?"

"You really are a wise guy. What're you trying to pull?"

"Nothing," I said, smiling at Tan Li. "Did she say she knew me? If so, bring her over, and we'll have some fun. Old friends are always welcome."

"If you're such good friends, what do you need me for?" The smile this time was ambiguous. "But I'll pass the word."

I returned the smile. "No need. You'll do just fine."

"Uh-oh, now he's hitting on you, Tan Li. Watch out, he's pretty bad."

Still smiling, Tan Li glanced back at her bearded companion, who was talking to frozen persimmon. "Why would I want to go anywhere with you?" she said. "I don't even know you."

"Strangers at first, friends at last. How long can it take to get to know somebody? Don't treat me like a stranger. The minute I saw you, I knew we were made for each other."

"You're scary."

"Scary? Let's take off and leave these people to their own games."

Smiling broadly, Tan Li neither took me up on my offer nor turned me down. Instead she kept up the banter a while longer, until they all got up to leave, and she flashed me a big smile. "Gotta go. See you around."

"You're not coming with me? Well, if that's the way you want it. See you later. Don't forget me, now. Think about me at night just before you fall off to sleep."

"Are you like this with everyone? Your regular line?"

"Good guess." I laughed and waved good-bye. By this time I'd forgotten why I was there in the first place, so I sat there a while longer, feeling bored, and finished my beer. After crushing the can, I got up and walked out.

A strong wind had swept the sidewalk clean of debris and litter. Pedestrians were bundled up, hats pulled down over their foreheads and gauze masks covering the lower half of their faces, leaving only their eyes exposed as they scurried along. Winter days are cruelly short, and dusk was already falling. The street-lights hadn't been turned on yet, but roadside shops were already lit up. I headed into the wind for a while, but the going was so slow I turned into a lane where a friend lived. He wasn't home, as I learned by pounding on his door for an eternity. After retracing my steps, I went into a café to eat a leisurely bowl of soupy dough balls, which they proclaimed to be "dumplings."

It was dark when I walked back outside. Up and down the street neon signs were winking, although by then most shops were closed for the day. The evening commute was over, the streets were cold and uninviting. I headed toward Dongdan, where it was livelier; Changan Street was bright with trams shuttling back and forth. Spotting a crowd around a festive doorway, I went up to see what was going on. It was, I recalled, a street market, and I wondered if people were stocking up for Chinese New Year, which was still two months off. But when I got close enough to see the flashy clothes and hear the music inside, I realized that the place had been converted into a dance hall. A friend of mine was laughing and talking loudly with a doorman as he ushered a group of friends inside. I went up and said hi. He slapped me on the back and propelled me through the entrance.

White ceramic water troughs and display showcases, where fish and meat had once been sold, were now lined with soft drinks. A band behind a vegetable counter was playing dance music. The space between bobbing heads and the ceiling was festooned with streamers and light bulbs. Dancing couples schooled among the fish-display troughs with rapturous looks on their faces. Just this side of the canned-goods shelves, tightly packed bunches of wallflowers sat or stood watching the dancers, suave and superior. I saw lots of people I knew, all happy as clams. They also asked if I had "made a pile." At first I denied it modestly, but after a while it sort of got to me. How come everybody was asking the same question? Was this some sort of conspiracy? I turned my pockets inside out. "Go on, search me," I said. "And if that doesn't convince you, go search my home. Anything you find there is yours." That shut them up.

Pretty soon some stag friends and I tried coming on to unattached girls. Whenever we saw a pretty one, we said, "How about giving a guy a break?" If she turned around, we hit her with, "Ugly guys like us shouldn't be allowed to exist around beauties like you." It was the rare girl who could resist that line, especially if she wasn't all that hot to begin with. Blushes, giggles. All we needed to say then was "I'm out of your league, but what the hell," and ten out of ten girls would spring out of their chairs and follow you to a secluded corner to do whatever you wanted. Our first perimeter sweep yielded respectable gains: A few of us found the dance partners of our dreams. Now I'm no dancer, but I did have some fun with a pudgy girl by telling her she looked like Hepburn. When the music stopped, some guys I'd seen around walked up with their dates, pretty girls for the most part. I tried some small talk, but no one took the bait, and when I saw I was getting nowhere, I made an excuse and walked off. But as I was leaving, one of the girls asked her date who I was. "That dumb fuck? How should I know?" Shit, that hurt, ruined my mood. So when the pudgy girl walked up smiling, I shrugged her off and sat down to watch the show of dancing feet and trim ankles between the legs and bodies of people in front of me while I smoked a cigarette. Life's all about change. Good times don't last forever.

A girl with a finely sculpted face sitting all alone in a quiet corner on the other side of the market was silently watching the dancers as if she existed outside all the noise and activity. The lights, the music, and the dancers were in constant flux; she alone remained still and unchanging. I went up to her, more taken by her graceful beauty with each step. Surrounded by the lingering stench of fish and raw meat, she invigorated all who saw her. Her eyes lit up as she saw me approach. I stood right next to her. "Would you look at those people," I said. "They're off in dreamland." A smile crossed her face like the outgoing tide passing over a reef. I saw pink gums, and teeth as white as mahjong tiles.

I left the pudgy girl in a stand of pine trees after pointing to the only window in the building with a light on. "Come up as soon as that light goes off. I have to get rid of some card players first."

"I'm cold," she whimpered. "Why can't we go up together."

"Do the words 'gang rape' mean anything to you?"

Leaving her where she stood, I clomped upstairs and flung open the door. "Cops!" I shouted. "The cops are here. Drop everything and don't move!"

"We're not moving. Come on in."

Three men in civilian blue overcoats sat around the table. They looked friendly enough. "You're Fang Yan, right?" one of them asked. "We thought you'd never show up." He introduced himself and his companions as policemen.

"How come you're shaking? No need for that."

I said I wasn't, and if I was, it was because I was wired, not scared. I asked if I could put a few things together before we left, since no one would be coming to see me in jail.

"Leave for where?" he asked. "We're not taking you anywhere. You sound like a man with a guilty conscience."

No no. I said I hadn't done anything, I just wondered what

three plainclothes cops were doing here in the middle of the night thinking that I might have done something and that the best place to determine whether I had or not was the station house.

"We're touched by your faith in the police," the cop said. "But there's no need to get excited. We just want to ask you a few questions."

"I'll tell you everything I know," I replied, thumping my chest.

Great just great. The cop suggested that I step inside and sit down for our friendly talk, since trying to settle things with them inside and me standing in the doorway made them nervous, like maybe I might bolt and then they'd have to take off after me.

With a loud, throat-clearing cough I stepped inside and sat on the sofa, then sprang right back to my feet and frantically searched for teacups, tea leaves, and boiled water. After steeping the tea, I tore open a pack of cigarettes and scrounged up some candy and melon seeds, all the while keeping up a stream of friendly chatter and making sure the cops took the comfortable seats.

"Take it easy," one of them protested. "You're making me dizzy with all that running around. This isn't a social call."

They wanted to know about a former friend of mine named Gao Yang. I told them I hadn't seen him in at least ten years. After a stint in the military, we hung out together until one day he just disappeared. I asked around, but no one, including his kid brother, Gao Jin, knew where he had gone. He hadn't been seen since, though there was no lack of rumors about what had happened to him, the most pervasive, and most credible, of which had to do with how he had made a pile of money, bought a phony passport, and gone to the Philippines. People joked about how he'd started up a tobacco plantation on Luzon, others said he'd joined the New

Popular Front, but it all seemed pretty far-fetched, since none of these friends had ever been to the Philippines.

The cop asked when and where and with whom I'd seen him last, and what we'd talked about.

I said it must have been summertime, since we were wearing short-sleeved shirts, and still we were dripping wet. I also recalled seeing ice cream vendors under canopies up and down the street. But at the time we were in our great nation's southernmost metropolis, and the temperature varies wildly from north to south in this vast land, which, if you're in the habit of looking at the calendar, might mean it was springtime, at least in most parts of the country.

I said that a bunch of us had just been demobilized, so recently in fact that we wore "cool" T-shirts over our uniform pants. We were drifters, totally carefree, a bunch of thrill seekers who ate all our meals together, gleefully wolfing down food and drinking as much booze as we could put away. Day in and day out, one restaurant after another, all over town. There must have been other attractions back then, and we probably took advantage of most of them, but eating is about all I could remember, and restaurants were the only images I could conjure up.

One of those meals took place in an open-air restaurant, and that was probably the last time I saw Gao Yang. . . . I forget the name, but it sat in the middle of the block, like a big courtyard, sporting an open-air courtyard of its own, and that's where we ate. Seven or eight residential lanes converged on the place, which we stumbled upon as we were cruising one of the old neighborhoods. From the outside it looked like a great big garage, with a heavy wooden signboard—black letters on a gold background—over the entrance. By standing next to the concrete utility pole near the entrance we could see down several lanes laid out like spokes;

at the end of a couple of them were streets wide enough for pedestrian and vehicular traffic. As many as a hundred metal tables with spotty green paint were arranged throughout the courtyard, which was surrounded by massive two-story colonial-type buildings, replete with etched concrete pillars, intricately carved bannisters, and arched windows. The stone facings had turned black under the assault of wind, rain, smoke, and grease. The restaurant itself was in an old-fashioned Chinese building, with carved beams and painted rafters and flying eaves and shuttered windows that boasted the handiwork of master woodcarvers: Flowers, birds, insects, and all manner of flora made the building look like a multitiered stage. I might be wrong, but I think it was deserted: no diners *and* no waiters. Open windows above us revealed an array of redwood tables and chairs that were polished until they shone. Landscape scrolls hung alongside specimens of fancy calligraphy. Large potted plants, many covered with gorgeous, odorless blooms, stood in the corners. It probably didn't register at the time, but now that I think of it, that aging but still fancy restaurant seemed to be waiting for someone.

Conflicting images of a courtyard drenched in the sun's rays and a courtyard cooled by dark shadows were both strong. Now if the former was the true image, then it would have been before noon; but if the latter image was accurate, then it had to have been after noon. A third possibility is that we arrived in the morning and were still there that afternoon.

To this day I can see the smiles, the gestures, the exaggerated toasting and drinking, and the looks on everyone's faces as conversations rose and fell. On the other hand, the substance of that talk, the words created by all those flapping lips and twisting tongues, had, I'm sorry to say, vanished. All those happy moments, and not a sound.

Eight of us sat at a smallish metal table, two to each side. Gao Jin and Xu Xun were opposite me; Wang Ruohai and a randy girl called Qiao Qiao—our group grope—were on my right. Another piece of public property, Xia Hong, was on my left, alongside Gao Yang, who was holding her hand. Next to Gao Yang . . . at this point, the words began to sputter: "No, no, it couldn't be him. That'd make it all wrong."

The harder I tried to eliminate Zhuo Yue's image from my mind, the more stubbornly my brain retrieved it: Dressed in white navy trousers, he beams as he raises a foamy glass of beer and bellows from his seat next to Gao Yang. . . .

I tried a recount, but Zhuo Yue stopped me cold again. It was the same every time—I couldn't get past him.

"Maybe my memory's gone haywire," I said by way of explaining to the cops why the last person could not have been Zhuo Yue. He wasn't even alive then. A year before our discharge he was lost to us in a shipboard accident. If he was there that day, it couldn't possibly have been the last time I saw Gao Yang. Besides, at that time—we were all still in uniform—we didn't know Miss Qiao Qiao or Ms. Qiao Qiao, or anyone like that.

"Take your time, think things through," the cop said. "You're probably just a little confused." Nervously I tried again, but I kept sinking deeper into the tenacious illusion of Zhuo Yue sitting at the table.

"Let's put him aside, OK?" the cop suggested. "He was dead, after all."

What bothered me was that if we put Zhuo Yue aside, we'd have to do the same with Gao Yang, since the two are inseparable in my mind, at least where that episode is concerned. And putting Gao Yang aside makes Xia Hong's image incomplete. They were holding hands, and her leg was touching mine, so without her, there's nothing to prop me up. Proceeding along these lines, if any link in the chain is removed the whole thing falls apart, and there's no one at all at the table. But that's absurd. Which leaves only one option, and that is to forcibly separate Zhuo Yue and Gao Yang. Which then creates another problem: With Zhuo Yue gone, there's a vacant chair between Gao Jin and Gao Yang. So who was sitting next to Gao Yang? It's like a boat tied to a pier: A weak link anywhere in the chain defeats the purpose. No, I couldn't let that chair stand vacant.

Cautiously the cop asked again if I might be mistaken about who was there that day, that maybe there were only seven people, not eight. "That would clear things up."

I was adamant. "Every seat was taken, I'm sure of that. Two at each side. I may be semiliterate, but I know how to count."

I could see they still had their doubts, but they switched from questions about who was at the table to eliciting my impressions of Gao Yang.

I told them he acted pretty much like everybody else—he ate, he drank, he had a good time. Even after he was a bit drunk, instead of turning sullen or mopey, he remained in high spirits. We were bragging about money and women, all our conquests, everybody but him, that is. He just sat there smiling and sipping his beer, seeming detached, indulgent even, like a contented man anticipating even better fortunes in the days to come as he listened complacently to the woes of poor slobs less fortunate than he. We were still partying when he asked for the check, paid, and walked off with his attaché case. I saw him to the door, where a red taxi was waiting, evidently arranged for ahead of time. We shook hands and he climbed in. I heard him tell the driver to take him to the train station, and hurry. I never saw him again.

I described my last meeting with Gao Yang like an eyewitness to history. Truth is, I could have gotten the same impression from someone angling for a promotion or planning to go abroad or whatever. In other words, I couldn't be absolutely sure who I was describing, but I didn't dare tell them I recalled nothing special about Gao Yang that day. They probably already assumed I was holding back or, worse, was afraid of incriminating myself; their frowns made that clear. My predicament was that while I had to gain their trust somehow, I couldn't recall much about Gao Yang at all, let alone his behavior at the table that day, even though we'd been thick as thieves. My last memory of him dated from an afternoon back in high school, just before graduation. Having just gotten up from a nap, I was so sleepy I had to force myself to head back to school. I was so late I didn't see another backpacking student on the street. Gao Yang came wobbling up on his twenty-eight-inch bicycle, with its missing rear rack, the seat raised as high as it would go. After stopping and resting his foot on the ground as he straddled the bike, he sized me up, then nonchalantly announced that he was joining the armored division of a certain military unit. Those big eyes of his, set in an oval face, seemed especially mature, aloof, and indulgent that day. Alongside his foot lay a brown turd, deposited there by some anonymous child, steam curling skyward from a wondrous little curlicue. Maybe it was because of this perfectly crafted little turd that the incident made such a lasting impression on me.

The pudgy girl chose this moment to come tramping upstairs. I'd been so intent on dealing with the cops I'd forgotten she was waiting expectantly in the pine grove for me to give the all-clear signal. I was as puzzled as the cops by the knock at the door. "Reinforcements?" I asked. They shook their heads emphatically. "Then it's probably one of the Gao brothers," I joked as I went to open the door. I nearly jumped out of my skin when I saw who it was; quickly blocking her way, I tried to get her to split. But she was in no mood to be cooperative after standing outside for a couple of hours with the wind whistling through the trees, until her lips had turned blue. "What's your game?" she demanded with a loud sniffle. I was about to tell her who else was in the room when one of the cops came up behind me. "Who is it? Ask her in."

"It's nobody." I turned and smiled. "I borrowed a book from a neighbor and promised to return it today. She came to get it herself, since it was past midnight."

"She must be quite a book lover to be retrieving one at this late hour."

"You call *this* late? No way. Maybe for common folk like you and me, but she's a writer. They don't get started till midnight. You can't expect eggheads and us common folk to have similar biological clocks."

I walked over to the bookcase, pulled out the first book my hand touched—*Meeting Business Emergencies*—and thrust it into the pudgy girl's hand. "I'm really really sorry to put you out like this," I said audibly. Then under my breath I gave her Fat Man Wu's address and told her to go straight there. "Same compound. Turn right, past the garbage dump, can't miss it."

She knew right off they were cops. So without a murmur she tucked the book under her arm and scooted downstairs.

"She's writing a book on reforms," I said. "Never sleeps. If that sort of thing interests you, I'll ask her to send you a copy."

"OK, enough of that. We don't give a damn about your private life, but please don't take us for idiots."

"Where does it say a woman writer can't be fat?" I protested. "Don't judge a book by its cover."

No response this time from the cops, who lit up and made some small talk for a few minutes before the questioning began again. They asked what I did after Gao Yang left. I said I went home and reported to the Veterans Placement Office, where I was given a job in a reputable pharmacy dispensing salves and ointments. One block over from the station house. "Who knows, you might have bought medicine from me. I always treated cops well. Soldiers and cops, cops and soldiers. To a veteran a cop is like his own brother. I almost became a cop myself. One day a recruiter came to the office and handed me an application. 'Want to be a cop? Fill this out.' But all I could think of was how someone as rowdy as me might bring discredit to the force. But that's how close we came to being colleagues."

The cops laughed. "That would have made it easier to keep tabs on you."

"Are you veterans? Normally veterans are easy to spot. They handle themselves differently. You know, that special look of valor."

That seemed to win them over. Smiles appeared on their faces.

"A lot of my friends joined the force after they got out. You'll find them at headquarters and all the district stations. Xu Xun, he's one. Then there's Wei Ren. You must know him. He's at municipal headquarters."

"Look, let's knock off the chitchat, OK? There'll be plenty of time for that after we've taken care of business. You can talk as long as you want then, but it doesn't do anybody any good to keep going off in all directions now."

"Sure, fine, whatever you say. Go ahead, ask away."

"You said you went to work right after you got out, at the

pharmacy. Was it a full-time job?" The cop flipped back through his notes.

"That's right. Except for holidays, of course. But I packed it in after three years. Variety is the spice of life for us veterans. We can't be stuck in dead-end jobs. Always itching for something new. How about you guys, did you have trouble adapting after you got out? Most people live dreary lives, until things that used to stand erect all by themselves have to be propped up. Maybe it's better for you cops, with all the danger and excitement, all those knives, all that blood."

"The way we've got it, less than a month after you went to work you turned up missing for a week. Hold it, no need to write down what he just said. Nothing that's unrelated to the case," the cop in charge chastised his two partners, who were taking down every word. "Where did you go?" he asked me.

"Where did I go? Nowhere. Did I go anywhere?"

"You went somewhere, because the pharmacy extended your probationary period three months."

"Oh, now I remember. I spent the week in Guangzhou. I borrowed some money from a friend and went down there to peddle some clothing. Gao Jin and Xu Xun knew all about it, because when I got back, I took what was left over to their place to sell. They wound up trading it for some nookie. Oops, peddling clothes is illegal, isn't it?"

"That was the year after. You took off for a week the next year to sell clothes, and lost money. What we want to know is where you spent those seven days during your first year on the job."

"Beats me," I said. "I can't recall. I was feeling pretty bad, broke most of the time, so I just walked around, you know, roamed the streets."

"Think hard, now, this is important." The cop stood up and walked over to my bookcase, where he picked up a marble pen holder and examined it. Then he looked down at my marble ashtray, filled with cigarette butts, and a couple of marble paperweights next to it.

"I need some time to think, OK? I doubt that I did anything so wild I'd still remember it after all this time."

"Ever been to Yunnan?" the cop asked.

"No. But I've always wanted to. I hear the native girls let you watch them bathe, and they can give it away to anyone they want any time they want. Better than us Chinese and our stuffy Han customs. Somebody gave me those marble knickknacks."

"Who?"

"Gao Yang."

All six eyes lit up like flash bulbs.

"Uh-oh, what did I say?"

"When did he give them to you? Before that meal or after?"

"It had to be before, since I never saw him again after. But I forget exactly when it was. He also gave me a sword and told me the scabbard was silver plated. I bragged about it until some jewelry expert told me it was just tinplate. It was Gao Yang who said that Yunnan girls bathe in the river and that you can swap a pair of stinky old plastic sandals for five jars of sugar."

"Where's the sword now?"

"Don't confiscate it. It's a decorative piece, not a weapon."

"We won't, we just want to look at it."

"OK, but remember, you promised."

I went into the bedroom and slid a silvery scabbard out from under the bed. I showed it to them. "Note the workmanship on the handle." I told them that the inlays on the scabbard were colored glass, not real jewels. "You know, fish eyes for pearls." I drew the sword. The dull blade was etched with a floral design alongside a narrow trough. It wasn't very sharp. I struck a pose and did a little sword dance for them. "Put it down." They backed off. "Right this second."

I laughed. "No sweat. If I wanted to kill you guys, I sure wouldn't use this. It's just for show. Crummy steel."

"That's not what worries us. We don't want you to hurt yourself." They approached me cautiously from three sides and took the sword, which they examined carefully.

"What are these nicks on the blade?" one of them asked.

"Oh, I got those from hacking away at some sugar cane. You see, even that nicks the blade."

"Sugar cane? Where'd you find sugar cane?" Suspicious looks all around.

"My little joke," I replied. "It wasn't sugar cane, probably a tree or something. Put a sword in someone's hand and he feels like hacking away."

"Look at this dark stain. Blood, maybe?" one of them said softly.

"Chicken blood," I said. "I killed an old villager's hen. It was great fun, like Japanese soldiers attacking a village."

I reached for the sword, but the cop stuck it back into the scabbard and handed it to one of his partners. "We'll take this with us."

"You said you just wanted to look at it. Is this how you keep your word? How am I supposed to trust you from now on?"

"I said we wouldn't confiscate it," the cop assured me. "You'll get it back after we've had a good look at it."

"This is very uncool, I mean it."

It was nearly daybreak—the horizon had turned fish-belly white—when the cops wrapped things up. We were drained, and the smoky room had us in tears. It was like the end of a family reunion, with everyone reluctant to say good-bye. The interrogation ended with more questions about how I'd spent those seven missing days. After swearing up and down that I couldn't recall, and that I wasn't trying to put anything over on them, they gave up, and agreed to give me time to think. They'd be back in a few days, and in the meantime I was to write down everything I'd done from the day I was discharged up to the time I started work, who I'd seen, and where I'd gone. I said I could write a novel, and still not get it all in, and if I did it in journal form, I'd fill three notebooks. "No fanciful sagas, now," they warned. "We're not here for a good time or to nurture new literary talent. Make up a story, and you'll wish you hadn't." Feeling hungry by then, I went into the kitchen to make some noodles and eggs. I asked the cops, who were yawning and picking up their mess, if they wanted some, but they declined my offer, saying they had to leave. I told them this was no time to be polite, since all they'd do at home was get something to eat and go to bed, now that their workday was finished, and that after staying up all night, it made no difference whether they went to bed early or late. "If you're afraid I'll put poison or something rotten into your food, then just forget it." "Well, when you put it that way, I guess we could take you up on your offer," the cop in charge said with a smile. "Now you're talking." I said I'd never heard of anyone using noodles and eggs to sugarcoat a bullet. Now that the cops were back in their seats, I prepared the noodles, even putting some extra sesame oil in their bowls. Then we all sat around slurping our noodles like four old friends. They oohed and ahhed, telling me how delicious everything was, even treated me to a smoke when they were done. How, they wondered, did I support myself without a job. I said I didn't know, but somehow the money was always there. "Keep it legal," they warned good-naturedly. "If it's dirty money, you can swallow it, but it'll turn up soon enough." I said I'd never done anything illegal in my life, that I was timid to a fault. I said I was scared of falling leaves, and that everybody called me "Do-good Fang." They brought up the matter of peddling clothes, and we all had a laugh over that. A youthful indiscretion, I said. "Young and stupid." Besides, peddling clothes was no longer illegal. "You can peddle anything you want now, except for your fellow citizens." When the cop advised me to stop the nonsense, I told him to lighten up. They asked how we'd paid for all our carousing back then, since our mustering-out pay "wouldn't have lasted you three days." I said we spent Gao Yang's money. "Did some overseas uncle die and leave him a fortune?" I said no, that his family had raised cattle for generations, until his father could no longer make a living at it and had to sell the farm. First he served the Nationalist Army, then the puppet forces, and finally the Communist Eighth Route Army. One of his uncles was captured by the Japanese for conscript labor and spent two years in a Hokkaido coal mine. Except for that, he had no other opportunities, not even as a slave laborer.

"So where'd he get the money?"

"That was his business." I smiled. "It was no concern of ours if it came via sticky fingers or a strong arm or a glib tongue, just so long as we could help him spend it."

By the time the cops left, the sun was up, and in the courtyard early-rising old-timers were already out jogging and practicing tai chi and walking around the tree and limbering up any way they could, heads bouncing and tails wagging. I saw the cops out to their waiting jeep, where we shook hands like old friends. They told me their names: Zhao, Qian, Sun.

"The next time I've got business with the police, I'll look you up."

"You see, one bowl of noodles, and he thinks he owns us."

"Scared you, didn't I? Just joking. I've got my own pals on the force."

2

Fat Man Wu, who had just dragged himself out of bed, opened the door and let me in: baggy underpants, blubbery torso, cigarette dangling from his lips.

"So, you're still alive and kicking. I thought the cops would have done away with you in the name of the people by now."

"Did you get that express package I sent last night? Your pal thinks of you any time something good shows up."

"Balls. How could you ship her over without calling first? What if my wife had come home unexpectedly? The breakup of our happy family would have been on your head."

I grinned and reached for the milk bottle on the dining table, opened it and took a swig. "Pleasant surprise, no? You must have thought she was some kind of fox fairy."

"A very *fat* fox fairy." Fat Man was grinning too. "Why the fuck send me such plain goods? Nothing foxy about her. Freezing outside, and she was still all hot and sweaty."

"I thought you went for fatty meat." I put the now empty milk bottle back on the table. Still grinning, I took a look around. Fat Man's bedroom door was shut tight.

"So, what did the cops want?"

"Nothing. Just some old army buddies over for a good time."

"Balls. Why would old army buddies take down our names and addresses?"

"What? You knew the cops were waiting for me, but instead of tipping me off, you let me make an ass of myself."

"Those cops weren't idiots. We couldn't have put anything over on them. When they were through with us they said, 'It will go real hard on anybody we catch hanging around a certain building instead of going home.' So tell me, what's up?"

"They wanted my advice on an unsolved case."

"There you go, blowing the ox pussy again. You'd do that if someone was holding a gun to your head."

I laughed and headed toward the bedroom. "Hey!" he shouted from behind me. "Take her home if you want to horse around. I don't need the grief."

"Grief is exactly what you need. If there's a snag, I'll say you let me use your place to knock off a piece."

The pudgy girl was dressed and sitting dejectedly on the edge of the bed. She started breathing heavy when she saw me.

"What's the matter, Hepburn? Don't get all hot and bothered. I'm just your average Chinese man."

"Don't you touch me! If you've got something to say, say it. If you need someplace to put your hands, stick them in your pockets."

"Well, well. Little goddess. Why the act?"

"Stay where you are. One step closer, and I'll jump out the window."

"What's that? Who do we have here, Lenin's security boss,

or maybe Dr. Tota?* Go ahead, jump. You'll owe me big time if you don't." I walked over, smiled, and grabbed her by the shoulders; she immediately laid her meaty hands on my shoulders, and the shoving match began. She must have been a stonemason's daughter to have that much strength. A foot sweep, a two-handed jerk, and I was flat on my back. The slats groaned as I thudded onto the bed.

Fat Man Wu ran in to see what was going on. "No rapes in my place," he pleaded.

After easing myself off the bed, I stood there rubbing my hip. "Just my luck to run up against a lady wrestler," I said in awe.

Defiant to the end, she tossed her hair and held her head high.

"What do you expect after the way you treated her?" Fat Man glanced at the girl, then turned back to me. "Hepburn's mad at you, can't you see that? Don't forget, you left her out in the cold last night with only a bunch of trees to keep her company. What if some lowlife had happened by? I know I'd have been pissed off if you'd done that to me. Isn't that right, Hepburn?"

"You're no better than him," she fumed. "And stop calling me Hepburn. Why didn't you come in when I screamed? How can you call yourself a man?"

I smiled at Fat Man. "Hepburn here is one unhappy comrade."

"You don't have to leave," Fat Man said with a smile.

"Why not? What's there to do here?" I said.

*In the Soviet movie Lenin in 1918, the security chief saves the beleaguered Lenin by jumping to his death to create a diversion. In the Japanese movie The Fugitive, Dr. Tota is forced to leap out of a window by his pursuers.

"If he doesn't leave, I will."

"Then leave."

"Punks." The pudgy girl ran out of the room looking very unhappy. *Thud* went the door.

"She called us punks," I said to Fat Man Wu. "Now that pisses me off."

"What are you and me to each other? And who is she? Pals don't let some bitch come between them." Fat Man Wu, his face shiny with grease, chuckled loudly. "Besides, what was I supposed to do about my wife with that one around?"

Fat Man called Liu Huiyuan to invite him and the gang over for a couple of hands. I asked what he planned to do about lunch. "Winner treats," he said. When the others showed up, he told them about my wrestling match, and they nearly died laughing. Then they asked what the cops wanted with me. Nothing, I told them, they were just bored. When they asked what I thought of the little bride, the question didn't register at first. Then: "Oh-oh, I forgot about them." Well we played till noon, then had some steamed stuffed buns in the cafeteria. They wanted to play some more, but I begged off, saying I had plans for the afternoon. "What could be more important than a game of cards?" I said I had a date, then winked obscenely. They laughed. "In that case, you have our permission to go."

From Fat Man Wu's I went straight to the subway and boarded a car that was so toasty I actually dozed off standing up, holding on to an overhead strap. Naturally, I passed my stop, plus several more, before I snapped awake, ran up to street level, and tried to flag down a cab. Plenty came by, but none stopped, so then I started walking, and after a couple of blocks I spotted several parked cabs, all but one of which were on monthly hire, and that one would only take foreign currency. I said I know I know, and showed him I had some; as he drove off he explained that he had nothing against local money, but until he met his foreign currency quota for the day he had no choice. Foreigners in Beijing had begun dumping their money on the black market instead of using it in cabs, and locals who needed it to buy foreign goods were nearly crazed enough to storm the foreign legations, just like the Boxers. We Chinese would have to swallow our pride, and that pissed this particular cabbie off.

I sat in the back with a forced smile, nodding in agreement. Though I was barely able to keep my eyes open, I knew I had to stay alert for the verbal exchange about to occur, and would be well advised to be wary of this genial cabbie. If I fell asleep, he could drive me out to the Great Wall and take all the cash I was carrying, maybe even my overcoat. He prattled on and on. What gets me is how some people ignore the foreign money that's out there just waiting for them. Wherever you look you see hale, hearty, and very horny foreign men, plus hordes of single young Chinese women who contribute nothing to the country. Liberalize, I say, spice things up. Out with deadening old intellectual fetters, down with feudal concepts! You're a true patriot, I told him, a man who puts country first, a good person with lofty ideals. So I guess you'll just have to count yourself among life's unfortunates, since I have no foreign money and can pay you only in RMB.* When we pulled up in front of the hotel, I peeled a single foreign bill off the wad of RMB. This is all I've got. Now you can take me anywhere you want if this won't do it—your cab company, the police station, anyplace. It's up to you. But it won't alter the fact that this is the only foreign currency I have

People's Currency.

and I can't even give you that, since I'll need it for the ride back. Not only that, I want a receipt *and* my change. I'll scream if you don't give it to me. You may think this is unfair, that it's a bad bargain, that I've tricked you, that your good deed has gone unrewarded—then go ahead, slug me if that'll make you happy.

At the hotel entrance I told the doorman I had an appointment with Gao Jin. He nodded and let me pass. It was a hazy day, and the lighting made the people in the lobby seem weary somehow, those on the move and those just standing around. Two rows of Seiko clocks behind the reception desk gave the time in cities around the world. Bright light shone through the welcoming doors of restaurants and bars, some with Western decors, others in the Chinese style; tables were laid out with elegant settings just waiting to be used, and the effect on anyone passing through the lobby was a leisurely mix of day and night. The mezzanine, with its bright, cheery walls, opened up like the sky. Sofas and potted plants set off the curves, the overhead was crisscrossed with steel beams and capped by a tea-colored glass ceiling, like a sports arena dome. The hotel offices were tucked behind a leather-covered door that opened onto a narrow T-shaped corridor with a low ceiling. Owing to the dim light and the closed doors on either side, it looked like a cruise ship passageway. Gao Jin wasn't in, which I learned after trying several doors, all of them locked, so I went back outside, picked up a house phone, and asked the operator to inform "General Manager Gao" that his guest was waiting for him on the mezzanine. Solemn airs rose majestically from a sprawling coffee shop with tables scattered amid artificial mountains and waterfalls and bamboo groves and betel palms and banana trees, where shadows and cheerful music merged. The only human sounds on the mezzanine came from tourist elevators silently whisking gaily clad guests up and down.

Gao Jin, dressed in a black suit, appeared around the corner and walked up on the lush red carpet. With a deadpan look, he waved to me.

"I thought you were coming for lunch. When you didn't show, I went ahead without you."

I said I'd already eaten—not there, someplace else—and asked if he was busy.

Don't worry about disturbing me, he assured me. I'm never too busy for you. He looked down at the coffee shop, then asked if I'd rather talk there.

I said it didn't matter. "This is your turf."

So we went downstairs and sat at a corner table in the all-but-deserted coffee shop. A waitress rushed up to take our order. Gao Jin opened the beverage menu and asked what I wanted. I said I didn't care, but he told me to go ahead and order. I asked what they had. Just about everything, he said, so I ordered a beer. "Mineral water for me," he told the waitress. As he closed the menu, he turned and stared at me, his pupils seemingly frozen in their sockets.

"The police came to see me last night. They asked about Gao Yang. . . ."

The waitress brought the beer and the mineral water, opened them at our table and filled our glasses, then walked off.

"Have you heard anything from or about him lately? What's he up to?"

Gao Jin took a sip of mineral water, then lowered his glass and puckered his lips. "He's dead. The police came to notify my folks that they'd found his body." He looked away. "They knew it was him from the discharge papers they found on him."

"He hadn't just died?"

"No," he said, shaking his head. "According to them, all that was left when they found him was a skeleton. The skull was missing, probably taken away by wild animals. Since his papers were laminated, they were still legible, more or less. So was the photograph. They figured he'd been dead at least ten years."

"In other words, back when they were saying he was in the Philippines, he was actually dead. Where'd they find the body?"

"Yunnan. In a remote gully near Mount Bao, not far from the Yunnan-Burma Highway. Apparently the driver of a vehicle that had plunged down the gully and somehow survived discovered the bones in a clump of grass.

"Have you got coffee?" I asked. "I could use a cup. I haven't slept in two days."

Gao Jin signaled the waitress. "Coffee, and make it strong."

"He didn't kill himself, did he?" I rubbed my face to get the blood flowing.

"No. The police said he'd been beheaded." Gao Jin swung his arm to demonstrate. "They could tell where the neckbone had been severed."

I straightened up abruptly, accidentally bumping into the waitress as she was walking up with the coffee, which she spilled on my pants. She quickly put down the cup, too embarrassed to move. Gao Jin glared at her and said in a low voice, "Go get some napkins to clean off our guest's pants."

"No no, that's OK, they're already dirty, they needed washing anyway."

"That's OK," I repeated when the waitress rushed up with a handful of napkins. "It's no big deal. No need for that, it's already soaked in."

Gao Jin kept glaring at the waitress, even after she was back at her station.

"It's OK," I said, "it's really OK. It wasn't her fault."

As if he hadn't heard a word I said, Gao Jin waved her over. "Where are you from? A trainee? What's your employee number?"

She was just a red-faced girl who kept her head down and her mouth shut.

"Forget it," I urged him, "just forget it. Let her go, I'm fine."

"No way. Whether you know it or not, this is a first-class hotel, and when the service doesn't match the facilities, I'm concerned. Nothing disturbs a foreigner more than having drinks or soup spilled on him. Our waitresses are so tongue-tied that even when they do manage to apologize, no one can hear them. I can forgive them for spilling something on a Chinese guest, but not on a foreigner. That's guaranteed to give the hotel a bad name."

Gao Jin summoned the floor manager, pointed to the offending waitress, and said, "Note this on her record."

We picked up our conversation after the floor manager left. Gao Jin asked what the police wanted.

"Mainly they asked about the last time I saw Gao Yang— when it was and where it occurred and who else was there. I told them it was when we all ate in that courtyard restaurant. You remember, you were there. A bunch of us guys and those two lays. That's about all I told them. Truth is, after all these years, I don't recall much about that get-together. About all we were up to those days was good clean fun, and if anyone says that something we did could have led to Gao Yang's death, I sure can't tell you what that was."

"That's what I told them, too," said Gao Jin as he drummed the table with his fingers. "He may have been my big brother, but as you know, we stayed out of each other's affairs. He was closer to you guys than he was to me. Things he might tell you he wouldn't let on to me, like women, for instance."

I laughed and Gao Jin looked up. I sipped my coffee. "My guess is that the cops think I killed him."

Gao Jin just looked at me, betraying no emotion.

"They took a Yunnan sword with them when they left my place. The blade was nicked and bloodstained. They didn't say a word about Gao Yang being dead or anything, and it wasn't until you told me just now that I realized they must think it was that sword that killed him."

"Well, was it?"

I laughed. "Gao Yang himself gave me that sword, the first time he came back from Yunnan. Remember? How could anybody give away a sword he used to cut off his own head? This is no tale from *The Immortal Monkey*."

Gao Jin just gazed at me for the longest time, then looked down at the table, picked up his mineral water, and took a drink. He leaned back in his chair and gazed at me again. "I don't know anything about that. Gao Yang went to Yunnan more than once, and he always brought things back for people. All I know is he was no nature lover. He could have spent his whole life in big coastal cities down south, where there's plenty of strong wine, good food, beautiful women, and the facilities to indulge his fantasies. When the police told me he died in a remote mountain gully in Yunnan I admit I was puzzled. If he had to die, it should have been in the arms of a beautiful woman in the soft bed of a VIP suite at a fine hotel or some place like that."

"For brothers, you guys hardly knew each other."

Beep beep. The pager at Gao Jin's belt sounded. He reached down and clicked it. A phone number and a name appeared in the digital readout window. "Sorry, I'm being paged. I have to make a phone call." He walked over to the reception desk, where I saw him dial a number and talk for several minutes, then hang up and make another call, a brief one, before returning to our table. Halfway there he stopped a cocktail waitress, pointed to a foreign couple who had just sat down beside the fountain, and told her to go take their order.

"Do you remember what we did when we returned from the south?" I asked. "The cops say seven days are unaccounted for during the time I worked at the pharmacy. They probably figure I took off for Yunnan, murdered Gao Yang, and returned without anyone knowing I was gone." I laughed. "I have no idea where I spent those seven days. I know I'd have let you in on anything that happened, since we saw each other a lot back then. Does anything come to mind?"

"I seem to recall you going to Guangzhou to peddle clothes. You did, didn't you?"

"That I remember, but they say it didn't happen till the year after. Soon after we returned to Beijing, I apparently took off for somewhere. Since they keep better tabs than us, I have to assume they know what they're talking about."

"Nothing comes to mind, except maybe you at that pharmacy near Front Gate selling anti-itch lotion over the counter. And the way you flirted with that cashier—did you ever score, by the way? And I remember how you stole rubbers and handed them out to your pals, saying they were 'on you.' You haven't really changed, still a bad egg. That was my first thought when I saw you on the mezzanine—once a bad egg, always a bad egg. It's like you've been in a deep freeze all these years and just reentered the world a couple of days ago." The trace of a smile finally showed on Gao Jin's face. His eyes flashed, a sign of contentment, the light of friendship. He was the Gao Jin of old—my staunch friend.

"Was I really that bad?" I asked with a laugh. "How come I remember being such a good kid back then?"

"Oh? You were a bad egg, all right. Skin an inch thick. You sweet-talked so many girls into the sack that I was tempted to turn you over to the authorities so they could put a bullet in that corrupt head of yours."

"Well, you've changed," I replied, laughing. "General Manager Gao, the sound of it gives me goosebumps. And seeing the way you are now, like some cocky bulldog, makes my heart race."

"*I've* changed?" Gao Jin straightened his suit. "I don't think so. This is how I've always been, like this transparent water here: Put something red next to it and it turns crimson, put it up against something black, and it goes dark."

His pager went off again. With a grumble he stood up. "That's how it goes," he said. "Someone's always looking for me. There's so much to do. But you can't take the job without the responsibilities that go with it."

"You've done OK for yourself," I said when he returned from this latest phone call. "Nobody would ever come looking for me, even if I asked them to. Except the cops, that is."

"The whole business sucks." Gao Jin ordered another cup of coffee, then added sugar and stirred it for me when it arrived. "I've just about had it," he said. "I'm not cut out for this boss stuff. I'll stay on for another year or so, then pack it in. I need my freedom."

"Don't say that. Hang in there. You're bound to move up, and that'll give me more reason to blow the ox pussy—hey, know that guy? He's my pal. And if you've got any good jobs, you can give them to me instead of someone else. Who cares who does the work, so long as it gets done?"

The pager went off again.

"I'm out of here. You're too busy. We'll talk later."

"I'll see you out."

"No need, I can find my way."

"But I want to. Wait here, I'll be right back."

Gao Jin trotted over to the registration desk for one more phone call. The waitress came up with our check, which Gao Jin took from her as he walked up to the table and signed with a ballpoint pen he took from his inside pocket. Then he walked me to the entrance.

We passed by upscale boutiques and fine restaurants. The employees greeted him with a respectful "General Manager Gao," which he accepted with the dignity fitting his position.

"You should get a job, have a steady income. A man over thirty shouldn't be riding the train one stop at a time. Knocking around in your twenties is one thing, but it's different in your thirties, and by the time you're in your forties and fifties, you wind up as a bum, an old beggar."

"How about taking me on as a waiter? I'm good at bowing and scraping."

"I don't want you, you're too old. But if you're serious about getting a job . . . ah, forget it, why should I worry? Do what you want."

"My best to your wife," I said at the entrance, where we shook hands. "I'll drop by to say hello one of these days."

"Now that you know where I work, don't be a stranger," Gao Jin replied. "And if you run into any of the gang, send them over."

"OK." I walked down the steps, then turned and waved good-bye.

"Hold on a minute." He caught up with me. "Don't treat this business with Gao Yang lightly. If you're not careful, the police might really think you did it."

"Don't worry. If it comes to that, I'll just tell them I was with you the whole time. You can be my alibi."

"Go ahead, if you can make it stick," Gao Jin said with a smile and a wave of his hand.

After saying good-bye to Gao Jin, I decided not to take a taxi after all. Having nothing to do and not averse to saving a little money, I set off into the wind and kept walking until I spotted a bus stop. Not so many years before, this area had been farmland, and I didn't know it very well. Each new high-rise looked like every other one, so did the crisscrossed streets, which were absent the signs that would have made things easier. Even the posted stops were new: such-and-such "inn" or some "cemetery." Obviously, this line would take me out to the sticks, so I decided to check with a woman who was waiting with me. She said to take the bus two stops, then transfer to one going into the city, that "It's the only way to get into town, no other bus lines nearby." I took her advice. Suburban buses don't come along very often, and they're usually crowded, which makes for slow going. By the time I was back in town, the evening rush hour was in full swing, and all the buses were packed with passengers in thick winter coats. You wouldn't catch me trying to squeeze onto one of those, not when I was this sleepy, so I stood on the busy street as dusk fell around me, wanting only to get some sleep until the rush hour had passed and I could be on my way. You'd think this was no time to be paying a visit to Zhang Li, but I didn't know anybody else in the area, so what the hell. As I feared, she greeted my arrival with surprise and anxiety. Her husband would be home any minute, she said, to which I responded, with a wink, "He can bump me off, but later." I headed straight for her unlit bedroom, sprawled across the bed, and was out like a light. I didn't even stir when she came in to cover me with a blanket. When I awoke, it was pitch dark, all warm and toasty, and so quiet I figured it must be the middle of the night. But when I looked at the Seiko clock on the wall, with its luminous dial and loud ticktocks, I saw I'd slept less than an hour. Out in the living room, Zhang Li was having dinner with a burly fellow sitting across from her. He stopped chewing, asked why I hadn't slept longer, and invited me to join them. "No, thanks," I said. I had to be on my way. "Are you OK?" Zhang Li asked. "You're not sick or anything, are you?" I said I wasn't sick, just tired. But her husband wouldn't take no for an answer, and when I said, "I appreciate your hospitality, but I won't dare come here again if you keep that up," he saw I was determined to leave and told Zhang Li to see me to the door. "If you're not well, don't pretend everything's OK," he said with genuine feeling. I said I was fine and walked out, with Zhang Li right behind me. When we reached the steps in the darkness, she said, "Sorry things didn't work out tonight. Come back tomorrow and I'll take the afternoon off." "We'll see," I replied. "I'll call if I'm free."

The streets were no longer crowded, but the subway was still packed. After squeezing aboard and finding a spot amid the bedrolls of a gang of laborers, I stood there about to doze off, recalling a dream I'd had back at Zhang Li's: We were in the courtyardlike restaurant, eating and laughing and drinking; everyone was there, but I was sitting in a different seat. I was on the other side of Qiao Qiao, and Wang Ruohai was on this side. Which meant that Gao Yang was sitting across from me, not Gao Jin and Xu Xun; and instead of Zhuo Yue sitting next to Gao Yang, it was someone I didn't know. His face was haloed in sunlight, so I could only see him from the neck down. The collar of his expensive striped shirt slid up and down each time he swallowed or laughed. In my dream I tried for a better look at his face, but no matter how close I got, all I could see was the haloed outline—his features were a blur. The fragmented dream shifted back and forth in time, like a videocassette that keeps fast-forwarding and rewinding. We got up from the table and retraced our steps to the entrance, where we hotly debated whether or not to enter the gloomy restaurant. Then we retraced our steps to the maze of narrow lanes, stopping to eat melting ice cream cones with chocolate sprinkles. I realized that the man with the blurred features and striped shirt was part of the group from the beginning, that he negotiated the maze of lanes with us, that he stood outside the restaurant next to the concrete utility pole with us, and that at each site he was positioned someplace where he couldn't be missed, saying nothing yet standing out from the crowd. At the metal table in the damp, mossy courtyard, he sat across from me, alongside Gao Yang, smack in the middle of bright sunlight. As we passed through the shadows on our way inside, I must have had a good look at his face, but that part of the dream was lost to me. The building, bathed in bright sunlight, took up all the surrounding space, like a multitiered stage, forcing out the other people and objects that should have been there, blocking them from my field of vision, or shrinking them, or collapsing them into one another, blurring their shapes beyond recognition. The more I concentrated on the images and people in my dream, the fuzzier, the fainter, or the weirder they got. It was like reaching into water with an oily hand to grab a sleek fish, then watching it squirm out of your grasp and disappear. In the end, the only clear image I salvaged from the dream was of Gao Yang talking the ear off the faceless man. The building, with its open doors and window, filled the space behind him, like a gigantic, silent eyeball or an enormous gaping mouth.

I wondered how much my dream reflected the realities of that moment.

3

Fat Man Wu was playing cards when I walked into my apartment. "My wife came home," he announced, "so we decided to move the Party group meeting to your place." He pointed to a stranger with large features. "We dug up a new member," he said. "Since we can never count on you to attend meetings, and you're always behind in your Party dues, we decided to place you on probation for the time being."

"You can take my place if you want," the stranger said.

"No, don't feel like it," I said. "I accept the Party's decision."

"What's up with you?" Liu Huiyuan asked. "You look like you just crawled out of a latrine."

"It's just possible," I said as I sprawled on the sofa, "it's goddamned possible that I'm a murder suspect."

Fat Man Wu took the cigarette out of his mouth, glanced at his cards, then looked up. "Lucky you," he said. "What trick did you use to turn yourself into a celebrity?"

"Don't think you're such hot shit," someone else said with a chuckle. "I advise you to hold on to those two ounces of meat down there. I doubt you could even give it away."

I laughed. "What's there to say to dumb fucks like you?"

"What can we say to a dumb fuck like *you*?" They laughed.

"Who knows what you're up to. You're like someone heading into the wind for an eight-*li* trip with a hard-on that'll be gone when you need it. Just you wait and see."

"Oh, right, you've got guests in the bedroom. They're not cops, and my guess is they're the darling couple Mingsong sent. When you didn't show up, they hoofed it over on their own."

"Go on, get in there," Fat Man Wu urged me. "The bride's a real looker, tender as a fresh clam."

"Don't give me that," I said with a laugh as I stood up. "I know you're making it up. If she was everything you say, you'd be hanging around her like a pesky fly instead of sitting here playing cards."

I went into the next room. The newcomers jumped to their feet. I'd expected a lot worse. Except for their gaudy clothes, which they assumed gave them a sophisticated look, but actually made them look foolish, they had the airs of southern gentility. Story time: I told them I'd passed out on the way to meet them the day before, and some good Samaritans had rushed me to the ER. I was an epileptic, I said. Impossible to predict when a seizure might hit. But I apologized for missing them at the station. The guy said that was OK. The cardplayers had already told them about my illness, so they weren't upset. The groom was real tight with Mingsong, who had sent them to me, since Mingsong was real tight with me too, and had them bring me a couple of pounds of mooncakes. I was so hungry I started in on one of them and asked how Mingsong was doing, if he'd had a windfall, if he and his wife had divorced, and who'd been given custody of the kid. The guy said that Mingsong was doing fine, that there was no windfall, and that his wife hadn't divorced him, since they'd talked a lot about getting married but had never actually gone through with it, and as for the kid, the one you saw was probably his brother, since Mingsong had a kid brother but had never actually raised a kid of his own, though his girlfriend had miscarried several times. I cleared my throat and said who cared if he had a kid or not since it had nothing to do with me, and so what if they were two different kids. Since you're so far from home and have no kin around here, you can count me as family. So tell me, what are you up for? The groom stammered that they didn't have anything in mind, they just wanted to have some fun. Since there was no one to meet them the day before, they'd spent the night at the home of some relative of the girl. But the place was too cramped, with a *kang* that filled up half the single room, which the relative let them use; she slept on the floor. "That was too much for us." I could see that, so I told them that if they wanted to see where Chairman Mao was residing, I couldn't get tickets, but I could put them up, if that's what they wanted. No meals, but you can turn handstands in the place, if you feel like it. The bride and groom grinned from ear to ear and even peeled the paper off a piece of candy and stuck it into my mouth. Enough of that. I'm not big on etiquette of any kind, it makes me uneasy. I've never been coddled, not even as a child, so when you give me such a warm reception, out of the blue and everything, I can't help thinking that maybe I ought to be a little more wary. There's nothing wrong with that candy, I swear. It's from the wedding. From now on, we're going to be great friends. I can't think of anything better than having a friend like you, since we have so much in common, like age and all. If you ever need anything back home, just say the word. "Enough already." I extricated myself from their enveloping presence. "Where does that friend of yours live? You can move into my place tonight." They giggled and buttered me up a while longer before taking off.

I went back to join the cardplayers, and sat there with a silly grin. I'd completely forgotten what it was I was supposed to be doing, so I asked the guys sitting around the table. "Any of you remember what I was going to do?" Out came one raunchy, midsection comment after another: "Propping up the wall with one hand to free the other for something else," and stuff like that, which brought some laughs, and that loosened my brain just enough to remind me that I had to make a phone call. The telephone rang and rang, until someone picked it up and a female voice asked who it was. The police, I said. Xu Xun's at work, she replied, so why was I calling his home? I hung up and dialed the police station. The duty cop asked who it was. I said I was calling from Xu Xun's house. He picked up the phone, and when he heard it was me, he told me to hang up. "I'm busy now. I'll call you back." He did, after a little while, this time from a different telephone. His voice was barely audible as he said he couldn't talk over the phone, and he told me to come to his place the next morning. "Make sure you're alone." "Are things that bad?" I was still treating it all as a joke, but he slammed the receiver down.

I must have looked pretty bummed out, the way everyone was gaping at me. "What's wrong?" Liu Huiyuan asked as he dealt a new hand. "Something bothering you?"

"It's nothing." I forced a smile. "Just making things hard on myself, that's all."

"Whatever it is, you can tell us," Fat Man Wu said without looking up from his cards, a cigarette dangling from his lips. "Bottle it up inside, and it'll only get worse."

"Really, it's nothing. Besides, I wouldn't let it bother me, not me."

"Don't tell us if you don't want to," Liu Huiyuan said before Fat Man could open his mouth again. "Let's play cards, guys."

There was a knock at the door, and I went pale. The others, seeing the worried look on my face, exchanged hurried glances. They asked me who it was.

"How should I know?"

"Who but our darling couple, back already." Liu Huiyuan threw down his cards and got up to answer the door. Following some confused noise, the newcomers appeared, sweaty-faced and loaded down with luggage. "Here we are."

"So you're here. Is that any reason to carry on like that?" Then I smiled, got up, and pointed to the bedroom. "It's a cozy room. You could walk around naked and never catch cold."

"Oh, let me introduce you. This is Li Jiangyun, my wife's cousin. She's the one who put us up last night."

"Pretty," I commented as a lovely young thing followed them into the room. "If I were you, I'd rather squeeze in with her than move over here."

"They like a good joke," the groom said with a laugh. "A great bunch of guys."

"Hah," Li Jiangyun said with a smile. "I've seen more guys like this than you have. The place is crawling with them. If you don't need me anymore, I'll be on my way. Let me know if something comes up."

"Can I let you know if something of mine comes up?"

"No," Li Jiangyun said with a little laugh as she shook her head.

"Where do you live? Far from here?" Liu Huiyuan asked her.

"No, not far," the groom said. "She lives on the next street over."

"What's your hurry then? Sit down, take a load off. It's not every day I meet someone like you." I moved out of the way to let Liu Huiyuan shepherd Li Jiangyun inside.

"Maybe you'd better go home, Yun." The bride didn't like the look of things; I could hear it in her voice.

"She's safer than you are," Liu Huiyuan said. "Yun knows her way around. See that smile—she's not worried. But you'd better look out for yourself. Before the week's out, your factory-equipped model here won't have anything to do. It's your own resolve you'd better concentrate on stiffening."

That broke us up. "Take it easy," the guy said to his wife. "Just some friendly banter. We're among friends."

"Not so fast. Friends don't count at a time like this, do they, Fang Yan?"

"That's right." I nodded. "Every man for himself."

Li Jiangyun confidently let herself be escorted into the room, smiling and nodding at Fat Man Wu and the others. Liu Huiyuan introduced her around, then poured tea.

"Did you say Li Jiangyun?" Fat Man lowered his cards, took a drag on his cigarette, and laughed. "Couldn't call you famous, since I've never heard of you."

"And who might you be?" Li Jiangyun replied laconically. "One of those people who couldn't make people hear of him if his life depended on it?"

"Ever hear of him?" Fat Man pointed to me with his cigarette hand.

Li Jiangyun turned to look at me. "Didn't I see you on a wanted poster a while back?"

"A wanted poster, she says." We all laughed. "Our pal here's a writer," Fat Man said. "You must have read his stuff.

The only book with a larger print run is *Selected Works of Chairman Mao*."

"Is that so?" She looked at me again. Keeping my eyes lowered, I nodded.

"What have you written," asked the bride.

"Not so fast," Fat Man broke in. "You'll answer your own question as soon as I tell you his pen name: Qiong Yao."*

That always got a big laugh, even from people who had heard it before. But this time I didn't laugh. I had some more tales in my bag.

"He does more than write books. He's an actor and he's made movies. What you call a Renaissance man. But he's better known in Europe than here in China."

"Who have you played?" The empty-headed little bride was falling for it, hook, line, and sinker.

"A young Gorky and a young Zhou Shuren†—before they grew moustaches."

"Really?" The bride *and* the groom both eyed me cautiously. By then I was smoking a cigarette, and I raised my head, as if posing for a portrait.

"You *do* look like them."

"His newest film is a joint-venture deal with the Czechs. It's called *The Mole's Story*. He plays the male lead. Also premoustache period."

The laughter this time was loud and hearty. And it included

---

*A writer of popular fiction in Taiwan. Her novels were enormously popular in China in the 1980s.
†The real name of Lu Xun (1881–1936), modern China's most famous writer.

Li Jiangyun, who turned to the empty-headed bride. "Haven't you figured it out yet that they're pulling your leg?"

"You married?" Fat Man Wu, suddenly a model of seriousness, asked Li Jiangyun.

"No." She smiled. Then she turned back to us and pouted.

"You ought to get married," Fat Man said with mock seriousness. "You're not a kid, you know. You're OK-looking now, but that'll go soon enough."

"Thanks, but I actually am married, so you can stop worrying." Li Jiangyun laughed.

"Glad to hear it," Fat Man said. "Now you should be thinking about taking a lover. Once you've fulfilled your marital obligation, it's time to think about yourself, about hooking up with somebody you really like."

"You've got an answer for everything, haven't you?"

"That's the primary aim of our party. If you were a member, we'd have to expel you, but since you're not, it's our duty to prepare you for membership. The one thing we can't do is let you remain idle."

I burst out laughing, my shrieks sending me sliding out of the chair and into a kneeling position on the floor. Everyone was staring at me. Li Jiangyun said to Fat Man Wu, "What makes you think I'm so eager to join your party?"

"Ah, now that's covered by party bylaws, which say: Whether or not someone asks to join the party, if members find that someone pleasing to the eye, that person becomes a member, and that, as they say, is that."

"Then how come he's laughing?" Li Jiangyun said. "You guys are just looking for someone to be the butt of your stupid jokes, is that it?"

"No, not at all." I stood up, still laughing. "A funny line from a Shandong skit just popped into my head: Anty fanties, arty farty, let me into your panties, and you can join my party. In the skit that's what the party secretary says to girls who are just aching to join up."

I doubled up laughing again.

Li Jiangyun turned to Fat Man Wu. "Do you think that's funny?"

He shook his head. "No, I don't."

"It sounds pretty raunchy to me. Why do you think that is?"

"Well, you're right," Fat Man said. "And we've already petitioned the local judiciary to take him into custody and punish him properly."

"With people like him, what else can you do?"

"Not so fast. With us it's instinct. Sooner or later every member of our party cools his heels in jail—that's how we keep things jumping politically."

Engulfed in waves of laughter, Li Jiangyun finally realized that there was no way out of her predicament, so she smiled and held her tongue, letting Fat Man Wu and the others carry out their performance without reacting to anything they said, thus shielding herself from further attack. As soon as they saw they could no longer get a rise out of her, they went back to playing cards. "You'd better go now," they said dismissively. "You'll tarnish our reputation if you hang around after dark."

"Are you always like this, sending your adversary off when you see victory slipping away?" You couldn't help admiring her spunk. "You guys are great at letting the situation dictate your actions."

"You're a smart girl, and if there's anything we dislike it's smart girls. Smart girls are dumb where it counts."

"It seems to me you'd like all guys to be gymnasts and all girls to be soft pads for you to bounce around on."

"I've never seen a virtuous man who's the equal of a lustful one."

"That's it, time to go." I picked up Li Jiangyun's scarf and gloves and forced them on her. "I've had enough ridiculous talk for one day. Impatient guys don't get started unless there's something in it for us. We prefer to snare the white wolf without lifting a finger."

"I'm leaving." Now all bundled up, she gave us one of those looks, then walked out the door grinning.

"Don't be angry, just pretend we never met." I closed the door behind her and walked back to where the stunned couple was sitting. "Off to bed with you two," I said. "No sense waiting up, since we're not sleeping together."

"If you ask me," Liu Huiyuan said after the couple had left the room, "that old maid wasn't bad."

"She sure wasn't, so how come our pal here didn't like her?" Fat Man Wu, his eyes reduced to slits, asked. "I joked around with her as much as I could. Feeling any better?"

"A lot better." I laughed.

We went back to our card game, but my attention was caught by a silver-gray Naugahyde bag hanging by its shoulder strap from a peg on the bookcase. Its natural luster was gone, covered by a layer of dust. Bags like that had been popular some years back. The game was heating up, and luck was with me—whatever I needed seemed to leap off the deck into my hand, and I swept the table. Even when I played the wrong card I won. That was not a good sign, since good luck in cards usually means rotten luck elsewhere. That's a tried and tested, axiomatic law of probability. Then I got a phone call from some woman. She said a girl named Ling Yu was in bad shape in the hospital. Her lupus was in the final stages, and she was asking for me. I tried but couldn't place the name. The woman asked if I was coming. I said no, I had to be on a flight for the U.S. early the next morning. I said I was sorry. After a pregnant pause, she hung up. I went back to the game, and my luck went straight into the toilet.

4

On the way to Xu Xun's house I stopped by Children's Hospital to see Jin Yan, who was handing out medicine to a bunch of rotund children. I told her to take the rest of the day off and come with me to the home of a certain director who was auditioning for a film he had written about women on the way up. Don't say a word when you get there, I told her. This director is a thoughtful man, not shallow, like you. If you open your mouth you'll disappoint him for sure. "The female lead's a mute, with no lines to memorize, so all you have to do is stare off in the distance, real thoughtful like."

When introducing Xu Xun to Jin Yan, I said she was a foreign girl who didn't know a word of Chinese. So instead of bothering with a lot of small talk, all he had to do was nod politely, smile, and offer her a cup of Chinese tea. He was sitting between two tall dark brown cabinets, whispering furtively to his wife. He nodded, smiled at us, and stood up.

"How come you brought a foreigner into this?" He eyed her suspiciously. "She dresses like a hometown girl. If you hadn't told me, I'd have taken her for some local tramp."

"She comes from an underdeveloped country." I sat down.

"A place called Roza, which means 'skin land.'* No matter what the people wear, their skin peeks through, which is how the place got its name."

"I see." Xu Xun glared at me. "No wonder."

"Throw on a video for our foreign visitor, why don't you?" I reached out and touched the VCR in one of the cabinets. "Give her something to do."

"I don't have any good ones," Xu Xun said. "Just martial-arts films."

"Nothing wrong with that. They don't have those where she comes from."

Xu Xun picked out a videocassette and put it in the VCR. Suddenly the room was filled with the shouts and grunts of shaved-head combatants going at it. Xu Xun's wife walked up with two cups of tea and placed them on the table in front of us. With a sweet smile she asked, "Are you a murderer?"

"Ai!" I exclaimed in exasperation. "Don't tell me even you know."

"What happened?" The idea obviously fascinated her. "Why murder?"

"Money," I said. "These days what other reason could there be? Certainly not to gain political power."

"Wow!" Admiration filled her eyes. "A lot of money, I bet."

"A *whole* lot. I wouldn't have done it otherwise."

"That's right. If you're going to do something, go all out." Xu Xun's wife looked over at him. "Not you, you don't have the guts."

*Roza (rouzhi, *using a variant form*) is a Muslim holiday. Here the author appears to be making up a country, taking as a model, perhaps, one of the small countries on China's western border.*

"Get away from me! What do you know?" Xu Xun glared at her. "Get away from me, and stay out of our business."

Xu Xun's wife stared daggers at him, pouted, and sat down to watch the video, which soon had her in its thrall.

"I told you to come alone," Xu Xun grumbled, his voice mingling with the shouts of the fighting monks. "Doesn't it concern you that she's a witness?"

"That's precisely what I want. No matter what I do these days I have to be ready with an alibi, in case a certain pair of eyes is on me. I'm better off saying I used your place to knock off a piece than to lie and say I never came at all."

"Does that mean they've already come for you?"

"They haven't been here yet? See what I mean? No matter what happens or how many people are involved, I'm the one who always gets the shaft, while you guys are off the hook."

"Who says I'm off the hook?" Xu Xun glared at me. "While you were out having a good time somewhere, I was stuck here not knowing which end was up."

"Which means they *have* been to see you. After that they came looking for me. Apparently you dodged the lightning and let it strike me."

"I can't say anything," Xu Xun said softly, "since others are involved. And lightning struck everyone who spoke to me. If I said anything to you, and word got around, it'd be my ass for selling them out."

"I don't need details. I just want to know where things stand. Am I about to be arrested? One word's all I need. Then I'll know what to do."

"But it's that one word I can't give you, since nobody has told me."

"Do you believe I murdered Gao Yang?" I asked, hoping he

would confide in me. "Do you think it's possible? Why would I do it? You know me as well as anybody. Can you think of a single person it'd be worth my time to murder?"

"Why lay that on me? I'd say you didn't do it even if I knew you did."

"Don't give me that." As I straightened up and fished out a cigarette, I glanced over at Jin Yan, who was engrossed in the video. She looked up; I smiled and lit up, then turned back to Xu Xun. "Don't give me that," I repeated in a low voice. "Don't you think I know you? You'd do anything I'd do, even if you have wrapped yourself up in a banana-peel police uniform."

"I'll tell you what I wouldn't do. I wouldn't put on a show as the reincarnation of Uncle Lei Feng* in front of a bunch of Young Pioneers."

"OK, OK, I admit I did that, to my eternal shame. But I've done plenty of good things too."

Xu Xun stuck a cigarette between his lips. I handed him mine, lit end first, then stuck it back in my mouth after he'd used it to light his. "Now give it to me straight," I continued, smiling. "The police never said it had to be me who did the killing, right? There are lots of suspects. You, for instance. If I were the cops, and I saw those black hands of yours, you'd be my prime suspect. When we played catch the killer as kids, you always wanted to be the bad guy. You were born to it. You had that look. Nothing could make you play the cop."

"You didn't tell them that, did you?" Xu Xun was smiling. "You've always considered loyalty important."

*Chairman Mao's favorite proletarian martyr, a PLA solider who died in an accident during the Cultural Revolution.

"Loyalty? Not me." I laughed. "I told them, all right. This time it's either you or me."

We both laughed. Xu Xun's wife and Jin Yan looked up at us.

"People like us don't go around making trouble. How could someone who's always helped others turn around and murder somebody? If I'd known that an ordinary meal with some friends would lead to this, I'd have choked myself before sitting down to it. Did you tell the cops that the last time we saw Gao Yang was during that meal?"

"Yes," said Xu Xun. "That was the last time I saw Gao Yang."

"What do you mean the last time *you* saw him? It was the last time *we* saw him."

Xu Xun pinched his lips, smiled, and puffed casually on his cigarette.

"How come you didn't say 'we'? Gao Yang left before the meal was over," I reminded him. "Later on the rest of us went to the zoo to watch the monkeys. While we were there we had trouble with some guys from the Northeast. You were so drunk you picked a fight with someone you thought was alone, only to find out he was in a gang, all armed with knives. When they started fanning out around us, we froze. Fuck if you weren't the first to hightail it out of there."

Xu Xun laughed. "No, you were the first to hightail it. And it was *you* who picked the fight, you always do when you're drinking. Once you start losing, your pals jump in to save your ass. I can't count the times I've taken a club or a brick for you, and you never said thanks, not once since we were kids." His smile vanished. "Let's stop trying to screw each other. That sucks. It's stupid and it's ridiculous. What you're talking about happened after another meal. The other time, that last meal we had with Gao Yang, you weren't with us when we left."

"What do you mean, I wasn't with you?" I asked with a laugh. "Where did I go? Are you saying I split with Gao Yang, and as soon as we were around the corner, I lopped off his head?"

"I don't know where you went or who you went with or what you did," Xu Xun said without getting ruffled. "All I know is you weren't with us. Five of us left the restaurant together: Gao Jin, Wang Ruohai, Xia Hong, Qiao Qiao, and me. We strolled around and looked at some of the vendors' goods, then they took off without me. I remember stopping at a street fair, where I popped some balloons with an air gun. You weren't there, believe me."

"I had to be," I insisted, staring at the ceiling. "I had to be. Eight of us went out to eat that day. . . ."

"Seven," he cut in. "There were seven of us: you, me, the Gao brothers, Wang, the two girls, plus . . . huh? Eight, how could there have been eight?"

"Plus who? You said 'plus.' Now who was it?"

"A stranger. I didn't know him."

"Wearing a striped shirt?"

"I think so."

"That's right then. The eighth person has been troubling me too. I kept thinking it was Zhuo Yue. . . ." I smiled. "He'd only just died, and I still hadn't gotten used to not having him around."

"You don't have to explain," Xu Xun said. "I felt the same way."

"The way you say it makes me the culprit." The bitter fight between the monks and the long-hairs on the TV screen ended and peace returned. Shouts of battle were replaced by a Cantonese song, gloomy music to accompany the scrolling of film credits.

"Did you think that as long as I kept quiet no one else would say anything?" Xu Xun was staring at me. "Do you think I was the first person they came to see? Besides, if that's all they had, you wouldn't be in any trouble. Just because you didn't leave with us doesn't mean you left with Gao Yang. This is just one end of a thread. Unless you appear at the other end, it can't hurt you."

"Is it me who appears at the end?"

"Ask yourself that. If you don't know, who does?"

"I appear, all right," I said with a laugh, "but not at the end of the Gao Yang thread you guys drew for me. No, it's one that veers off from the other. At a ninety-degree angle. Gao Yang headed southwest, I went north, just like the rest of you. Now if you want to say there was a rape that night in Beijing, I'll admit to being there."

"What about later on? Are you sure you didn't draw a diagonal line on the map of China?"

"I knew you'd bring up those seven days." I laughed. "I really have no memory of that week. But one thing I'm sure of is that I didn't go to Yunnan. I've never been there, not that week, not ever."

"Cool it," Xu Xun said, "just cool it. I'm an easy mark, but I'm not the one you have to convince. What about other people, will they believe you? Someone saw you and Gao Yang in Kunming. You don't think hotels just toss away their guest registers after a couple of years, do you?"

"Who saw me?"

"Who did you see?"

"I saw the back of my own head."

"Forget it, just forget it." Xu Xun straightened up. "What are we arguing about, anyway? This is no interrogation or anything like that. You can say you saw whoever you wanted. It makes no difference to me."

By now a TV program—a rerun of some entertainment special—had replaced the video. Movie and TV stars, and singers—some famous, some not—were sucking up to a foreign film personality with songs, dances, and feats of contortion by someone who could stick her head between her legs and look up her own ass. Jin Yan had a pained expression as she turned to look at me; she was a fan of some of those people.

"Doesn't anybody tell them how stupid they look?"

"You're assuming people like that have brains to begin with." Xu Xun's wife spun around, startled. She looked at Jin Yan and said, "Hey, you can speak Chinese!"

"Chinese people speak Chinese, so what?" I blurted out. Then I realized my mistake. "All right, so you've seen through our little game," I said with a hollow laugh. "I'm in real trouble when I can't even carry out a simple deception. That sucks, it really sucks."

"Did you honestly think we believed you?" Xu Xun asked. "You're out of your league here. We could teach you a thing or two about deceptions."

"All right, you know I'm a terrible liar, so when I say I didn't kill Gao Yang, you can believe me."

"So what if you killed him?" Xu Xun's wife said. "Why can't you just admit it? You really disappoint me."

"Your wife sure takes things in stride," I commented to Xu Xun. "Since she's so laid back, how about we let the lightning come down on your head? You can have the glory this time." I turned to Xu Xun's wife. "You be the murderer and take all the credit. Women these days are really something."

"Why are you always shooting off your mouth like that?" Xu Xun asked his wife. "If dying is what you're after, let me count the ways. I'll even help. We've got rope and poison here. Both do a nice, neat job."

"Here's what I think," I said to Xu Xun. "Since I know I didn't *kill* anyone during those seven days, I must have actually *saved* someone."

Xu Xun gave me a contemptuous look. I laughed and continued, "All I know is I'm not someone to run off to some craggy spot to study or meditate or get a bird's-eye view of the land. I'm not the philosophical or mission-oriented type."

"No, you're not, and even if you were to take off for some craggy spot, it wouldn't be to save anybody, but to take a flying piss."

"Why are you so hard on me? Fang Yan always stands with the masses. A fish needs water."

"What you mean is, Fang Yan always stands with the female masses. This fish really needs its water."

"That's me," I said with a laugh. "So if I did take off for seven days, it was because of some girl."

"Maybe," Xu Xun said with a smile. "The only force that could keep you in check for seven days is a woman. Try to quiet a dog by chaining it up, and it'll bark and jump around till you give it a bone."

"Were there many girls after me back then? Help me out here. Tell me which one was hottest on my trail, someone with a bedroll on her back who wanted to shack up with me."

"Can't recall ever seeing anyone like that, but I did spot you standing in the street with a bedroll on *your* back, looking right and left, with no one paying any attention."

"Says who? I was damned handsome back then. In fact, if it

hadn't been for Alain Delon, all the girls would have been drooling over me."

"Is that right?" Xu Xun asked his wife.

"Hardly," she said, glancing over at me. "Back then we were all drooling over Sun Wukong, the Immortal Monkey."

"Come on, I wasn't that bad. Jin Yan, you can come to my defense, you know. At the time, all you nurses were dueling over me."

"You were that bad, all right," Jin Yan said with a laugh. "We felt sorry for you, given the fact that it's our job to save the dying and cure the injured. It's a children's hospital, so how could we not duel? Whoever lost got stuck with you. And the poor soul who did was me."

"There's no justice in this world," I said to Xu Xun. "Any girl I fell for back then would have had to fulfill the following conditions: face like a goddess, independently wealthy, learned in things Chinese and foreign, warm-hearted and decent—or so my palmist said."

"The person you're describing—she hasn't been born yet."

5

I left Xu Xun's place after lunch, sent Jin Yan on her way, then called Wang Ruohai from a pay phone. His mother said he'd gone out early that morning and wasn't back yet. After hanging up, I went to the subway station. It was noontime, so few people were waiting. I sat down, and it was just me and the service personnel. After a while I got up and boarded a train heading home. I knew I was wasting my time—I wasn't naive enough to think I could actually dodge my shadow. The powers of the police know no bounds; once you're on their list, it's like you're already caught in a dragnet. But I needed to see for myself: If they weren't on my tail at the moment, I had a brief reprieve.

The first thing I noticed when I got off at my station was the man sitting across the way looking right at me. I flashed him a smile, he returned it. Then he stood up and walked through the crowd toward me.

"Waiting for me?"

"I've been waiting all morning." We walked out of the station together. "Where you headed?" he asked.

"A new restaurant is opening. They want me to calligraph their name."

"Oh, so you've learned how to write," he remarked,

crinkling his brow, apparently unaware that I was pulling his leg.

"How many years has it been?" I asked, cocking my head to look at him. "I thought you rotted in prison."

"Just got out." A wan smile. No longer the happy-go-lucky fellow I once knew, Wang Ruohai showed the effects of his long prison stay, which had aged him and drained him of his vigor. When we emerged at street level, I saw him stiffen with nervous unfamiliarity; we were engulfed by noisy pedestrians and automobile traffic.

"Did you know Gao Yang's dead?" he asked urgently as we walked.

"No, how'd he die? Swallow his own fist?"

"Haven't the cops been to see you?"

"Nope," I said. "This is all news to me."

"He was murdered," Wang Ruohai said. "They came to see me yesterday, mainly to ask about you. They wanted to know what happened after we got out of the army. They said that's when it happened."

"Do they mean to say I murdered him?" I took out my keys as I climbed the stairs.

"It appears so." Wang Ruohai was right behind me. "I told them they had to be wrong."

"Why'd you say that?" I unlocked the door, opened it, and invited him in. It was quiet inside. The newcomers must have gone out. The telephone rang, but I let it ring, and after a while it stopped. "You must know who did it, then."

"I didn't mean that," he said after sitting down and looking around. "Your place looks the same." Then he turned back to me. "I didn't mean that. I meant you don't have what it takes. What I'm getting at is, you don't have the balls to go out and kill somebody without thinking about the consequences. You're no professional hit man. Someone might kill you, but you could never kill anybody, not even if you were cornered. It takes nerves of steel to kill a person."

I laughed and sat down across from him. "Are you maybe underestimating me?"

Surprise showed in his eyes. "Is this some kind of game to you? This is one time I wouldn't seek out the limelight if I were you."

I handed him a smoke. After lighting one for myself, I remarked smugly, "The way things look, I'm the only one who had the opportunity to kill Gao Yang. Among our group, that is."

Wang Ruohai smiled and looked at me with mounting interest. "You really have changed. Being locked up all those years has dulled me. I never figured murder would become cool."

"I just wonder why you think I couldn't kill anybody."

"Oh, have I wounded your pride?" He looked away, then turned back to me. "OK, then why'd you kill him?"

"For money," I said with a laugh. "What better reason is there?"

He looked doubtful. "So you know everything," he said after a moment.

I nodded and smiled, but held my tongue.

Wang Ruohai knitted his brow and gave me an inquisitive look. "You're joking, right?" he asked, sizing me up.

This was great. "How could I possibly know? What do I know? All I remember is taking a trip down south with you guys and having a great time. Now, ten years later, people tell me I killed somebody. And I'm so spooked I can't recall a thing that happened back then. If they said I tried to overthrow the Party I'd probably have to admit it."

"Are you saying you don't remember what we did?" Wang Ruohai was obviously relieved. "Not at all?"

"All I remember is eating and drinking and getting laid, until we split up. Gao Yang took off you guys took off I took off."

"That's what happened, all right." Wang Ruohai smiled. "We threw a lot of money around. We can back each other up on that."

"But I can't help thinking," I said, looking right at him, "that maybe all that eating and drinking was just the tip of the iceberg, and that beneath the surface we did lots of other things, stuff that wasn't so innocent. The cops asked a very interesting question: 'Where did you guys get your money?' Know what I mean? We were a bunch of naked eggs, how did we manage to live so high off the hog? To the best of my memory, we headed south with only our mustering-out pay in our pockets."

"Apparently the cops have been to see you."

"Yes." I nodded spiritedly. "How could they ignore their prime suspect? This time they went easy on me, but one of these days I might find myself wearing Li Yuhe's handcuffs and shackles.* Not only that . . ."

I stood up and took down the silver-gray Naugahyde bag that was hanging from the bookcase by its shoulder strap. I dumped out the contents—cosmetic case, mirror, toilet tissue, barrettes, some odds and ends.

"I wonder where this came from. It's been hanging here for ten years. Obviously it belonged to a woman, so where is she?

*_The hero of the Cultural Revolution drama_ The Red Lantern.

How come she left it here? I'll level with you—there used to be money in this purse, and I spent it." I sat down. "Who is she? I wish I knew. I have no idea what she looked like or how she happened to leave her purse at my place. You'd think that she and I must have been pretty tight, but I've asked all the girls I know, and they insist it's not theirs. I'm not a purse snatcher, am I?"

"Don't make yourself out to be worse than you are," Wang Ruohai said. "There are plenty of people out there only too willing to do that for you."

"But this purse seems linked to some dark aspect of my past." I stared at the purse. "I feel creepy every time I look at it, like I'm surrounded by fog so thick I can't see the nose on my face, which keeps me from recalling anything I've ever done." I stared at Wang Ruohai. "Well, say something. What the hell did we do back then? Eat a little snake meat and guzzle some alcohol, and that's all?"

"Me, yes, but not you." He smiled. "You did more than that. In fact, other stuff is mainly what you did."

"Stuff not exactly permitted by law, for example?"

"You were hitting on a girl." Wang Ruohai laughed. "In a way that could have landed you in jail for hooliganism. You were head over heels in love, out first thing in the morning and not back till late at night, talking to yourself till you were red in the face, but keeping us in the dark and making us promise to keep our mouths shut. You swore you were just out for a good time, but you fell for the girl and you figured we were too dumb to catch on."

"I did *that*?" I felt my face turn red beneath the smile.

"That and more. You wrote love letters every day, like

someone right out of a classic romance, coming up with mushy phrases like starry skies and the world in all its glory. You made our skin crawl."

"Oh, the shame, the shame!" I smiled at him. "The girl, who was she? Some raving beauty, I hope?"

"Nothing special, if you want the truth," Wang Ruohai said. "Not much to look at, and I still can't figure out what you saw in her. Back then we assumed you had been fired in the mighty, meatless furnace of revolution until fatty drippings were all you thought of. That's the best I can come up with, since you did everything possible to keep us from seeing her. You turned so pure and decent I was embarrassed to say anything to you. We teased you about it a time or two, and you almost bit our heads off. All I remember about her was that she carried a gray shoulder bag. Can't say if this is the one or not, since bags like this were all the rage—every girl had one."

"Now that you mention it, I do recall something," I said with a smile. "If I'm not mistaken, some girl tagged along wherever I went."

"I think you've got it backwards."

"So? What difference does it make who tagged along after whom? I'll bet she wasn't as bad as you say, in fact, not bad at all. I wasn't the only one on her tail. You guys were like a pack of wolves on the prowl."

"Hardly. We hid from her like she was the wolf."

"Don't be so modest." I was getting excited. "It's all starting to come back now." I picked up the cosmetic case, opened it, and took out a lipstick, then slid a sheet of newspaper over and drew a girl's face on it. "About like this?" I asked Wang Ruohai as I held up the newspaper. "Broad forehead, large mouth, deep-set eyes."

"You've got it all wrong," he replied calmly. "That 'sweet-heart' of yours looked nothing like that. She was one of those flat-faced Hong Kong types."

"Right." I flung the newspaper away. "I knew that. She was beautiful. OK, we've solved that, now back to the love story. Do you recall why we, um, split up?"

"You got me," Wang Ruohai answered with a note of irrita-tion. "I don't remember the two of you ever being *that* close."

"No way. I'm sure I dumped her. It's getting clearer all the time. She was real sexy, so why did I dump her? I pulled some pretty stupid stunts when I was young. Do you remember her name or where she lived?"

"Why?" This caught Wang Ruohai off guard. "You aren't planning to look her up, are you?"

"Why not? First of all," I said earnestly, "she and I have fond memories to share. Second, she might be able to tell me where I spent those seven days. I'm eighty or ninety percent sure I spent the time with her. Weren't you just saying how much in love with her I was?"

"I never said you were in love with *her*. I said you were in love with that flat chest of hers."

"Whose flat chest? I hate it when you talk about the love of my life that way. So, do you remember her name?"

"No," he said. "Not a clue—I really don't, and that's the truth."

A noise at the door was followed by the young couple, who looked travel-worn and weary. Seeing that I was home, they turned on the charm again, and I told them (charmingly) that this was my home and there was no need to wish me well every time they saw me, that not everybody in Beijing was a member of the Manchu aristocracy. After they'd gone in to wash up and rest,

Wang Ruohai and I continued our conversation about Gao Yang. Referring to that last meal we had together, he said:

"After the meal was over, you didn't leave with the rest of us. I agree with Xu Xun on that score. As I recall, there were seven of us at the table, although I can't shake the image of that person in the striped shirt you mentioned. He was always hanging around us. I think Gao Yang brought him along. But then he dropped out of sight. He was a shady character, and we just about had to pry the words out of his mouth. You were working in the pharmacy then, and I really can't tell you where you spent those seven days. It's possible you didn't go anywhere, but spent the week holed up with some skirt. Still there's no denying that somebody said she saw your and Gao Yang's names in the guest register when she checked into a hotel in Kunming. She even went up to say hello. Gao Yang was there, but you weren't. She said you were avoiding her, that someone was in the bathroom though Gao Yang said you'd gone out. She was so pissed off that years later there was still anger in her voice. She called you a jerk who had this crazy fear that every girl who laid eyes on you wanted to be your wife, when in fact the only ones who'd consider marrying you were Chinese farm girls or women living in the African bush."

I laughed. "Is Qiao Qiao still peddling pastries?"

"Don't know," he said. "I've been out of touch so long I can't tell who's who anymore. The last time I heard her voice was at the police station. She was in the adjoining interrogation room, complaining loudly that she was being framed. According to my information, the police had been looking for an excuse to bust her, and finally sent her away to be reeducated over some minor offense."

"If it was just reeducation, she must have gotten out long ago."

"Who's to say she didn't go out and get into more trouble? All I know is, I haven't heard anything. And you won't catch me hanging around people like her now. If I saw her on the street, I'd cross to the other side."

"Let me ask you this," I said with a broad grin, handing him another cigarette. "What were you in for, anyway? I've heard burglary and I've heard dealing in hot rubies. Which was it?"

"I got a raw deal, I can tell you that," Wang Ruohai said with a wry grin. "It wasn't burglary and it sure wasn't dealing in hot rubies. If I'd had any rubies, I'd have held on to them. I went to see some guy I knew from Hong Kong, and walked out with his wallet, just in time for a hotel residency check, and I was no sooner past the corridor than they dragged me back. A measly few thousand Hong Kong dollars cost me eight years. Those were tense times, politically, and no one would give me a damned break. I was railroaded, and I've been thinking about getting the verdict reversed."

"That's not the way I heard it." I laughed and looked him right in the eye. "I heard you got your hands on a big ruby and showed it off all over the place, until you were busted and the ruby was confiscated. It turned out to be a national treasure that had been inlaid in one of your granny's tiny shoes. She was a palace girl and your grandpa was a eunuch, and when the dynasty was overthrown they fled the palace with their precious rubies."

"Bullshit. If my grandpa was a eunuch, where did I come from?"

"Honest, I mean it. If he wasn't a eunuch, then he was a Qing dynasty 8341 palace cop.* People say that's why you got

* *"Left-supporting" troop-unit teams organized by Mao to protect China's top leaders and assigned to areas in and around Beijing. One of them arrested the Gang of Four in 1976.*

hit with such a stiff sentence. Your problem is you're evil. Selling a gem is one thing, but out of your own granny's smelly shoe, which you try to palm off as a relic worth thousands? It's people like you they need to do away with, making the country look bad like that. I'll bet there isn't another profiteer anywhere in the world as despicable as you. If some foreigner had got his hands on that smelly shoe and stuck it in a museum somewhere, there isn't a son of Han anywhere in the world who could hold his head up. What you did was a crime against the Republic, and you'd have been jailed even if they'd busted you in Taiwan."

Wang Ruohai laughed. "You've turned into an orator, I see."

"But what about the other stone? Your granny had two feet, so she must have had two stones. In the imperial court everything comes in pairs, isn't that what they say?"

"There are three more. My granny had four feet."

Nighttime. I was fiddling with the contents of the gray handbag under a lamp. I tried fastening one of the barrettes in my hair, but it was too closely cropped, and the thing kept slipping off. I opened the cosmetic case, walked over to the dressing-table mirror, and started making up my face. First I put on blue eye shadow, making my eyes look like the sunken eyes of a panda. Then I added blush and traced the outline of my ample mouth with lipstick. When I smiled, I looked like a giant clam. By doing myself up that way, looking at a cat to paint a tiger, I was in touch with the image of that certain someone. I sat down and began flipping through an old address book. Every page was filled with names and phone numbers. Some were of friends from the past whose faces I could more or less recall, but far more meant absolutely nothing to me; I couldn't tell you who they were or how

I'd known them. It was a safe bet that the girl's name was hidden in there somewhere, but it didn't jump out at me. All those Little Lis and Little Mings, common as can be, told me nothing, not even who was male and who was female. That night I slept terribly, nightmares coming fast and furious. I dreamt I was eating and chatting with a bunch of people I didn't know and flirting with a girl whose face was too blurred to recognize, but everything was so disjointed that I was all hot and sweaty, like I was in a vat of boiling water or suspended in the void of heaven. And no matter what I did, some guy in a striped shirt was always in my field of vision, a ruby the size of a goose egg on his finger. Gao Yang appeared at one point, never looking more alive, talking and laughing and gesturing, carefree as can be. In my dream I could tell he wasn't dead, and I felt just great.

6

A man in a black leather overcoat stood in the post office doorway across the street, watching me through window glass stamped with reflections of pedestrians and traffic. He probably thought I didn't see him. After I crossed at the intersection, his face was reflected in the glass door of a tailor shop. It made no difference which street I took, the face floated past storefront doors and shop windows like one of those movie posters that's plastered everywhere. Plainclothes cops dress just like the people they bust these days, I was thinking. Talk about cool, they know cool. I went into a grocery store and stood at the counter. The face appeared in the window of a café across the street, bigger than life, eyes glued to me. Like someone caught in the beam of a searchlight, I turned to block out the eyes with my back. "Excuse me, miss," I said softly. A young salesclerk, eyes lowered, walked up holding a pair of metal tongs. "What do you want?" "I'm looking for someone. Does Qiao Qiao still work here?" "Qiao Qiao? Who's that?" She scowled and walked off. "Nobody here by that name." "Wait a second, hold on. Qiao Qiao's not her name. Qiao's her family name, I forget the rest. She sold pastries." "There's nobody here named Qiao," the salesclerk said over her shoulder without looking back. She began weighing out some "candy ears" for a middle-aged customer.

I left the grocery store. The heavy gaze of that huge, ubiquitous face slowly fell in behind me. A tour bus passed, momentarily blocking the view, and giving me just enough time to slip into a pharmacy. I smiled and walked up to the counter. The large miragelike face was transformed into a man in a black leather overcoat running frantically down the street, hesitating briefly at each shop door. A girl walked up and asked what I wanted. I said nothing, just smiled. She looked behind her and saw Zhang Li, who walked up with a smile. The first girl slipped away tactfully.

"What are you doing here?" Zhang Li asked.

"I came to see you."

"Sure you did. Something's up, I know it. We're out of aphrodisiacs."

"Now that our Chinese citizens are leading better lives, male virility has suffered." The man in the black leather overcoat was heading this way. "Can we continue this in the back?" I asked Zhang Li.

"Come on." She retreated to the rear of the store.

I walked quickly around the counter and disappeared behind the storeroom curtain just as the man in the black leather overcoat walked in.

I sat in the lounge area with a cup of tea. The place was warm and comfortable. Zhang Li smiled and felt my icy hands. "What have you been up to lately? Bumming around, as usual?"

"I killed a guy. The cops are after me."

"Be serious." Zhang Li laughed. "You haven't got the guts."

"So Zhang Li understands me after all." I laughed and sipped my tea. "Let me ask you something. Do you remember what I was up to back when we were working at that Front Gate pharmacy?"

"What made you think of that? What else would you have

been up to? When you weren't shooting off your mouth, you were on the phone."

"Who was I talking to?"

"What's with you? Tell me what's going on."

"Don't ask. I want you to think back and tell me who I spent most of my time with. Who came to the pharmacy to see me?"

"Lots of people. Just about every bad egg I can think of. How do you expect me to remember who came and how often? I didn't know any of them."

"I'm not worried about lots of people. Somebody had to come more often than the others. Don't tell me nothing registered. You kept an eye on me, and if anyone came to see me, it was you who sent them packing."

"Who did? When did I ever keep tabs on you? You've got a pretty high opinion of yourself."

"Honest, I mean it." I looked around; we were alone. I reached out sneaky-like and touched her. "You must remember something."

"What if someone's watching?" She backed away, looked down at her feet, and thought for a moment. Then she looked up and smiled. "I remember you were always calling some girl."

"Who? What was her name?"

"Liu, I think." She looked away. "Liu something or other. You called her several times a day, and once you got talking, you never stopped. Very tacky. How could you forget that? Don't play games with me. Are you thinking of starting that up again?"

"You're not jealous, are you, after all these years?"

"Get away from me. This is my workplace, show some class. Jealous of her? That hippopotamus? I was embarrassed that you could fall for something like that."

"You met her? Did she come to the pharmacy?"

"Are you going to try to find her?"

"Yes. And what the hell business is it of yours? Oops, sorry, didn't mean it, don't get mad please don't get mad. Where did you meet her? Tell me, I'm begging you."

"This is how you always treat me. Any time you need something, out comes the sweet talk, down on your knees and all. But the rest of the time, you won't even look my way." Zhang Li was hurt. "I can read you like a book."

"I didn't mean it," I repeated, trying to patch things up. "You know me as well as anybody, the way I can hurt people's feelings without even trying—low self-esteem, you know."

"Stop that. Don't go wagging your tail at me." Then she softened. "A good horse doesn't eat the grass behind it. If you're really serious about wanting to find someone, I know a great girl, daughter of a high official, lives in a big three-room flat with a northern exposure."

"What are you talking about? I say I've got a great life, and you say what you need is a wife. I'm not looking to get married. And if I were, why look any further? I couldn't do better than you. No, I'm planning to write some memoirs. Haven't you noticed all the handwringing in the papers these days, how the old comrades are dropping like flies? If we don't hurry up and help them write down their experiences, it'll be too late. Their lives are at the core of our revolutionary experience, and recording them for posterity will be invaluable in instructing the younger generation in our nation's history."

"I love you so much."

I sneaked out through the back door. The neat, tidy lanes were nearly deserted. Rooftops of traditional neighborhood houses were bathed in sunlight, the air was cold and crisp. I walked slowly, neck scrunched down, hands in my pockets, happy to have learned the girl's name. "Looked like a hippopotamus." Even taking into consideration the source of Zhang Li's smear, it occurred to me that the girl must have had a pretty large mouth; that was it, she had a large mouth. Images of all the large-mouthed girls I'd known paraded through my head: some flashing their thirty-two pearly whites, others with pinched smiles that hid their teeth behind a narrow gash, lips covering uppers and revealing lowers . . . they came and they went, until only she remained. I continued down the lane until I was in another neighborhood, the best-preserved section of old Peking: narrow streets lined with elfin shops, traditional houses converted into privately run cafés. Pedestrians and cars had to edge past delivery trucks parked at produce stalls. Scattered among the old Peking residences were Western homes, run-down cottages, and red-tiled apartment buildings, all dating from different eras; plaques on some of the grander buildings showed they once housed royalty or wealthy merchants. These homes, to which garages had been added, were well maintained for the powerful and famous people who lived in comparative luxury behind closed gates and tall trees. Zhang Li said that one summer evening ten years earlier, she was riding her bike through this neighborhood when she spotted me and the "hippopotamus" emerging from one of the many lanes, wearing sandals and holding hands, which meant that the "hippopotamus" and I had to have been hanging out in this neighborhood. Now I know this city like the back of my hand, having visited every inch of it over the decades, and I can tell you how monotonously similar its neighborhoods can be, sort of like a bathhouse, where one naked body is pretty much the same as all the others. Each neighborhood has the feel of home, since I've had dealings of one sort or another with people from all over the city. I can never pinpoint what took me to any one particular area, because there's hardly a lane in the city I haven't lived in at one time or another, mostly with a whole bunch of people, and not all of them female. I walked up one lane and down another, passing all kinds of gates, some open, some shut, some locked, and wondered which girl might live where. What I felt like doing was making a sweep up and down the street with a loud gong, so the residents would stick out their heads, and I could examine their goofy expressions. I was curious and anxious at the same time. All those gates closed me off from segments of my past, and I ought to have been able to push them open to retrieve what was mine. I was haunted by strong feelings that part of me remained trapped within these sunbathed compounds, like smoky odors in a room—invisible yet detectable. Or like a just-vacated sofa, where the warmth remains even with the person gone.

I stopped at a corner café for a bowl of bean porridge and some stuffed flatcakes dipped in vinegar, which I ate as I watched pedestrians pass by the glassed-in storefront. The warmth of my body and the taste of the food and the sights around me made me feel that I had sat in this very same spot more than once at some time in the past, eating the very same snack and taking in the very same sights from the very same perspective.

I glanced through my old address book for all the Lius, as well as the other family names that sounded similar, like Niu and Yiu. I failed miserably at the process of elimination. We Chinese have gotten so sophisticated at choosing names for their meaning that you can no longer tell at a glance if someone is male or female. And not just people named Liu either. So I went ahead and picked a name I liked.

*   *   *

It was an ordinary Beijing compound, complete with date trees and so many add-ons there was barely room for the walkways. Thick layers of ice surrounded the white putty wraps of waterpipes; the area under each family's eaves was reserved for strings of garlic and stacks of charcoal briquettes and heads of bok choy. At one time I'd been a frequent visitor to this compound, and now I stood there filled with emotion, having brought with me an abundance of happy, contented feelings (I must have been happy and contented back then). It all seemed so alien yet so familiar. I could almost picture the captivating Liu Xiaoli who lived here: perfect Beijing accent, colorful body-hugging jacket, slender and sexy, her laugh as crisp and mellow as silver bells. I'd been so hung up on her that I'd phoned her several times a day.

I climbed the steps of the main building and knocked on the curtained glass door. A slender girl in a colorful, body-hugging jacket opened the door and greeted me with a broad smile. I smiled back. Something was wrong here. She was just as I had pictured her, but many years too young. Either I'd gone back ten years in time, or she needed to, which would put her in diapers. The smiling girl told me that Liu Xiaoli lived in the west wing, then shouted from the steps, "Hey, Buddy Liu, there's somebody here to see you."

Buddy Liu? Uh-oh, something was *very* wrong here. A stubby guy with long hair emerged from the tiny west-wing kitchen holding a drippy eggshell in his hand. He stared at me.

"I'm, um . . . I'm . . ." I nearly ran over, grinning from ear to ear, but not knowing what to say.

"Hey, it's you." With a toss of his head, the stubby guy laughed and waved to me. "Come in," he said, "come on in. What brings you here? Hungry?"

"No," I said as I stepped into his room, "I just ate. You go ahead. I was passing by and thought I'd sneak a look inside. It's been so long I wasn't sure you were still around."

A little old lady in the room was regarding me with a watchful eye.

"We went to school together, Ma," the stubby guy announced. "He's a big shot now, a regiment commander. Graduated from a military academy. Hey, how come you're not in uniform?"

"Oh, civvies make things more civilized," I answered easily, wondering who the hell he thought I was.

The old lady made a puffing noise as she gave me the once-over, then curled her lip. "Well, at least somebody's mother has something to brag about. Look at him, then take a look at yourself."

"That must have been some battle in the Old Mountain region," the stubby guy said excitedly, ignoring his mother's remark. "How many'd you kill?"

"Well, as regiment commander, I don't actually do the fighting. Besides, it's an artillery regiment."

"Fighting those fucking Vietnamese, every time I read about kicking their butts, I get a rush. We can't let 'em get away with stuff. Besides, what else does the people's army have to do these days?" He didn't pause in his rantings as he stood in the middle of the room quickly slurping a bowl of noodles and dumping a raw egg into his mouth. "This is great," he said. "Since you've already eaten, I get it all for myself. Raw eggs are very nutritious, the essence of an animal. You should have come to see me before this. I think about you all the time."

"It's been ten years, hasn't it?"

"More than that. You took off right after high school. I wondered what a crazy motherfucker like you was up to. You were such a pussy in high school, the girls knew they could slap you around." Another raw egg slid into his mouth. "All right," he said with a look of satisfaction, "you're all right, coming to see me like this. You're the first regiment commander who's ever done that. We were out of line, really out of line to kick and slap you around in high school. You don't remember, do you? My life ended the day I graduated. I've been a stinking laborer ever since. Not like you—a regiment commander. Shee-it! And at your age, you're bound to keep going. A division, hell, maybe even a brigade."

"I just dropped by to say hello, no particular reason."

"What's your hurry?" Seeing I was about to split, the stubby guy slurped down the last egg. His breath fouled the air around him. "Stick around a while as long as you're here. I've got nothing else to do. I don't know who I'd go see if you hadn't dropped by."

"Our house is too dirty for the likes of him, can't you see that?" the old lady hissed as she glared at me. "Why would a regiment commander want to hang around a place like this? Putting his foot in the door is a great thing already."

"That's not it, old mother. I'm supposed to be visiting the homes of my troops. As a senior officer, whenever I'm on home leave, I'm expected to call on the families of my soldiers, let them know everything's fine. You know how anxious old folks can get when their sons are off fighting a war."

"You don't know shit!" The stubby guy turned on his mother. "You don't expect a regiment commander to think like you, do you? If he did, he'd never have become a regiment commander. Don't mind the old witch. You and I know what's what."

The stubby guy walked me outside. "Drop by any time. You're a lot better than Fang Yan. As soon as that low-down motherfucker's ship came in, he turned his back on all his friends. I saw him with some girl once, and he looked right through me as they walked into a hotel. Who the fuck did he think he was? I was really mad. Selling your ass for all the money in the world doesn't make you hot shit."

"When was that?" I turned to the stubby guy. "It must have been someone who just looked like him."

"No way. He hadn't changed a bit. Hadn't had time. I ran after his ass and yelled Fang Yan Fang Yan, but he was too fast for me."

"Do you remember my name?"

"How could I forget?" He thumped me on the back and grinned broadly. "You're Zhuo Yue. Who'd you think you were?"

7

After leaving the stubby guy's place, I headed down a series of lanes, hugging the walls as I went, dejection gradually claiming me. It was just past noon, and sunlight washed the lanes like water spilling out of a trough, the glittery rays penetrating the surrounding haze. The street was my destination, but I kept circling through the network of lanes; where one ended another began, and it was sort of like walking on a rolling ball, going round and round with no end in sight. People noises, mixed with the whine and bumps of electric trams out on the street nearby, were clear as a bell, that and the amplified shouts of ticket collectors, but it was out there and I was in here, emerging from one brick-walled lane only to find myself in yet another. Seeing no other people around, I was beginning to panic, with the blinding sunlight hitting me squarely in the face. I looked down and spotted a pointy, steamy, wondrous turd on the damp ground close to the wall. . . . A middle-school student with a heavy backpack was coming my way. Then, as if a curtain of haze had been lifted, a swarm of boys and girls came toward me, silently, their heads lowered. A middle school appeared before me. The athletic field was deserted; a basketball wrapped in a net rested at the base of a pole. Every window in the cinder block building was broken, the angular shape of each black hole unique. A few snack shops, vegetable stands, and barbershops dotted the T-shaped intersection. Women buying groceries looked familiar, and when they saw me they nodded. I realized I'd wandered into one of my old haunts. It hadn't changed in the ten years since I'd last been there. So I began walking briskly, sensing that something was about to appear up ahead. Sure enough, high above me emerged an iron eagle, wings outstretched, a stone-carved earth clutched in its claws. The eagle was perched upon a magnificent arched gate made of stone. The surrounding rooftops of squat homes created a perfect setting for the stately buildings, the artificial mountain and dense green shadows, a smattering of little pavilions, and the lush canopy of tall trees in the mammoth compound beyond the arched gate. At the turn of the century it had been the residence of a high official for the northern warlords, later converted into the headquarters of intelligence agencies for a succession of governments. Until the Cultural Revolution, that is, when military intelligence moved out and the compound served as a barracks. Musty grand halls were divided into a patchwork of tiny rooms for the dependents of cashiered officers. As I walked, I felt more and more at home in a place where, ten years earlier, I had hung out with Gao Jin, Xu Xun, Wang Ruohai, and others, male and female. But I thought that it had been torn down in the wave of new construction sweeping the nation a decade earlier, that the artificial mountain had been leveled, the stones from Lake Hu sold off to public parks, the trees cut down, the goldfish pond filled in, and the heating pipes buried. The army had built a tract of identical apartment buildings on the site. After passing beneath the eagle unchallenged by the sentry in his gatehouse and through the three impressive gates of the awesome main hall, I headed down a passageway with peeling red paint, past a large flower garden bathed in murky afternoon sunlight. A giant hydrangea, its lofty branches covered with snowy blossoms, cast its shade over a petal-strewn path. In the middle of the garden, behind a stand of emerald-green cypresses, plum and pear trees were in full bloom with red and white blossoms that covered the compound like a quilt of gorgeous colors under a blue sky. As I turned down a dark path between outlying buildings, I detected the familiar odor of an outhouse. Suddenly there was a flash of light in front of me, and I found myself in a small open-air courtyard in the middle of a two-story building with concrete pillars, an odd mixture of Western and Chinese architecture. Every room was occupied, with children running up and down the hallways, and laundry of every description hanging from lines stretching from one pillar to the next. I hesitated, as the sights before me merged with mental images of another place I'd been, and for a moment I wasn't sure where I was, as if I'd stumbled into an alien realm. The courtyard was made up of numerous enclosures, each with its own gate; you opened one, and you were in a new, yet identical courtyard, except that they kept getting smaller, until finally the patch of sky overhead seemed no larger than a handkerchief, and when I gazed skyward, I felt wedged in a deep well. The brick flooring was coated with moss, doors and windows around me were shut, and not a sound anywhere. I've been here before, I thought as I walked toward the western wing; not just been here, but often, and in my dreams. In that sense, I'd been a regular visitor over the years. I knew the door would be opened by a pale young man and that I'd see a smoky interior dimly lit by a fluorescent bulb: two rooms with hollow floorboards and as many beds as could be crammed into them, the space beneath the beds cluttered with empty, filthy beer bottles. Crumpled cigarette packs would be strewn across the one and only table in the cramped room, that and a butt-filled fishbowl serving as an ashtray. In a corner would stand a large mahogany-colored bookcase brought over from some government office. The furniture would be chipped and scarred. I could even recall what I came in my dream to do: play cards with three pale young men, the same game I played so well with Fat Man Wu, Liu Huiyuan, and that bunch.

After rapping on the door of the western wing, I was about to knock for the second time when it opened without a sound; I was face-to-face with a pale young man. I entered a smoky room lit by a single fluorescent bulb, the floorboards creaking under my feet. I sat down across from three pale young men who stared at me with blank expressions. They were acquaintances, my friends, except I couldn't recall their names. The words were right on the tip of my tongue but I turned mute as soon as I opened my mouth.

"Let's play," one of the pale young men said, his voice sounding as if it had come from the far end of a tunnel. One of the other pale young men took out a new deck of cards and shuffled them, fingers flying. Then we cut the cards. I drew the ten of clubs, higher than the others. My deal.

We settled down to some serious card-playing. I started very conservatively, and for a while that paid off. But caution seldom produces winners, and miscues are inevitable. I remember drawing several good no-bid hands, when I could trump all four suits, but I lacked the king. So I'd lead with my ace and someone would trump me with the king. Or two of the kings would be out, tying up those suits, and a hand that was good enough to be a winner would come up short. If I failed to take one suit, I'd move to another, only to be trumped. One bad hand after another took its toll, emotionally, and I tried every trick I knew to start winning. So what happened? I finally got a good hand, and I misplayed it—as I discovered after it was too late.

During that game, I recall, a young couple was in the next room talking in whispers. I couldn't make out what they were saying, but they kept it up the whole time, until the sound reminded me of a lonely wasp; the weak but persistent buzz made me tense up and ruined my concentration until I couldn't focus on what I was supposed to be doing. Later on, whenever I thought back to that incident, the image I had of the room was one of noisy chaos. I recall that for part of the time a girl stood next to me watching me play, a graceful, proper-looking girl, and now it occurs to me that she was the one whose face I so often sketched in my mind and on paper and even on my own face. I can't recall if she had come in from the other room, but the muted talk didn't let up even while she was standing beside me. Apparently we all knew her, since we talked and joked with her between hands, and she giggled and chattered away the whole time, although I can't tell you what she said. In fact, from start to finish, the only comment I can recall—and I don't know who said it—was: "Haven't we met somewhere before?"

It was just past noon—the sky was bright and clear—when I entered the little courtyard, and the handkerchief-sized patch of sky was a dazzling blue; but it was dark by the time I emerged. I didn't think I'd been in there *that* long; we'd only played a few hands of cards and chatted a while. Retracing my steps down the dark narrow path, I negotiated one courtyard after another; the doors and windows were all shut tight, although from time to time thin human voices penetrated the darkness. Now the place seemed so unfamiliar; I had no memory of ever walking down such a winding, twisting, inky-black path before, and I had the strange feeling that the room with its dim fluorescent bulb and the pale young men and those hands of cards we'd played might never have existed at all, in the same way that the odd girl hadn't existed. When I made it back to the brightly lit, largest courtyard, the sense of strangeness abated, and once again I was in the grip of a feeling that this was one of my old haunts. Night was falling and a couple of soldiers were setting up a movie screen in the compound; two rows of seats—everything from stools to rickety bamboo chairs—were in readiness; a cluster of girls stood beside one of the pillars nibbling melon seeds and gabbing. People— men and women, young and old, laughing and talking—entered the darkened path from the lit area at the other end, turning into silent moving shadows until they reemerged into the light. . . . Now I remembered, I'd been here before, no doubt about it. It was summertime, and a movie was being shown then too. Night was closing in, but since it was summer, it would have been a little later than tonight. It was a black-and-white movie: Chinese officers and soldiers in summer uniforms, minus insignia, armed with .50-caliber assault rifles, obviously a movie about the Aid Korea and Resist America campaign. From where we stood beside the gate, talking and smoking cigarettes, we could see the illuminated outlines of small wooden buildings behind the thin movie screen. Muffled movie dialog swirled and echoed in the courtyard, punctuated every now and then by the deafening rumble of tanks and cannons. Bursts of rifle fire, rockets exploding amid clusters of shouting soldiers, and other related noises blended into a heroic symphony . . . there was alcohol on the breath of the people around me. We had just finished a big meal, but where? I had a bellyache from all that rich food and strong wine. In fact it was the first time in my life that too much good wine and stir-fried meat hadn't agreed with me. A sour, slightly sweet taste rose up into my mouth. That's right, we'd eaten Western food. At the time, there were only two Western restaurants open to Beijing residents: One was way out near the zoo, so if we'd eaten there, we wouldn't have gotten back until much later. . . . I know where I'd eaten. She was standing next to me, and even though I couldn't see her face, I smelled her violet cologne. No wonder I get a peculiar rush whenever I smell violets. I was standing in the dark getting turned on, which proves she was there with me. The scent of violets wrapped itself around me the way the musky odor of a she-animal in the wild attracts a mate. Everything is a blank from that moment till we were in bed. I'd been drinking heavily, so I was pretty woozy. My next recollection is from much later that night. The movie was long over, and a heavy rain was falling. Flashes of lightning lit up the room; the white body lay beside me like a fallen sheep. The rain fell noiselessly. Someone opened the door and came in, but went right back out; the floorboards creaked. Now an image is forming: Her posture is that of a mighty steed, and that position must be the one that left such an impression on me.

Who were all those boozy people talking to me in the gateway? I tried but failed to conjure up images of their hazy faces, and had no success in figuring out the connection, given their diversity, in what can only be described as a scene of chaos; I also had no luck restoring my own voice amid the cacophonous buzzing all around me. It was sort of like watching swaying figures in a dimly lit ballroom across a vast empty space, so even though you know the people, all you can see are strange silhouettes.

After the passage of years, the restaurant now sported a different sign, but that was the only visible change. It was still a long, narrow arrangement within a square, cinder block building, like a theater aisle. The owners had opened a new and quite splendid entrance on the side street, and the old-style revolving door had fallen into disuse; it now opened onto crates of empty beer and soft drink bottles. The cars lined up in the shade of tall trees were covered with dust, their windshields turned filthy under the onslaught of the elements. People had etched personal tags and obscene graffitti in the grime.

I stood across the busy street, looking through the windows at diners as they ate, drank, and talked; faint strains of music reached my ears. I knew without being told that this was no longer the fine restaurant of earlier times. It had been converted into a trendy Western-style fast-food joint geared to turn a fast profit for its Japanese investors. Diners filed past the long serving counter, kept in line by a stainless-steel railing, taking whatever caught their fancy. It reminded me of a subway entrance or a hospital registration desk. The good old days were gone forever. I'd gone back a few days earlier, and just sat there for the longest time, like a solitary cigarette in a pack.

Numbly I sat drinking alone in a crowd: Bearded European tourists, bespectacled students, and clusters of rosy-cheeked girls faced me or looked away, heads down or faces raised, laughing or pouting, you name it. I drank I nodded off my eyes ached I opened them wide I daydreamed, while all around me people muttered. I saw a bespectacled guy with disheveled hair and wearing a loose-knit sweater go to the bar get a soft drink spin around and be transformed into an old friend of mine, coming toward me with a smile and asking why I was drinking alone "instead of joining him and the others." I got up and followed him across the dining hall, as if it were empty, to a private room where I knew every single person. Happy diners at each table acted like friends at a reunion. I saw Gao Jin, Xu Xun, Wang Ruohai and

Qiao Qiao, and Xia Hong; I saw Fat Man Wu, Liu Huiyuan, and the pudgy girl; I saw the three cops who had come looking for me, Zhang Li, Jin Yan, even the young couple who weren't part of our group, but who sat there looking radiant. And I saw Gao Yang, Zhuo Yue, and the stranger in the striped shirt sitting at the same table. How could I have missed all these familiar faces when I entered the restaurant? Figuring this was my chance to clear up some matters face-to-face, I approached the tables, but not a word emerged. They stared at my smiling, silent mouth. With growing anxiety, I went from table to table with a beseeching look on my face one moment and a yearning one the next, but no one seemed to notice. Zhang Li waved to me, so I headed toward her. Yet inexplicably I sat down at a table next to the disheveled, bespectacled guy. He poured me a beer, and kept pouring, even after the suds overflowed the rim of the glass, puddled on the table, and dripped onto my pants, sending a chill down my legs. He asked why I hadn't brought my girlfriend along, and I sputtered something about her staying home to entertain a relative, before it dawned on me I didn't know who he was talking about. So I asked him. Liu Yan, who else? Then, strangely enough, he asked, Didn't you two just return from Yunnan where you'd supposedly gone to see the stone forest but in fact had other things in mind? Did I go to Yunnan with her? Can you prove it? I asked. Don't be silly, he said. As if Liu Yan shacked up with me and not with you as if you didn't know. Liu Yan I muttered trying my damnedest to place it. Are you saying her name was Liu Yan? Are you drunk? he asked me. Or hallucinating? No no, I said I hadn't seen her in ten years, and couldn't recall what she looked like. He laughed. I remember her face clearly, but not her body. Not bad, you've got nothing to be ashamed of. Details, I want details, I said, I need an exact description. I'm trying to find her and can't unless I know exactly what she looks like. Sorry I can't give you a detailed description, he said. But I might have a photo of her at home. I'll try to dig it up for you. Now do it now I said and you can finish eating when we come back. He lived in a narrow lane, and after groping around in the dark for the longest time, we wound up in that same court-yard. I've been here before, I said. I gazed blankly at the ruins of the once lovely compound. Broken bricks and tiles lay all over the ground; the artificial hill and flower garden and buildings were gone, and only the remnants of a wall marked the bound-aries of the place. A small building stood alone, dim light emerg-ing from within. We went in. No trace of the pale-faced young men or that woman. He took down a cloth-covered photo album from the bookcase and began flipping through it. It was filled with yellowing black-and-white photos: men and women of all ages and all types caught in a variety of poses and settings. I ap-peared in some of the photos, a sour look on my face and a red bandanna around my neck, rowing a boat in a sailor outfit, long hair and smoking a cigarette. The people with me kept changing: First it was my parents, then Gao Yang and Xu Xun, and finally Fat Man Wu and Liu Huiyuan. Included too were many people I had long forgotten and some who were mere chance acquain-tances. I appeared in photos mainly with Gao Yang and Zhuo Yue. Nearly every phase of my life was marked by photos with them: from a crew-cut little boy sticking out his puny chest all the way up to adulthood with photos in uniform and civilian clothes taken at scenic spots throughout the country and always with the trace of a smile. I pretty much grew up with those two and even the expressions on our faces evolved together from in-nocence to cynicism. Then Zhuo Yue simply vanished, never to reappear; after that it was Gao Yang, his face absent among the images. I appeared in more and more photos alone, older and older, my smile more and more forced, until, in the last few my head was bowed. The lens had shifted, focusing now on crumbling walls and dying trees and decaying temples and windswept oceans and weed-covered ruins and hilltop foliage. Girls alone or in groups showed up in a few of these nondescript photos, their various smiles and poses, some sexy, others demure, simply adornments to the sunlit scenery behind them. Only one was taken indoors, on a gloomy day: A girl is standing in the dim light, everything behind her a blur, her mouth is open as if she is about to say something; toward the bottom of the photo where the light is brighter you can see her folded hands. Bad though the photo was, making it difficult to see the person clearly, I knew it was her. I recall removing the photograph and pocketing it before heading back to the restaurant, which was hot and stuffy and blindingly bright and just as crowded as before. My palms were sweaty, but Gao Yang, Fat Man Wu, and the others just kept eating as if nothing were wrong; those familiar faces danced and swayed and as I surveyed the scene like a movie director with a zoom lens moving in for close-ups, I discovered they weren't who I thought they were. The distinct, familiar features and magnified pores of all those faces began to fade and evolve into unfamiliar noses, eyes, and mouths, forming shapes I didn't recognize, layers of alien faces. A graceful girl stood by watching me, and it was as if I'd taken out the photograph and laid it on the table beside me. I wasn't sure if I'd entered the photograph or if she'd emerged from it. Darkness enclosed me, objects around me grew fuzzy, and it was drizzling outside, a gloomy day. We sat lazily across from each other, her hands shining bright and sleek under the table, loose straight hair falling over her shoulders like a black waterfall, eyes lowered and lips slightly parted. I believe I made small talk for a long time but she never uttered a word. Lighten up, I said, you're always complaining about never getting a break in life, but when one finally comes along, you let it get away. If you knew who I was you wouldn't act this way. I let her know that I was no common lout even though I toot my own horn immodestly, like a gourmet dish that can't wait to be carried out and proceeds to the table on its own, but since we seem destined for each other, if you can't be a little forward, leave everything to me. I told her I never approved of separating people into social classes, and why can't celebrities come on to commoners? I never considered it slumming. She was convulsed with laughter . . . that's probably when things started getting weird. I told her I was a writer, author of *The Weeping Camel* and *How Many Blossoms Fell in My Dream?** Don't turn goofy on me, she said. You've already played this tune for me at your place. "It's a stale routine." She wanted me to take a good look at her. We've met before. You threw me out of your house once. Caught by surprise I sat like a wooden chicken frozen in place gradually coming to the realization that she was none other than Li Jiangyun the girl who had escorted the honeymooners to my house that night. I tried slipping away but she shouted me to a halt. "Embarrassed? No need to be. Don't pretend it's the first time you ever did anything like this, it doesn't work on someone who knows you're an old hand at it." I forced a smile and coughed out of embarrassment and looked around as my face turned bright red. "There's innocence in everybody," I said. What the hell did I mean by that empty phrase? If I'm not mistaken, I sat with her for a long while,

Both written by San Mao, a popular writer in Taiwan during the 1970s and 1980s. She committed suicide after the death of her Spanish husband.

mostly listening to her taunts. Lots of wordplay, with all kinds of hidden meanings, which I should have jotted down but never did. One thought stuck out clearly the whole time, and that is I wanted to leave and go back to the moment before Li Jiangyun appeared, but I stayed right where I was sitting across from her. I recall snippets of what I said: "I went to look up their superiors. . . ." "Once you're out of the loop, people who worked for you treat you differently. . . ." By rights, all this should have been spoken later on when we were waiting for the subway, but I have this vague feeling that I said it all in the restaurant and that we could already foresee that we were in for a long wait at the station. Other things were said, but their implications elude me since I reverted to the classical Chinese of pedants: "Alas, the night is filled with dense mist, the day replete with dark clouds . . . with grief in his bosom, Xiang Heng gazes afar . . . abandoned by honest scholars . . . how can any tender heart endure? . . ." After that came a bunch of gibberish, French or something like that, which puzzled me, since I don't know French. I must have been dreaming, but everything and everyone seemed so real—if I hit something I heard the thump—so it couldn't have been a dream. We rode the subway home, yet I can still see lit streetlamps and shadowy roadside trees whizzing by. As if it were the most natural thing in the world, I went with Li Jiangyun to her place, where we sneaked down the dark hallway and slipped past a colorful door curtain into her tiny flat. I could sense her moist lips and the hot breath on my face in the darkness, but I could also see her seated calmly under a lamp, dressed in a skintight maroon sweater. She descended out of thin air, like a child slipping down a slide. I gazed at her as if I were being enfolded in a swaddling blanket, soft and cozy, the contentment of ripples washing over me. Down deep I was aroused, enlivened. A wave descending from the distant heavens, ever clearer, ever more powerful. For the moment, I was in complete control of my faculties, alert as a bed-wetting child. But my senses wanted to roam, I couldn't stop them, and the release was coming. . . . I grabbed a meaty handful of taut quivering flesh. It was real, all right. I remained in that critical state for the longest time, like a shell in the barrel of a cannon that won't fire, lethal yet impotent. Then bursts of fireworks lit up the sky, releasing spurts of hot energy, the night trembling, I was a delicate glass tube melting in a fiery oven—too late for regrets, all thoughts stilled. . . .

8

My head ached.

Long after the sun's rays had filled the room, I dragged myself weakly out of bed. For some reason I felt I'd soiled the sheets, so I was understandably puzzled to discover that the bedding was perfectly clean. The honeymooners were warming some milk when they saw me walk in, so they poured me a bowlful. After finishing breakfast, quietly for my sake, the man said it was time for them to head back home, and they wanted to repay my hospitality by hosting a dinner for me and my friends. They had already bought everything they needed, and all I had to do was invite the others over. I nodded and said That's fine with me, if that's what you want, then went out and dialed Fat Man Wu's number to extend the invitation.

I was packing my toothbrush, toothpaste, and a change of clothes when Li Jiangyun came over, looking quite stately and confident as she waved hello. Long time no see, I remarked with a smile. Except for last night in my dream. Really? she replied casually before asking where I was off to. I told her I was turning myself in. I was being framed and there were hard days ahead for me. You didn't dream about me last night, did you? I asked. She blushed and looked away. What do you have planned for our dinner tonight? she asked the bride. I stood there dumbly for a moment before turning back to my simple task of packing. Fat Man Wu and Liu Huiyuan and the others walked in, and wasted no time in having a raucous good time at Li Jiangyun's expense. They said that after spending the last couple of days looking everywhere for her, they'd gone to her place the night before, but she wouldn't answer the door, leaving them to freeze in the cold air. She smiled but said nothing. We sat down to play cards, leaving Li Jiangyun to kill time by flipping through some magazines. I kept glancing over at her, and our eyes often met, though I couldn't tell what those looks meant. And where were you last night, Fang Yan? Fat Man asked. We spent the day looking for you too. You weren't hiding in Li Jiangyun's room, were you? I said Yes, we had a great time. I go out and win the revolution, Fat Man said with a smirk, but you get to sit on the throne. I told her to come sit next to me to give the others an eyeful. After muttering something in reply, she came over and sat down beside me. Oh? I said with a smile. Were they right after all? Her face darkened and her eyes rounded in anger as if I'd given her the ultimate insult. Get away from me, go on, I said in mock terror. I don't want to upset you. She stared out the window and ignored us. Liu Huiyuan asked if there were any developments in the Gao Yang case. I'm done for, I said, my goose is cooked. I can't find any witnesses and I can't cut myself loose from suspicion. If I run it's like admitting guilt, so now all I can do is wait for the cops to come haul me away, and let that be the end of it. You can't be serious, Liu Huiyuan said. You don't even know where you were at the time. No I don't, I said. And that's not the only thing I don't know. I recall being in Beijing then, but a parade of witnesses insists that I was in Yunnan, and I can't find a single person who'll admit to being with me. Apparently there was a girl, but I'll be damned if I can find a trace of her. I don't know what she's been up to all these years, or if there even was such a girl in the first place. I turned to Li Jiangyun, who appeared to be deep in thought. We were not being fair to her. A pretty girl, still she was a bit too standoffish for my tastes, attractive yet hard to get close to. You ought to get serious about finding her, Liu Huiyuan remarked. The smell always lingers long after the fart, so if there was such a girl, she must have left a trail. The first order of business is to determine her identity, so everyone can start looking. What's her name? That's the problem, I don't know a thing about her, except that she's Miss Liu, and there's a basketful of those. It's all perfectly clear in my dreams but what good are dreams? She's in your dreams? Liu Huiyuan laughed. You've got everything covered. That's why I said I'll be a raving lunatic before long.

The young groom, sleeves rolled up and all sweaty, came in to announce that lunch was nearly ready and told us to wash up. First we went in to see what was being served, and there on the table was a dazzling display of glistening, inviting cold cuts. After loudly voicing our approval, we washed up, moved chairs and stools over to the table, and dug in. Li Jiangyun tugged on my sleeve and said she needed to talk to me. So I followed her into the living room, where I saw her eyes redden and watched her light a cigarette instead of coming right out and saying what was on her mind. After a couple of deep drags, she glared at me and said in measured tones, What's wrong with me? How come everybody treats me like I'm invisible, like just having me around is a pain? Tell me, and I want the truth. What's so disagreeable about me? It's me not you, I said with a smile that withered before her forlorn expression. I tried to smooth things over by saying how much we all like you, how nobody has ever said anything bad about you, and how we agree that you're terrific. Those guys and their gutter talk, that's their problem not yours. I'm talking about you. Li Jiangyun was steaming. How come I can't make an impression on you? You're always putting on an act, nothing seems to matter to you. You impressed me right from the start, I said, feeling more perplexed by the minute. You're never far from my thoughts, but I don't do anything about it for fear of upsetting . . . ah, to hell with it! Li Jiangyun flipped away her cigarette and stood up to go. Fuck you!

Fuck me? Who did that bitch think she was, talking to me like that? What did I ever do to you? I grumbled as I returned to the other room, where the diners were grazing the table and toasting each other. Li Jiangyun sat down across from me with the cold glare of resentment in her eyes.

This is our last time together, so here's farewell to you all. I raised my glass and laughed, and so did the others, except for Li Jiangyun. After draining my glass and sitting down, I poured another drink and clinked glasses with my friends, one after the other, fixing Li Jiangyun with a searing smile. Suddenly something dawned on me; I began searching my pockets frantically.

"What are you looking for?" Fat Man Wu asked. "I've got a light, if that's what you want."

"No, I'm not looking for a light." I jumped up and ran into the bedroom, opened my closet, and rummaged through the clothes hanging there. That day, I recalled, I was wearing an old brown leather bomber jacket with a fur collar, one of those air force jobs that were so popular at the time. One after the other, I slid the hangers across the bar, until, way back in the corner, I found what I was looking for: my dusty leather jacket. I dug through the pockets and came up with that photograph; sunbeams in the closet filled with swirling dust motes. The dark background framed the hazy face of a girl in old-fashioned clothes. The photograph was turning yellow, its corners curled inward, and a crease cut right across the girl's face, distorting her smile.

I carried it back to the table, and gave Li Jiangyun a long, hard look. With her head lowered, she kept at her food, refusing to look up at me.

"Where'd you get that?" Liu Huiyuan laid down his chopsticks and took the photo from me, holding it to the light for a better look.

"It was in the pocket of an old jacket," I said, looking back at Li Jiangyun. "I've been turning the world upside down, and it's been right here all along. I think that's who I've been looking for, the girl everyone says I was with back then."

"Let me see it," said Fat Man Wu, who was chewing lustily. "If you ask me, this is a younger version of Li Jiangyun. Well, now, don't tell me you two have a history."

"How could that be Li Jiangyun?" I laughed and took back the photograph. A quick look at Li Jiangyun, then the photograph. "This isn't Li Jiangyun, although there is a slight resemblance. This was the girl of my dreams. Not bad, hmm? If I remember correctly, someone told me her name once. It's it's it's Liu Yan." It came to me in a flash.

"The girl of your dreams, and someone else has to tell you her name?"

"I forgot it a long time ago." I laid the photograph down on the table to study it from a distance. "A person's youth is like a river," I said with a smile. "On and on it flows until it becomes a muddy soup."

"You're the dizziest person I've ever seen," Fat Man said with a laugh. "You lay the egg, but somebody else has to sit on it for you."

"You'd be dizzy, too, if you were in my shoes," I said. "If

all of a sudden somebody started asking you about things that happened back in your great-great-grandfather's time, I doubt you'd have much to say either. What worries you is that they'll come to settle accounts after many autumns. Things that were clear once aren't clear any longer." I stared at the photograph, lost in thought. Then: "But there was someone, a royal consort, I think, though her face is blurred and her name escapes me. But then we knew our dear Chairman Mao better than anyone, didn't we? And still if I don't head over to Tiananmen Square for a look every once in a while, I can never remember how the old fellow combed his hair, straight back or parted."

I held out my glass to Li Jiangyun. "A toast, just you and me, no hard feelings. With all that's been happening lately, I don't know if I'm coming or going. It's like a bad dream."

"What's this?" Fat Man Wu asked, smiling. "Is there something you two aren't telling us?"

"He probably hasn't emerged from that dream yet," Li Jiangyun remarked coolly as she laid down her wineglass and motioned for the photograph. After giving it a quick look, she handed it back. "Where is this raving beauty now?"

"I don't know." Acknowledging that fact was deflating. "What good is her photograph if I don't know how to find her?"

"You could stick an announcement up on a street corner," Fat Man Wu said with a laugh, "or you could send the picture to the newspaper and take out an ad: Lost: one dotty girl . . ."

"Must you always get your kicks out of other people's suffering?" Liu Huiyuan asked Fat Man Wu. "I hate that."

"Are you suffering?" Fat Man nudged me.

"Of course I am," I replied, edging away from him. "My poor heart's broken." As I studied the girl in the photograph, in my mind I knew that she and I had once been more than just friends, but no powerful emotions swept over me. Something was hidden there, I sensed, probably because the lowered lids shielded her eyes. To say that she had an indifferent look would be closer to the truth than to say that her face was devoid of any expression. Maybe she was in the midst of divulging something so important that only an indifferent look would do, or maybe she was repulsed by the person she was talking to. That thought forced me to consider the possibility that her eyes might be lowered because she was too lazy, or too bored, to look whoever it was in the eye. It seemed perfectly reasonable to assume that the person she was talking to, the individual beyond the borders of the photograph, was me. Obviously, there was another person in the room as well—whoever took the picture—and since the angle was slightly off and the mood especially somber, it was apparent that the photographer was listening closely to the conversation, was in fact making a game of it by capturing it on film. I couldn't tell by the setting whose house it was, although it looked familiar. A chairback visible over the girl's shoulder appeared to have a glossy finish, like the wall in the darkness behind it, as if made of the same material; for a moment there I racked my brain to come up with a commonly available material used in making both walls *and* furniture, and bamboo was all I could think of. Now I've already indicated that the girl's hands were bright, and that she was holding them in a funny way—at first glance they appeared to be folded, but a closer look revealed that she might be holding something. Unfortunately, whatever it was blended in with her dark clothing, and the best I could come up with was a dark-colored billfold. I can't say why, maybe I had money on the brain, but I couldn't help feeling that the conversation involved money.

Lunch lasted well into the afternoon, until there was nothing left but dregs in the bottles and crumbs on the plates. We sat around lethargically, barely able to keep our eyes open. Before leaving for the station, the honeymooners started clearing the table to halfhearted good-byes all around. In a whisper, I asked Li Jiangyun to stick around, but she said no, she wanted to take the dopey honeymooners to the station. I all but begged her to stay, but she turned a deaf ear. "Then I'll go with you," I said.

We got up from the messy table and went outside. It was a sunny day. Fat Man Wu squinted in the bright sunlight, a cigarette dangling from his lips, and made an ass of himself with the young bride, while Li Jiangyun helped the groom check their belongings. While all this was going on, Liu Huiyuan nudged me and led me off to the side, as if to have a smoke.

"I didn't want to say anything back there," he said. "Too many people." With his cigarette hand he pointed to my pocket, the one with the photograph in it. "I've seen that Liu Yan before, and I think I can help you find her."

"How do you know her?" I was thrilled. "Do you know where she lives?"

"No," Liu Huiyuan said. "I don't know her and I don't know where she lives. But I know someone who might. It was many years ago, but I recall seeing that girl often at a friend's house. I'm pretty sure they were an item. In fact, she might have been living with him, though I can't be sure about that, since I don't like to pry. She and I didn't talk much, but she seemed right at home there. She knew where everything was, and on nights when I hung around later than usual, she made us something to eat."

"It's OK," I said with a smile. "I don't care how many guys she's made it with. All I want from her is proof that for one particular seven-day period she was with me."

"She's no ordinary girl," Liu Huiyuan said. "Impressed the hell out of me. Witty easygoing good dancer good skater even knew how to say some things in a foreign language. She was always making a scene over how she wanted to marry that pal of mine. Then I lost track of her."

"Are you coming or not?" Li Jiangyun shouted. "We're going, with or without you."

"I'm coming." I turned to Liu Huiyuan. "We'll continue this later."

All the way to the train station, Li Jiangyun and I stuck close to each other, in the subway station and on the subway, keeping our distance from the honeymooners. Even after they had boarded the train, Li Jiangyun and I gabbed on and on, standing on the far end of the platform as if we didn't even know them. "Give me a break," I kept repeating. "First of all, I didn't think anything like that was possible, and I wasn't using my head. I was afraid of making a fool of myself, confusing the true with the false. So I refused to believe the obvious." "I think you're still confusing the true with the false," she said. "I don't know what sort of conclusion you've reached, but obviously you're someone who doesn't know which end is up. You go from one extreme to the other. I'll bet you can't tell the difference between have and have not. Either you deny everything or you accept everything, then you make up some cock-and-bull story so you can accept things as fact, and that's what gets you into trouble." "I know you're a proud woman," I said. "And I realize it's hard to snap back after a setback. But I mean it this time. I'm less interested in restoring a measure of face for you than in repairing the damage caused by my stupidity. I don't want you to think I'm acting on some impulse or that I'm just following the mule down the slope, out of habit. I like you, I really do, and if I'd used my head at the time, I'd have acted like it. From the bottom of my heart, I want to act like it, in fact, I'd be your servant if you'd let me." "I believe you," she said. "If I make some gesture, no matter what state you're in at the time, whether you're using your head or not, you'll react, react well, you hope. And not just to me. You'd do the same with any female of the species. Don't think I'm putting you down. You're no different from most men. It's not evil, it's your nature." "You see, you have no idea what I'm saying." "Sure I do, I know exactly what you're saying, so don't waste breath trying to explain yourself. You have a pretty good idea what you're all about right now, but you don't know a thing about me. Everything you've said so far comes from a mistaken impression of me. You have no idea what I expect from you. I never wanted us to be anything but friends. I don't know what I did to make you think otherwise. What happened between us is a complete mystery to you. You took some things that happened, some things that never happened, and some things that couldn't possibly happen, and mixed them all together. As always, your attitude is based upon experience alone, that and conventional wisdom." "You consider yourself different from other people, don't you? You think it's no big deal if something like this happens to them, but when you're involved that makes it special, right?" "I never thought that."

The train started rolling, the honeymooners waved through the window, and we were still standing on the platform after everyone else had left, oblivious to our surroundings. Even as we walked out of the station we were still talking, having completely forgotten our purpose for being there in the first place.

"You're so vain," I said. "You're in love with yourself. Most of the time that's considered a virtue, but sometimes it's stubbornness, pure and simple, and that's what turns people off."

"That's where you're wrong. Vanity isn't something I've cultivated or anything I'm happy about, it's just there. I know it turns people off, and that it comes back to haunt me. Speaking from the heart, I'd love to have a little humility. I hate the idea that I come across as affected and proud. I don't try to give that impression, it just happens. Admittedly, I have lots of self-respect, I value myself, and while I don't think I'm any better than I am, at the same time I'm not about to let people step all over me. You can call it vanity, self-worth, or whatever you like."

"Do you think that you and I are not equals?"

"No, I think we are. But being equals doesn't mean we have to always return a favor with a favor. I've got my space to protect and you've got yours. It doesn't bother me that you come across as, or shall I say, try hard to give people the impression that you're an imbecile, a real moron, because deep down you're no dummy. You've got qualities other people can't match."

"You think so?" I laughed. "I don't. I see myself as a person who just goes with the flow, someone who takes things as they come."

"There you go again, skirting the truth," Li Jiangyun said. "For a while there you were taking this to heart, but no more. I'm being truthful, and I expect the same from you. Or we can just joke around if you'd rather."

"All right, all right, the truth it is, even if it's like looking for a needle in a haystack, or a pearl in the stomach."

"You have a very high opinion of yourself, don't deny it. Otherwise, why is it so important to get to the bottom of things that happened so long ago? Let people talk. . . ."

"If I don't get to the bottom of these things, young lady, it's my head."

"That's just an excuse. I can tell by the extent of your concern that there's more to this than just clearing your name. It's mainly self-knowledge. Your anxiety comes from not understanding some aspect of yourself, as if you've lost something, as if your image of yourself were somehow incomplete. If you can learn what happened back then, I think your anxieties will disappear, even if you find you've done something horrible. Nothing's more important than having a thorough understanding of yourself. At the very least, it gives you an idea of what to do next, and how to do it, since there's nothing worse than having your future controlled by others."

"You know me pretty well, better than I know myself. How come I didn't meet you sooner? I'll bet you even keep a diary."

"I do. I'm not one to entertain self-doubts over what others say."

"People like you scare me."

Li Jiangyun smiled for the first time in a long time. "No more talk, is that it? You've lost interest in ideas, right? OK, we'll stop here, I'm tired myself."

"Let's get serious now," I said.

"I thought we *were* being serious."

"Serious, right, we were. What I mean is, let's talk about practical matters." I held the subway door for her, then followed her in. "Well? Quite the gentleman, no?"

"It doesn't count if you say it yourself." She laughed. "It ruins the effect."

I laughed too as I grasped the swaying overhead strap. "I can't go home, the cops might come busting in at any time. You said there's nothing worse than having your future controlled by others, and I agree. Let's say the cops are so good that they eventually break the case. That still doesn't mean we should pin our hopes on other people's skills. We're the masters of our own destiny. And what if I really did kill him? Wouldn't that be a shock? And there's not a thing we could do about it."

"Stop with that 'we' business," Li Jiangyun said with a laugh. "You make it sound like we're in this together."

"That's how I see it," I said. "If they bust me, you won't get away scot-free. I'll say your diary is a fake, that the murder was all your idea, and that you were in it for the money—what'll you do then?"

"You're hopeless." She laughed. "But I wouldn't mind seeing how someone else's bullshit could affect me. So who was the ringleader in all this?"

"You were. But the imperial troops are still the big ringleaders. Come on, let me stay at your place for a while. Nothing up my sleeve, I just need to hide out. Plus you and I can have intellectual discussions morning, noon, and night. We can talk about life, about the world."

"Spare me." Li Jiangyun closed her eyes and laughed. "I can't let you stay at my place. Nothing up my sleeve, either, it's simply not safe. Just think, a single woman—my neighbors' eyes would pop out of their heads. And if one of them reported me for harboring some guy off the street, forget what they'd do to me, your life would be on the line. I couldn't bear the thought of that."

"I didn't think you cared," I said. "I've got other friends, but I can't stay with them. It'd be the same as turning myself in."

"How about this?" Li Jiangyun said. "I'll find you a place. A girlfriend of mine has her own apartment. I'll talk her into letting you stay there for a few days."

"I'm not big on staying with people I don't know."

"You and she will hit it off right away," Li Jiangyun said with

a laugh. "And she's not vain at all—just what you've been waiting for."

"Where she and I are concerned, I'm a eunuch."

We went to my place so I could get some clothes and other
necessities. "Don't forget your toothbrush," she said. "Don't forget your washcloth, don't forget your skin lotion, and what about
a bib? Don't forget your bib, my little baby."

With a laugh I took down the dusty gray handbag. "I didn't
have time to get you anything, so this'll have to do. I'll buy a real
gift tomorrow."

Li Jiangyun took the handbag and felt around inside. "My
poor little baby," she said with a laugh. "Is this the sort of prop
you use when you're playing house?"

"Your 'sister-in-law' left it here. It's full of things she used to
topple the three mountains of imperialism, feudalism, and
bureaucratism."*

"And you held on to it as a keepsake, right? I'd like to hear
this slice of history. Take your time."

The telephone rang. "Hello," I answered. Nothing.
"Hello?" Finally a girl's voice. "I thought you went to America."

That stumped me for a moment. Then I figured out who it
was. "I did, but they kicked me out. Immigration authorities
found out I had hepatitis A."

"Since you're back," the girl said, "and won't be going anywhere for a while, I think you ought to go see Ling Yu."

"I will, tomorrow," I said sincerely. "I'll be at the hospital
tomorrow afternoon, three o'clock."

*The three major enemies of the people, they appear in the preamble of the
Constitution. The "sister-in-law" refers to Madame Mao, Jiang Qing.

"You're going where tomorrow afternoon?" Li Jiangyun asked between applications of the lipstick she had found in the handbag.

I hung up the phone and walked over to her. "Nowhere," I said. "I was just bullshitting the little dope. I'm too busy to play their game."

"You're terrible." Li Jiangyun checked her lipstick in my mirror. "What do you think?" she asked.

I didn't know what to say, so I moved her face this way and that with my hand. "Are we dreaming?"

She pushed my hand away and rubbed off the lipstick. "I never use this stuff," she said with a laugh. "Instead of making a girl look sexy, I think painting lips till they drip red makes her look hideous."

9

If you ask me, the whole thing was a chance occurrence. While Li Jiangyun and I were strolling in and out of sunbathed lanes, I was hanging on her every word, not paying attention to where we were headed. So it wasn't until we walked into a lane crowded with raucous middle-school students on their way home with their backpacks that I looked up and noticed the school building up ahead, that and a T-shaped intersection occupied by tiny shops.

"Where are we?" I had to raise my voice to be heard over the kids.

"Baishan's place." She smiled serenely. "Up ahead."

We turned at the intersection, where a public square surrounded by apartment buildings, all very tall and all exactly alike, came into view. Their shadows threw half the street into darkness. As we walked among the buildings, we left the sunlight, and the warmth it carried, behind. Strong gusty winds whipped around the corners.

The hallway was quiet, deserted even, devoid of the market baskets, cardboard boxes, and bicycles normally found inside apartment houses. The doors were closed, all the way up, although as we climbed the stairs we felt a steady cold draft. Strong winds on the top floor made the landing window bang loudly. Li

Jiangyun took out a ring of keys and opened the door of one of the two apartments.

The apartment was stifling—poor ventilation. Everything—desk, chairs, beds, dressers—was in perfect order, and when I peeked out the bedroom window, I saw an expanse of rooftops, like the overlapping scales of a fish; the gray middle-school building rose above neighboring squat houses lining the narrow lane all the way to the intersection, with its tiny shops.

"Your girlfriend, what's her name, Baishan, doesn't seem to be home." I sat down on the neatly made, feminine-smelling bed. "I expected her to welcome us on bended knee."

"She's at work." Li Jiangyun unpacked the things I'd brought with me, busily putting the clothes in the dresser and the toilet articles in the bathroom. "Stay here, I'll go get her. Your problems are solved. You'll be as comfy here as you are in your own home."

"I've never been comfy in my own home."

"Then you'll be comfier here than in your own home." With a smile, she unlocked a drawer in the desk. "Anything you don't want people to see you can put in here."

I looked down at the drawer, then let my eyes roam about the room to see how it was laid out. There was a bottle of cologne on the bedside dresser. I picked it up, I opened it, I sprayed it in the air. "Does Baishan snore?"

"What makes you think you're sleeping in the same room?" Li Jiangyun walked up and took the cologne from me, capped it, and put it back where it belonged.

"Then who do I sleep with?"

"Here's your roommate." She picked a fuzzy object up off the bed and tossed it to me. A cute, smiling teddy bear.

"Don't you live here?" I asked.

"I've got my own place." She smiled. "I've never done anything so bad that I had to quit my job and move away."

"The more people living together, the merrier," I said earnestly. "Being around close friends makes life interesting. Living alone is a drag."

"I know all about you," she said, her eyes glued to me. "You're someone who cherishes all the traditional virtues."

"I do," I said as I hugged the teddy bear to myself. "I have nothing in common with the modern crowd. They get on my nerves."

"Then why not settle down and start a family? Eat simply and live a traditional life."

"That's what I've been thinking of doing, but I never get the chance. When I was young, nobody fit the bill. Now I've met you, but you're not interested. Just my luck."

"Can the act. I really think it's time you canned it. We know each other too well for you to waste time and energy playing that bit."

"I mean it," I said as I walked up to her, looking pouty. "I've got all this bitterness stored up inside me, and who can I pour it out to if not you? I, ah, a bitter wanderer, tramping through China." I walked over to an orchid planter and bent down to smell the flower.

"Bitter wanderer."

I turned around. Li Jiangyun came up to me, head down, purse in hand. "I'll go get Baishan. You wait here."

"Tell her there's a new 'man-in-waiting' waiting for her at home."

"I'll tell her she's got a new little orphan to take care of."

Li Jiangyun went out smiling. I lay down on the bed with my hands behind my head, engulfed in silence after the door slammed shut. Somewhere in the room I detected the delicate aroma of violets. I examined the cologne bottle on the dresser. After checking the label, I opened it again and squirted some in the air. The smell of violets got stronger.

The apartment reeked of violets. Carefully I checked out each room. In the bathroom I found every imaginable kind of shampoo and bath oil, plus jar upon jar of face cream, all unopened, full to the top, though the labels were turning dark. From there into the kitchen: appliances pots and pans spatulas spices cooking oil salt vinegar, it was all there in front of me, all brand new, never used. The door of the second bedroom was closed. I tried it; it was locked.

Back in my room again, I strolled out onto the balcony, where I leaned against the railing to take in the view. Street noises in the distance never stopped, but the apartment complex was deathly silent. A window curtain in the building across the way fluttered; I was being watched, so I went back inside. A young woman was standing in the room.

"I'm Baishan," she said, her eyes large and vacant like those of the blind. She had bright red spots high on each cheek, rough around the edges, which made her nostrils look like a butterfly about to soar in the air; her tiny capillaries were visible. She was not pretty, but she had a great body.

"Have a seat." She was pacing back and forth silently. Could be trying to shake off the chill she'd brought in from outside. "Li Jiangyun told me what's up. Make yourself at home. If you act like a guest, you'll just make me uncomfortable."

"Sorry to put you to all this trouble."

Again she looked at me as if she were blind. She had big eyes but her pupils weren't clouded, and I couldn't say why I had the impression that she was sightless, except maybe because the pupils were gray and lusterless as dead cinders.

"It must be nice living here all alone."

Baishan walked up to the bed as if she hadn't heard me and straightened the covers where I had lain on them. Then she moved the cologne bottle back to where I had found it. "My place is your place," she said. Then she smiled. "It's nice having someone around for a change."

She walked out of the room, and I heard her unlock the second bedroom door. Then the lock clicked, returning the apartment to silence.

Li Jiangyun didn't come back that night, and Baishan didn't show her face. I slept like a baby. Until the middle of the night, that is, when something woke me up. Someone was in the living room making a phone call; I heard every click of the dial. Then silence. A moment later, the dialing recommenced, and again no one said a word. Finally, after the longest time, whoever it was hung up the phone, and I heard a woman sobbing loudly. After that came a loud scratching on the door. That did it. "Who's out there?" I shouted. "Is that you, Baishan?"

The scratching and sobbing stopped, so I got out of bed and opened the door. The room was as dark as it was quiet. The telephone on the dining table was covered with a handkerchief. Baishan's bedroom door was shut tight.

Northwest winds blew in from the plains that night, covering the city with a blanket of yellow dust. When I opened my eyes in the morning, the sky was a murky yellow and tons of fine dust had settled slowly and evenly to earth. My room had not been spared: Dust had found its way in through the cracks to blanket the windowsill, the tables and chairs, the floor, even my covers. Getting out of bed was like climbing out of a sand pit.

Outside the dust was still settling like a rainy mist, as if a fleet of heavenly dump trucks were releasing loads of fine sand onto people's heads, cars and trucks, and rooftops, until everything was little more than a blur. The yellow mist became a vast sandy quilt, creating a nightmarish scene, as if the city were being buried alive. At a local dairy shop I called Liu Huiyuan to tell him where I was staying. Then I found an empty chair and sat down. The shop had only a weak fluorescent light, which turned everything inside pale: the large food chiller, the clerks' aprons and caps, the ice cream containers and other products on top of the food chiller, even the people's faces, all of it made worse by the contrasting murky yellow sky outside.

When Liu Huiyuan walked in, I was drinking a warm bottle of dark soda, so agitated I was shaking.

10

Liu Huiyuan's friend, Li Kuidong, a broad-shouldered thick-waisted urbane fellow, a department head in some government office, was waiting for us in the tiny reception room. He and Liu Huiyuan were pretty tight, as I could tell from their friendly banter while I sat quietly off to the side feeling sorry for myself. I had just learned from Liu Huiyuan that police, carloads of them, had searched my house the night before, going around the compound telling everyone I'd fled to avoid arrest for some serious crime. From there they went to see him and Fat Man Wu to find out where I'd gone; both insisted they didn't know. The police seemed to know a lot, since they asked about the young couple and a woman, obviously Li Jiangyun. They told them what they could about the couple, but said they didn't know who the woman was. I was worried that the police would try to get to me through Li Jiangyun, and I assumed they had more than one way of keeping tabs on me. I was even suspicious of this urbane department head, who knew nothing at all about me.

He and Liu Huiyuan kept up the friendly talk for a while before picking up the photograph I'd brought with me. "Why do you want to find her?"

I gave him my prepared speech, a pack of harmless lies: "A

friend of mine angling for a promotion needs his diploma back. They lived together."

"That's it, that's the only reason," Liu Huiyuan pitched in helpfully. "It's all on the up and up. But so much time has passed, and there have been so many changes. We tried her old address, but no luck."

"I don't know where she's living these days," Li Kuidong said. "We split up years ago. Shortly after we met, she lived with me for a while, but I couldn't tell you where she is now."

"When you and she were together, what year was that? Where was it? What was she doing at the time?"

"At the time . . ." He paused. "What do you want to know all that for?"

"I think you'd better tell him the truth," Liu Huiyuan urged me. "It'll make things easier."

"OK." I moved on to the second set of lies. "She's my big sister. Our parents died during the ten chaotic years,* and I went to live with relatives in the provinces. She was sent to a farm in the Northeast, and that was the last I saw of her. I've been looking for her ever since, but no luck. All I've got to go on is this photograph, and I don't even know when it was taken. Without it, I'd have forgotten what she looked like long ago. Life must have been hard on her all these years, a girl alone, drifting from place to place, lucky if she can find a decent person anywhere along the way. Just thinking about it nearly breaks my heart."

"He's been through hell," Liu Huiyuan said. "This pal of mine has really been through hell, which is why I decided to help out."

"Um." I blew my nose before going on. "I'm not looking

*The Cultural Revolution, 1966–1976.

to settle scores or anything like that," I said to Li Kuidong. "What's past is past. Besides, like they say, in the end all accounts have to be settled with the Gang of Four. I just want to find my sister. To you folks who took her in, all I can say is thank you."

"It was ten years ago," Li Kuidong said, blinking uncertainly. "I'd just returned from a production corps, and didn't have a job, so I hung around the house most of the time. We lived near Red Tower Auditorium, where they showed foreign films all the time, and I used to try to scrounge up tickets. I think it was early spring, still cold enough for an overcoat. I'm not sure what was showing that night, maybe *The Bold Adventure*. Anyway, I was standing in the entrance without a ticket when the movie began, and people with tickets filed inside, leaving the rest of us to loiter in front of the auditorium. I was about to leave when she—your sister—brushed past me in an army overcoat, her hands tucked in the sleeves. When I asked if she had an extra ticket, she looked up and nodded yes. But instead of giving it to me, she handed them both to the ticket-taker, who tore them in half. So I followed her in. Although I offered to pay for the ticket, she said No need, so we watched the movie together, shoulder to shoulder. After it was over, I asked if she had any plans. She wondered what I had in mind, and I said, Nothing, maybe get a bite to eat, and after thinking it over she said OK. . . ."

"Then what?" I asked, thinking he might not go on. "That can't be all."

"Then we got to know each other," he said, starting to get a little fidgety. Probably reluctant to discuss such things with a total stranger.

"We always agreed on when and where we'd meet the next time before saying good-bye, and somewhere along the line, she moved into my place. She said she had just returned from a production corps, and that she had no family. My experience in one of those places told me that she had labored in one too, so I never doubted her, never had any reason to. A tough life had taught her to take things in stride. One look, a subtle change in expression told her everything she needed to know about where she stood and what the other person had in mind. She was never willful, never intentionally made things hard on anyone. Always gentle and easy to get along with, she made my life a carefree one. But don't get the idea that she was some taciturn, unfeeling marionette. She talked a lot, she loved to laugh, and she had a great sense of humor. Crowds didn't bother her, she handled herself with ease. Liu Huiyuan knows what I'm talking about. She wasn't one of those petty, affected women who feel sorry for themselves or are always acting coy. What set her apart from all those naive, unpolished girls out there was that she could enjoy herself without becoming self-indulgent, was poised and natural without appearing to be flighty. You could tease her all you wanted, until it turned nasty or disrespectful, and she'd know right off. Not that her expression would change all of a sudden, just that she knew without letting on that she knew. So when I say she led a tough life, I mean she had a certain aloofness that kept her from getting ruffled or losing her cool. Though the cover is worn, it still keeps the contents clean. Whenever she lowered her eyelids, you could take her in your arms or enter her or whatever, and still you knew that she was a free spirit, off someplace far away."

"Did she call herself Liu Yan when you were together?"

"Right, though I could never shake the feeling that it wasn't her real name. Even when things were going great between us, she was like a stranger, a girl who didn't want me to know her real identity. She was incredibly elusive."

"Is that why you broke up?"

"No. I'm not someone who has to know everything about people he's close to. Some things you're better off not knowing. Take me, for instance. I've got this minor official post, and I understand the importance of keeping my distance from the people who work for me. Fair and equal treatment leads to harmonious relationships. No, that wasn't the reason."

Li Kuidong took a drag on his cigarette, then another before putting it out. He looked at me.

"She lied," he said, "and that's one thing I can't tolerate. I tried, I really did, but it was too much for me. I guess it was something in her makeup, but she'd lie when she had no reason to. I never showed any interest in anyone or anything but her, but she went and lied to me anyway. Maybe it had become a habit. And while most people lie purposefully, to get something or to protect themselves, especially girls, she did it for no apparent reason, probably wasn't even aware of it. That's what bothered me. Say it's something you have trouble talking about, or tell me you have good reason to lie, I can understand that. I'll give you an example. We're walking past some buildings and she points to one and says that's where her folks live, door such-and-such, number so-and-so, x number of rooms furnished with this and that plus a dog or a cat or whatever. So one day I decide to drop in, you know, surprise her by showing up unannounced and all. So who should open the door but some guy I hate, and he says he doesn't know her, never heard of her. She made an ass of me, pure and simple. But when I brought it up, she had this blank look on her face like she didn't know what I was talking about. Another time she told me about this darling puppy she had, how cute it was, with long scraggly hair that covered its eyes, and how she had to trim it so the dog could see where it was going. When she took it to the park, she was stopped by a policeman, so she said 'Tell uncle you're sorry,' and the dog goes 'bow-wow,' and on and on, as detailed as you could imagine. I said I'd like to see the dog, and she kept promising to bring it over, but never did. After moving into my place, one day she came home and, with a great show of pomp and flair, handed me a bundle that held the dog, or so she said. I opened it and found a toy dog."

I laughed. "She sounds intriguing."

Li Kuidong eyed me uncertainly. "You'd find it hard to be intrigued if things like that happened every day. I told her, 'You make it impossible for me to know if anything you say is true.' She said, 'I'll change.' But a couple of days later she said someone had invited her to a reunion with a bunch of friends, so I told her Go ahead, and she went. I had some things to take care of at Xidan that day, and as I was passing through Muxidi I saw her sitting on a park bench, playing with some kids. There were no friends. In all that time, the only people I ever saw her with were my friends. Whenever she said she was going somewhere with friends, she wound up walking the streets alone. But before long she'd be telling me once more that she was off to see some friends.

"It must have been our second year, and this is something I definitely want to get out into the open, I never had any intention of marrying her, your sister, that is. I'm sure she knew that, and one day she went out and never came back. I waited for her for the longest time. For a while there, if there was a noise at the door, I thought it was her coming home, but it never was. As time passed, I thought about her less and less. A man's got to get married, after all, and that's what I did. I'd have forgotten all about her if you hadn't come by." Li Kuidong lit another cigarette.

"You never saw her again?"

"Once," he said. "Sometime in the summer, in Master Wang Lane or Bastard Wang Lane, I forget which. My wife and I were riding along on our bikes when I saw her coming out of the lane with some guy in sandals. She didn't see me and I didn't call out to her. We rode on, and that was it. A friend of mine said he ran into her at a dance somewhere and that she spent a few nights with him. But he's a playboy who's always bragging about how many women he's slept with, so I'm not sure I believe him. But who knows? Wang Kuanglin. Know him?" Li asked Liu Huiyuan.

"No," Huiyuan said. "Doesn't ring a bell."

"Got his address? Could you write it down for me?"

"I've got it," Li Kuidong said. "But don't tell him you got it from me."

"No problem." I watched him copy out the address, then slipped the scrap of paper into my pocket. "We'd better be going. If you hear any news of Liu Yan, I'd appreciate it if you passed it on."

"How'll I find you?"

"Liu Huiyuan will know how to find me."

"Your sister's got good qualities." Having gotten into the swing of things, Li Kuidong seemed reluctant to bring the talk of Liu Yan to a close. "There isn't much she can't do. Good dancer, great skater. If there were amateur rankings for skaters, she'd be right at the top. Out on the ice she was the center of attention, the best skater around. She could do a pirouette that would knock your eye out, like somebody who'd spent a lot of time in frozen, snow-covered regions."

11

"What do you mean you're trying to find your big sister? Whose leg are you trying to pull? The country's at peace the people are content and human tragedies like that are a thing of the past. I've seen you around, pal. Since when have you got a big sister? Any sister of yours was flung over the wall by your old man long ago."

Wang Kuanglin, a hideous cripple, was wearing a dark, trim, Western suit, and tiny, spit-polished shoes, one with an elevated heel, to make him look more impressive when he stood up. Liu Huiyuan and I found him in the bicycle shed downstairs, talking on a pay phone. "Do you know where Wang Kuanglin is?" we asked the parking attendant. Wang stuck his head out of the phone booth, receiver in hand, and shouted, "Over here over here Wang Kuanglin's over here." Then, in a bossier tone, he added, "Wait till I've finished this call, and we can talk." He pulled his head back into the booth, leaned against the window, and continued his long-winded conversation: "You guys have to get moving. That seventy thousand U.S. has already been transferred from the Paris bank into a Swiss account. I've seen the bank draft with my own eyes. Monsieur Balloon is mighty upset about having such a large sum of money moved from one European bank to another without earning a cent of interest. I was morti-

fied to hear it. You can stick it to all the foreign devils you want,
but not Monsieur Balloon, he's one of China's biggest supporters.
He gave me a car, a *Tit*roën, just because I asked him for one.
This is bigger than you and me, so if you muck things up, I might
just have to place a call to Boss Zhao or Boss Li. . . ." The parking
attendant whispered, "That cripple, who is he? He's always on
the phone and the conversation is always the same." "He runs
the Crippled Citizens office for the State Council," we replied.
By then Wang Kuanglin had hung up and was emerging from the
phone booth, face red and shiny. We stopped laughing and told
him why we'd come to see him. That's when more of the same
lies began pouring out of my mouth. But the crippled prick saw
right through me. He didn't believe a word I said.

"Do you know who you're dealing with? You're no match for
Master Wang, a man whose mind is as bright as a polished mirror."

I laughed awkwardly. "Since Master Wang knows what's up,
I'll give it to you straight. That line was intended for some dumb
prick not Master Wang. We need to find her because she owes
me money, and even if I didn't need it, I wouldn't want her to
have it. I'd rather see it go to our Master Wang here."

"You guys go about these things all wrong." The cripple sucked
on his teeth. "Where women are concerned I take pride in always
using their money. You'll never catch me spending any of my own."

"Sounds good to me. Master Wang is one of a kind."

"How's this," the cripple said as he hobbled out of the bicycle shed. "I could use some lunch, why not join me?"

"Whatever you say."

"Someplace nearby." We followed him to a car parked in
front of the building. He patted the trunk. "The damn thing's
out of gas, so we'll have to walk. Any place around here will do.
I avoid rich food, so let's get something simple—what do you

think of the car? Not bad, eh? It's French. One of the four best cars in the world, a *Titr*oën, the only one in Beijing."

"No doubt whose car *this* is."

We followed the crippled prick out of the apartment complex, crossed a street where a road crew was laying some bubbly asphalt, and entered a decent-looking café. We took a private booth and started bickering about what to order. Instead of looking at the menu, we took the crippled prick's lead and looked to the waiter. "What do you recommend?" He suggested sea anemones and giant prawns. We exchanged glances. "They suck, no good." He moved on to other items: meatballs, pork tendon, grouper. Each was met with, "Too common, that's all we ever eat." He closed the menu. "Then what do you feel like?" I jumped in before the crippled prick. "Fried tofu steamed hyacinth beans braised eggplant." The waiter said they had no seasonal vegetables. "You can eat that stuff at home." I turned to the cripple. "That's the trouble with cafés. They never have what you want." The waiter walked off and sat down. "Call me when you're ready," he said. So much for recommendations. "Our turn." We opened the menu, started at the top, and ordered sliced pork and minced meat, to which the crippled prick added enough rice to go around. We had to pay up front, and the dumb fuck fought with me over the bill. I had the money out, but he grabbed my hand and shoved it back into my pocket. He was determined to pay, he said. But once his hand found its way into his pocket, that's where it stayed.

"This is ridiculous," I said as I handed the money to the waiter.

"No, it's not right," the crippled prick objected, cupping his chin and looking pouty. "This is my turf."

The crippled prick's mood lightened considerably with the

arrival of the food. He motioned for us to dig in before deftly scooping up slices of pork and cramming them into his mouth.

"Who told you guys I knew Liu Yan?" He asked confidently, smacking his lips over the tasty meat. "The news apparently made the rounds in spite of my attempts to squelch it."

"It's common knowledge," I replied fawningly. "It's all over Beijing."

"Can't be," he said, cunningly confident in his knowledge and deductive abilities. "Li Kuidong's the only one who knew, so that's where you heard it."

"No," I objected protectively, "no way."

"Nice try, but when you eat grapes, sooner or later you have to spit out the seeds." A derisive tone crept into his voice. "Master Cripple's no fool. You don't think I made it this far without knowing who's who and what's what, do you . . . but that's OK, Master Cripple doesn't care where you heard it. Li Kuidong must have told you that the Liu girl had plenty of good qualities and how great she was, and all that. But for the peaches crowd,* with their rotten skins, the meat inside has to be just as rotten. For somebody like him, who's never seen a real-life pussy, he's like a guy nibbling melon seeds under the covers who figures that anything finding its way into his stomach must be good. I'm telling you guys that Liu Yan was the cheapest, dirtiest slut in all Beijing, as scummy a piece of goods as you can imagine. She made herself up like a proper lady in order to prowl the back alleys, and you think I didn't know her? Her dad's got a pushcart, her mom's a ragpicker, and she's never brushed her teeth or washed her snatch, which is the repository of crap you wouldn't believe. She has to cover up the stench with gobs of deodorant, and anybody

*Prostitutes.

who sticks it in her could bathe for three days, until his skin bled, and still not get rid of the smell, like food that stinks so bad you can't swallow it without loading it up with onions and sopping up lots of soy sauce."

Wang Kuanglin said he had picked Liu Yan up at a dance years before and still regretted it. I showed him the photo, and asked him to be absolutely sure. He took a good long look and said it was her, no mistake. "Have you ever seen anything so disgusting?" He told us he'd organized a dance, a real classy affair for high-ranking cadres, and a girl who called herself Five Grain Alcohol had brought Liu Yan along. "She figured she could work the place like some call girl." The muted lighting and smoky air made it hard to see or smell and he thought she was some kind of fairy princess.

"I was dancing up a storm," the cripple said, "when Five Grain Alcohol shoved Liu Yan into my arms and said She's all yours. Well, Liu Yan stuck to me like a skin plaster. She spoke to me in Flemish. With all the time I spent in Belgium it was like talking to me in my native tongue, so I threw it back at her and we'd see who came out best. Well, she right away switched to Hebrew, but again she'd met her match, since I grew up in the old Jewish enclave of Kaifeng. After Hebrew it was southern Fukien, after that the language of the Lisu minority. . . . By then I was starting to squirm, since this was supposed to be a dance not some birdcall contest. What nest did you come from? Out with it, and that'll settle things. Well, she hemmed and hawed out of embarrassment for a while before saying she was a Beijing native, and too bad there was no one home when the foreigners entered the city during the Boxer Rebellion. I said Chinese shouldn't be putting on an act like they were hatched from foreign eggs. What the hell, we take a backseat to nobody. I told her that the Empress

Dowager and a bunch of emperors of the Eastern Han were all members of our clan, until just about everyone who mattered was named Wang. But all this talk, what I'm saying, means nothing because that's not where a person's social standing comes from. I ran into her again somewhere near Wei Villa, you know, where you find all those song and dance troupes, and she was parading up and down the street like some performer. When she saw me at the public market entrance, she started in about music, first this then that, passing herself off as some kind of cultural insider. I can't begin to tell you how I felt. Oh, I said, so that's what music is. I've known about it all along, I just knew it by a different name. You call it music, I call it chicken squawks."

At that point I broke in: "How long did you know Liu Yan? When was that? Who did she hang out with?"

"Not long," the cripple said. "With someone like that, a little goes a long way. I've got one bad leg already, I sure didn't want another. But when all is said and done, she wasn't bad, if you know what I mean." He winked lewdly. "She knew how to take care of a guy."

"She was good at what she did." I nodded in agreement. "You don't happen to know who she went with after that, do you?"

"You, I thought," he said. "You treated her like a disposable cigarette lighter, something no one can refill after you've used it up. But she went through so many men it's hard to say who came next. You weren't the first and you sure weren't going to be the last, so why worry yourself sick over her? Women are all alike. They dust themselves off, wash off the dirt, cover themselves with stuff that says 'Made in China,' and palm themselves off as brand new."

"That's not what I meant," I said. "I don't care who she

hooked up with or when. What I need to find out is how I met her. Do you know?"

"You lost me there." The crippled prick eyed me suspiciously. "Tell me what's going on here, and don't say one thing when you mean another. Now did you just ask me how you met her?"

"That's right," I replied nervously. "I wish I knew, but I've drawn a blank, it's all tied up with something else and I . . ." I was on the verge of becoming incoherent.

"You two, you, that is, met her in Guangzhou." The cripple was guarded as a fox that's spotted a chunk of meat on the ground and wonders what it's doing there, but doesn't sense any immediate danger nearby. "You guys were going from one guesthouse to another, pretending you were there on business, while what you were really up to was ripping off Hong Kong tourists. You went down the line till you found an unlocked door, then cleaned the place out. Or you'd tell the hotel staff you'd left your keys in your room, go inside and dress up in nice Hong Kong clothes and expensive Hong Kong shoes, then take off, suitcases and all. That's when you picked up athlete's foot—what they call Hong Kong rot—and B.O. You were living like a king, with all the good food, good drink, and great women you wanted, bashing people's heads in and pulling off all kinds of scams. About the only thing you didn't do was drape explosives around the necks of your Hong Kong tourists."

"Me? I did that?" I laughed. "How come I don't remember any of it?"

"Liu Yan flew to Guangzhou on her own, in response, she said, to the nine-point communiqué by Central Committee member Ye Jianying for people to expand relations across the

Taiwan Straits and support the three contacts.* In fact, she expanded it to four contacts by setting up a 'Taiwanese Brethren Reception Center.' You met in the lounge of Guangzhou's White Cloud Airport. You were there to buy a plane ticket to Kunming, she was seeing off a Nationalist secret agent, and when you heard hometown accents, you hit it off right away. You sat in the lounge area talking up a storm, and when you left together you were beaming."

"Where were you? You talk like you were watching us the whole time. How come I don't recall seeing you?"

"You don't recall seeing me because you didn't. Oh, I was there, sitting nearby. Liu Yan saw me, but didn't let on. She kept glancing at me out of the corner of her eye while she was talking to you. Actually, you saw me when you turned around to see what or who she was looking at, but since you didn't know who I was I left no impression."

"Then what?"

"You'll have to ask yourself that, since she hooked up with you, not me. You spent most of your time with Gao Yang, Xu Xun, Wang Ruohai, and Gao Jin, and nobody knows what you were up to better than you. Not one of you acknowledged my presence, which in your case was no big deal, since you didn't know me, but I helped Gao Jin and Xu Xun lots of times, and Wang Ruohai pretended he didn't know me either, but that was OK with me, since I had other fish to fry."

"Are you saying that Gao Jin, Xu Xun, and the others saw Liu Yan too?"

"Just what kind of skirmish are you fighting here, pal? Don't worry, I'm not interested in your affairs. If you want to find Liu

*Postal, transportation, and trade.

Yan, start by looking up Five Grain Alcohol. One's as scummy as the next, they know all about each other. Sparring like this with me is a stupid waste of everyone's time."

I asked him some more questions, but he refused to answer, repeating over and over, Don't know. And he wouldn't give me Five Grain Alcohol's address. Check around, he said. "Ask anybody about her, they'll tell you." I wondered if he'd had any news of Liu Yan in recent years. He said he'd heard she was seen on Ten Crossings Mountain with Wang Ruohai, and that someone else had spotted her with Gao Jin doing the butterfly stroke in Guanting Reservoir. I didn't quite believe him because Wang Ruohai had just gotten out of jail, and while I might have believed him if he'd said Mount Kunlun, Ten Crossings was out of the question. And as for Gao Jin, what with his career and his temperament, it would have been unthinkable for him to find the time to fool around with a woman, even though he did know the butterfly stroke. But to practice it in Guanting Reservoir meant he'd have to have been deposited there by a helicopter, and I figured the crippled prick was jerking me around. He and Liu Huiyuan moved on to other topics. He said, There's a horny chick over there who can't keep her eyes off us. What would you say if I told you I could get her to come over here without breaking a sweat? We turned and, sure enough, there was a real looker sitting alone at a nearby table, chopsticks in hand in anticipation of the food that was coming. The crippled prick pumped himself up and smoothed some wrinkles out of his suit, with Liu Huiyuan sitting there saying, Don't don't don't make any trouble. The cripple asked, What kind of trouble do you mean? Don't be so gutless. He flashed a winning smile at the girl, who hadn't moved a muscle, and said "Come here, I have something to tell you." I was too busy thinking my own thoughts to pay attention to what happened next, and by the time I looked up, this mountain of a man was standing right in front of the crippled prick. "You can tell me whatever it is." The crippled prick flexed his muscles and started rolling up his sleeves without even standing up. "Are you looking for a fight?" That was more than the big guy could take. He picked the crippled prick up by the scruff of his neck as if he were a scrawny chicken. "Your bones are just itching to get busted, is that it?" Liu Huiyuan and I jumped to our feet to keep things from getting out of hand. "No fighting no fighting." Liu Huiyuan turned and said to the big guy softly, "Our comrade here isn't well. He just got out of Anding Hospital." The big guy dropped the cripple, who bounced hard on the floor. "Anyone as disgusting as you shouldn't be pulling that shit." The cripple stumbled around until he managed to sit back down on his stool. "I'm only backing off because of you two," he said. The big guy spun around and headed back, but we managed to block his way and keep the two of them apart. "Let me at him, I'll show him how to cry without tears." "Keep that up, and you can forget about getting any help from us," I told him. "Help? You're nothing but punks," he swore. Liu Huiyuan grabbed me by the arm. "Let's go, come on, let the fucker alone." As we walked out of the café we heard the cripple screaming like a butchered pig.

"That was some story the crippled prick told," I said with a hollow laugh when we were out on the street.

Liu Huiyuan looked at me and smiled. "You seem to have kept your secrets pretty well hidden."

"Um." My chest swelled. "Who'd have thought I'd done all that? I guess I've taken my share of walks down the dark road. All this time I'd assumed I'd been a wimp ever since I was a kid, but no, I've done some awesome things, ridden on the backs of a person or two."

"Are you saying the crippled prick was telling the truth?"

"He said he saw it with his own eyes, so I assume he was telling the truth. But then, what about the money? What happened to all the loot I supposedly took from those well-heeled visitors? How come I'm still the same old naked egg? And how come I can't remember ever having that much fun?"

"Back to Liu Yan, who do you tend to believe, Li Kuidong or the cripple?"

"For sure, not the cripple. I've never been one who likes to wallow in filth."

After leaving Liu Huiyuan, I bought a ticket at a local theater and went inside to turn my imagination loose in the darkness.

It was one of those foreign whodunits about an urbane young man who carries on with two quite different women at the same time. It had been shown so many times that the color was unnaturally dark and the film was nicked and spliced. The movie seemed to take place after a downpour, with fancy-dressed couples in some far-off exotic country spouting gibberish inside the house or out in the garden. My interest quickly waned, and I watched in fits and starts. A man sailing on the ocean, a woman on the shore gazes out at him; a car races through a rainstorm, a couple is talking in a brightly lit summer cottage; an empty bedroom, sheets and blanket crumpled on the carpet; people caught up in intimate conversations, a background of soft music; passengers milling about an airport terminal, a young woman in a windbreaker stands in the middle of the crowd gazing intently at something offscreen. . . . My imagination takes over as I meet Liu Yan in just such a noisy airport terminal. I'm talking to one of the lounge attendants when I turn around and there she is, standing on the other side of the terminal; our eyes meet through the crowd. She smiles brightly. On a sofa nearby sits the cripple, who looks up as I stride toward Liu Yan. She and I talk excitedly, then move to a quiet corner to sit down and continue the conversation, me doing most of the talking, she occasionally saying something that makes me laugh. Foreigners in tuxedos and gowns take their places at a long candle-lit table in a private dining room. The men hold the women's chairs for them. . . . . A bunch of us are talking and laughing with Liu Yan as we pass a row of tables in a spacious restaurant; the cripple, who is sitting at one of the tables, looks up as each of us passes, but we ignore him and take a table at the far end, where I make sure that Liu Yan's plate is always full. . . . The couple on the screen walk down a hotel corridor; so do we. They go into their room and sit down; so do we. They climb into bed, and so do we, and we wrap our arms around each other and we moan and the curtain flutters . . . and the movie is over. Beams of orange light stream down from the vaulted theater ceiling, and I'm sitting there, and I'm pissed off. That wasn't about me and Liu Yan. Sure, like them, we ate together and had our talks and slept together, but none of what we did falls under the shroud of criminal behavior, like theirs does. I actually believe that I met Liu Yan in a crowd of people and that our eyes met quite by accident, but I also believe I wouldn't have been laughing about it at that time in that place. . . . I took out the photograph and looked closely at Liu Yan, frozen in time with lowered eyes in a darkened corner, and I was sure that when I was in love I was a different person altogether—unless of course the whole business is a bunch of bullshit.

I walked out of the theater with a single image in my head that simply wouldn't go away: me sitting in a dimly lit hotel suite playing solitaire. It's too quiet for anyone else to be there. I stand up abruptly, jerk open the connecting door, and there in the next room, seated under a pale overhead light, are Gao Jin, Wang Ruo-hai, Qiao Qiao, and Liu Yan—the cripple is standing in the corner, facing the wall.

12

A Beijing jeep was parked with its doors open under a tree; it had been there a long time. The driver was smoking a cigarette, the tip glowing every now and then. It didn't take a genius to know it was a police vehicle, even without markings. As the sky darkened, a few stars winked softly on the horizon. People across the street were watching TV, light streaming out of windows as if from a common room. Hallways were quiet and dark, except for tiny green lights on the switches. TV chatter and sound effects seeped through cracks in doors and traveled up and down the dark hallway: a nasty argument someone crying someone laughing, every channel featuring people in different moods.

An apartment door opened, releasing loud conversation into the hallway, followed by hurried footsteps down the stairs and out the door—the three cops who had been to see me once already headed for the parked jeep in the company of a fourth individual who smiled and said good-bye as they climbed in, closed the doors—*thump thump*—and drove off. The man turned and walked back inside the building. His slow ascent resounded up and down the hallway. I was waiting for him at the door.

"What are you doing here?" Wang Ruohai asked when he saw me, not surprised in the least. "The cops just left."

"I know. I waited till they were gone before coming down."
I smiled.

He looked down the dark hallway before opening his door.
"Were you at the end of the hall all the time?"

"No, I flew in. While you were talking with them I was chatting with the Man in the Moon. The Yanks had stuck an American flag in his and his better half's vegetable garden, and she was arguing with them."

The TV was on in Wang Ruohai's apartment, but the volume was turned all the way down. The picture flickered. It was a European Cup soccer match, and the spectators—white men and women in bright, summery tank tops, shorts, and sunglasses—jumped and shouted and clapped and whistled happily; just no sound.

"Friends of yours?"

"The old guy was one of the bunch that ran me in that time."

"Are you telling me that this business is related to what happened way back then?"

"That's what the dumb cops think. To them everything is linked somehow."

"So we were wrong, is that it? The government said we were no longer at war, that we were supposed to coexist, but we couldn't stop being soldiers and beating up every member of the bourgeoisie we saw."

"What the hell are you talking about?" Wang Ruohai gaped at me. "Were you and the Man in the Moon ranting about this so long you don't know how to put on the brakes?"

"Did we or did we not agree that we'd keep our own activities secret from ourselves, so no one would know what even he was doing? It was an ironclad pact."

"I was never a member of your reactionary clique. Why not just say we all sat around drinking chicken blood?"

"That's right, that's what it was all about. Anybody asks, we say we don't know. Without that spirit, we'd have been in their clutches long ago. You've had a rough go, taking so much on your own head all by yourself, and I'll bet it leaves a sour taste."

"Are you trying to get out of going to jail by being sent to a mental hospital instead?" Wang Ruohai stuck his face up next to mine. "If not, then what are you doing? Instead of being a good little boy, you decide on a life of crime, so you can bring a bucket of shit down on your head. I did the crime, so I did the time, my bad luck. But why do you have to go looking for trouble? We do everything possible to keep you out of this, just so you can bore your way back in. Are you really that tired of living?"

"No, I just think that a man's got to own up to what he does."

"That's your vanity talking." Wang Ruohai walked off, stopped, and turned to glare at me. "This is neither the time nor the place for it."

"Why do you insist on saying I wasn't part of what went on, when I was?" I was starting to lose my temper too. "Are you saying I was an outsider?" I felt terrible. "You guys sure treated me like one."

"OK, have it your way, you were the central figure, the backbone." He looked at me like I was crazy. "You know, you've got a problem."

I laughed. "I'm just teasing you. Don't make it sound like an election campaign, where the winner celebrates and the loser slinks away. I mean it when I say I agree with your viewpoint, that what's past is past. They didn't get me then, so maybe they'll get me now. It doesn't make any difference, but I'll admit nothing, and that's exactly what I tell everybody."

Wang Ruohai sucked on his teeth as he turned back to watch the TV.

I walked up behind him. "But I'm innocent, and that's the truth. I'm on the track of that girl, the one I told you about last time, the one you said didn't exist. Well, I've got a picture of her. Do you recall if one of the girls we hung out with back then was named Liu Yan?"

With his hands clasped behind his back, Wang Ruohai kept his eyes fixed on the TV screen. "No."

"Look." I took the photo out of my pocket and handed it to him. "I met someone who says you knew her. She used to hang out with us."

He took the photo from me and glanced at it. "Never saw her before," he said as he handed it back with a deadpan look.

"Impossible." Carefully I put the photograph away. "She ate with us and sat around talking with us maybe even went to bed with us. A pretty girl with a high nose and sunken eyes, and you insist she was flat-chested. What's up with you? How come no one ever mentioned her all this time? And how come, when I do, you make fun of me? What was she to me? Are we talking broken hearts here? Don't worry, I can take it. I'm strong enough, especially after so much time has passed."

Wang Ruohai sighed. "I envy you, I really do. I don't know how you manage to feel so good about yourself, but it's a heart-warming story." He sat down on the sofa. "If you're so sure this girl was your true love, why ask me about your relationship? I don't understand why you keep coming to me for information."

"I forget, remember?" I grinned as I sat down next to him. "Like the saying goes, a good horse doesn't eat the grass behind it. No, wait a minute, that's not it. Any man worth his salt doesn't eat . . . that's not it either. I can't find the right words, but what I mean is, there's no looking back. Is she dead?" I asked, turning serious. "Lots of people die for love."

"How should I know?" Wang Ruohai replied lazily. "Don't expect me to remember, if you can't."

The TV camera panning the soccer fans in the stand stopped at a golden-haired beauty. Miss Golden-hair, who was wearing shades, looked into the lens and waved. I waved back at her. "See you when it's over.

"Ever hear of Five Grain Alcohol?" I asked Wang Ruohai.

"Of course."

"Where should I start looking?"

"Anywhere. As long as you've got the money, it's there for the asking."

"I'm talking about a person, a girl. Apparently you don't know either."

"You're right, I don't."

"You don't know anything. How about Gao Jin and Xu Xun, will they know?"

"Don't know."

The phone rang. It sounded shrill in the darkness. I picked up the receiver and handed it to Wang Ruohai, who pressed it against his ear and said nothing. Whoever it was talked for a long time before he said, "Can't make it." Then whoever it was talked some more, to which Ruohai responded with a series of Nope's. Then silence, followed by a terse Right here. Whoever it was hung up in a hurry. Wang Ruohai held the receiver up, then slowly placed it back in its cradle.

"The path of life, how come it's so hard to travel?"

Wang Ruohai looked up, held the pose for a moment, then lowered his eyes.

"Am I getting on your nerves?" I stood up, stuck my hands in my pockets, and made a couple of slow turns around the room, singing a little tune: "I luh—vuh yo—u, do you love me . . .

"Actually, I get on my own nerves." I smiled. "Over the past few years I've become a fucking dustbin, and now I'm suspicious of everyone. I think they're after me. I don't believe a thing anybody says. And the more passionately they say something, the less willing I am to accept it. Maybe it's like you said, maybe I've got a problem. It's terrible, I know it's terrible, but I can't do a thing about it. Fortunately, by admitting I've got a problem, people who know me take it in stride. So I'm a bastard, big deal."

I turned the TV volume all the way up, swelling the apartment with soccer sounds. The sportscaster was breathlessly trying to keep up with the action, while the crowd jeered whistled made their bugles blare.

"Did we start drifting apart after I returned from down south?" I held my smile as I looked at him. "What happened between us? Did I do something awful to you guys? How come you all started avoiding me?"

"We didn't," he replied moodily. "What makes you think we were avoiding you? We had jobs, lives to lead."

"Let's be honest with each other, just this once, OK? We've been pals for a lot of years. Even if we aren't any longer, we can still be honest with each other."

"But you've come to the wrong person," he said. "I was just a spectator. My conscience is clear, so don't try to engage me in a war of nerves. It won't do you any good. You know exactly what happened. If you think it was my fault and you want revenge, I won't say a word. Do what you want, I won't lift a finger against you."

"What are you talking about?" I laughed. "Why would I want revenge?"

Wang Ruohai held his tongue.

"Come on, say something that makes sense."

"Doesn't what I said make sense?" Wang Ruohai said. "We're not stupid, you know. You think nobody knows how Gao Yang died, right? OK, forget it, just forget it. Gao Yang's dead, let it be. Why try to screw your pals over something that happened years ago? Maybe it's time to forget about settling scores."

Amid the raucous sounds of the TV, I heard a key turn in the door, followed by a woman's voice: "Why do you have the TV so loud? You can hear every word out in the hallway. Are the police gone?" The woman walked into the room.

I turned the volume all the way down. The flickering TV gave our faces—mine, Wang Ruohai's, and Qiao Qiao's—an ashen appearance. Qiao Qiao held a little girl with a bow in her hair in her arms. She bent down, and when the girl's feet touched the floor, she waddled over to Wang Ruohai, who scooped her up in his arms. "Daddy." He gave her a hug and kissed her on the cheek. The girl squirmed in his arms so she could see me. She had big, dark eyes; black grapes is about the only way I can describe what they looked like—a description that works for children, but not adults. I smiled weakly and said to Wang Ruohai and Qiao Qiao, "I'd better be on my way."

"No, don't go." Wang Ruohai stood up with his daughter in his arms. "It's time to tell him," he said to Qiao Qiao. "I'll take the little one inside for a nap."

*   *   *

"We've been married two years."

"That's great, really."

After Wang Ruohai took his daughter into the bedroom, we turned the TV off and the lamp on, then sat in armchairs separated by a tea table, our eyes glued to a bookcase against the opposite wall.

"Where to begin?" Qiao Qiao mused as she turned to face me.

"I don't know, I really don't." I was studying the titles on the spines of books lined up behind the glass doors. Between the covers of each book was a stirring tale straight out of someone's imagination.

"I didn't see you in Kunming." Qiao Qiao stared at the tips of her shoes. "I saw your and Gao Yang's names in the guest register of a certain hotel, but when I went up to your room, Gao Yang was alone. He said you were out, but I could tell that someone was hiding in the bathroom. I assumed it was you. Now that I think about it, maybe it wasn't, maybe it was someone else. The hotel wasn't particular about its registration procedures, and anybody with a letter of introduction could sign in with any name he pleased."

"What were we doing?"

"Couldn't say. Remember, I was only hanging out with you guys back then, and you wouldn't discuss your private affairs with some girl you hardly knew. And I never asked. In all honesty, I was an outsider as far as you guys were concerned, even though we were together just about every day, having a good time and all. We never talked, not really, and we knew hardly anything about one another.

"You seemed shy. You blushed around girls. Wang Ruohai

and Xu Xun weren't bad either, easygoing. Oh, they talked like predators, but I never saw them do any of the things they talked about. Just hung around the guesthouse and played poker. Gao Yang was OK. Bragged a lot, liked to party, lots of people came to see him. Gao Jin was the one to watch out for. No casual talk or laughter from him, and you never knew what he was thinking. He'd take off without a word to anyone and stay out half the night, then come back as if nothing had happened. If I had to choose one person capable of making trouble, it would be Gao Jin, he'd be my prime suspect. One particular incident left a deep impression on me. One night I went to another guesthouse, just for kicks, and there was Gao Yang in the bar with a bunch of Hong Kong Chinese, drinking and having a grand old time, bullshitting right and left. Wang Ruohai and Xu Xun were there too, fighting alien invaders on video machines on the mezzanine and sharing sinister laughs every time they shot one out of the sky. But I didn't see you or Gao Jin. Later I went upstairs, where I spotted Gao Jin sneaking out of one of the guest rooms carrying a suitcase with a combination lock. He froze when he saw me, but before I could say hi, he flew downstairs, skipping the elevator, without even a how-do-you-do. I went back downstairs to look for Wang Ruohai and Xu Xun, but they were gone. Gao Yang was still in the bar talking a blue streak. When I got back to our guesthouse, Wang Ruohai and Xu Xun were there ahead of me, having a great time in the room, doing I don't know what. Gao Jin didn't come back till much later, about the same time Gao Yang walked in, and I heard them whispering in their room for the longest time."

"What about me? You didn't see me that night?"

"I saw you, all right. You never left your room. Wang Ruo-

hai wouldn't let me go up to see you, said you were busy. I figured you were with Xia Hong, so I went up anyway and tried
your door. It wasn't locked, and when I opened it, I was so
shocked by what I saw that I slammed the door and ran out of
there."

"What was I doing?"

"You were crying. There was a girl with you, but it wasn't
Xia Hong. It was someone I didn't know."

"I was crying?"

"That's right. And I mean really bawling. The room was
dark. The curtains were drawn, and the only light came from a
table lamp. You were crying and talking at the same time, but I
couldn't tell what you were saying. We knew you had a girlfriend, and we joked about it when you weren't around."

I took out the photograph. "Is this the girl?"

"No," Qiao Qiao said as she handed it back. "I'd never seen
that other one before."

"But you've seen this one?"

"Sure. She wasn't staying with us, but I remember seeing her
sometimes around the table."

"This girl, the one in the photograph, is her name Liu Yan?"

"No," Qiao Qiao said after a brief pause. "That's not Liu
Yan."

"Then who is Liu Yan?"

I looked at Qiao Qiao. She returned the look.

"Her name's not Liu Yan."

"What is her name?"

"Don't know." Qiao Qiao shook her head.

I stared at the photograph. The girl remained aloof and
indifferent.

"What else do you remember?"

"I remember that you left not long after that. They said you went off with your true love."

"I left first? Not Gao Yang? Then what can you tell me about that last meal we had together?"

"We were all wrong on that one," Qiao Qiao said. "We weren't talking about the same thing. It was actually two separate meals. Two separate send-offs at the same restaurant. The first was for you, and there were eight people present. The second time it was for Gao Yang, and there were seven of us—you weren't there. That's why no one is sure who you left with. We thought it was Gao Yang, when in fact the person who left with Gao Yang after dinner and was never seen again was the guy in the striped shirt. You weren't at the table that night, and for all we knew, you were already back in Beijing. So not only were you not the last person to see Gao Yang alive, you were actually the first one to say good-bye to him—that is, if you didn't return to Kunming."

"If I'd returned to Kunming, then you'd have seen three people there. Do you recall the name of the guy in the striped shirt?"

"Feng, Feng Xiaogang," Qiao Qiao said clearly and confidently.

"And you didn't see his name in the hotel guest register?"

"No. I'd have remembered."

"Do you know where he was from, this Feng Xiaogang?"

"Nope. He had a Beijing accent, but I'd never seen him before. The reason I remember so clearly is that he had the same name as someone at the TV Arts Center. This other Feng Xiaogang was an actor who played Vietnamese officers, criminals, roles like that—he was perfect for the parts."

"I'd better be going." I stood up. "One last question. Ever hear of Five Grain Alcohol?"

"No." Qiao Qiao blinked.

I laughed. "I mean the liquor."

Qiao Qiao laughed too. "More of your jokes."

"Your daughter," I turned to say at the door, "she takes after you."

Qiao Qiao smiled to keep from looking too pleased. Not very successfully. "Don't be angry with Wang Ruohai. He's a good man. People used him like a weapon. That's why he spent all those years behind bars."

Shadows flickered across the lights of Baishan's apartment that night, so when I entered the lane and was confronted by a skyline of bright windows, it looked like there were people inside dancing the night away; either that, or someone was ransacking the place.

Once inside the building I heard noise upstairs, including music, but it stopped when I knocked on the door. Li Jiangyun was alone in the apartment, nothing had been disturbed. She flashed a smile, a very alluring smile. She said she'd been waiting for me, and now that I'd returned safe and sound, she had to be going. You can't go, I said, not tonight, I need company, I'm lonely. I heard the noise again, faintly this time, emanating from every corner of the apartment. If we kept very quiet, we could hear it floating around us: whispered conversations among people of all ages, male and female, in different tones of voice, now laughing now crying, all mixed together with music, the thud of furniture being overturned the scratching of matches on emery paper bowls and plates being smashed doors opening and closing footsteps running faucets stuff like that which sounded like a tape

recording of everything that had happened here during a particular month in any given year.

As I undressed I said to Li Jiangyun, This apartment has a
memory, doesn't it? Was some tragedy played out in this room?
Where are the people who lived here then? She said that they
had long since forgotten the place, that the memory of what had
happened existed only in cracks between the bricks in the wall,
echoing in the room on gloomy or windy days. My shirt was off,
and I shivered. Where was I at the time? I asked. Where were
you? You were up in the air and I was in a swamp. Have you
forgotten how clear the sky was? Li Jiangyun asked me. Like it
had been washed clean, and you and I were transparent. Now I
remember, I said with a laugh. A breeze brushed past my face;
you and I were locked in an embrace. We bent over gravely to
look at the golden fields below and inhale the mist lying between
heaven and earth. The essence of sun and moon were sown together on the tassels of grain whose kernels were threshed and
bagged and milled and eaten and recycled and secreted—I guess
we were pretty close at one time. I took her hand. Since we've
been here before, together, there's no reason to feel awkward.
She let me hold her hand, but didn't stand up. I've let the wolf
in the door this time, she said with a smile. I guess escape is out
of the question, right? I walked over and sat down, pulling the
covers up around my shoulders. "You can relax," I said. "I've
got AIDS, and I'm not the type to spread it around."

"Not that you could," Li Jiangyun laughed. "That's a special
skill only Westerners have."

"Let's stay up all night," I suggested earnestly.

"No need for that," she said with a laugh. "Quitting smoking
doesn't depend upon whether you chew nicotine gum or not."

She started undressing without a hint of modesty. I stared at her skintight maroon sweater. Then the light went out, throwing the room into darkness, except for moonbeams passing through the curtain and outlining its pattern.

Out of politeness, I offered her my hand as she climbed into bed. She took it, then pushed it away. "Thanks."

"Is this what it's like to be caged with a snake?" I grumbled, holding on to the bedding. A cold foot slid beneath the covers. I shivered. The second foot followed. It was just as cold.

Later, once our breathing was back to normal, I heard what sounded like a long, drawn out note from a distant flute, loud one minute soft the next, carried on gusty winds that invaded the apartment; it stopped at the window, then circled the room. The earlier sounds returned, like a chorus of taut strings snapping and depositing their echoes to linger in the room.

Seemingly fast asleep, at the same time I was climbing out of bed and walking barefoot into the next room, drawn by a sound. The room was all lit up. A girl with bright red butterfly spots was making a phone call. She dialed the number, then held the receiver to her ear, over and over. Each ring on the other end swirled around the apartment like the rhythmic beat of a massive heart. I don't think I said anything to her, nor did she so much as look at me, but it did seem as though someone was talking, and I intuited that she was calling the number of an old boyfriend, something she'd done night after night for a long time; the call always went through, but no one ever answered. A sound, a single utterance, repeated itself in the room, like something I was saying to her but also like something she was saying to me, a muffled sound that kept getting louder all the time, as if an enormous face were speaking into a microphone, or a phonograph record were spinning round and round under a stationary needle. I went back into the bedroom, yet felt somehow that I remained stand-

ing in the brightly lit room, where the girl was waiting for someone to answer the phone and the sound kept swirling. I lay down
next to Li Jiangyun and fell asleep. The bedroom was dark and
gloomy; the girl stood beside the bed looking down at me, her
butterfly spots showing up bright red even in the darkness. She
lay down between me and Li Jiangyun; I tried to nudge her out
of bed yet felt strangely indifferent at the same time. She reached
out for my face, and as her hand drew closer, I intercepted it in
midair. It snapped off below the elbow, as if it had been pasted
on. The room's sound, that single monotonous sentence, had not
died out, not even by morning, when I awoke, but the girl and
the severed arm and the sound of it snapping off had vanished.

Sunlight filled the room. Li Jiangyun was gone, and I was left
to lie in bed to think about that sentence. My dream was losing
its focus, but that sentence was perfectly clear: "There's something on your body that I know quite well."

I got up and walked into the next room. Baishan's door was
closed tight. I tried opening it, but it was locked.

I sat on the bed with my legs crossed and cried until my face
was wet with snot and tears.

13

"The cripple said Liu Yan had changed a lot, and it was pure luck that he was able to pluck her out of the crowd like that. If we hadn't just been to see him, he probably would have walked right past her without any idea who she was."

Liu Huiyuan and I were racing down the street under sunlight that had begun to melt the surface of the ice rink in the park. Skaters glided nervously across the slippery surface, like children walking unassisted for the first time. It had been a mild winter, and there were stories of skaters who fell through the ice.

"He's a man of many talents. That gimpy leg is the only thing that stands between him and the supernatural."

"If he weren't a cripple, the laws of heaven would be violated." I laughed. "What concerns me is whether this time he's been crippled for good."

"Do you think Liu Yan will remember what happened back then? What if she's forgotten everything, like you have? That could present a problem."

"Then I'll go find the nearest outhouse and dive in—no need to keep on living then."

"Did you really, um, have a thing for her?" Liu Huiyuan grinned. "The idea that you've actually done stuff like that really knocks me out."

"We knew what was going on." I kept walking, tense with anticipation. "Back then we didn't do anything halfway."

I knew I'd been suckered the minute I entered the cripple's hovel. Several people, all apparently waiting for me. He was very pleased with himself. His oily face showed no signs of any injuries. He smiled. "I can't say much about your public spiritedness the other day, pal."

One of the men stood up. I'd seen him somewhere before. Liu Yan was not among those in the room.

"Too bad you didn't stick around to watch me take care of that tub of lard," he laughed. "I beat him up so badly you couldn't bear to look at him."

"Where is she?" Liu Huiyuan asked. By then I could place the man who stood up as the person in the black leather overcoat who was tailing me. His coat was draped over the sofa.

"Where is she?" the cripple asked Black Leather Overcoat, grinning from ear to ear. Then he turned back to us. "He knows."

Black Leather Overcoat smiled. "While you've been looking for her, she's been looking for you. All that wasted energy. I've taken care of everything."

"Cripple," I said, nodding in his direction. "We'll meet again someday."

"No we won't," he said, turning his hands palms up. "That's where you're wrong."

"What's going on?" Liu Huiyuan demanded. "We didn't come here to chitchat with a bunch of gorillas."

"This has nothing to do with you and me," the cripple said to Huiyuan as he pulled him to the side. "Come with me into the other room. I'll show you Master Cripple's pride and joy."

"Get your hands off me." Huiyuan sent him reeling.

Two thuglike creatures sitting off to the side rose out of their chairs, very menacingly. I had to laugh. Seated, they looked very intimidating, with thick upper bodies. But once they were on their feet, they only came up to my armpits. One was bowlegged, the other knock-kneed. My mirth lasted only as long as it took them to reach under their seats and draw out knives that seemed taller than they were—as it turned out, they were bayonets from World War II Japanese thirty-eight Carbines. One was pointed at me, the other at Liu Huiyuan. What was going on here?

"Since when do cops carry spears?"

"Cops?" This stopped Black Leather Overcoat momentarily. Then: "No more games. You could be as fast as a camera shutter, and the cops would still be too late to help you."

"Hey, take it easy," I complained, arching my body and taking a couple of steps forward. "He stuck me with that. Take charge here," I said to Black Leather Overcoat. "Put away the instruments of torture and we can talk this out."

"Talk? Sure, I'll be reasonable, I'm always reasonable. I'm a civilized man." He turned to his cohorts. "Back off a bit," he said. "He's our guest."

"I didn't hurt him," the one behind me defended himself.

"Don't forget, he's taller than you. It wouldn't take much to run that thing through him." Black Leather Overcoat glared at the man then turned back to me, smiling broadly. "Have a seat. Polite and amiable, that's the way to do things."

The two thugs put away their bayonets, but remained standing.

I sat down, looked them over, and nearly laughed out loud at how they were standing there holding those bayonets, tips to the ground, with both hands, like officers' swords.

"How come you use people like that?" I asked Black Leather

Overcoat. "Don't tell me there aren't any respectable-looking thugs around."

Black Leather Overcoat turned red. With a wave of his hand he dismissed the two men. "Wait in the other room."

"We'll join them," the cripple said to Liu Huiyuan as he dragged him into the other room on the heels of the two sinister-looking creeps.

"Those are his pals," Black Leather Overcoat said when they were out of earshot. "They disgust me too."

I lowered my head, trying to get my bearings. I wanted to say something cool, but didn't know the lingo. "What gang do you belong to?" was all I could manage.

Black Leather Overcoat cupped his fist. "One ox on a high mountain."

I just stared at him for a moment. "Two anything goes and three trees," I said hesitantly.

Black Leather Overcoat didn't know what to say to that. Finally: "You're one generation up on me."

I smiled sanctimoniously.

"I've offended you."

"So what? It doesn't make any difference," I replied amiably. "Just tell me what's going on. With all the sword dances and spear chucking, this looks like the beginning of the next Boxer movement."

"Since we're both organization types, I'll give it to you straight," he said. "The truth is, I told her not to assume that everybody's bad, and that you wouldn't separate her from her money. If you needed a little, no harm in a loan, so long as you paid it back, right? We're all Chinese, we know about justice and humanity."

"Who did I borrow money from?"

"It wasn't your fault," Black Leather Overcoat replied. "How could you know that she and I were friends? You wouldn't have done what you did if you had. I told her not to worry, that Fang Yan and I are friends, and one word from me will do the trick."

"The girl, where is she? Is her name Liu Yan?"

"I really can't say what her name is. Besides, what difference does it make? A person's name is like clothing, you can change it at will. Call it what you want, cerumen is still earwax. That's what this is all about."

Black Leather Overcoat stuck his forefingers in his mouth and let out a shrill whistle. A girl walked in. I looked at her with considerable interest. Made up like a beauty pageant contestant, she was barely in the room before her eyes were darting all around, as if she were looking for someone.

"Apparently I'm not the only one with a bad memory," I said. "You can stop looking. The person you're looking for is right here."

"You?" She looked me over, then smiled coyly. "You're joking."

"Why would he do that?" Black Leather Overcoat broke in, seeing I didn't know what to say. "You were looking for Fang Yan, so we went out and found him for you. Don't be afraid. If it's him, just say so. I'm right here."

"Him? How could he be Fang Yan?" She sized me up. "This guy? Fang Yan? In cheap knock-off clothes like that?"

"Pardon me!" I stood up. "If I'm not me, then you and I have a big problem. When did I borrow money from you?" I walked up to her.

"This must be a mistake." Black Leather Overcoat stepped between us. "Forget it, just forget it. The whole thing's a big mistake, the person who took off with her money had to be somebody else."

"I have some questions, and I want answers," I said as I shoved Black Leather Overcoat away. "I'm not going to do anything to this girl. She's no raving beauty, you know."

"What sort of questions? I said it's all a mistake." Black Leather Overcoat stepped between us again. "You can ask me your questions."

"This is none of your business," I said. "If another Fang Yan is involved I'd like to hear about it. This is getting very interesting. There's another Fang Yan, is that it, little rich girl?"

I told Black Leather Overcoat to sit down, smile, and listen to the story. "I have a bigger stake in this than you do," I told the girl, "because that other Fang Yan owes me quite a sum of money."

"I met Fang Yan in front of the Friendship Store," the girl began. He was a tall heavyset man with a crew cut and black-rimmed eyeglasses, and she took him to be Japanese. She told him, in Japanese, that she was in the market for Japanese yen or Foreign Exchange Currency or anything else he might have on him; in other words, she'd exchange what she had to offer for what he had to offer. Speak Chinese, he said. I know you're speaking Japanese, but I don't understand a word of it. In other words, he was huffing and puffing like a bushy-tailed wolf. I thought he was an old China hand from Japan. With an abashed look, she continued, He told me to get into a taxi and I said Sure and he said his name was Hogen Taro or Big Brother Fang Yan— Fang Yan Taro, if you mix the languages. This Fang Yan Taro said he was a half-breed—Chinese father and Nipponese mother—so he knew his way around both cultures. He used so much Beijing slang that I couldn't understand most of what he said, and before I knew it I was under his spell.

The girl did it all: went with him to the hotel and drank with him in the bar and went up to his room and did what you might expect there. She discovered that this non-Japanese was a bona fide jet-setter, a big spender who wore nothing but expensive 120-thread fine-cotton striped shirts.

What she found particularly bizarre was that he never stayed in any hotel for more than one night, like a man trudging aimlessly from place to place. She never knew him to engage in any proper activity or saw him in the company of another person in his never-ending travels. He was a chain smoker but didn't drink. Wherever he went, whether he was walking or standing or sitting, he never stopped people-watching. Once, when he was asleep, leaving me with nothing to do, I picked up his glasses from the bedstand and tried them on. The lenses were plain glass but the marks alongside his nose proved he wore them most of the time. He knew his way around Beijing, and sometimes on cold windy days he'd hire a taxi to tour the city, having the cabbie weave in and out of narrow lanes and telling him to stop along the way so he could sit there and watch people coming and going, typical residential areas, nothing special. But they so completely captured his interest that he wouldn't make a sound, and he'd return to the same place over and over. At least once I'm sure I saw tears in his eyes, and he told me these were places where his father had once lived.

One afternoon I awoke from my nap, and he was gone. I went downstairs to window-shop in the hotel's arcade, and spotted him in the bar with some man. I shopped a little longer, and they were still there when I came back. So I went in and sat at a table behind him, within hearing distance. But several minutes passed without a word; they just sat there. I don't know what this man was to him, but he was obviously a regular at the hotel, since the staff all seemed to know him and treated him with deference. I figured he must be pretty rich.

I walked out of the bar, and didn't look back till I'd put some distance between us. Fang Yan Taro was watching me through a glass partition. There was a cold glint in his eyes.

Not long after that I answered the phone in the room, and some man asked "Is this Fang Yan?" When I said "No," he hung up. Well, Fang Yan went through the roof when he learned I'd taken one of his phone calls—I couldn't believe it. Then late one night I woke up and he wasn't there. It didn't seem important, so I went back to sleep. The next morning he had split, along with all my stuff of any value. He hadn't paid the hotel bill either. "I was really pissed!" the girl said as she glared at us. I laughed. "This Fang Yan Taro seems pretty cool to me."

"Despicable is more like it," the girl said angrily. "Chinese wouldn't do something like that."

"Then what?" I asked with a laugh.

"Then nothing. All I could do was get the hell out of there. At least he had the decency not to take my clothes along with everything else."

"So no one paid for the room."

"After all I'd lost?" she said with an ingratiating smile. "There were times I suspected he was using a phony name. Fang Yan may have been something he dreamed up. We were out walking one day when someone yelled out Fang Yan, and that so unraveled him he didn't even turn around. He didn't run, but neither did he stop walking for a long time. I figured he was avoiding some former acquaintance, and I was beginning to doubt that he was part Japanese. Now I'm pretty sure you must have been the person being hailed, that you happened to be walking somewhere nearby at the time."

"If you ask me," Black Leather Overcoat cut in, "that other Fang Yan was someone you knew, maybe a friend. If not, how come he didn't shout *my* name?"

"Hard to say," I replied somberly. "Everyone wants a cool name. My family name was highly celebrated at one time. Our humble clan produced a respectable number of renowned officials, one of whom has a sinecure in the current cabinet."*

I went into the next room to get Liu Huiyuan, who was sitting between the two bayonet-toting thugs and confidently bending their ears with: "If this had happened in the past, I wouldn't have let you get away with it."

There was a Fang Yi who served as Executive Chairman of the Chinese People's Political Consultative Conference.

14

The place was so dark and so quiet I thought I'd stumbled into an empty room, but then a bright light flashed, framing a crowd of heads and turning the place smoky orange as waves of music rolled up and set the crowd in motion beneath the throaty sounds of a man's voice: "My heart is waiting forever waiting, my heart is waiting forever waiting. . . ."

I rose up and charged headlong into the throng, giving every girl I passed the once-over, until I was face-to-face with one who was writhing almost drunkenly, like she was suffering from cramps. I leaped and twisted around her like a chicken hawk circling its prey.

"Tan Li, Tan Li!" I shouted. "Look over here. Remember me?"

The girl opened her eyes and gazed sluggishly at me, then shut them again and continued swaying to the music.

"I'm Fang Yan, Sha Qing's good friend. Now do you remember?"

She opened her eyes again, then closed them and nodded.

"Where is Sha Qing? I have to find her. It's important." I glanced at the other dancers, whose flailing legs occasionally connected with my backside. "How come this song's so goddamned long? Let's go outside where we can talk."

As I led the giddy girl through the crowd, her head lolled, her legs jerked spasmodically.

Once we were outside the dance hall, I let go of her. The music wasn't quite so deafening out there and the dance floor looked like a misty blue ocean.

"I'm Fang Yan. I need Sha Qing's address."

The girl, dripping with sweat, gave me a dazed look, as if trying to figure out why I was spewing all these words into her face.

Three skinny guys elbowed their way out of the crowd and surrounded me. They started shoving. "What the hell are you up to?"

"Nothing." I tried to defend myself. "I'm just asking her about someone. As soon as she tells me what I want to know, I'll be on my way."

"Asking what? What's to ask?" They started hitting me and forcing me backwards.

I shielded my head the best I could. "OK, enough," I said. "I'm going—Tan Li, where does Sha Qing live?"

"Come on, ignore the prick." One of them took her arm. "Let's dance."

As Tan Li was being led away she shouted: "La sol fa mi re do."

"Music Academy?" A fist in the stomach knocked the wind out of me, but as I stood there doubled over it came to me: a phone number.

"He dressed a lot better than you."

I was standing beside Sha Qing at the Dashilar cinema complex, a spherical entertainment structure where two film shorts featuring high-speed travel were shown continuously on the wrap-around screen; for the price of admission you could watch for as long as you wanted. My phone call to Sha Qing, a petite girl whose face showed no signs of wear, took her by surprise, and she would only agree to meet me in a public place; we chose a busy place that still allowed for a measure of privacy. There was nothing inside the domed structure except the railing up front, and most viewers stood against the back wall, leaving us and a few scattered children alone at the railing.

We were seated next to each other on a flight from Beijing to Guangzhou one spring when I was traveling around lining up manuscripts for a publishing company. In a soft voice, a half tone lower than most, he told me he was a writer, and he certainly looked the part. With a straight face he said he was the author of "Eyes of Spring," "Bells of Lightning," and *Movable Parts.* He was calm composed modest unassuming. I'm so glad to meet you, I said. I've read all your books, even edited one of them. You've put on weight you're taller your lenses aren't as thick as they used to be. Did I not recognize you or have you changed your image. He looked up and calmly said, You didn't recognize me. That government official is a fraud, the real author is heavyset, like me. He never smiled, not once. He talked about the student movement and about exile and about writing, and even though his speech was dotted with phrases like cloudy crags and misty marshes, he spoke so logically so convincingly that I was enthralled. I've never met anyone so self-assured or one who spoke with such passion, refusing to change his tune even in the face of solid evidence, a man who could admit there were tigers on the

Two novellas and a novel by Wang Meng, China's Minister of Culture, who was sacked in the wake of the Tiananmen incident in 1989.

mountain then charge up the mountain anyway, someone who gave new meaning to the term stubborn ox. Sha Qing said that from the moment they took off until they landed two and a half hours later, she was mesmerized by the tall heavyset Fang Yan in his black-rimmed glasses Western suit and striped shirt who talked the entire time. When they left the terminal together, the person who was supposed to meet Sha Qing either hadn't shown up or didn't spot her in the crowd, so she shared a taxi with Fang Yan. They checked into a hotel, separate rooms. She was nervous and edgy, he was happy as a clam. He took her to lunch treated her to a sauna showed her how to play squash shot pool with her, generally acting as if he were in a game room at home. He was so good at pool he could run the table over and over, spending hours comfortably engaged in this pastime. And he stuck to his story that he was a writer. "I'm exactly the same as all the others, except they actually write and I don't. I can make my point by selecting any one of their literary works to illustrate the meaninglessness of social standing." He said he liked Sha Qing, without making it sound indecent. She said, By liking me he meant he liked the sound of my voice, that hearing a hometown accent when he was on the road brought him great joy. A professional man like me, who's always on the go, eventually begins to feel that wherever he happens to be at the time is home. When he told me that, he didn't sound at all like someone who had just left Beijing, and there was something strange about the way he talked, like he was hiding something or like he found it difficult to talk about something.

He and I spent most of the day together, until I started getting bored, and recalled that I was here on business. I sneaked off to call the publishing house. The person I spoke to was gnashing his teeth because nobody had met me, especially since I was a girl in unfamiliar surroundings and he was worried I might have run into some unsavory character or been spirited away, and he didn't know what he'd do if that happened. Ecstatic that she had called in, he told her to stay put and he'd send a car right away. Before long, two men, one old and one young, showed up. They looked around the hotel lobby, and when they spotted Sha Qing and the man, they walked up shook hands with her and urged her to come with them, keeping a watchful eye on her neatly dressed companion. They weren't very friendly or particularly courteous. Later they told her they didn't like the looks of the guy and figured he was up to no good. But he didn't appear to feel out of place or concerned about being scrutinized like that, and just sat there smoking a cigarette without even standing up. When I said good-bye all he did was nod before looking away indifferently like he'd never seen you before and like the conversation never happened.

Some days later I went out for dim sum with one of the editors, a college student who had just started working there, and who treated me like royalty, accompanying me anywhere I wanted to go. We really hit it off. There was a sort of old-school romanticism in the way he took care of me, you know. In a city saturated with fancy restaurants, he took me to one with neither much of a reputation nor particularly good food. The customers were mainly local, us included, since the publishing house was right across the street. It was a hot, steamy morning, with slick streets covered by dappled sunlight filtering through the lush, broad leaves of kola nut trees. Clumps of duckweed floated on the surface of a river whose mossy bank ran parallel to the street. Everywhere you looked—the island separating the fast and slow lanes on the street the area just beyond the restaurant window in front and in back of houses on the other side of the river—you could see lush foliage: banana trees cycad trees fishtail trees all anchored in a sprawling net of white mist. I kept wanting to call Fang Yan and see how he was doing, that was the least I could do even though we had met in passing like floating duckweed. I did it, I called, but his room had a new occupant, and I kept thinking about what had happened, and where he might be occupying himself now.

The restaurant was packed with people eating and drinking and talking. I studied the passing dim sum trays, with their dainty little pastries and meaty snacks, and quietly rejoiced. I tried them all, they were delicious. My local guide's chest swelled with pride. Just as I was sampling a shrimp dumpling and examining a piece of transparent horse hoof cake, neither of which I'd even heard of, I spotted a face in the crowd, a round face minus the glasses; he was eating a fancy oil fritter. He blended right in with the local diners, with their paper fans and T-shirts and sandals, their cups of tea and their pastries and their snacks and their breezy manner. Apparently some of them knew him, since he spoke with them in Cantonese. When he looked my way, I smiled and pointed to a vacant chair beside me. He put on his glasses walked over and sat down but didn't eat anything. When he realized I wasn't alone, he spoke to my young companion courteously, almost humbly. I asked what he'd been up to since I last saw him. A smile but no answer. Instead he talked to my companion in a worldly-wise tone about work and its hardships; it was an exhausting conversation, and the boy was just humoring him. I think the man must have known that, but he kept at it, his confidence never dwindling, his energy never flagging. When I announced that he was a writer, the boy turned sarcastic, barely masking his contempt with shallow compliments, and making a big show of how tight he and I were.

He said good-bye to us, very elegantly, I might add, saying he had a flight to catch. After hailing a taxi at the curb, he waved good-bye, and we crossed the street, brushing perilously close to a group of schoolkids with backpacks walking toward us. Florists' shops and fruit stands gave the street some color, a jewelry store window made it glisten. The boy told me there was no flight and that the man would take the taxi to a park where he'd sit on a bench by the lake for a while, then hail another taxi and take the long way round town to wherever it is he lives, somewhere in this neighborhood. He'd seen him lots of times, out for a morning stroll or cooling off in an evening breeze, and recognized him because he always wore a striped shirt just like the one he had on now. He's a con artist, a guy who takes advantage of women, a gigolo whose phony Cantonese accent proves he's no native. Wanting to make sure I was well warned, the boy told me that eight or nine out of every ten migrant birds from the north nesting in this city were no good. I assured him I'd be careful, looking as grateful and as innocent as possible. You don't have to pass all your experience on to me, little brother, I was thinking.

I never told the boy that I saw the man again after that. It was my last day in town, and I went out for one more nostalgic stroll in the cool evening breeze. I saw him coming toward me. The boy was probably right when he said the man must live nearby, but that didn't lessen my joy over running into him like this. As we walked together, I told him what the boy had said, seemingly unable to hold anything back from him. He said the boy was right, that everything had its own intrinsic pattern and rules of behavior, people included, and that stale phrases and conventions would always be around. But a firecracker can't pop forever, he said, and after an earthquake the threat of danger passes. That firecracker may not like the idea, but there's no fight left in it.

He called himself a "survivor," a scrap of charred paper carried on the wind's currents after an explosion. He talked about the excitement and anticipation that precede one of those explosions and the pervasive silence after the bang. . . .

The streets were growing dark, cars and pedestrians were weaving in and out. I saw the three cops approach slowly—mere armlengths away, shoulder to shoulder, then right on past. I was wearing a gauze mask, looking over it the way a soldier peers through a pillbox slit. Xu Xun and Qiao Qiao came my way, then walked on by; the cripple and Black Leather Overcoat came toward me, then walked on by; Li Kuidong, Wang Ruohai, Fat Man Wu, and Liu Huiyuan came and passed, one after the other. I couldn't continue, I lacked the nerve, assuming I'd meet up with Zhang Li, Jin Yan, the pudgy girl, and everyone else I knew. Sha Qing was beside me, biting her lip and not saying a word. Then all of a sudden she turned and walked in the direction all the others were taking—she had seen Tan Li, who was right behind the pudgy girl. I kept walking, all by myself now. I saw Gao Jin, saw Xia Hong and the newlyweds and the tough guy and the burly guy and a whole bunch of other people male and female some I knew and some I didn't. I reached an intersection where the stream of people thinned out; shops were closed streetlamps lit up the deserted vista. The lids of fruit crates snapped open in the wind and a scrap of paper was sent swirling down the street in fits and starts. A man in an overcoat crossed the street, and when he passed beneath the streetlamp I got a good look at his face. It was Gao Yang. Someone lumbered up behind him, and I could tell by the uniform that it was Zhuo Yue. They walked on without even pausing, then disappeared into the night. I stood at the intersection waiting; a tall slim well dressed woman strolled leisurely up to the streetlamp. It was Liu Yan, looking just like her picture, eyes lowered and devoid of any discernible expression. When I called out softly, she turned my way, lifting her eyes as she came closer. She was surprised to see me, and at that moment I knew who she was.

"What are you doing here?" Li Jiangyun asked.

"Waiting for someone," I replied as I looked around. "How about you?"

"Who could you be waiting for at this hour?" Li Jiangyun glanced down the dark street. She smiled. "Not me, I suppose."

"Where did you come from?"

"Where are you going to?" She put her arm in mine, spun me around, and walked me back the way I'd come. "Let's go. The person you're waiting for won't be coming."

She held my arm so tightly I had to struggle to turn my head back. "Everybody but that one person."

The street was deserted. That one person didn't show, not a trace.

"Gone already," Li Jiangyun said as she dragged me along by the arm. "The person you're waiting for is gone already."

15

"This is illegal."

"So it's illegal."

"You can't wait just a little while? Till I catch my breath? I just got here."

"I don't feel like talking. Once you get me started, who knows where it'll end up? We've talked enough."

"Here, I'll get it let me get it. Easy now, or you'll break it. There's a hidden hook. They put them there to make things hard for people like you."

"I say we cut the ceremony. Make things simple."

"You don't seem to have what it takes to gild the lily."

"Me, well, I don't like to be distracted. If you're too caught up in the means, it's easy to lose sight of the end. Don't move, this is the critical moment."

" . . . "

"Well? How'd I do? Do I get a passing grade? How come you're looking at me like that? Stop acting like all this had nothing to do with you."

"Don't you think you're talking a little too much? You ought to learn to shut up at times like this."

"I don't want you to be too tense. I need to talk to loosen you up."

"You've been running around a lot the past few days. Get anything done?"

"I've made progress, but it's still too early to tell."

"Does that mean you're beginning to understand certain aspects of your past?"

"Yes, and reaching that understanding has been a real eye-opener. You should feel honored to be in the presence of such an extraordinary person."

"What about your past?"

"I'm told that all the signs point to the likelihood that I was some sort of merciless gangster."

"Were you really that impressive? You could have fooled me."

"You're right. When I look back over the years, I see an ordinary guy."

"Tell me about your past. Did you murder that man or not?"

"I don't want to talk about the past. I'd rather let it lie, since I'm content with my life now. A person can't act like a raving lunatic forever. When you're young you can go off half-cocked and sow your wild oats and feel good about yourself. But as you get older, it's time to cultivate moral character and live your golden years in quiet contemplation."

"You sound like a man who's seen a lot of what life has to offer."

"I have. I think back to those days when we had just been discharged, all primed and ready to go. There was nothing we didn't want to try or were afraid of doing. The proverbial masters of the nation. If we wanted love, we went out and took it, if we felt like going on a rampage, we did it. No one could stop us. But the times weren't right for outlaws. A few decades earlier we'd have been warlords. Hey, are you awake? Say something."

"Oh, I guess I dozed off. Your lyricism put me to sleep."

"What's with you? I thought I could keep you awake by talking. I'm not like I used to be. You can't make me lose my temper these days. If you slap me in the face, I just smile and turn the other cheek. But back then, I'd come after you with a cleaver if you looked at me cross-eyed. No holds barred, and that went for all of us. We did whatever we had to."

"Sounds like fun. Was it?"

"Of course it was fun. So is lying here talking and rolling around and keeping all the parts moving. What could be better?"

"Here, I'll make some room for you."

"No, don't move."

The light snapped on, and Li Jiangyun and I sat up in bed. She looked me over closely.

"Don't, don't, don't pretend you're full of passion, that you're all infatuated."

"I'm so ashamed. I'm over the hill. I used to leave them breathless and asking for more."

"Don't let it get to you," Li Jiangyun said as she fondled me. "Things change whether we want them to or not. No one can be top dog forever, everyone comes to the end of the line someday. You've tasted glory. If you haven't killed a man you've sure bedded plenty of women. Either one of those would make you the envy of lots of men. No wasted life there. Take a look at others. Some have killed more men than you and bedded at least as many women, and most of them are now law-abiding folks who practice their tai chi or take up disco dancing. They drink a little, sleep a little, and when you look at them with a cold eye, all you see are doddering old farts. When you reach a dead end, that's the time to show what you're made of."

"But there's plenty of mileage left in these limbs of mine, and lots of things I want to do yet."

"Then go do them. But you've got to leave something for other people to do, don't you? Actions are like a cake. No matter how small you cut the pieces, there's still never enough to go around, let alone for you to have seconds."

"Do you mean to say I've done enough for one lifetime, and there's no reason to go on living? It's beginning to look as if I should bitch if I *didn't* kill him."

Li Jiangyun just looked at me and smiled.

I returned her look, and kept looking until a long sigh escaped.

"No, don't sigh like that. I hate it when people do that."

I kept staring at her, but no more sighing, just staring.

"What is it?" she asked with a little laugh. "Why are you looking at me like that?"

"Can we still be serious?" I asked her. "You and me, the two of us, can we be completely frank with each other?"

"Don't go weird on me now," she said in a comforting tone. "Take it easy. Of course we can. Tell me what's on your mind. I'm here to listen."

"If I can't talk to you," I said, "I don't know who I can talk to."

"Go on," she said, sitting up straight to show she was serious. "I won't laugh, I promise."

"I . . ." I stammered, my face turned crimson, I lowered my head. "It's nothing, forget it. It'd sound stupid."

"Then lie back and get some sleep. You can tell me later."

Li Jiangyun lay back, and so did I. Then I rolled over toward her. "Do you think I'm a bad person, that I'm shameless?"

"Truth?" she said, opening her eyes. "No, I don't. You haven't got what it takes to be really bad. I know what it means to be bad."

"Really?"

"Really."

"Would it sound creepy if I said I find that very touching?"

"Yes, it would," Li Jiangyun said with a smile as she closed her eyes. "Now get some sleep, your soul can use the rest."

Li Jiangyun was fast asleep, and I was wide awake. I climbed out of bed, followed by a hulking shadow. I lit a cigarette, closed my eyes, and let my thoughts roam; new tableaux, in all shapes and colors, some beautiful and bright, others gloomy and dark, slowly permeated the boundless darkness: I am walking in the mountains as the blood-red sun sets; a shadowy figure is pushed off the mountain by another; arms and legs fly as a body tumbles, the sight of legs kicking the air is imprinted on the red sky; I am walking gingerly down a scarlet-carpeted corridor bathed in muted yellow light, carrying someone else's suitcase when a striped shirt appears where the staircase turns, and Gao Yang, suitcase in hand, walks gingerly from the far end of the corridor toward my reflection in the mirror; Liu Yan is sitting next to me, her heavy perfume filling the inside of the car as we leave one deserted street behind only to draw up to another, and as we pass each intersection, shadowy storefronts radiate outward, their stainless steel roll-down gates reflecting the light. Everything is distinct and illusory at the same time, and I am hard put to distinguish the real from the imaginary. We kick open the gate of a walled-in compound in a neighborhood lane and spray the inside with invisible assault rifles, *brrp brrp brrp;* we tie a young Gao Yang to a willow tree whose branches sway in the wind, then whip him with willow switches, grins on the faces of assailants and victim alike; as the young Gao Yang lies motionless on the ground, his face drained of blood, Zhuo Yue sprays a mouthful of water in his face, and he quickly sits up. This is the game we played as kids: Some of us were killers, the others were the police; the police gave the killers a head start, then went after them. Torture lay in store for the killers when they were caught, and still we all fought to be the killers, because when they were on the lam, they could torment their pursuers, and after they were caught, they could put on a real show. They were the stars, the ones who made the game. Without exception our killers were characters you could be proud of.

I took out Liu Yan's photograph and laid it on the table; it glowed in the faint lamplight. The dappled face seemed more blurred than ever, as if shrouded in mist. Thoughts of a long lost past flashed through my head: I'm walking down a narrow lane, the thick snow crunching beneath my feet, wisps of steam escaping from the door curtain of a little café directly ahead; hanging from the chimney rising up through the exhaust window is a blackened kerosene bucket. . . . I sit down at a square table with a plastic tablecloth to eat some cocoa-filled dumplings, all soft and sweet-smelling, the backpack with my ice skates inside keeps slipping around to my chest; crowds of skaters glide silently across the murky ice rink, blades scraping the icy surface. As I bang against the protective reed mats on the wall off in a dark corner, I lose my footing and crash into someone who steadies me, and we exchange smiles; I stand under a snow-covered pine tree grinning, nearly blinded by a flashbulb, and I hear laughter like tinkling bells, while off in the distance yellow glazed tiles and gargoyles and swallowtail eaves rise above the scarlet palace wall; we are enjoying a seafood meal in a restaurant with pillars adorned with wood-carved couplets, as people outside walk past the window; a felt-capped boatman poles his black-sailed boat, manning the tiller as he passes beneath the arched bridge on his way downriver, his dog and his daughter resting on their haunches alongside the cabin, while the opposite bank is blanketed by golden rape as far as the eye can see; we are sitting in the spacious hall of a mountain temple eating vegetarian snacks and nibbling melon seeds as rain like dripping oil falls intermittently, and all around us mountain peaks poke holes in the swirling mist; the still mountains and serene forests are backdrops for a raft poled by a man in a bamboo hat, behind him the mountain path is slippery, the bamboo forest emerald-green; we hold on to each other to keep from falling, our clothes are soaked and above us two characters have been carved into the rock and painted red: Cleanse Heart. We listen to the rain from our bed beside the window and hear a woman's voice: "It seems . . . it seems . . ." I can see it all, I can hear every sound, but when I look down again at the face in the photograph, everything suddenly drifts away, breaking into pieces; the woman simply does not blend into any of those tableaux, not even the barest outline, is at odds with all the other fuzzy images, and the more I study it, the more alien it becomes—for the first time I feel that this Liu Yan is a complete stranger.

Out there the wind howled, as if someone far away were whistling in the night air; a cat in some dark corner screeched sadly, ceaselessly; crows perched silently on forked limbs; something moved, but I sensed rather than saw it. A gust of wind blew the window open and set the curtain dancing. A moment later the door swung open, first one leaf then the other, letting the wind sweep in and whistle its way into every inch of space; the photograph was whisked off the bed and onto the floor. I stood up and looked down at Li Jiangyun, who was still fast asleep, her bloodless face looking like death. I went into the living room, where the door to the hallway stood wide open, and was surrounded by swirling cold winds that chilled me to the bone. Whatever it was, I felt, was here in the room with me, and I detected the smell of violets, faint but unmistakable.

It moved, and the wind currents underwent a change.

"Is that you?" I asked softly as I walked toward the darkened hallway. "Come in here, why don't you?"

I stepped into the hallway; it was deserted. So I went downstairs and stood in the doorway. Stillness all around me, but then I heard the door upstairs bang close, one leaf then the other, like two explosions.

16

"You remind me of someone."

We were eating lunch in a crowded restaurant, with noise and commotion all around. Li Jiangyun had brought along a middle-aged man with an easygoing manner who was wearing a stylish wool overcoat; every time our eyes met, he smiled. Lunch was his treat.

"Li Jiangyun is always talking about you, so I said I'd like to meet you, you know, shoot the breeze."

I smiled politely and said to Li Jiangyun, "If I'd known earlier, I'd have held on to that horn.* But the people at the Chinese pharmacy wouldn't give me a moment's peace. They said their prescription required horn for it to be effective. And patients kept coming to see me, asking me on bended knee to mix some horn in alcohol for them. What could I do? I shaved some off for them."

"Amazing!" The middle-aged man said with a laugh. "Very interesting." He sized me up. "You're just like a young fellow I used to know. The way you talk, your gestures, your expressions, they're all the same. And like you, he preferred older women. He was always happy as a clam."

*An aphrodisiac.

"Here we go again with that stale old love story of yours. I must have heard it eight hundred times."

"So what?" I said to Li Jiangyun. "Let him talk."

"Actually, I only saw the guy once, but what an impression he made on me," the man said.

"Don't get the idea that this is *his* story," Li Jiangyun said. "He heard it from somebody else, but goes around telling it like he was there."

"It's not just something I heard, dear," he said with a gentle look at Li Jiangyun. He smiled at me. "The girl in the story was a friend of mine, first back in school, then in the production corps. We returned to the city together, and we still keep in touch."

I looked at Li Jiangyun. "This isn't about Li Jiangyun, is it?"

"No names, all right?" he said, with another glance at Li Jiangyun. "We'll just leave out the names, what do you say?"

"You don't know her," Li Jiangyun said. "No one's heard from her for years—saying they keep in touch is a way of showing how important he is."

The man smiled to show he wasn't offended.

"If you want," he said to me, "you can treat this like a tale from *The Arabian Nights*. It's an old story, and I'm only telling it now for its entertainment value. It has nothing to do with any of us here today."

"Yeah, right, we'll just pretend we left our brains at home, that we're not real people. There are no people here, we're just a bunch of flies landing on manure that an old farmer has spread over his field—buzz buzz—and who cares whether the crops grow or get harvested."

"You two are just like the guy who says, I *haven't* buried

three hundred ounces of silver on this very spot," Li Jiangyun said with a laugh.

"We have to be," I responded earnestly. "That's where it gets its authenticity."

"Her father was a famous linguist," the middle-aged man said, "maybe the most famous one of his time, but you wouldn't have heard of him, since he committed suicide shortly after the Cultural Revolution was launched, he and his wife both. The person I'm talking about was a little girl at the time, suddenly orphaned, the poor thing. Later, in fact just recently, we learned that she had a kid brother, and people said he was looking for her, though I don't think he has a chance of finding her. Li Jiangyun was right when she said no one's heard from her for years."

"He wouldn't recognize her if she was standing right in front of him," Li Jiangyun said.

"I'm afraid you're right," the man said. "At the time we knew nothing about any brother, and just seeing her all alone, with no one to care for her, just about broke our hearts. So we took her along when we were sent to the production corps, though she wasn't really qualified. Eight years we spent in the Northeast Production Corps. They were trying years, but we survived somehow, and when we made it back to the city, we got our lives back on track, believing that our suffering had ended, and that now we could accomplish anything our abilities would allow. The worst was behind us, then suddenly she fell apart. Up till then she'd been so good, always doing her share of the work and keeping up with all of us, even talking about going to college. And now that she had her chance, she fell apart. We were all pretty busy at the time, busy going to school busy working busy getting married busy looking for housing, too busy to worry

about anybody but ourselves. I recall—so do a lot of the others—
that she came to see us once, but we were too busy to listen to
her, and after some small talk we sent her packing. After that, she
stopped coming. By the time we were ready to take a breather
and reestablish contact, she had changed. First she moved in with
the biggest wimp, the biggest loser from the entire corps, then
she left him and got friendly with a bunch of shady characters,
hanging out in dance halls and restaurants, making herself up like
a whore, drinking and smoking and lots of filthy language, interested only in eat drink man woman. She went from being a tal-
ented girl who played the piano and knew a couple of foreign
languages and was a good dancer and an even better skater to
someone who put all her talents to uses for which they were
never intended. Calling her a slut was no exaggeration. I ran into
a wretched cripple once who talked about her in language too
filthy to describe. Even a piece of garbage like that treated her
like dirt.''

"This part always upsets him,'' Li Jiangyun said with a laugh.
"Can you sense it? He really liked that girl at one time, but he
was a weakling, burdened with such a powerful inferiority complex that he didn't have the guts to declare his love for his goddess. By the time he figured he'd saved up enough to propose in
a manner that suited her regal stature, he discovered that the
woman of his dreams was worthless goods, ripe for the picking
by any con man or thug who came along.''

"You young folks don't appreciate old-fashioned romance,
do you?'' The middle-aged man smiled and looked at me, and it
was obvious that Li Jiangyun's barbed comments had had no effect
on him. "Compared to you, we must look hopelessly weak-
willed and fickle. Well, we're a product of our times. In our personal pursuits we weren't nearly as bold as you. You go through

life armed with prodigious courage, willing to sacrifice everything for the right cause, while we look at all sides of an issue to
get the proper balance, having been taught to consign the individual to a position of insignificance. That may be our tragedy,
but it's what we're accustomed to. We understand it perfectly,
yet there's nothing we can do about it."

"I've told Li Jiangyun the same thing," I said. "There's no
need to draw a distinction between our generations."

"Oh, I'm afraid it's still two separate generations, whether I
draw it or not," the middle-aged man said. "What grade were
you in at the beginning of the Cultural Revolution?"

"Drawing the line that way is unscientific."

"Don't think I'm putting you down. If I could choose, I'd
love to be your age and have some of that courage."

"Nobody's stopping you." I turned to look at Li Jiangyun.
"We went from being part of the herd to being the herdsmen."

"Spoken like a true youngster," the middle-aged man said.
"There's plenty to stop me. You'll find that over the years more
and more barriers will be erected to stop you too. But back to my
story. One day, after we'd stopped inviting that schoolmate of
mine to our get-togethers, she showed up on her own, in the
company of a young man, the one you remind me of."

"It wasn't me?" I asked with a laugh. "Maybe I was that
young man."

"No no," the middle-aged man said with a laugh. "You look
alike, but it wasn't you, I'm sure of that. So is Li Jiangyun. She
was there that day."

"It wasn't you," Li Jiangyun said, looking away.

"He was handsome, real sharp, well dressed but not flashy,
polite and well behaved, with an occasional hint of dread in his
eyes. You can imagine the cool reception he got from us, since

we assumed he was a one-night stand or, even worse, one of those disgusting, pretty-faced dandies who always hang around women. We ignored him, and some of the women made no secret of how they felt about her inviting someone like him. But that didn't faze her. She laughed and talked just like anyone else, even made a point of saying things intended to shock or embarrass us, which we took as further proof that she'd become a shameless tramp. Although we tried to shut her out of our reunion, she forced her way in, disregarding the contemptuous looks and actually turning herself into the main topic of discussion. But the poor guy she'd brought just sat awkwardly in a corner, nursing his drink and staring at the tips of his shoes. It pained me to see an innocent bystander suffer all that neglect. And as host, I didn't want him thinking we were barbarians. So I went over to talk to him."

"I was there, I saw it all," Li Jiangyun said. "And this is what makes my friend here such a hypocrite. He can't stand the guy, and yet he treats him like an old friend. He wants people to think he's refined and courteous, someone who never offends anyone."

"I admit it," the middle-aged man said with a laugh. "Sometimes I'm nice to people who don't deserve it, but it seems necessary somehow." He turned back to me and went on with his story. "When he saw me walk up and sit down beside him, he smiled bashfully. I still remember what he said: 'I'm fine, don't worry about me.' I asked how long he'd known the woman, and he said not long, 'a few days.' He fielded my question on age by saying he was in his twenties. And when I asked what he did, he said shyly that he'd just gotten out of the army and hadn't 'found a job yet.' By then there was no doubt that he was a decent young man, innocent as a little girl, and I was convinced she was corrupting him. But I couldn't say that, so I just smiled. 'You're a lot younger than her.' He smiled and said something about how he preferred older women, that girls his own age didn't interest him. They didn't know anything and by the time they did, they'd be older women and 'I'd be older, too, just like them.' I found him to be intriguing, straightforward and sincere. Each time I mentioned his lover's name, his eyes lit up and he looked over at her, while she entertained the others with crude comments and coarse laughter, clearly moved yet trying to conceal his emotions, just like a young man in love. He said we didn't really understand her, that 'a diamond achieved perfection through countless polishings.' I asked if he thought he really understood her. Comparing a woman to a diamond was inappropriate, I remarked, and I preferred to think of them as white mourning silk. I confess there was contempt in my comment, I admit I was contemptible. He blushed, the kid actually blushed, and said he knew what I was getting at, but that he understood her perfectly, because she hid nothing from him, so there. 'Don't think I'm some babe in the woods. I'll bet I know women better than you do, which is probably the main difference between us.' I was so ashamed. The words were barely out of his mouth, and I was ashamed of myself genuinely ashamed. To cover my embarrassment I asked if he planned to marry her. He looked at me in astonishment. 'Of course, why else would I have said so much?' But he went on to say that he had no immediate plans to marry, since he realized that happiness depended upon several factors, none of which could be absent, and that conditions weren't quite right for him yet. 'But you just wait and see, I'll manage, I'm not as wet behind the ears as you think.' He laughed loudly, a threatening yet somehow endearing sound. I knew he was talking about money, which is yet another difference between my generation and yours. You young folks are too practical; there's no romance in your soul. I asked him how he was going to manage, since 'talk is cheap.' He said he'd 'be like a diamond, unyielding.' Wasn't he worried his feelings might change? He just laughed and said, 'Only if I don't carry this out. Have you ever seen a kite in midair with no string attached?' That took me by surprise."

"What's so surprising about that?" I asked. "He was just stating the truth. As I see it, he couldn't have been more sensible if he'd tried. He'd thought things out carefully and with great seriousness. Only dilettantes believe that love conquers all. They solemnly pledge their love to win over the objects of their desire—I can't think of anything more dishonest than that."

"He used the word 'diamond.' " The middle-aged man looked straight at me. "Several times, in fact, comparing women to diamonds, and the many facets of the metaphor had me thinking that diamonds were more than a casual symbol, that they lingered tenaciously at the core of his brain. Our dreams often become metaphors in real life. The more we talked, the more confident I was that I had not misjudged him. He wouldn't say exactly how he'd manage, and I had the feeling he wanted to tell me what he had in mind, but held back, not because he was afraid of revealing his secret but, like all people with a flair for the dramatic, he wanted to appear enigmatic. That way his little secret would gain more credence than it warranted, and he'd be seen as mysterious. He said he had the inside track on a path to riches, 'a sure thing, a precious gem.' Some friends were down south waiting for him, 'Guys just like me.' He hinted that these friends were engaged in criminal activities. When I said that was dangerous business, he laughed, the way you laughed just now. That's why I say you and he are a lot alike, sincere yet ruthless—that's what I saw in his eyes then and what I see in yours now."

"You're right there."

"And that's the same thing he said to me then: 'You're right there.' "

"You didn't happen to notice the type of shirt he was wearing, did you?"

"What?" A puzzled look.

"Was he wearing a striped shirt?" I asked with a laugh. "I might be able to tell you his name."

He laughed and put his finger to his lips. "Remember what we said, no names. This is just a friendly chat."

"Right right. Just some totally unrelated anecdotes and gossip about other people." I tapped my temple. "Go on with your story."

"After a while I left him and walked up to the heroine of our little drama. 'Congratulations,' I said, 'on finding the man of your dreams.' She didn't know what I was talking about, so I said it again. This time she laughed. 'Worth waiting for, wouldn't you say?' Then she turned serious, looking across the floor at the young man as he sat there, and nodded to me without another word. Later on, long after our reunion, I heard they were going around borrowing money from everyone they knew, and it was only a matter of time before my turn came. She said she'd pay me back real soon, even set a date a month later. It was springtime when they left, and we never saw them again, they never came back. It's been ten years. I don't know what happened to them, whether they caught the brass ring or not. Oh, I asked around, but nothing came of it. They vanished like puffs of smoke. Somebody spotted them with a bunch of young guys down south once, then there was word that they'd gotten into trouble, with some arrests, even a death. That was the last I heard. I've thought about them over the years, and I can still see them if I close my eyes, him in particular. There was no need for them to get involved in whatever it was. They might have been poor, but they were still better off than most Chinese. The risks far outweighed any possible benefits. They weren't kids, so they should have known better—still, I'd like to know what became of them."

"How come you're not telling him what else you told the girl back then?" Li Jiangyun said. "You said you thought no good would come of her plans, and that she was foolish to think otherwise, that it was all wishful thinking."

"I did indeed say that." He smiled. "Not only that, I told her that the young man wasn't right for her. I said he could be dangerous, if not to others, then to himself, and after all these years, it was time to be cautious."

"What did she say to that?" I asked.

"She said," Li Jiangyun replied, " 'What are we most afraid of in life? Living a lie, that's what!' "

"I'll give you my dreams and my freedom. . . ."* The barely audible strains of a song oozed from the restaurant speakers.

"Great lyrics," some guy sitting behind us said to his dinner companion. "Just hearing them makes my hair stand on end. '. . . and my freedom,' that's so stirring. When you go that far, what else is there to give? If I were in his place, I'd give you my democratic rights and earnings."

"Now you're pushing it," the girl said. "I don't need those. Give them to somebody who really wants them."

"She's a tough nut," the man said. "And that guy sounds desperate."

We laughed, but said nothing. One by one we lowered our heads.

*Lyrics from the song "I Have Nothing" by the rock star Cui Jian.

17

The wind howled all night.

The next morning I went out for a walk. The temperature had dropped, and chilled air sent everything that had thawed for the new day, or was about to, back into the deep freeze. People scurried along with hands over their faces to protect them from the cold. Leafless branches trembled in the cold wind.

Some youngsters in knit caps, ice skates slung over their shoulders, were sitting behind me, laughing and talking as they drank warm milk. They were praising the skills of some skater. "Like an old pro. With her out there, who needs the rest of us?" "I've never seen a girl do a leaping split like that before. I was afraid one of the blades might catch her in the face." "We should get to know her. She could teach us a thing or two. She's faster on figure skates than we are on speed skates. How does she do it?"

Through the steamy glass of the café I could see past the iron railing into the rink across the street. The sky was pale, the sunlight muted. Clusters of skaters circled the dark blue ice. Some were bent over, their arms swinging very fast, which, obviously, increased their speed dramatically. The rink was a machine with all its gears moving at different speeds. Some skaters executed flying camels as they sailed around the rink, others leaped into the air, then took off like a shot when their skates hit the ice again; one line of skaters stopped abruptly, all in a row, sending a mist of ice chips skyward. The rink went round and round, along with the shimmering blades of skates on the feet of boys and girls who laughed and shouted when they bumped into each other. Sounds could not make it across the street, so for me it was like watching a larger-than-life mime play.

Tan Li, her cheeks bright red, walked past the café. She tapped on the window when she saw me. I smiled, and she put her mouth up close to the glass and yelled something. After backtracking to the entrance, she parted the curtain and came inside. I stood up and invited her to join me, accidentally bumping into one of the youngsters behind me, spilling milk onto his army overcoat.

"Sorry, sorry," I said. "I didn't see you."

"Why have eyes if you won't use them?" he snarled.

"I'll wipe it off." I searched my pockets for tissue or a handkerchief.

"Wipe it off and that's it? Wipe it off and no harm done?" He banged his cup down on the table and turned to his friends. "This guy won't even let us drink a cup of milk."

One of his friends, a big fellow by the look of him sitting there, said, "Come here."

"I said I was sorry. It was an accident." I didn't move.

"I said come over here. What're you scared of?" he asked. "Where you from?"

"Di'anmen, right around the corner."

"Well well, Di'anmen." He grinned. "How come I've never seen you around?"

"Yo, Tan Li." The fellow with milk on his coat spotted Tan Li. "You know him?" he asked with a glance at me.

"Who the hell do you think you are, treating one of my pals this way?" She walked up to me frowning.

"I didn't know," he protested. "We'll just forget this ever happened. Come on, guys, let's go," he said to the others. "He's a pal of hers."

They stood up. On his way out, the big guy patted me on the shoulder. "No offense, we were just messing around with you."

We sat down after they'd left. "Calm down," Tan Li said. "Just look at you." She laughed. "I've never seen you like this before."

"If this had happened in the past, well, why talk about that now? But I'll tell you, I wouldn't have let a bunch of rat-faced punks like that get away with it." I laughed. "I'm a little tense, that's all."

"Have you found the person you're looking for?"

"What? Oh, yeah, I did, and I have you to thank for that."

"I don't mean Sha Qing, I mean the other girl, Liu Yan."

"How did you know I was looking for Liu Yan?"

"How could I not know?" She laughed. "Everybody's talking about it, saying you have to find her to keep out of jail."

"I wish *good* news traveled this fast." I sighed. "That's right, I'm looking for her. Know her?"

"Heard of her, but never met her. A girlfriend of mine is real tight with her, though. She's always talking about her."

"Your girlfriend? What's her name?"

"Don't know her name." Tan Li laughed. She stuck out two fingers and wiggled them. "Got any smokes? I'm having a nicotine fit."

I handed her a cigarette and lit it. She took a drag and yawned, bringing tears to her eyes. She smiled. "Not a girlfriend, really, just someone I hung out with for a while. She never told me her name. All I know is you guys call her Five Grain Alcohol. That's awful-sounding."

Tan Li then proceeded to describe Five Grain Alcohol in great detail: "Face shaped like a melon seed, big eyes, a dimple, bad teeth, wears braces, usually dresses in white, probably some kind of reverse psychology." She asked if I knew who she was talking about. "She knows you, says you two are pretty tight. I ran into her a couple of days ago. She said she'd seen you recently."

I nodded. "I know who you're talking about."

"I hear you've got a picture of this Liu Yan," Tan Li said. "Can I see it?"

"Sure." I took it out. "You seem to know everything. No sense trying to hide anything from you."

Tan Li took the photo. "Yes, I know everything," she said with a smile. "And there's nothing I like better than a little gossip." She studied the photo carefully, then looked up and said, "Not as pretty as I figured."

I laughed. "Just a girl."

"Let me see that again." Again she studied the photo carefully, then handed it back to me. "I've seen that picture somewhere."

I looked at her but didn't say anything.

Tan Li stubbed out her cigarette and rested her forehead in her hand. "Let me think, where did I see it? It was at somebody's house. I remember it was one of several, a whole album, all black and whites. Now, where was that?"

"Take your time," I said. "Want another cigarette?"

"No, one's plenty." She smiled and thought some more. Then a flicker of recollection. She looked up and laughed. "Now I remember, his name was Gao Jin, lived in an old residential compound, a pretty place, I recall a veranda and a garden and a miniature mountain, supposedly the residence of some government bigwig before Liberation. A bunch of guys were playing poker in the living room, where the air was thick with smoke. I was alone in the bedroom looking at photos."

"What else do you recall? Was Gao Jin there?"

"Yeah, sure, in the living room. Before I got through all the pictures there was some noise out there, so I got up to see what was going on. Some guy had just come in and was talking to Gao Jin and the others."

"Was he wearing a striped shirt?"

"Yes, he was." That surprised her. "I figured he'd just come from someplace where it was pretty warm, because he was only wearing a suit coat over his shirt. Beijing was really cold then, in fact, one of the guys had on a bomber jacket with a fur collar. The new guy had brought a lot of stuff along, in boxes and little packages. I remember he had a sword in a beautiful scabbard with silver inlay. The guy in the fur collar took the sword, but the guy in the striped shirt wasn't happy about that, since it was the only one he had. But the guy in the fur collar wouldn't take no for an answer, and since they seemed to be good friends, the guy finally let him have it. The guy in the bomber jacket started hacking away at imaginary targets in the air. . . ."

"Then what?"

"I went back inside to look at more pictures, picking up where I'd left off when I was interrupted. This one, the picture of Liu Yan, had been removed. You couldn't miss the empty spot in the photo album. I don't know who could have taken it, but I think the guy in the fur collar was the only one who went into the room while I was standing in the doorway. He'd have had to walk right by me to go in."

"Who else was there?" I asked Tan Li. "Can you recall?"

"Five Grain Alcohol, she was there. She's the one who brought me. And there were two or three people I didn't know, all men."

I lit up and took a couple of melancholy drags. "All men, you say."

Tan Li laughed. "You must have really loved her."

"Huh? Who? Oh, yeah, I guess so. It wasn't easy, but I loved her anyway. Even if she didn't love me."

"You're OK in my book. You know, people your age."

"Huh?" I looked at her.

"Nothing." She looked down and fidgeted with a corner of the tablecloth. "To me love means something, no matter how it turns out."

"We're in love with love, and that's enough for us."

"They say you tried to kill yourself over her."

"That's absurd." I laughed. "Where'd you hear that? It never got that far, we were never that serious. I just wanted a snack, not a full-blown meal. I had some feelings for her, but that's all. No no, none of that for me, I'm not the suicidal type. How would that make me look?"

"Why be ashamed of that? I find it very moving. Awesome! To die for someone, just think. I should be so lucky. Every man I meet is more disgusting than the last one. If I had my way, they'd all drop dead."

"Me, too. I can't wait for other people to die."

"I'm not laughing at you, I'm really not. I respect you, you say what's on your mind. In my eyes, you're one of those soulful, heroic types."

"Me, soulful? Heroic? No way, that's praise I don't deserve. I don't take compliments well, and if you keep it up, I might actually have to go out and do something soulfully heroic."

"Such as? Maybe you can teach me." Tan Li leaned over conspiratorially. "I'd like to do something like that, but don't know how."

A young guy in an army overcoat parted the door curtain and entered the café, bringing the wintry air in with him. He spotted Tan Li.

"What are you doing sitting here?" he shouted at her. "If I hadn't run into Fats Two, I'd still be cooling my heels at the skating rink."

He eyed me suspiciously. "What are you two up to?"

"I ran into an old friend, and we just started talking." Tan Li flashed him a smile of pure innocence. "You go on. I'll be there in a minute."

"Make it quick," he said, looking at me. "I'll wait for you outside."

He left the toasty café and paced back and forth, stopping to look inside impatiently from time to time.

"Take that kid, for instance," Tan Li sighed. "Think you could get him to die for me?"

"Who can say? How old is he?" I glanced out the window. "I'd say he's about the right age to climb a mountain of knives or leap into a pot of boiling oil."

"Him?" Tan Li flashed the young fellow a fetching smile, then turned back to me. "Guys like that aren't in your league. You're a free spirit."

"I've never been in a pot of boiling oil myself," I said. "Times have changed. So have the rules. You can get him into the sack if you like."

"I prefer men who treat me rough." Tan Li stood up and straightened her clothes. "See you later. Call me a masochist if you want."

*   *   *

"Little brother."

As soon as I stepped inside, a haggard-looking girl wrapped her arms tightly around me, nearly smothering me. She was sobbing. Tears and snot coated my cheek, shoulder, even my chest. It was a struggle, but I managed to peek over at Liu Huiyuan and Li Kuidong, who were standing like statues off to the side, seemingly moved and apprehensive at the same time, and more than a little embarrassed by the scene they were witnessing.

"Let me look at you," the girl muttered, roughing up the skin of my face with her coarse hand. "How many years has it been? You've changed so much I hardly recognize you."

"I know I don't recognize *you*." I turned to Liu Huiyuan. "What's going on?"

"Your sister," Li Kuidong said. "You've been trying to find your sister, haven't you? Well, I found her for you. She got everything right, even your nickname."

"Winterboy," the girl uttered tearfully. "That's what we used to call you, Winterboy."

"Not so fast," I said, pushing her away as gently as possible. "Let's think back now. No crying until we've got a clear picture of things."

"What? Wrong again?" Liu Huiyuan asked uneasily.

"I'm eighty or ninety percent sure," I said, "that I don't know this woman."

"How could you?" the woman said, obviously sick at heart. "You were so young."

"But I have no recollection of any big sister." I turned to Li Kuidong. "Where did you find this woman? Is this Liu Yan? Don't you know anything?"

"She came to me, said she was looking for you." Li Kuidong

appeared to be at his wit's end. "She said she was looking for a lost brother, and came running when she heard I knew someone who was looking for a lost sister. I knew it couldn't be Liu Yan, but you kept saying you were trying to find your sister, and I figured that Liu Yan probably wasn't your sister, that somehow you'd gotten the two of them—your sister and Liu Yan—all mixed up together. I gave her a real grilling, and her story had all the parts in all the right places. Everything matched perfectly with the story you told me about your missing sister."

"When old Li here came looking for me," Liu Huiyuan interjected, "at first I knew he'd made a mistake. But the woman insisted she was your lost sister, and even had me believing her. Who knows, I thought, maybe you really do have a sister, one you haven't seen in so long that you forgot her—anything's possible."

"You're disowning me?" the girl said, looking up with her sad eyes.

"No no," I said, "it's not that. It's a misunderstanding, that's all. They made a mistake, you're not my sister."

"But you're my brother," she persisted. "I'd know you anywhere."

"How can that be?" I said, throwing my arms up in exasperation. "I don't have a sister. I said I was looking for my sister, but I don't actually have one. The sister I'm trying to find isn't my sister, just someone I call my sister. In trying to simplify a complicated situation, I wound up making it more complicated than ever. What else can I say?"

"When Father was alive, his favorite hobby was raising birds. He hung the cages in his study."

"Never happened. My father used to shoot birds with an air rifle."

"Mother's thousand-layer round cakes were the best."

"Don't make things up. Oh, sorry, I didn't mean you're making this up, just that it has nothing to do with me. I don't know anything about you or your family."

"You've got a mole on your belly. You're not afraid to take off your shirt and let them see for themselves, are you?"

"I'll catch cold. Besides, I have a mole, but it's on my calf, not my belly."

"So I'm a little off on the location. You've got a mole on your calf. You're not afraid to take off your pants and let them see for themselves, are you?"

"You won't give up, will you? Why in heaven's name do you insist that I'm your brother? We don't look one bit alike."

"You're my kid brother, and I don't have to look at you to be sure of that."

"Here's the truth. I do not have a big sister, I have no sisters at all, and my parents are still alive to prove it. I was lying when I said I was trying to find my sister, understand? There's no way I could be your brother, mole or no mole."

"I understand." She nodded.

"I'm terribly sorry, it was a stupid thing to do. I didn't mean for this to happen, I wasn't thinking. I hope you'll forgive me."

"Don't worry, I don't hate you," the woman said calmly. "You've got your own problems. I'll leave now, and I won't bother you any more. But don't you ever forget, you can refuse to accept me as your sister, but I'll always remember you as my brother."

"Are they all like that these days?" I asked Liu Huiyuan and Li Kuidong after the woman had left. I was nearly shouting. "They won't believe you no matter what you say!"

18

As evening fell, I bought a bagful of rolls at a hotel bakery and ate them as I walked down the sidewalk, gazing from time to time at the bus stop close up ahead. Hotel restaurants lit up the darkening sky, taxis drove up and disgorged couples dressed for dinner; shop interiors were dazzlingly white, people streamed in and out, and merchandise of all shapes, sizes, and colors was displayed in such a way that it was easy to distinguish the clothing stores from the general stores and appliance stores; crenellations in the distant city wall and beyond them the dark, overlapping roofs of palace buildings at the edge of the square formed a dim skyline; pale yellow light from streetlamps seeping through pine branches followed the progress of bicycles, columns of them, heading down a maze of streets into the night. Pedestrians kept blocking my view, yet I never lost sight of the graceful young woman walking toward the bus stop. I weaved through the pedestrian traffic and came silently up behind her. In the dim light her glowing face, her radiant eyes, and her sleek fur-collared white leather coat and brown leather boots drew admiring looks, even from girls who turned back to look after she passed.

She stopped beneath the bus stop sign and looked down the street to see if a bus was coming. The cinched belt of her white coat accentuated her hourglass figure. I drew up until we were virtually shoulder to shoulder and said with a smile:

"Haven't we met somewhere before?"

She spun around, a guarded look in her eyes, then, obviously relieved, smiled to reveal crooked teeth encased in wire braces.

"How's it going, Qiao Qiao?"

"What are you doing here?" she asked, turning to look behind me. "Out for a walk in the cold or waiting for someone?"

"Waiting for you." A bus pulled up, so I took her by the arm and stepped back. "We need to talk. Let's find a place to sit down."

"What's wrong with right here?" Qiao Qiao had an imploring look in her eyes. "I have to get home."

"No, let's go someplace." I steered her toward a nearby hotel snack bar. "We can talk in there. This is much too involved for a short conversation."

We found a quiet corner. "What would you like?" I asked her.

She frowned. "Nothing, I'm not hungry."

"Some orange juice, then." I went up to the counter, ordered two orange juices, and brought them back to the table. I sat down across from Qiao Qiao and just looked at her.

"You first," we said at the same time.

A pause, then we both said: "Out with it, whatever it is."

Qiao Qiao turned her head. "This is silly. You go ahead."

"Don't you know what I want to ask?"

"No," she replied, obviously irritated. "I've already told you everything I know. I have no idea what you want to ask me now." She leaned over and looked me square in the eye. "No more of that business about the police investigation, all right? Tell me whatever it is and stop beating around the bush."

"All right, if that's what you want." I sat up straight. "I want to hear about Liu Yan."

Qiao Qiao returned my look, then lowered her eyes and took a sip of orange juice. "I've already told you I don't know who you're talking about."

I spread my hands out on the table and shifted in my chair. "You see," I said with a sigh, "you still won't tell the truth."

She didn't say anything.

"Come on," I said. "Everyone says you not only knew her, but that you were real tight with her. Why pretend otherwise? We're just wasting time."

"You heard it from Xu Xun?"

"That's right." I blinked. "And Gao Jin."

Qiao Qiao picked up her glass and took another sip. "They tell me not to say anything, then they go ahead and blab it them-selves. Why ask me, if you already know?"

"They didn't give details. They said to get the rest from you, since you knew more than anyone."

"They always give me the nasty jobs. That way they can be the good guys."

"How come I don't know your nickname? You never told me, did you?"

"Why would I want to go around telling you a terrible name like that? Just so you could have something else to call me?"

"How about Liu Yan," I said, "did she have a nickname?"

"Yes," Qiao Qiao said, curling her lip. "Polar Fox. You have to be pretty mean to give someone a nickname like that."

"Where is she now?" I looked down at her long nails. "This Polar Fox."

"I don't know. How come you're always asking about her?" Qiao Qiao stiffened her neck and glared at me. "Do you really think that finding her will solve your problems?" she asked softly. "I'll tell you, what did you in was that sword. They found traces of human blood on the so-called silver-inlaid handle. It was Gao Yang's blood type. Finding Liu Yan won't keep you from being implicated. That sword is solid evidence. I don't know who you think you're kidding by telling people that Gao Yang gave it to you."

"Gao Yang *did* give it to me."

"Whew!" Qiao Qiao threw up her hands contemptuously. "Say what you want, then. Go talk to the police. If they believe you, everything's fine."

"Gao Yang didn't *give* me the sword—I sort of wheedled it out of him."

"Stop looking for Liu Yan." Qiao Qiao leaned back and looked me in the eye. "She can't do you any good. You weren't with her those seven days, so stop wasting your time. If you want to know where you went that week, you should be looking else-where, thinking about other people."

"You saw me take that sword from Gao Yang. You were there."

"What you're driving at," Qiao Qiao said with a sigh, "is that you won't stop until I give you an alibi, testify that you saw Gao Yang after you returned from down south, right? We've backed you up all this time, swearing you were the first to leave after saying good-bye to Gao Yang in Guangzhou, and to that end, I even moved up the time I saw Gao Yang in Kunming to when you left him in Guangzhou as proof that you were in Beijing then. Do you have any idea how big a risk I took? To protect you, I moved up the date of Gao Yang's death one whole month. Obviously, you don't appreciate that. Instead, you're hell-bent on bringing everything down on your own head. Well, if you want the truth, then you'll get it. Yes, we can all testify that you ran into Gao Yang again in Beijing. Not only that, we can swear that you took possession of the sword he had bought as a decorative piece but wound up being a murder weapon. He left after that, and you disappeared for seven days. I was the only one who saw him in Kunming during that time. Whoever he was with signed your name in the hotel guest register. Then you resurfaced in Beijing, but there was no word of Gao Yang. Then years later his body is discovered in the Yunnan mountains, hacked to death by the sword he gave you. Have I got it right? Are you pleased with the tale I've spun? It's what you've been waiting to hear, the real story."

"I'm very pleased, and no matter how you put it, I was never a strong suspect. I still say I spent those seven days with Liu Yan."

"No you didn't. I should know, since she was with me. We went to Kunming together."

"What did you go there for?"

"Someone was waiting for her." Qiao Qiao looked up at me. "Liu Yan went to see her boyfriend. She was frantic for news from him, since they had been out of touch for so long. When they said good-bye they agreed to meet up in Kunming. But he didn't show. She was sure something had happened to him, but we all knew that he had simply left her. Things like that happen all the time, but it's hard for some people to accept."

"Where did her boyfriend go? Why did she think something had happened to him? Was he on some sort of dangerous mission?"

"Don't know. She didn't say. But I think that if someone goes off alone and doesn't return, it's natural to assume the worst, to think that something happened, especially if you're a woman.

I mean if your husband's a little late coming home from work, you worry. A car accident, another woman, bad stuff like that is always out there for us."

"So you think her boyfriend dumped her for another woman?"

"I don't know, there's no way to tell."

"Who was her boyfriend?" I asked. "One of our crowd?"

"I knew him, and so did you."

"So she never did find her boyfriend, right? I mean in Kunming."

"No, she didn't."

"He must have been avoiding her."

"You could say that." Qiao Qiao looked at me. "And you could also say that he avoided everyone, not just her."

"That boyfriend of hers must have been a real heartbreaker." I laughed and flicked the long, drooping ash from my cigarette into the paper cup that had held my orange juice. "Did she give up when she didn't find him right away?"

"I think she kept looking," Qiao Qiao said. "She got sick, and even though she knew he wanted nothing to do with her, she was hoping she'd see him again. She kept calling, but by then he'd forgotten her. He'd either refuse to take her calls or agree to whatever she said, then stand her up."

"Were they ever real tight?"

"The word 'tight' doesn't begin to describe their relationship. They were lovebirds. No, frenzied lovers is more like it. It was impossible to see them together and not be deeply moved. They were like a nut and a bolt that had rusted together. . . ."

"Then why did it end like that? I mean, what caused the cracks in their relationship?"

"Same old thing, he fell for another girl. Have you ever seen a man who's content with what he's got?"

"You said she was sick, didn't you? What'd she have?"

"Lupus. And she kept making phone calls, all the way up to the bitter end."

19

It was late when I headed back down the narrow road. After the little stuffed-dumpling shop at the intersection, I passed the produce market, the grocery, the bicycle repair shop, and a succession of gloomy lanes, unable to shake the feeling that a pair of eyes was following me. I kept looking over my shoulder, but the street, its asphalt pavement gleaming in the murky yellow light of streetlamps, was deserted—no pedestrians and no vehicles. I gazed into the cold, clear, moonlit night sky for no particular reason, and there, at the intersection ahead, the naked branches of a scholar tree were mantled by perching crows; that's where the disturbing gaze was emanating from. I passed beneath the tree, the crows maintaining a stony silence that settled heavily upon me. After being swallowed up by a dark lane, I heard the distant sound of flapping wings as the crows left their branches and wheeled into the sky like a black cyclone; when they flew overhead they slowed down to match my pace. The farther I walked down the pitch black lane, the closer I drew to the dark buildings rising into the night sky. A bright red butterfly appeared in front of me, lazily fluttering up and down and in and out of view.

Someone must have been following me that night, because so much that happened afterward shows obvious signs of human intervention. Someone, it seemed, entered the building before I reached it, because I saw lights snap on, one floor at a time; then someone, it seemed, followed me inside, for as I walked upstairs the lights on the lower floors went out, again one at a time. I stood on the top floor for a while, but no one appeared and no footsteps sounded. The hall light stayed on the whole time I was there. But as soon as I opened the apartment door and walked in, the light went out. It all seemed so carefully planned, even though whoever it was would have had to be quick as hell.

Everything in the apartment was in fine working order at first: A wall switch turned on the lights, the stereo tuner made music, water flowed from the taps, and I could make a phone call. I lifted the receiver and got a dial tone. First the lights went out, then everything else shut down. I thought it was a power outage, but at the window I saw lights in the building across the way, and all the neighboring buildings as well. Then I discovered that the water faucets didn't work and the telephone was dead, and I knew I was the target of all this activity.

I sat waiting quietly in the apartment, figuring that these measures to cut me off from the outside world were but a prelude to something larger. All I could think about at the time was my own personal safety.

No one came upstairs, nothing stirred all night long, at least while I was awake. Eventually I fell asleep, and at some point the electricity came back on: The room was flooded with light, someone was talking and laughing, the telephone was ringing insistently, and water gushed from the taps; it was, in other words, pretty lively in there. Unable to tell if it was real or if I was dreaming, I didn't give it much thought before drifting back into a druglike sleep.

I awoke in the morning to blinding light, feeling somehow

unrefreshed, my bedding having slipped away to points un-
known; I reached down to find it—nothing but dust and an icy
floor. I opened my eyes to a ceiling that seemed too high, and
felt something hard and bumpy pressing against my back. I sat up
quickly and discovered that I had been sleeping on the floor. The
room was empty, the floor dusty, the corners nested with cobwebs. All the furnishings were gone; my backpack lay on the
floor. I jumped up and ran out the door, only to find that the
apartment was empty of all but a layer of dust; the pipes were
rusty, the toilet and bathtub pitted; no cleaning implements no
telephone not a single object I'd ever seen there before. The door
to Baishan's bedroom was, as always, shut. I pushed, but it didn't
budge, so I kicked it, and heard something heavy shift on the
other side. The door opened a crack. Another kick, and the object crashed to the floor. The door swung open, sending dust
from the frame raining down and wreaking havoc on a mass of
cobwebs. I stepped inside. A large mahogany bookcase lay on a
floor that was covered with shards of glass from a goldfish bowl
and cigarette butts. There were three beds, with dust so thick on
the covers I couldn't make out the colors or the patterns. A bar
of soap in the washstand behind the door was hard as a rock, the
face towel curled up at the edges; a deck of playing cards, yel-
lowed with age, lay scattered on a table, whose legs, and those
on the beds, were nicked and gouged, leaving ancient scars that
blended in with everything else in the room. I walked gingerly
back into the bedroom, leaving footprints in the dust, sort of like
trekking across virgin snow. I bent down and picked up a photo
album. After flicking the dust off the cover, I began flipping
through the pages: One had a blank spot, so I took Liu Yan's
photo out of my pocket and placed it over the spot—a perfect fit,
alongside a rectangular group shot of me, Gao Yang, Xu Xun,

Wang Ruohai, Qiao Qiao, Xia Hong, and Feng Xiaogang, a
runty guy with a sheepish smile. I noticed we were all wearing
identical striped shirts, like a team uniform. I noticed too that
Baishan was standing beside me, her face beaming. Liu Yan was
at the other end, next to Feng Xiaogang, forcing a smile, her eyes
lowered just as they were in the one of her alone. One person
was missing from the group photo. I searched the album, and discovered that this particular individual appeared only as a youngster, that there wasn't a single photo of him as an adult; everyone
else appeared in all sorts of poses, everyone but him, everyone
but Gao Jin.

I closed the album, then tried to shut the door, but it
wouldn't stay that way; the bookcase must have held it shut, so I
left it the way it was.

Someone had gone through my backpack, since the gray
handbag I kept inside it had been removed, leaving an empty
space in a pack that was normally stuffed full. I crammed in the
photo album, zipped the pack shut, and walked out the door
with it.

I questioned every old-timer, every child, and every young
girl I saw, upstairs and down, about their neighbors, but they all
said they didn't know either Baishan or Li Jiangyun. An old
woman who lived across the way told me she knew of no tenants
in that building. The entire block had gone up at the same time,
but to her knowledge no one had ever lived in that building, it
had been empty since day one, which got the neighbors talking,
given the critical housing shortage. They'd even gone to the
housing office, only to be told that the building had been assigned, and it was no business of theirs if the tenants ever moved
in or not.

When I went to the housing office, I learned that that particular apartment had been assigned to someone named Gao Yang. They weren't aware that he wasn't living there, because he paid his rent and utilities on time, sometimes six months in advance, so no one had ever had to go collect from him. I was even shown the rental agreement with the signature of the person called Gao Yang.

20

New Year's Eve, streets and lanes throughout the city were thick with exploding firecrackers; that must be what a coup d'état sounded like, with firefights lighting up half the sky.

I searched all over town for Li Jiangyun, checking every place she'd ever been or might have been, but not a trace of her; I asked everyone who had seen her or might have seen her, but no news.

All hell broke out that night, as if an army were being routed. Streets were littered with scraps of charred paper, and the infrequent car just zoomed past. No women or children anywhere in sight, just pockets of young men; my ears rang with the popping of firecrackers, punctuated by dull thuds when rockets lit up the sky before exploding above rooftops or vacant lots. I didn't know where the person I was looking for had gone; her door was locked, the hallway was a cluttered mess.

I ran across the smoke-choked street at a crouch, little explosions erupting all around me, fireballs dropping at my feet. After locating a public phone booth, I closed the door behind me and dialed a number just before my streetcorner booth was ambushed: firepower was unleashed from all directions, incandescent traces streaked through the night sky; brilliant flashes of light flamed out spectacularly when they struck my protective shield, then turned into brilliant purples and reds that rode the slippery glass to the ground. I called everyone I knew; telephones ringing in every murky corner of the city confirmed the fact that no one was home.

Liu Huiyuan, asleep in bed until his phone rang off the hook, got up in a grouchy mood and answered it in his bare feet. He couldn't tell me where everyone was either. According to him, over the past few days, right up till yesterday, thousands upon thousands of people had swarmed to the train station, loaded down with luggage, frantic to get away; there were reports that railway authorities had added dozens of cars to departing trains.

The duty clerk at Gao Jin's hotel, oozing charm, said that "GM Gao" had begun his holiday early, and it took all my persuasive powers to get her to ask around and determine that he had bought a ticket for the south. Normally he went by air, but this time, uncharacteristically, he had reserved a first-class berth on the train.

"The reservation was for tonight," she said helpfully. "GM Gao is probably on his way to the station at this very minute."

A taxi pulled up to the terminal. Out stepped a man in a black suit carrying a hard-shelled briefcase with a combination lock. The taxi drove off as the man walked into the brightly lit terminal. In contrast to the frenzied chaos of the city, the terminal was tranquility itself, a cold and cheerless place, virtually deserted by travelers since early that afternoon. Most of the escalators leading to the platforms were still, merchants inside the terminal had closed up shop for the day, and policemen and service personnel had dispersed to the four corners of the large building to stand around or sit idly by.

I watched Gao Jin take the stairs to the second floor and, rather than enter the first-class lounge, cut across to the economy-class waiting room. He seemed preoccupied, looking straight ahead; if he'd turned his head just a bit, he'd have spotted me, but he didn't. A big man for a Chinese, he stood out in a crowd, a head or so taller than most of the people around him. To compensate for his height, he stooped a bit as he grew up, and now leaned forward slightly when he walked, which gave him the appearance of a man meeting his future head on.

I went up to the timetable alongside the ticket counter, but the train wasn't listed. As a matter of fact, trains originating from this station had all left by midnight.

I rapped on the window of a closed ticket booth. The sleepy clerk asked if I wanted a ticket. When I said yes, he took my money tossed a ticket at me slammed the window shut, *bang*.

There was no announcement to proceed to the gate, and Gao Jin and I appeared to have the train to ourselves. Moments before the departure time, he stood up, showed the gateman his ticket, and headed for the platform. I stood up, had my ticket checked, and followed him. On my way across the covered overpass, I gazed out at the city, which had settled in for the night; the darkness was broken only by a few flickering lights on tall buildings.

I hadn't even boarded the train, and the city already seemed far far away.

A dark green, silent train, with only a few cars, sat alongside the murky yellow platform, closed and curtained windows muting the lamplight inside. Conductors who normally stood by the doors were conspicuous by their absence, as were other platform personnel; it looked like a private train or one that was going nowhere. No sign of Gao Jin; he must have boarded already, since this was the only train around. Even so, I walked from one end to the other, checking each car for originating and terminating stations before actually boarding.

Apparently I was alone; in car after car, tier after tier, the berths were snowy white and undisturbed. After putting my things away, I stood at the window. Nothing had changed: The platform was still deserted, and no attendants came to change the signs. *Thud!* The door slammed shut and the train lurched forward, then gradually picked up speed: no announcement, no music, no train whistle; we just slipped quietly out of the station and out of the city into the darkness of open country. The lights went out, leaving only the night lights at the base of the corridor to form a dim walkway that strung together a row of blackened sleeping compartments. The train was on its way, with me the only passenger in my car, yet I couldn't hear the rumble of the wheels on the tracks below; surrounded as I was by total silence, it was as if I had suddenly gone deaf. I coughed and the sound was perfectly clear, yet no track noise. Only the gentle rocking motion proved that we were moving. I lay down without taking off my shoes, pulled the blanket up, and closed my eyes. I fell asleep at once, although my senses remained keen, as if I were standing at the window watching the blackness of the countryside whiz past, the winds sweeping in from the fields through the window and mussing my hair.

By the time I awoke, the sky had turned light, and the countryside whizzing past my window was just as I'd dreamed it. Someone had opened the window across from me and the wind was whipping in. Sunlight spread slowly over the barren fields, the wheels rumbled rhythmically on the tracks below in perfect cadence with the now not so gentle rocking of the train.

Passengers who must have boarded during the night sat on

pull-down seats next to the windows; some were fairly old, the rest were gaunt and sickly young people like me. All of them put as much distance between themselves and their neighbors as possible, preferring to stare gloomily outside rather than acknowledge one another's presence.

Now the fields were shrouded in bright sunlight, and the icy cold land was gradually suffused with gentle, warm sunbeams. The gentle warmth and the icy coldness coexisted easily, drawn together without commingling, like a mismatched couple that stays together because they have lost the ability to go it alone.

We crossed northern plains, which in the wintertime offer a panorama of naked earth, frozen rivers, bare trees, and scarce signs of life.

A passenger-laden train rushed toward us; windows flashed by, the rumbling noise was deafening, and then it was gone, leaving in its wake only the vast countryside. All told, we met several trains traveling in the opposite direction. They popped up from time to time and were just as quickly gone. Then the scenery started turning green: stands of pine trees throwing dark shadows over mountains; emerald green paddy fields whose water glistened. More and more rivers and streams came into view, the water in constant motion; in villages chimney smoke rose into the sky, where birds and clouds vied for space. These changes in scenery signaled our arrival in the south.

At some time after noon we crossed the first of several bridges. Calling upon my knowledge of geography—the width of riverbeds, the amount of flow, the surrounding terrain—I guessed the names of the waterways we crossed: the Yellow River, the River Huai, the Yangtze. . . . But just when I had confidently surmised that we had crossed all the main rivers of central China, those dividers of north and south—the Pearl River was still a thousand

li away—a broad, turbulent river appeared up ahead. The bridge
approaches ran for at least ten li, carrying us higher and higher,
past villages and tributaries and mountain ranges on the horizon.
Several hundred li to the east, across the plain, sat an enormous
industrial city under a canopy of smog that turned the clouds a
dirty gray and weakened the sun's rays. Given its size and apparent population, plus the location, I assumed it must be Shanghai,
though this line should never have allowed for a view of Shanghai, not from any vantage point. I'd taken this line before, so
I knew.

The train crawled up the bridge incline. Beneath me were
pilings, thick at the top and tapering off as they broke the surface
of the swirling waters. Upriver, off in the distance, stood tall
mountains and dense forests, and I could not have told you which
province we were leaving or which one we were about to enter,
since none of this bore any resemblance to the south-central
China I knew.

The river roared beneath us, flowing all the way to the horizon after veering off in a wide arc, where the opposite bank vanished in a water haze. The vista of whitecaps above emerald
waters as far as the eye could see created an illusion of being alone
on a vast lake, without a sail in sight. A light drizzle raised ripples
that quickly turned into watery troughs. Now that we had begun
our descent, we seemed to ride on the water itself, as the windows
were hit by cresting waves, which misted them up until the lake
was one big watery blur. It was getting dark inside, and the lights
came on; it felt like I was on a boat in a driving rain. Then no
more water splashed against the windows; the mist congealed into
sparkling liquid beads, and the view through the glass went from
blurry to crystal clear. Slanting rays from the setting sun lit up the
water, then sank beneath the surface. Water all around: emerald

waves, transparent ripples, rising and falling, snowy seagulls soaring above the surface. The moon climbed into the sky, bright and silvery, turning the lake into a vast jade-colored field, paddies waving before the wind, now east, now west; with the moon as my companion and the sound of waves in my ears, I fell into a dreamy sleep. Early the next morning, bright sunlight streamed into the car as we sped across the sunbathed land. Outside the window lay the same watery vista, as far as I could see, but these were real rice paddies bending in the wind, waves of green all the way to the horizon. Far off, where the rice paddies ended, a large, populous city of tall buildings rose out of the plain. A pall of smoke filled the sky above the city, through the center of which meandered a shimmering river bordered by houses and trees and crisscrossing streets, a neat, orderly place where people and vehicles came into full view.

Our train snaked through the outskirts of town, where lush tropical flora passed by the windows: tall betel palms, clumps of hollyhock, fruit-laden banana trees, and squat, thorny cacti. Rural cottages in the southern style were interspersed with Western houses; the highway was shared by cars, buses, and trucks. As sunlight baked the land, the temperature inside the coach shot up until the heated air nearly roasted my face. When we pulled into the station, my fellow passengers changed clothes and took their belongings down from the luggage racks, all in the bright light of day. This was the first movement I'd seen from them so far; their faces came alive as they opened windows and stuck their heads out to see if anyone was waiting for them on the approaching platform.

Even after the train had pulled up alongside the long platform and come to a complete stop, I couldn't be sure if this was the city I'd wanted to travel to, even though it looked like it.

21

I was the last person off the train, disembarking right after I saw Gao Jin pass beneath my window. A woman at the far end of the platform came up to him; they smiled and spoke briefly before she took his briefcase and walked with him to the exit. Someone was there to meet all the passengers, all but me. A policeman with his hands clasped behind his back froze when he spotted me. "No one here to meet you?" he asked.

"Out on the street," I said. "Where you from?" I gave the name of a stop along the way and moved on, sensing his inquisitive stare boring into my back.

Typically, the station exit was swarming with people there to meet relatives, all of them holding signs: "So-and-so, your (fill in the blank) is here to meet you." Parents waiting for sons and daughters, children waiting for fathers and mothers, or (even more common) wives waiting for husbands and husbands waiting for wives. I never could understand why they were holding up signs. Were they afraid their own kin wouldn't recognize them? Some seemed to have been waiting there for years, their signs were so weather-beaten, the words barely legible; the people themselves were scruffy, bedraggled, weary. As I exited the station, I was surrounded by people asking where I'd come from, which train I was on, and whether or not I was the last one out.

The answers obviously disappointed my interrogators, who kept looking behind me, reluctant to disperse and go home. A young man holding up a sign for his wife saw I was all alone. "How come nobody's here to meet you?" He was the second person to ask me that. Guardedly I sized him up. "This isn't my home, I've got no kin here." With compassion in his eyes, he said, "Then you must be the first in your family to arrive."

From there I crossed the square to the curb, where a rainbow assortment of taxicabs pulled up, sometimes two or more at a time, stopped long enough to pick up a fare, then took off again like a flock of great garish birds.

Gao Jin and the woman climbed into a red cab, which made a turn around the grassy center of the square and took the freeway on-ramp into town. I jumped into a white cab and took off in pursuit.

The freeway passed through and above the city, giving me a bird's-eye view of busy clerks—male and female—in offices, and the mixed decor of apartment complexes. Old buildings that dominated the landscape were losing ground to modern high-rises. Billboards and neon signs vied for attention, downtown streets were lined with shops; people crowded the sidewalks, vehicles streamed back and forth, creating a world bursting with life and color and energy, all bathed in sunlight. From the extraordinary bustle of the scenes below, plus the people's dress and behavior, even their accents, I believed I was where I was supposed to be, but couldn't shake my feelings of strangeness and alienation. Maybe that was because of all that rich, blinding sunlight, that and the looks of smug satisfaction on people's faces, a marked contrast to what I was used to seeing in most inland cities. I was struck by the air of carefree prosperity as I sped past upscale boutiques and fancy restaurants that were a feast for the eyes, and all of them filled with shoppers and diners. The lack of anxiety was palpable, unchecked, and so obvious it seemed artificial, extravagant even, as if it concealed a trap for the unwary, set by residents of the city, knowingly or not. The sun's spreading rays carried a sense of doom.

The red taxi weaved in and out of traffic.

We took the freeway off-ramp and slowed down as we entered a canyon between tall buildings, where we merged with the bumper-to-bumper traffic. Windows on tall buildings and ground-floor shop windows reflected the sunlight like mirrors. Pedestrians formed unbroken lines of motion that propelled snippets of conversation and peals of laughter into my cab.

Turning into a shady avenue, wider than the street we'd just left and all but devoid of shops and pedestrians, we picked up speed as we passed a roadside park with lakes and hills and flower beds; it was encircled by a low, wavy wall topped by green tiles and the shade of tall bamboo; every few paces a hole opened up in a unique shape. After we left the park behind us, a riverlet of dark green, seemingly stagnant water appeared beside the road; clumps of duckweed floated on the surface; moss covered the path running next to it. Banana trees and iron trees and hollyhock filled spaces around houses on the opposite bank, where one tall white building displayed the signs of several publishing houses. The red taxi had stopped in front of the arched entrance to a nightclub directly across from the publishing houses. We sped past just as Gao Jin and the woman were climbing out of the taxi, and when she turned to look down the street, I saw it was Xia Hong, the woman we'd hung out with all those years ago. She was the last of the group I'd lost track of, and eventually I'd forgotten her altogether, though obviously she hadn't forgotten us. My cab turned the corner and pulled up to the curb, where I paid the driver and walked toward the nightclub and a noisy crowd of people on the sun-drenched street. A heavyset foreign man looking earnestly up and down the street stood where I'd seen Xia Hong and Gao Jin just a moment earlier. The red taxi was long gone, its place taken by a silver Volvo. I kept going, feeling as if I were walking through clouds, despite the sunlight all around.

I saw people converge on the nightclub like schools of minnows being sucked into the gaping mouth of a large fish. I too felt drawn to the entrance, and the minute I stepped inside, I had the distinct feeling that I'd been there before.

It was a dark, murky dining room, even with the lights on, with four or five hundred diners eating and drinking in silence. Shadowy figures moved among them, merging and separating in helter-skelter fashion; they too were eating and drinking and gesturing, also in silence. The diners shared a single room, yet each was an island; it was like a multiple-exposure photograph on which each individual had been captured separately.

Gao Jin and Xia Hong sat in a corner beside a French window, their heads lowered. Ignoring the soft drinks and pastries in front of them, they appeared to be waiting for someone; diners who tried to sit in the empty chair at their table were told it was occupied.

I sat all the way across the room, where I could watch what went on at their table.

The room darkened, and I turned to look at the entrance, just as a husky fellow stepped in out of the blinding sunlight. His features, haloed by sunlight, were indistinguishable, but once he was standing inside the dimly lit room, I noticed he was wearing a striped shirt. It was, I saw, Gao Yang.

The place was dark as dusk, yet hundreds of diners kept eating and drinking, like extras in a long play, who seemed prepared to sit there eating and drinking for as long as the show went on.

22

"You knew it was me all along, didn't you?" Gao Yang smiled. "You weren't surprised at all."

"Not after I heard that girl describe the Japanese man who came on to her."

We were walking shoulder to shoulder along the lakeshore. Ripples glimmered in the waning sunlight, the woods around us were somber and silent—all bird sounds had died out. Beyond the trees on the opposite shore evening lights snapped on and dinner was on the table in all sorts of homes, where shadows moved behind shaded windows. Bursts of laughter and conversation drifted across the water.

Gao Jin and Xia Hong were walking several paces behind us.

"Then when that editor told me about the odd, morose writer she met, I all but knew it was you. Only people like us know how to pull off stunts like that."

"My skills failed me. If I'd been a bit more professional, I might have gotten away with it."

"The sword was the key. Once it became the murder weapon, you could no longer have been the victim."

"That's where I slipped up," Gao Yang admitted ruefully. "If I'd chosen not to let you have it, you'd probably still be in the dark. At the very least you'd suffer a few more setbacks before finally figuring things out."

"But then the police wouldn't have come looking for me, and we wouldn't have met, since I'd still think you were on some tobacco plantation in the Philippines."

"Yes, and if you believed that, we could have kept the game going a bit longer." I noticed a faint smile on Gao Yang's lips. "Eventually I tired of the game, but ending it with no real drama is disappointing. When we decided to include you in our plan, Feng Xiaogang warned us to be careful, saying you might turn our elaborate scheme to your own advantage and have a good time at our expense. I didn't believe him, because you were running around with your head in the clouds over some girl, and wouldn't be distracted. It was still our show. You were a minor eddy among vast rapids, a tiny swerve amid countless watery twists and turns. It took the police a long time and a lot of energy to finally discover that someone else had been using your name, and that you knew nothing about any of this."

"You underestimated me," I said with a laugh. "I've never passed up a starring role."

"I should have guessed," said Gao Yang. "There isn't a single dim bulb in our group. We want people to know how important we are, want to be the star of every play. So tell me, in all these years, have you ever found a more interesting starring role?"

"In all these years, this has been the *only* interesting starring role I've had. From out of nowhere I learned that I had been somebody once, a guy who did something important. I had both a reason and the guts to commit murder. For me that was a real high, just knowing I wasn't some mediocrity. I wish it had been true. We kicked butt, didn't we? A little thieving here, some smuggling there, even a big-time robbery. Maybe I didn't murder anybody, but I took part in all those other things. We were in it together. Somebody called us a gang once, a spirited, self-indulgent, criminal gang."

"There was no thieving, no smuggling, no big-time robbery, no criminal gang, none of that. We just hung out, stuffing ourselves and getting drunk and concocting bold schemes we wouldn't carry out in a million years. We were a bunch of gutless wonders, kids in grown-up bodies who played at being bullies and killers. We all wanted to be stars, we wanted to rule over a craven world, while in fact we were destined to be little fish capable only of making tiny ripples in a big pond." Our walk had taken us to the opposite shore, where China firs, with their straight trunks and evenly spaced limbs, towered over us; now that the sun had set, the sky, trees, and lake had turned dark and filled our eyes with a verdant solitude. We stopped, and were gradually enveloped in cold winds sweeping off the lake and out of the woods.

"After lunch that day, our last rowdy lunch together, we left the others and came down here." Gao Yang smiled like a blind man, his eyes two dark holes. "We pretended everything was cool, that we had urgent, important business to take care of, mysterious dealings far away. In fact, we had no place else to go. Our money was gone, so we couldn't stick around here any longer. We'd screwed everyone we knew out of their money in order to get here. We said we were about to score a cash toad, and they all thought we were on to something big. But there were no toads here, and all those grandiose words were pure bullshit. If we had to slink back to Beijing, what bothered us wasn't our inability to pay back the money, but the loss of our credibility. Who'd ever believe another word we said?"

"Once a wimp, always a wimp."

"No, not us. We knew we had to go all the way. Where that led us was all Feng Xiaogang's idea."

. . . That evening, some friends were hanging out when Feng Xiaogang, who had been gazing out over the lake, turned and said with a laugh, "What do you think people would say if you and I strapped ourselves to a big rock, jumped into the lake, and sank to the bottom?"

"They'd probably think they had two new American cousins." As he leaned against a fir tree, Gao Yang lazily puffed on a cigarette; blue-tinted smoke curled out of his mouth and mingled with the mist settling around the trees. The moon rising above the dark arboreal canopy created a mottled tableau of shadows. Every word sounded like a hoarse sob in the misty night.

"Let's do it, then." They couldn't see Feng Xiaogang clearly as he came toward them, but they heard the laughter in his voice. "We'll make a game of it. The kind of life we're living sucks, maybe dying's a way to spice things up."

"What's so great about that? I say it stinks. I thought we had a rule that we could run around screwing anyone we wanted, just so we didn't get screwed in the process."

"Well, I think it's a good idea. What rule? We're playing for thrills. We're not going to screw anybody, are we?"

"Depends on how we do it." *Splash!* A rock hit the lake and sent water spraying. A hazy figure walked up. "Too shallow. We'd bob to the surface in a day or two. If we're going to die, let's do it without leaving a trace. This isn't the place."

"Where then? And how?" Two people turned to look at the speaker.

"Someplace no one's ever been, someplace no one will ever

go, someplace where you can rot in peace. You can only act out a historical romance as long as you're not discovered doing it."

"No good." A female figure walked up. "Where do you expect to find a place like that? Climb a high mountain until you think you've found a primeval spot, then look in any clump of weeds and you'll find that someone's already taken a leak there. If you ask me, you have to be discovered for there to be any excitement. And you need to mess up the body so people will know it wasn't a natural death. Now that's worth doing. You'll drive people nuts trying to figure out what happened. That's going out in style. There'll be no peace for anyone."

"Everybody's got an opinion, it seems, almost as if this has been in the works for days." Feng Xiaogang's voice.

"I agree that it should be murder. First comes the disappearance, then the saga can unfold any old way, till the murder itself happens. The climax of our drama will offer no clues whatsoever. But we have to divide up the labor. We can't all die, so one person will be the victim, another the killer. We must have a killer—if there's going to be a murder, that is—to be realistic."

"Are you saying I'm to be the victim?" Feng Xiaogang laughingly asked Gao Yang. "And you'll be the killer? How come you always get the good parts?"

"Being the killer's a lot tougher than you think," Gao Yang said with a laugh. "Just think—hiding out, being chased, and, if you're unlucky enough to meet up with some empty-headed official and can't talk your way out of it, you might pay the ultimate price. Being the victim, on the other hand, is a snap. Jump into the river, close your eyes, and wait for all the excitement. While everyone else is running around like crazy, you lie there and take it easy. But we can swap if you're unhappy."

"Hey, I didn't know you cared. All right, I'll be the victim. Whose idea was this anyway? Mine, of course."

"We expect a lot from the killer," the woman said. "If we're going to make a game of it, let's do it right or not do it at all. No run-of-the-mill killer, someone who only knows how to hide out. It should be a person with brains, somebody who can weave an intricate web. Here's something to think about. Our killer assumes different roles. A phony name, for example. Before anything happens he appears as someone else. That way, when the investigation begins, the police will be off on a wild goose chase. We don't want to make it too easy for them to get their hands on the killer."

"How about Fang Yan?" the man said. "He lives an exciting life. We can throw a monkey wrench into it to keep him from getting cocky."

"Not so fast," Feng Xiaogang said. "You're making things so complicated nobody will be able to break the case. Then you guys'll get off scot-free, and I'll have died for nothing."

"You must trust your government," the woman consoled him. "No case is too hard for the government."

"And I don't think we should involve an outsider," Feng Xiaogang whined. "I don't trust Fang Yan. What if the prick gets pumped up by all this and turns the game to his own advantage? After all our plans, we still get the shaft. A guy like that's always looking for a few thrills."

"Good point," Gao Yang said. "But who would be any better? Can you think of anyone we know who actually avoids stuff like this?"

"I say, since life and death is no longer at issue here," the woman said coldly, "why worry about the phony name?"

"I'm telling you I won't lay down my life just to become an

anonymous hero. I want a guarantee that after I die I'll be a hot topic of conversation. That'll be up to you guys."

"You have our word that if the day comes when we never see you again, we will tell your story to everybody, whether they knew you or not, placing the blame for every unacknowledged misdeed on your head, telling how you robbed and plundered, what a playboy you were, and how you're now enjoying yourself in a better world. That way you'll become a folk hero, a legend embodying all of mankind's longings and fantasies. Then when the discussions and the rumors begin turning stale, and you're fading from people's memories, if no one has found your body, we'll do it for them and report our discovery, which will start people talking about you again, until you're the hottest topic in town. Anyone who's still breathing will cringe when they think about what happened to you. You have our word that for the next ten years you'll live in the people's hearts. After that, it's out of our hands. You know how hard it was for our great revolutionary pioneers to live for more than ten years in the people's hearts, so you have nothing to complain about. Ten years is damned close to immortality, so you can reside down in the Nine Springs with a smile on your face."

"I hope I die with dignity. I don't want to suffer, even if it's only symbolic pain."

"As your killer I'll give you complete freedom to choose the way you depart this world. Even if that makes me unworthy of the calling."

"You can jump in the river leap off a mountain be hanged garroted, it's up to you. Try them all if you want," the woman's voice said. "It's your call. Sample all the avenues of death, then take that knowledge to your grave."

"I want to thank you warmly for your kind wishes. You can't

beat pals at a time like this," Feng Xiaogang said with a laugh. "I say, let's do it."

"Let's do it," Gao Yang echoed him. "This is going to be a lot of fun. We'll totally confuse those dumb assholes. When it's over, no one will know what it was all about. They'll have no idea why we did it, not in their wildest dreams."

"Since there's nothing more to talk about, I say we go ahead and do it." The woman's voice again. "Not like the old days, when all our big talk led to nothing, and all our chances to have some fun were wasted."

"We're really going to do it this time, really. Primed and ready," Feng Xiaogang said. "We're punks if we don't."

"Let's commemorate this momentous discussion with a group photo." The man's voice, silent for so long, drew the words out slowly. "It can serve as proof of the gathering."

"There's a kiosk," the woman's voice said. "Let's go over there."

In the moonlight four figures walked up to the lake, where the water shimmered. They were swallowed up in the darkness as they stepped inside the kiosk. *Click.* The shutter snapped and a flashbulb lit up the inside with its strong light. Gao Yang was smiling, his face white as a sheet of paper, mouth and eyes like gaping holes. Another flash. Feng Xiaogang's face was like a sheet of paper, mouth and eyes like gaping holes, briefly, before returning to darkness. A third flash, Liu Yan's eyes were lowered, her hands folded, her lips parted slightly. Every time the shutter clicked, light flooded the kiosk. Liu Yan seemed frozen in the dazzling brightness that defined the colorful, glossy grains of the bamboo posts and the railings behind her.

"Don't you want your picture taken?"

After the kiosk returned to darkness, the surface of the lake shimmered again. The photographer replied: "Out of film."

A column of people walked along the shore of the moonlit lake past dark stands of trees. Gao Yang's voice carried from the distance:

"This time we're really going to do it, aren't we?"

One cloudy, drizzly day followed another; streets and houses and trees were drenched; water dripped from eaves and forked branches; pedestrians wore raincoats or carried umbrellas to keep their heads dry. The street scene was clear one minute, hazy the next. Electric wipers rhythmically kept automobile windshields clear of fine raindrops.

Taxicabs prowled the rainswept city streets, down one street and up another, past building after building, going this way and that. Lights inside the gloomy buildings turned their windows pale yellow or ghostly white.

Four people were packed into a taxi, all slightly drunk, even though it was still early in the morning. Gao Jin sat up front staring blankly at the miragelike scene ahead and at pedestrians crossing the street. Gao Yang, a goofy smile on his face, sat in the backseat. Feng Xiaogang was squeezed between him and Liu Yan, so sleepy he could barely keep his eyes open; his head kept flopping down on his chest as he sagged sideways. Each time he slumped over, Liu Yan righted him and cupped her hand under his chin. "Where are we?" he asked.

"Thailand," Gao Yang giggled.

"Don't make fun of a pal." Feng Xiaogang looked out the window and saw they were still within the confines of the city. "I'm not stupid," he said angrily. "I'm bright as a shiny mirror, so don't think you're so funny." Feng looked at Gao Yang then at Liu Yan. "What's so funny?"

"Who says it's funny?" Liu Yan said. "If anybody does, it's you."

"I say it's funny," Gao Yang commented earnestly. "The whole idea of what we're doing is a blast. I know we're going to have a great time."

"You're a fucking blast. I'd like to see how fucking funny you'd think it was if I decided not to die after all." Feng Xiaogang's head drooped again and he slumped to the side, only to be righted once more by Liu Yan.

"Leave me alone," he grumbled. "Just because we're riding together doesn't mean you can push me around."

"We want you to look outside. This may be your last chance," Gao Yang said.

"Shut up, Gao Yang," Liu Yan said. "Why do you have to make a joke out of this?"

"Stop calling me Gao Yang." Gao Yang looked over at Liu Yan. "From now on, I'm Fang Yan, so call me by my new name."

"What do you mean, you're Fang Yan?" Feng Xiaogang struggled to raise his head. "I'm Fang Yan now. I'll pass it on to you after I'm dead."

"Keep your facts straight, you two," Liu Yan said calmly. "Don't screw things up before we even get started."

Gao Yang laughed foolishly, once more angering Feng Xiaogang. "You think it's fucking funny, don't you?"

"I think it's funny about Fang Yan," Gao Yang said. "We've got him hog-tied and he doesn't even know it. When the time comes I'll use his name all over the world, and the prick won't have a clue."

"You're a bastard, you really are," Feng Xiaogang laughed. "You love the idea of taking advantage of an honest man."

Once the taxi left the city limits, it sped down the pencil straight highway. Glistening white water flowed through irrigation ditches, dark clouds skittered across the sky, and off in the distance a sleek silvery airplane sat in a clearing at the foot of a mountain.

It was an old but recently redecorated hotel whose facade and interior had begun to fade under the onslaught of the elements and the ravages of human traffic. Narrow corridors with scarlet carpets made of synthetic fiber and chocolate-colored wallpaper, scenes of constant foot traffic, were murky even with the lights on. The noisy lobby was cramped, cluttered with Naugahyde sofas whose springs sagged from years of service, and dusty potted plants with droopy leaves. Every corner was packed with men and a few women here and there, some standing, others sitting, the artificial light turning their faces pale. They were puffing away on cigarettes and gesturing and talking loudly, lively, ever-changing expressions of joy or sadness on their faces. Every room, private and public, was filled with people, morning, noon, and night, all of them carrying on noisily, totally unconcerned, lights on, smoke rising.

Four guests occupied separate top-floor rooms. No one paid them any attention when they appeared in the corridors or the lobby. All four of them reeked of alcohol, especially the two men, who were often so drunk they could hardly utter an intelligent comment and could barely stand on their own two feet. They weaved in and out of the crowds, flirting with waitresses and talking to people they'd never met, sometimes starting arguments and nearly getting punched by strangers, until, at the urging of by-

standers, they backed off smiling and handed their would-be opponents cigarettes or offered to buy them a drink. One guest,
named Mingsong, or "bright pine," got to know one of the two
men through just such idle chatter; the man, who called himself
Fang Yan, gave Mingsong his address and said, "Look me up next
time you're in Beijing."

The women generally stayed in their rooms gazing out the
windows at a lush green hill across the way, site of the city's zoo.
Each night, when the streets were deserted and quiet, they could
hear the screeching of monkeys and the roars of tigers emerging
from the dark woods.

A tour bus, packed with passengers, sped between emerald
green mountains against the flow of a river whose waters ran red.
Rolling hills stretched to the horizon. Four seated passengers rose
and fell as the bus negotiated the bumpy road. Suddenly they
were at the crest, where heaven and earth spread out magnifi-
cently before them, mountain peaks filling their eyes; then just as
suddenly they were in a gully with thick underbrush, dense
woods, and the roar of water. A little mountain town appeared
from time to time across the river, rooftops merging and overlapping amid swirling fog, like a landscape painting badly hung,
throwing its perspective out of kilter. But mostly the view was of
endless mountains, unbroken streams of flowing water, vegeta-
tion, now withered now lush, some brown some green, and rolling white clouds that changed shape as they merged and moved
on, their shadows mottling the sunlight in mountain valleys.

It was an old city moat that had recently undergone repairs;
at the foot of a mountain, the gate towers rose majestically with
golden double-eaved roofs and a forest of crimson pillars. A pan-

orama of fertile land lay beyond the city wall, dotted by villages, herds of livestock, stands of tall trees, clouds of chimney smoke, and peasants on tractors wriggling through the fields along irrigation ridges. The air was clean, the sky blue, and all around as far as the eye could see stood a range of snowcapped mountains, the lakes at their bases shimmering with rippling water and an occasional pagoda made sparkly and bright by light from the sun and the snow and the lake waters.

The two main streets, one east-west the other north-south, intersected in the center of town, connecting the four city gates. Old-fashioned shops and teahouses and public houses and cafés and general stores, all painted the same color, lined sidewalks with tables on which were displayed marble utensils ashtrays brush holders paperweights flower pots garlic mortars rings, pure and clean and eye-catchingly beautiful, like watercolors, with clouds and mist and mountains and streams.

The four people strolled past the shops and stores buying a little of this and pilfering some of that and giggling and laughing out loud as they walked along with their pockets stuffed their arms loaded down their hands full.

The two men, not yet sober from the last binge, were guzzling rice wine, their faces changing from red to white, eyes watery, barely able to walk, but laughing like crazy.

It was a prosperous little town located where the plains meet the towering mountains, perched at the edge of the nation's borders, beyond which lay territory belonging to a neighboring country, one saddled with serious instability, whose government troops launched repeated assaults on communist guerrilla forces and minority secessionists. At dusk the sound of artillery fire echoed amid mountain peaks. But in town dusk was a time for the local residents; sandaled men and women in the traditional dress of many nationalities packed streets where colorful clothing was displayed, and where peddlers hawked products from around the world: clothing digital watches costume jewelry cigarettes and keepsakes. Included among the buyers and sellers were foreign men and women, but appearance and dress and accent made it impossible to distinguish between them and the locals, since they were all of Malay-Mongol stock, wore identical togas, and spoke Chinese. Sold on the next street over were cooked meat stewed eggs fruit coffee and all kinds of soft drinks plus fried stir-fried boiled and baked foods. The next street after that was all but deserted, the sidewalks lined with wood-carved Buddhist icons strangely shaped wild animal horns piles of knives and scabbards and all kinds of swords.

That night an old woman sold a sword with a handle of galvanized steel inlaid with shiny glass beads that turned it into a magical sword under the streetlamps.

That night a wild dance party was held on the top floor of the town's only high-rise, where flashing red and green lights rained down on the town's motley elements well past midnight. Some out-of-town men drank rice wine at a roadside stand until they puked, then after beating their breasts and stamping their feet, they switched from wine to lemonade, filling their stomachs with glass after glass of it, before walking off with a splendid sword.

Late that night an argument erupted in one of the town's small inns. A man vigorously defended his position, insisting he was joking all along, that he was never all that serious, that there was no need for anybody else to be so earnest, that he had never entertained the idea of actually going through with it. Half of what came out of his mouth was pure bullshit, and anyone who took him seriously was a fool—heh-heh. A woman said she didn't like joking around, and even if others did it, she still took them seriously, and if that made her a fool, then so be it. She ridiculed the man for having to get his courage out of a bottle, for joking around so he wouldn't have to face the music once he sobered up. She said that now, after all these years, she appreciated his talent for making jokes when he was drunk. The man, not at all angry, and not wanting to wrangle, laughed and said, You're just now figuring me out? I thought you knew all along. If not for that particular talent, I wouldn't have lived this long. Then he turned to the other two men in the room. Have you got something to say? Then say it. If you want to gang up on me with this woman, go ahead, since I'm pulling out of the game anyhow. It's no fun anymore. Commoners like us have no use for glory or self-esteem, so there's no disgrace in heading home with egg on my face. I say to hell with everybody. One of the men, who resembled him in a way, said it was all the same to him whether they kept the game going or not. The woman turned to the man sitting on the bed as he tested the sharpness of the sword with his finger and asked, What do you say? You've got the lead role here, if you want to keep the game going, they'll have to play, whether they want to or not. Once everything's in place, events will unfold, no matter where they run off to. I'm beginning to think this game stinks, the man with the sword said. It's too simple, too contrived, and it'll be over when I die, anyway. After that it's up to others to join in. So you guys can step things up and play on, that is, if you have the interest and the will. But the game comes to a screeching halt if any one of you slinks off. You can walk away any time you want, but what about me? Once I'm down I can't get up again. I guarantee you I won't walk away, the woman said, and as long as I stick around, none of the others will be able to either. She looked at the other two men. I don't trust guarantees from anyone, the man said, chopping the air a couple of times with the sword. Guarantees don't pay the mortgage. As far as I'm concerned, the game can continue, but the rules have to change. Everyone joins in. I've thought it over and the only way to make it possible for people to play along conscientiously yet conservatively is to change the rules. By that I mean we have a series of murders, with each of us calling upon all our resources to hunt down the others. The last one left alive is the smartest, the one with the right to the throne of killer king. That'll cause a sensation, it'll spark interest and make it a game worthy of the name. Deciding who lives and who dies seems fraudulent, unfair somehow. Playing for thrills is what it's all about, and that means everyone.

The man with the sword stood beneath the light smirking and watching the other three as they sat on the edge of the bed; the sharp edge of the sword in his hand glinted coldly in the light.

"We can't all die," the woman said after a momentary silence. "Someone has to live to tell the story, since the murderer's lips are sealed. Besides, if lots of people die, you'll be lumped together with everyone else."

"How come I can't be the last one left alive?" the man with the sword said as he stuck the point up under the woman's nose. "I see no need for a designated propagandist. The creative energies of the masses are boundless. We must combine our efforts to draw upon this creative energy."

"Count me out," one of the men said. "I know when I'm beaten."

"Then let's all count ourselves out," the man said, sheathing his sword. "Either that, or we do it my way."

* * *

Later on, the story goes, the four people headed home in high spirits, talking and laughing at themselves. None so much as mentioned the game again, not even as a joke. They traveled by day and slept by night, always together, never touching a drop of alcohol, even though all the mountain inns readied the finest rice wine for them; if one of them laughingly suggested a drink, he was greeted with silence by his companions. The bumpy mountain road was combed by the wind and washed by the rain; the four travelers had bags under their eyes their skin hung slack the hard trip down the mountain showed in their faces. But they got their second wind each night when they put up at an inn and played poker all night long, with me laughing at you and you joking with me, and no one sleeping.

One night a minor incident caused a bit of an uproar. One of the travelers signed the name Fang Yan in the guest register. His companions said there was no longer any need for phony names and told him to change it. The man said he'd already written the name and changing it would only make the innkeeper suspicious, so for now it was better to leave it as it was. His companions said he could change it without the innkeeper noticing. The man said that if the innkeeper wouldn't notice, why change it, since it didn't matter either way? The other three laughingly insisted that he change it, and if he thought it was too much trouble, they'd change it for him. The man laughingly insisted that he wouldn't change it and he didn't want anyone else doing it for him, and he wondered out loud what harm was caused by using the name Fang Yan.

Later that night it rained, setting the trees rustling in the noisy downpour. Well after midnight it really started coming down, accompanied by thunder and lightning; they heard the pounding of water all around them as it cascaded down the rocky mountains. At daybreak the rain stopped, and a soupy morning fog curled up around the mountain peaks, enshrouding them like roiling smoke. Off in the distance, out of sight, cresting waters roared down mountain streams; the road was littered with broken branches and fallen leaves as the bus noisily rumbled along, past dense foliage that was broken through in places by tall trees felled by the wind and rain, revealing brief snatches of earth and sky that were just as quickly swallowed up again by the fog.

Vehicles negotiated the mountain road cautiously, headlights on, like a succession of blurry eyes.

That morning a head-on collision between a truck and a tour bus occurred at a highway curve near Mount Bao. Fortunately neither vehicle was traveling fast, which kept both from going over the side, and saved the passengers from death or serious injury; the front ends of both vehicles were damaged, and the bus driver sustained minor injuries. But since the accident blocked the highway, traffic in both directions was held up for four hours. While they were waiting for traffic-control personnel to come from Mount Bao and determine who was at fault, a tow truck drove up to drag both vehicles over to the side of the road and allow traffic to pass. Hundreds of vehicles, passenger and freight, were backed up a good ten li, the blaring of their horns rising and falling; some of the drivers had climbed down out of their cabs and were talking among themselves or walking around, they and their trucks all but hidden by a blanket of fog not quite dense enough to stifle the constant clomp of footsteps or the chatter of human voices or the slamming of truck doors, and from the trees lining the highway came sounds of branches snapping leaves rustling and piss streaming. Some of the people answering nature's call or strolling just to keep limber not only went in among the trees but past them all the way to the edge of the cliff to look down into the valley, where the sound of rushing water from the river cut through the soupy fog and gave the illusion that it was flowing right past their feet, when in fact it was hundreds of feet below them. A young woman squatting in a clump of grass near the ridge to relieve herself thought she heard a single scream from somewhere nearby, followed by silence, so she stood up and walked over to take a look, but the fog was too thick to see anything, although she heard a rustling noise off in the distance, followed by the sound of more than one person tramping through the underbrush. After that she heard the roar of engines starting up back on the highway, now that the road was open again, and out of the fog-enshrouded woods people came running and shouting as they searched for their vehicles. She was one of those people out on the road, and she climbed into the cab of her truck and fell in behind the truck ahead.

The fog lifted, the sky was clear, and the range of green mountains beyond the ridges came to an abrupt end; as they drove through the pass, the world opened up for them. The sun was suspended high above the flatlands, sending its shimmering rays down on farms and towns and factories and rivers. Water that had roared and crashed its way down the valley now flowed meekly across the plain and into a gigantic lake. The bus sped down the flat highway, the watery surface sparkled on the distant lake, long then round then flat then narrow. Long cottony clouds filled the sky above the lake, as if they had been stretched and twisted by a huge invisible hand into all manner of lifelike shapes, singly and in clusters: now a pride of lions manes flung heads raised, now a herd of galloping horses hooves flying, now a towering snowcapped mountain, now alabaster pillars forming a corridor through the sky. The clouds grew and grew as the bus neared the lake, until they filled the sky like a cathedral dome, wispy figures undergoing countless transformations as if the Creator were giving the mortals below a microcosmic view of the world. The snowcapped mountain crumbled, the alabaster pillars toppled, tigers and elephants and lions and leopards were swallowed up by smoke and dust, clouds billowed then spouted and formed a massive human head looking majestically into the sky, showing only the whites of its eyes. As the bus rounded the lakeshore, the head followed its progress with its eyes, now happy now sad now angry now exasperated, abruptly looking straight down into the bus then abruptly cocking itself to gaze off into the distance. When the bus came to the end of the lake the head still hung in the sky, reluctant to leave.

Three passengers, two men and a woman, sat in the bus, their faces pale as paper. . . .

23

Lights inside the resplendent nightclub dimmed and went out. A white taxi turned the corner and sped down the tree-dappled avenue as people poured out through the arched entrance with its raised red lanterns, like minnows expelled from the mouth of a large fish, water and all. They crowded about on the moonlit street, where traffic flowed parallel to duckweed floating atop the murmuring stream. Leaves on banana trees and iron trees around the moonlit houses rustled, a low wall around the park rolled like a petrified wave into the dark of night.

The taxi turned off the tree-shaded street and drove into a valley between tall buildings. People streamed past ground-level shops lit up like a hall of mirrors like schooling fish in an aquarium, blazing with color.

Bright city streets came and went; at each intersection, more bright city streets spread out like spokes, all black with people converging this way or dispersing that way, shops and roadside trees alternating between light and dark. As we crossed one street after another, I saw at the far end nightclubs and shops I'd already driven past, with their bright neon lights; I spotted the elevated freeway heading out of town, and beyond that crowds of people and palm trees in the square fronting the train station. High-rises kept getting shorter and older and less numerous; streets and lanes kept getting darker and quieter and more sparsely populated.

The taxi pulled up in front of a gray guesthouse on a dark, secluded street. I stood there with my satchel and looked up at the gray building, the very guesthouse where we had once stayed for thirteen days. I remembered it as being a fancy, imposing building that dwarfed everything around it, a crane among chickens; but now I could see that it was squat and run down, more a residential hostel than a real guesthouse, and though there were no new high-rises nearby, it no longer stood out even among stodgy old buildings. I assumed it must have been a haven for people who were down on their luck even back then.

The interior was just as seedy; no elevator, so I climbed the uneven concrete steps all the way to the top. The staff I met on the way up had emaciated faces and wore filthy white jackets; the guests were mostly swarthy crew-cut middle-aged men dressed in no longer fashionable blue-gray tunics and carrying black Naugahyde satchels, or pretentious young men in double-knit Western suits and gaudy ties, plus some flighty show-offy young women in heavy makeup and flashy costume jewelry.

I was given the same room I'd stayed in the first time, an eighth-floor corner. Spacious and very old, it had all the necessary equipment—TV telephone bathroom facilities—but it was third-rate stuff. The windows on two of the walls had no screens or curtains, just wavy steel bars welded to the frames, thus allowing the wind to swirl freely inside. The toilet was broken, it didn't flush and there was no seat; no toilet paper no towels, the inside of the porcelain bowl was grungy and rust-stained, and it didn't take much to imagine what the caked-on filth had once been. No water emerged from the taps, the mirror above the wash basin was cracked so badly that the twisted face staring back at me belonged to a fiendish clown.

It was late, and I was exhausted, so I lay down on the sagging bed without washing up or getting undressed and fell into a groggy sleep. Wind kept gusting past my face, chilled by the night air; beyond the open windows the starry sky was a resplendent cupola inlaid with precious stones. Even with the lamp turned off, you could make out the ghostly shapes of furniture in the starlight. I slept like a camper on the edge of wakefulness.

The room filled up with a fine-edged din: rustling leaves, chattering insects, chirping crickets, the hollow reverberation of loaded trucks rumbling down the street, and the distant sound of footsteps and muted conversations. Wind sliced across the room carrying the pungent aroma of grass and trees along with the acrid night smells of asphalt and auto exhaust, plus a whiff of the odd fragrance of a refinery. Echoes of familiar voices swirled amid snatches of graceful muted conversation. In the midst of this cacophony of sounds and jangle of smells I detected a familiar manly odor and sensed the lingering heat of a body no longer present here; this heat formed the intermittent yet discernible outline of the body from which it had come. I watched the figure pace the room and drink some water and sit down to smoke a cigarette, and after it rose from the sofa and left the room, the shallow impression of a body remained on the cushion. . . .

Day Thirteen

The telephone rang just as I was dropping off to sleep. It was like a rhythmic tap on the door—tap tap tap, then a pause, then tap tap tap. In my groggy state I figured it must be a wrong number, since none of my friends knew where I was sleeping at the time. But I picked it up anyway, and from deep inside came a woman's voice. "Hello hello" she said anxiously. Then: "Can you tell who this is?"

I gave some sort of reply, I think, or maybe not.

"Say something, I know it's you." The voice was plaintive. "I'm outside, on the corner. Can you come down?"

"What else is there to say?" I asked, as if talking to an old friend. "I need my rest, I'm tired. I just got into bed."

"You're leaving," the voice said. "From where I'm standing I can see the taxi parked in front of your hotel."

"OK, I'll be right down," I said. "Where are you?"

"On the corner," the voice replied. "You'll see me as soon as you walk out the door, and I'll see you."

After hanging up, I climbed out of bed and, still foggy-headed, went in to wash up. Water gushed out of the taps when I turned them on, and continued to drip when I turned them off. I washed my face, then flushed the toilet on my way out of the bathroom.

By then the sun was up and shining. Cars drove up and down the streets, pedestrians moved about on the sidewalks. Neighboring buildings were much older and a lot grayer than they had seemed the night before. People were dressed in the most unfashionable clothing imaginable: if not black, then white, the occasional "personal statement" nothing more than cheap double knits or bell-bottom jeans that swept the sidewalk. A red, mudspattered taxicab was parked in front of the hotel. I looked up, and there were Xu Xun, Wang Ruohai, and Qiao Qiao coming out of a smoke shop across the street, laughing and talking and taking cigarettes out of fresh packs and lighting up; the two men were wearing identical striped shirts and navy blue trousers. A domed green and white bus passed by, blocking them from view; but after it had turned the corner, they looked my way, not at me but at the hotel entrance behind me. A noisy bunch of people in striped shirts walked out of the hotel. Gao Jin, Gao Yang, Xia Hong, and I were all carrying suitcases. I went up to the taxi, set down my suitcase, fished a pack of smokes out of the pocket of my striped shirt, passed them around, and lit one for myself.

"See you back there," I said. "When do you think you'll leave?"

"Soon, maybe," Gao Yang said with a smile. "Then again, maybe we won't leave. Who can say? But we'll call you if we do."

"You'll get by just fine." I smiled. "Better than me. I'll wait to see what you make of yourself."

"Pharmacy isn't so bad," Gao Jin said. "If we're ever in need of medicine, can we come around to you and get it for free?"

"No problem. I'll pay you to buy from me."

"Hey, here's Feng Xiaogang, coming to say good-bye," Gao Yang said as he stepped aside and looked over his shoulder.

A gaunt, sickly-looking fellow in an identical striped shirt squeezed through the gathering; smiling broadly, he walked up and shook hands with me. "What's your hurry?" he asked. "Why not hang out with us for a few more days?" In the daylight his face was very animated.

"Can't. Besides, what's to keep me here?" I smiled. "We'll meet up again, that's for sure."

"Do Gao Yang and the others have your address?"

"Yes. They'll know where to find me."

A younger Li Jiangyun, who had come with Feng Xiaogang, stood beyond the circle of friends and smiled. We called her Liu Yan at the time. I reached out to shake hands with her and said with a laugh, "Meeting you has been one of the highlights of my stay. If you and Feng Xiaogang ever decide to break up, make sure I'm the first to know about it."

She didn't reply, just smiled. Another girl rounded the corner and came up behind her. She had a flat profile, but a moon-shaped face that glowed; not a blemish anywhere. A silver-gray Naugahyde handbag hung from her shoulder. It was Baishan, a very young Baishan. Her arrival brought smiles all around, as everyone turned to look at us. A forced smile made her look as if she were crying. She walked slowly up to me.

"What's with you?" I said with a sense of annoyance. "If you're going to cry, let it go and let's have some tears. You should see yourself now."

"Don't, don't be like that," Gao Yang said with a pat on the back.

"No, tell me, what'd I do? For three days now she's been giving me that same look. What did I ever do to you?" My neck was thrust out, my head cocked. "It's not all right for me to go home, is that it? You have my address and phone number. Who's stopping you from coming to see me? It's not like I'm off to Taiwan, and we'll have to gaze across the straits for the rest of our lives. I'll be here in China, right where anyone who wants to can find me."

"All right, that's enough," Gao Jin said. "You won't be happy till you've got her bawling again, will you? Then you'll start bawling, and while you two are crying your eyes out, the rest of us will stand around feeling terrible and looking it."

Everyone laughed. "Who?" My face was turning red. "Who's going to bawl?"

"Don't give me that," Gao Jin said, still laughing. "We know what you're capable of." He turned to Baishan. "He gave you his address, didn't he? What else do you need? Go see him. He can't run away, he's got nowhere to go."

"It's you he's thinking about, if you want the truth," Gao Yang said to her. "He may act like an asshole, but we know how he's been crying into his pillow the last couple of nights. In the mornings his eyes look like peaches. He's a very emotional person."

"Shut the fuck up." I shoved Gao Yang.

They all laughed, including Baishan, who gave me a tender look. I turned away in disgust. "Are you folks about finished? If not, stay here and keep it up, I'm going."

"Not so fast." Gao Jin took a camera out of his bag. "One last picture together."

"Not me." I waved him off. "When did you turn into a damned tourist, always wanting to take a damned picture? Like a monkey, spraying the area with piss to leave his mark."

"Picture time picture time." Gao Jin backed up to frame the shot. "We're all together, maybe for the last time—tell Xu Xun and that bunch to join us. What are they gabbing about? Call them over."

Xia Hong shouted for them to join us. Qiao Qiao led Wang Ruohai and Xu Xun across the street by the arm.

"You still here?" Xu Xun laughed. "I'm getting sick of you."

"And I can't wait to get away from you." I laughed. Gao Yang dragged me over to line up. Xu Xun pushed Baishan up next to me and held her there.

We stood shoulder to shoulder facing the camera and talking all at once: "Hurry up, we can't stand like this forever."

"Just a second." Gao Jin focused the camera, then looked up. "Smile."

We smiled. He lowered the camera and said to Baishan: "Sorry, Ling Yu, try again with the smile."

That was what we called Baishan at the time.

Finally, with awkward smiles frozen on our faces, Gao Jin snapped the shutter.

We broke ranks. I shook hands all around and climbed into the taxi. At everyone's urging, Baishan tried to get in after me, but I stopped her. "No scenes now. I hate seeing people gazing in or out of cabs and waving good-bye."

She stared at me through the window.

The driver turned on the ignition, eased the taxi through the gathering and out onto the street, then drove off, leaving the gang in front of the hotel yawning, smoking, gabbing, and wondering where to go now. Baishan walked off alone. Li Jiangyun watched her go, but no one else was even aware that she had left.

Day Twelve

Traffic was heavy under the scorching sun's rays; ice cream vendors at stands under white awnings were all over the place. People strolled along the sidewalks in front of buildings on both sides of the street. I left the public phone booth in front of the corner grocery store and crossed the street, where I stepped onto the sidewalk under some stone pillars. An ice cream vendor had staked out the spot. My friends were buying ice cream cones. Qiao Qiao held up one with flakes of chocolate and handed it to me. Already beginning to melt, but still plenty cold, it was wonderfully refreshing. Without a word, we walked past some stone pillars, ice cream in hand, toward the sunbaked intersection. Small, frail Feng Xiaogang trailed along behind me as he ate his ice cream.

We headed down a cobblestone lane, single file, hugging a shadowy wall. At every open window we scrunched down to pass under or walked around it. Doors stood open behind steel gratings or stout bamboo poles. Murky though the interiors were, we could still see wizened old men in undershirts or stout housewives in pajamas and plenty of skinny kids with big, dark eyes. Some of the residents were drinking tea, others were washing clothes, to which bamboo poles draped with soggy colorful laundry flapping

in the wind bore witness. Music from radios and cassette record-
ers swelled and abated.

Narrow, winding lanes crossed and recrossed, and from time
to time we spotted a street bustling with cars and pedestrians at
the end of one of them.

The restaurant's arcadelike entrance resembled that of a
garage, except for a heavy signboard—gold letters on a black
background—that said: View of Heaven. Inside the central
courtyard—half in shadows, half brightly lit—a hundred or more
metal tables and chairs, mottled green paint showing their age,
awaited customers.

My friends and I took seats at one of the tables. Close at hand
was a row of open windows, behind which we saw redwood tables
and chairs, scenic scrolls hanging on the walls, potted plants in full
bloom, and lofty towers with carved pillars painted beams and
upswept eaves. Our conversation and our laughter and the clinking of glasses echoed in the all-but-deserted courtyard, like shouts
in a mountain valley.

"Tomorrow at this time I'll be home be home. . . . Where
will you be you be tomorrow?"

"How come you didn't invite Ling Yu over Ling Yu over
how come?"

"I'm tired of her tired of her, why should I invite her. She's
no fun anymore, I'd rather sit here and look at Qiao Qiao look
at Xia Hong look at Liu Yan. In sight but out of reach or within
reach but out of sight."

"Liu Yan said she'd come said she'd come but she stood us
up like some cunt and brother Feng ought to give the cunt a
real beating."

"Who can say who'll beat whom our brother Feng here doesn't know mantis boxing boxing."

"When you get back to Beijing check into rubbers into rubbers for me. Buy up as many as you can get I don't plan to sell them as balloons some guy from Roza wants them since you can't buy them in Roza where the people want birth control even if the government doesn't we sell them for five Rozan dollars five Rozan dollars apiece. Spend nothing and make a bundle make a bundle that guy from Roza his dad's a Rozan field marshal."

"No problem I don't see any problem we'll cut costs I'll mark the boxes Aid for Roza* and ship them to the river bordering Roza so we can make a profit while we're furthering international cooperation what could be more fitting you pick up the goods there and tell your Rozan operators I'll take one dollar one dollar Rozan for each one."

"No problem I don't see any problem one Rozan dollar that's too cheap too cheap we can do better I'll bargain with them five Rozan dollars was just for openers we can bump the price up we've got what it takes we don't have to treat our Rozan cousins too good too good friends are friends but if we have to we cut them down tomorrow you'll be a Rozan millionaire millionaire."

"I don't want cash what good does it do to be a millionaire of a neighboring country no you tell your Rozan pals to buy up nylon herringbone suits and ship them across the river to swap with our stuff our stuff stuff stuff."

"You can have it all I don't care whatever you want from Roza it's yours and we don't want a penny for our efforts it's all

*A spoof on the aid sent to North Korea during the Korean War, 1950–1953.

for you that way you get fat today and tomorrow we share a little of it and that's fine with us fine with us."

"No no, we all get fat together fat together, if we're going to do it let's really do it and no more of that all talk and no action. As soon as I get back there I'll start collecting rubbers. Are used ones OK? No no let's do things right. We don't want to jeopardize future deals by bungling the first one. Instead of talking about Zhang Three or Li Four or Pockface Wang Two, they'll be saying that the Chinese are unprincipled, so how could they stick together through thick and thin."

"Rozans are principled, they say what they mean and mean what they say. I've already made the contact, so we're punks if we don't go through with it. Right right we not only make a profit but we get people to sing our praises, we're no profiteers. When you've got ten cases send a telegram, and I'll hop a plane to Roza."

"It's our turn to get fat, but how did they manage without getting up off their asses? I think this is doable, and if we make a profit, we donate some of it to the disabled,* which should help. Is there any risk going to Roza? Because if you get stopped, there's nothing we can do. Rozan prison food can't be as good as ours."

"I've got a way in, and I'm determined to go through with it. All that's left now is to see if you've got the nerve to go through with it."

"You bet I've got the nerve. I've been wanting something easy like this for a long time. We're always talking about things

---

*A not so subtle reference to graft, since Deng Xiaoping's son, Deng Pufa, who lost the use of his legs during the Cultural Revolution, heads the Association for Disabled Citizens.

but never doing them. There's nothing you can't accomplish if you're set on doing it."

"It's a deal then. I'll wait for news from you."

"It's a deal. As soon as I've got news, you'll hear from me."

"You guys sound like you mean it. Don't forget us if you've really got something cooking. Even if we can't manage the precision jobs, we should qualify for some kind of protocol position, shouldn't we? As citizens of a major power, we can't let other people think they're better than us."

"Everyone gets something everyone gets something. When the money comes, all our friends will be called in."

"We've got to go out and do something. If you want the truth, I've been wanting to tell you guys how much I miss Zhuo Yue. We weren't in his league in stuff like this. No one can dispute that. He'd walk up and smack a guy, then ask who he was. Truth is, that's the spirit we're lacking, the spirit of those war years."

"I agree we've got to go out and do something. If we don't do it to people now, they'll do it to us when we get old. Being broke when you're young is no big deal, since you can always fall back on your looks or your line to get by. But once you're old and your body's shot and your line is old hat, without money, forget about getting a girl. Who'll give a damn about you then? That'd drive us crazy, wouldn't it? Take that pleasure away, and where are you going to find happiness?"

"That's how it is. You can't rely on your sons and daughters. We're sons and daughters, and we ought to know. So you need money. That way, if you can't find happiness, you go buy it."

"I really miss Zhuo Yue. We'd already be in great shape if he was here. We could just sit around waiting to put meat on the table, and he'd go out and get us some. Tell me what good that third-grade commendation of his is. The *Awa Maru* was refloated, but there were none of those gold ingots we need for our four modernizations, nothing but eight thousand Japanese cremation urns. What good did that do us? All those so-called treasures of General Yamashita Tomoyuki* were dreamed up by the Japanese to trick us into refloating the ship, and they vanished like so much fertilizer. Our pal was part of the mission, and got crushed by Sea Eagle Number 1."

"What's that? I thought you said Zhuo Yue died by banging his head on a ship's ladder as he was running into the galley to get some stuffed buns hot out of the oven."

"That's bullshit. We fired a missile at a Taiwanese ship, and the damned thing did a one-eighty and came right back at us. Everybody ran, everybody but Zhuo Yue, who stood on deck and tried to catch the incoming missile. The dumb fuck, how can you catch a flying missile? It blew him to bits."

"No no that's not what happened, that's the official explanation. What really happened is that they scheduled target practice for hundred-thirty-millimeter guns, and Zhuo Yue, who was on the tow ship, was afraid the gunners might be off target, so he ordered a ten-thousand-meter cable from the factory. Well, they aimed at the target tow, but the shell headed straight for the tow ship, off target by ten thousand meters, and blew our pal to bits. You should know, you fired the shot, and when you saw where it went you stood on the platform like an idiot."

"Those were the Gang of Four days, after all, so you could say just about anything you wanted, right?"

Commander of attacks on Singapore and Bataan, and defender of the Philippines against MacArthur, he was later hanged for war crimes.

"Hey we've got to kill these two bottles of white lightning. You say I fired that shot? No way. I fired at the enemy. I was the finest gunner in the fleet. It was Gao Yang who fired it, now I remember, he was the pointer for the forward gun, I was the pointer for the aft gun, I hit the target, he hit the tow vessel. You punk, I've got a beef with you, you prick, you'll pay with your life for what you did. You had it in for Zhuo Yue all along because when he went aboard your ship he kept taking your rations, and you hated him for that."

"It wasn't Gao Yang. He wasn't even with us. He was a tank gunner. He fired a cannon, all right, but at Vietnamese villages. You're thinking of Gao Jin."

"Gao Jin, I've got a beef with you. You had it in for Zhuo Yue all along because he kept taking your rations, and you hated him for that."

"Nobody did anything to Zhuo Yue, he killed himself when he banged his head on a ship's ladder because all he could think of were those meat-filled buns. He already had arteriosclerosis."

"You always had it in for me because I kept taking your rations, and you hated me for that."

"Come on, let's go. We're out of food and haven't got anything to drink. Why sit around here any longer?"

"Did you hate me or didn't you? I mean because I wouldn't share my rations with you until you finished your own. And because I didn't help you when those soldiers from Dalian kicked your ass. Tell me, how was I supposed to help? They all knew kick-boxing, and all I'd have gotten for jumping in was get my ass kicked too. Xu Xun and Wang Ruohai were there that day, how come you don't hate them? They had a fire ax, but what did they do with it? They hollered all night how they were going to use it on those Dalian soldiers, and how they'd be punks if they didn't. Lucky for me I had my wits about me and didn't fly off the handle like you."

"Are you saying you weren't out there hollering too? That first night in the cabin, who was the most fearless, the most radical of all? You. It was you who swore that anyone who turned and ran was a punk, and it was you who was up front with your meat cleaver, heading straight for them. We were right behind you. But when we were face-to-face with them, you smiled and greeted them like old friends. Then off you went, leaving Gao Jin, with that murderous scowl on his face, to get his ass kicked. If not for Zhuo Yue's reputation with those Dalian soldiers, the dumplings we ate that night would have been stuffed with minced Gao Jin. Who'd be crazy enough to pair up with you?"

"Ask him if that was the first time. Back at school we had a beef at Chaoyang with a bunch of young thugs from another neighborhood. The night before he ranted and raved about how he was going to clean up on those punks, so he rushed out brandishing a knife and a club, until he ran into the father of one of them, who drove him and thirty of his friends back with one lousy hoe. And who was at the head of that retreating pack? He even lost a double-knot-tied shoe he ran so hard."

"Come on, let's go. We can talk on the way to the zoo. I hear they've got a new bunch of monkeys they retired from the circus, so they know how to smoke and nibble melon seeds and even shake hands and laugh at each other."

"Yeah, let's go. I don't care where. I'm not scared of Gao Yang. Maybe he slipped off because he's afraid I'll punch him out."

"Punch who out? What's up with you? Why don't you punch

me out instead? I haven't said a thing the whole time, while you're talking yourself into a rage. Sorry, I don't buy it."

"Did I say I wanted to punch you out? Did I? I didn't say you, so why get so uptight? What's up with this guy? Gao Yang may be your brother, but you don't have to get so uptight over a pissy little matter like this. All these years we know each other this sucks this sucks this really sucks, from now on no more joking around with you."

"Yes, no more joking around with me."

"That's some good-looking monkey, I'd say as good-looking as you. If it was a little bit darker out here I couldn't tell you which was the older brother, you or the monkey."

"You're worse-looking than that monkey! Take it home with you, and your folks might think it's one of your siblings. Hey, look, your kid brother's laughing. He looks better smoking than you. . . . Hey, who do you think you're shoving? Stick your neck in the monkey cage, why don't you? What's the idea laying those sweaty paws on my shoulders? If this happened over at bear mountain I'd have to think one of the inmates climbed a tree and escaped. So what's the idea, tell me that? Keep it up and I'll have to throw you into the monkey cage. Hey, guys, this prick's bugging me. Should I kick his ass or not?"

"No, let him go. You whip him, and it'll cost me to have him fixed up."

"Look at him. He's just asking to be whipped. Let's go find some deserted spot. We don't want to injure the innocent masses. Know how to swim? Then let's go to the lake. First tell me where you can't take a punch. Show me the meatier spots on your body."

"What's going on here what's going on? Who's looking for a deserted spot?"

"Let me see who this is, see who's got such a big mouth. So it's you, is it. You're not the man of steel. To the lake or in the lake, it's all the same to me."

"Sorry sorry, our comrade here isn't well had too much to drink isn't usually like this. Don't do what you're thinking, fellows. We'll teach him a lesson."

"Don't listen to him. They were all screwing around just now."

The circle of people arguing by the monkey cage suddenly dispersed and took off in all directions, me in the lead, with a bunch of mean-looking toughs hot in pursuit. We ran across lawns and over bridges and through lush flower beds. Bamboo standing in our way parted noisily as we flew down the park's main path and out the gate, where we lost ourselves in the bustling crowds.

The mud was strewn with ruined red petals, the bamboo grove was a welter of footprints, cars plied the street as if it were a loom, pedestrians streamed this way and that, everyone was in too big a hurry to worry about anyone else. The setting sun was blood red; the city, alive and raucous, was enveloped in a golden iridescence.

Day Ten

Baishan walked down a veranda beneath a vaulted white-wood trellis hung with wisteria and covered with trumpet creepers, her figure appearing and reappearing in the gaps between twisted vines; a silver-gray shoulder bag bumped her hip as it swayed to the motions of her body. Afternoon sunlight spotted the slippery flagstones. All around her the area was lush with flowers and trees; cicadas chirruped in the cool shade of banyan trees; no one else was anywhere in sight. It was a long and winding veranda that ran past exquisite floral side rooms, wayside pavilions, open balconies, and bamboo cottages, with chains of smaller rooms inside much larger ones, some with their graceful interiors hidden from view, others airy and bright; tiered structures, each with its own garret, were scattered here and there, complete with curtained windows and bench railings, the elegance and simplicity in perfect harmony. There were people frying fish and grilling delicacies from the sea, other people chewing pork and salivating over mutton; and always the faint clinking of glasses and the smiling faces.

The veranda followed the downward curve of the hill to a covered landing with jadeite railings and vermilion eaves on the edge of an emerald-green clearwater lake. Seated by a window at a table laid with a teapot and a fresh setting of chopsticks and utensils, I was enjoying a cigarette, the smoke curling up like a coiled snake, then mushrooming outward. Baishan took a seat beside me, but neither of us spoke. After a waiter walked up with a second place setting, Baishan ordered from the menu. "No wild game," I said. She looked at me before pointing to what she wanted, then handed the waiter the menu and fixed me with a stare.

"Gao Yang didn't come?"

"No, he hasn't shown his face since I've been here."

"But I told my uncle already, seven thousand at forty, and he said for us to come to his place at three-thirty."

"Then you go at three-thirty and tell him no deal, forty's too high."

The waiter walked up with a delicious-looking plate of cold cuts. I reached out with my chopsticks, nabbed a peacock head made of radishes, and began chewing crisply. The plate immediately lost its integrity, its vitality.

"How am I supposed to tell him that? Forty isn't high. He only gave that price when I said it was for me. For everyone else it's forty-two or forty-three."

"You're the only one around here who takes this so seriously. Anyone that serious can just sit here until she turns to hardened wax."

"But he said he'd do it. I don't like getting involved in these things, I only did it this time because it's your friend. Does he really know someone who wants to buy Hong Kong dollars?"

"Maybe yes maybe no, then again maybe it was just a bunch of talk, you know, the affairs of some friend of a friend. He barely mentioned it, so who gave you the green light?"

Baishan looked down at the plate and moved some slices of pork around with her chopsticks.

"But he seemed so earnest when he told me, I figured this was a good opportunity for you guys to make a little money. Always eating out and renting hotel rooms and taking taxis, I don't know how you manage. All you do is sit around talking big. Weren't you the one who kept saying I should do it?"

"I always tell people they should do one thing or another. How far do you think trusting me will take you? If you don't know whether you should do it or not, who does?"

Baishan glanced at me, then looked up angrily at the waiter, who was bringing over a plate of pig knuckles, a specialty called "wild boar forest."

"From now on don't believe anything they say." I gnawed on a pig's knuckle. "Remember what I'm telling you. Hear them out and agree to whatever they say, then put it out of your mind. Taking them seriously is just asking for trouble."

"How about you? Should I take you seriously? How much of what you say is the truth? Are you also one of those who just talks and that's it? Simply puts it out of his mind after that?"

"More or less. Seven or eight out of every ten sentences that come out of my mouth are pure bullshit. Maybe I start out by telling the truth, but sometimes not even that."

"To anybody at any time and any place?"

"To anybody at any time and any place."

"Why? Why are you like that? Because the truth cracks your teeth, or do lies just roll off your tongue?"

"They just roll off my tongue. The truth can't crack my teeth, because there isn't any truth to speak. What's there to say? And what's so great about the truth anyway? For me, of course, it's become a habit. Once I get started, I can't stop. After the first couple of truthful sentences the lies just gush out. I'd feel like a fool if I couldn't make some noise."

"Is it just people like you or is everyone like that?"

"You'll have to ask the other people. Try striking up conversations with any of them, you'll know right off what's true and what's false."

"Could you tell when I was telling the truth and when I was lying?"

"What's that?"

"The things I said to you. I told you lots of things and you told me lots of things too. Assuming you've already forgotten everything you told me, does that mean you've also forgotten everything I told you?"

"Tell me again, tell me what you said."

"Why should I? You should remember."

"I've forgotten, tell me again."

"I said I love you after you said you love me. . . ."

The waiter came up with a bowl of stewed chicken and turtle and set it down carefully. He said the dish was called "heroes gathering."

"I was telling the truth." Baishan looked at me. "I was being honest."

"A lie." I laughed dryly. "I could tell right off it was a lie."

"You might have been lying, but I wasn't."

"All lies." I stared blankly down at the chicken and turtle steeping immobilized in the soup. "Enough already, talk like that makes my skin crawl."

"But you were all teary, don't deny it."

"If so, I'm doubly ashamed. Was I really?"

"I swear you sprayed me with so much mucus and tears it took three scrubbings with soap to get it off. I should have saved it for you."

"Don't take things so much to heart. I can cry any time I want. Sometimes I cry and cry and couldn't begin to tell you who or what I was crying for."

"That time it was for real, that I know, like it was for real with me."

"No no, it wasn't for real, it really wasn't. Stop saying that. You weren't the girl for me. I like full-figured girls, you know that. Oh, I liked you OK, but that's all. And that's the honest truth."

"If that's how you felt, you should have said so. Any decent person would have."

"Let's not turn this into something vulgar, OK? We're not kids, we have to bear responsibility for our own actions. Right off the bat you should have thought about the risks a woman takes. I assumed you were prepared to accept those risks, since you're nobody's fool. How come you expected me to be so noble, to have such high moral standards? I'm not, I don't! I've never been sensitive to other people's feelings, and I don't know the meaning of the word remorse. So stop appealing to my conscience. Deal with me at your own risk, don't try to bluff your way around me. I choose only those who are willing, and they get what they're looking for, exactly what they deserve. And that goes both ways. I don't want anybody turning their conscience loose on me either."

"I'm dead."

"Don't give me that. Dead how? Who's dead? Who isn't dead? How many are dead? Everybody who's not dead is alive and kicking. I tell you, I don't buy it. If I see a single tear, I'm out of here. Tears don't move me."

Baishan looked up at me, her eyes wide, the skin around them taut, like someone trying to get a clear view of my face in stormy weather.

"Don't look at me like that, I'm not that easily intimidated."

"This isn't you."

"It's me, all right." I laughed. "Can't you come up with anything better than that? That's a cliché even in the mouths of the barely literate."

"This isn't the same you as before."

"No difference, and it's still a cliché, no matter how you say it. How do you know what I was like? You've known me, what, a few days? I'll tell you, this is how I've always been, since I was a kid, since the day I was born. You say I was different somehow? All an act; now you see me for what I am."

Baishan's head drooped in dejection. I told the waiter to bring some rice, then poured the thick soup from the "wild boar forest" over the snowy-white grains and began shoveling them into my mouth. Breezes from the lake came in through the curtained doorway; the scenery changed as sounds rose around us. The lake was still, a carpet of green; red flowers were mirrored on the surface; raindrops washed the shore, where tassels of weeping willows and banyan trees fluttered and green branches swayed with every breeze. Baishan held me tightly amid a profusion of branches and sobbed, tears bathing her cheeks.

"I'm not asking for much, just to be with you."

"The problem's not you, it's me. After the talk we had today, there's no way I can stay with you. I don't feel safe."

"No demands, I promise, and no questions. If you find somebody else, I'll leave."

"Show a little self-esteem." I grabbed her arms, which were coiled around me like a snake, and pried loose her fingers. She resisted despite the pain. From a distance, we must have looked like wrestlers. "You're spineless. Talk like that is what you hear from a slave, certainly not what I'd expect from one of China's 'new women.' Don't you care if I respect you or not?"

Day Nine

Gao Jin walked down the sunbaked street with a younger Li Jiangyun, who was holding a parasol to ward off the searing rays. He was talking and laughing and taking an occasional quick look to note her reaction. Even holding her hand over her face could not hide the meaningful smile.

A passing electric tram blocked them from view, then moved on. By then they had turned and were coming across the street toward me.

Taxis whizzing past made them disappear from view, then reappear, over and over, but had no effect on either the smiles on their faces or the gaga looks in their eyes or the way they were talking—yackety-yak, nonstop.

In the blinding sunlight the gray hotel was little more than a blur.

An electric fan sent cool air this way and that, back and forth.

The windows were wide open to a lush canopy of trees under a sky so bright and so blue it seemed almost transparent, all of it blistering in the sun's rays.

Xu Xun, Wang Ruohai, Gao Yang, and I sat around a card table letting the cool air sweep across our bare chests and backs as we played poker, slapping the cards down noisily and laughing raucously and making a mess of the table and floor with melon seed husks and cigarette butts. Qiao Qiao and Xia Hong were sprawled on the bed behind us, dead to the world, a knotted mosquito net suspended uselessly in the air above them; their skirts were hitched up around their sweaty thighs.

We were playing a game that tests knowledge and cunning. After placing his cards face down, a player reveals what was in his hand. Anyone who doesn't believe him turns over one of the cards; if it corresponds to what was said the challenger picks it up but if it doesn't it belongs to the bluffer. Jokers are wild, and the players are free to call anything they want. One important rule is that a player may not be completely honest when announcing the cards in his hand, something called a "cop-out." You must mix truth with deception, shout east and attack west. The name of the game is "liar's poker." The winner, that is, the most believable liar, is the first one to have no cards left in his hand. Once all the rage, partly because it was so simple, it gradually lost much of its popularity to more complex card games. Outside our circle it wasn't played much, since you can't bet, a fatal shortcoming in a game of chance. No seasoned cardplayer worth his salt would be caught dead playing it. Why cheat, if you can't bet on it?

With innocent exuberance we bluffed and we challenged, working up a mighty sweat.

"Five twos, and five more twos."

"Three eights, plus five eights."

"Take 'em back, save your lies for somebody else. I've got two eights in my hand."

With a giggle I picked up all eight cards, and now had more than the other three players.

"Where's Gao Jin?" I asked as I studied the cards in my hand.

"He's busy, something good came up," Xu Xun said mirth-fully, a cigarette dangling from his lips.

"Did you wear out Liu Yan last night?" Gao Yang asked.

"No," I said. "We talked all night long."

"Talked? Why waste all that time?"

"Don't believe him. Ask him what he was talking with."

"Honest, I'm not lying," I protested. "She told me her life story. So heartbreaking."

"Heartbreaking? Says who?" They laughed. "Boy, are you dumb."

"When I sent you over there, didn't I tell you, As soon as you're in the room, head straight for the bed and take off your shoes? You can do your talking up there, after you're finished. Where sex is involved, the less said the better. Who doesn't have a sad story to tell? But once the talk starts to flow, pretty soon the subject of right and wrong comes up, and how are you supposed to take off your pants then? There you are, doing something naughty, and wrestling with your scruples. If you come on like God or something, who's going to get it on with God?"

"This asshole with his holier-than-thou attitude is too shrewd for us!"

"No, I just thought it might be awkward to jump into bed as soon as we walked in the door and lay her out flat without at least saying something. We barely knew each other, after all, and a little atmosphere, something to get things started, seemed like a good idea. We started talking, and the next thing I know, she's crying."

"You were supposed to rescue her body, not her soul. Why turn her into a penitent?"

"I suppose you cried too, you asshole! I'll bet her tale of woe had your tears flowing."

"No way, not me. I was cool as can be while she was talking. Oh sure, it kind of got to me, and I felt sorry for her, but not enough to cry."

"Yeah, right. Qiao Qiao saw you. She said you were both sitting there crying your eyes out. With a heart so full of mercy and pity, maybe we should be calling you Do-good Fang. Right, Qiao Qiao?" Wang Ruohai nudged Qiao Qiao, who was still asleep.

Qiao Qiao opened her eyes, squinted in my direction, and managed a sleepy smile as she made waterfalls down her cheeks with her fingers. Then she rolled over and went back to sleep.

I turned beet red. "If you'd been there to hear what Liu Yan had to say, you'd have done the same thing. I mean really heart-breaking. Nothing's gone right in her life, except for meeting Feng Xiaogang, who treated her better than most people. They had strong feelings for each other, which was just what they both needed. She told me all about their relationship. Very touching. Feng Xiaogang loved her, he really did."

"Oho, he loved her, did he? And how about you?" Xu Xun touched my cheek. "Let's see here, let's see if a saint pops up out of this basket."

"Knock it off." I pushed his hand away. "I couldn't bear the thought of her hating me for the rest of her life as some lowlife just out to get his kicks."

"Dumb ass." Gao Yang, who was chewing on the end of a cigarette, forced the comment out with a laugh. "She's given that same line to everybody. Ask Qiao Qiao if you don't believe me. And Qiao Qiao can even top Liu Yan, if that's what you're in the market for. Oh, the searching! Oh, the feelings! Longing for happiness since childhood, the death of ideals, society's snubs, one bad person after another, adding up to a lifetime of pain. All the dumb assholes, the losers, every screwup, that's the story you'll hear from them. How come you didn't ask her why she sneaked off and came here instead of sticking with Feng Xiao-gang? Did somebody tie her up and drag her here?"

"I know she piled it on a little, I knew that at the time. Some of what she got she asked for. But the emotional pain was real. Maybe she did some of those things because she wanted to, but that doesn't mean she can't regret them now. I'm telling you guys, what got to me and made me feel a sense of responsibility was how she lost control, with all those tears and the runny nose, when she expressed her remorse over things she'd done. If she had just laughed them off, well, I'd have been all over her. But it was remorse, deep remorse, and even though nobility is beyond me, I could at least act human and give her another chance. What kind of animal would I have been if I'd added frost to the snow, if I'd tossed rocks down the well?"

Gao Yang, Xu Xun, and Wang Ruohai just leered at me. Heh-heh. They tossed down their cards.

"Honest." I sat up straight to show my sincerity. "I may be a rotten guy," I said, "but this time I did the right thing. All night long I just talked, without getting a thing. You guys used the word rescue. Well, I wouldn't go that far, but I did give her soul some comfort, just to prove there are still some good people in this world."

My face lit up as I patted myself on the chest and exclaimed, "I'm a lot more content than if I'd gone ahead and done her. I learned that I've still got decent qualities, that when the chips are down, if you rub me with a cloth I shine like anyone else. I'm capable of sacrifice."

Gao Yang stifled a laugh. "You know that soul you com-
forted," he said, "that long-suffering person you gave a chance
to start over again? Where do you think she is now?"

"I don't know. She said she wouldn't be seeing any of you
guys again," I said proudly. "I told her this was a bad crowd."

"Don't be too pleased with yourself," Gao Yang said with a
laugh. "Go knock on the door across the hall. See who's in there
and what's going on."

"Who's in there?"

"Don't ask me." With a laugh, Gao Yang waved my question off. "See for yourself."

Xu Xun and Wang Ruohai looked at me with mysterious
smiles.

With a laugh, I stood up. So did they, also laughing. I smiled
at them as I went to the door, opened it, and stepped into the
hall. Strong gusts of wind blew playing cards off the table,
drowned out the whir of the electric fan, and ruffled the skirts
and hair of Qiao Qiao and Xia Hong as they slept. Leaves outside
the window rustled loudly; the door across the way blew open,
glided across the floor, and nestled up against the wall. Forest
green georgette curtains, which had been pulled shut, fluttered.
The room was dark; a standing fan swiveled back and forth, sending gusts of air over to a bed that was partially hidden behind
the outcropping of the bathroom, then down the wall past two
armchairs decorated with men's and women's clothing and un-
derwear; a brassiere hung from the wooden armrest like a dangling hand. The curtains fluttered, the bed creaked, people
moaned, sounds and more sounds. Someone laughed loudly
opened and closed a door, a faucet was dripping, water gurgled
down someone's throat. . . . Gao Jin, covering his nakedness,
stuck his head out the bathroom door, then emerged and ran up

to us, a weird smile on his face. *Slam* went the mahogany-colored door. The wind inlaying the space between the walls stopped; the hall returned to silence.

I shut the door and turned around with a sheepish grin. My friends, weird smiles still on their faces, hadn't moved.

"Boy, am I stupid," I said with a laugh. "I really fell for it."

"You are stupid," my friends said with a laugh. "You're too young. Now what good did letting her off do?"

"Yeah, what good did it do?"

"If you don't take what heaven offers, the blame is yours. Strike while the iron's hot, or chaos follows. Women are all the same."

"The same, they're all the same."

"Including your Ling Yu."

"Including her."

"Don't assume she's devoted to you. I could get her to go off with me right in front of you. We surrounded her but didn't press the attack because you're so small-minded, not because she'd stand up to us. I'll call her over if you don't believe me."

"We'll just see about that," I giggled. "Go ahead, call her over."

"And you honestly don't care? Didn't you say you really love her? If you still feel that way, the deal's off. I don't want to make my move and get you pissed off."

"Be careful, now, anything could happen."

"I don't care, I really don't. I wasn't raised in a society that recognizes private ownership."

"All right, we agree that nobody gets pissed off."

"Nobody gets pissed off."

With giggles all around, we stared at each other to see who could act the most natural. Gao Yang picked up the telephone and dialed a number. Someone answered. He turned his back to me and spoke into the receiver:

"I'd like to speak to Ling Yu . . . Ling Yu? No no, this isn't Fang Yan it's Gao Yang. I'm fine, how are you?" He turned to us, winked, and turned back around. "Yes, there's a reason I'm calling. Do you mean I can't just call to say hello? I can. Oh, that's good. That's right, close friends like us. Can you come over? Here, to my place. Of course, my place." Gao Yang turned to look at me. "Him? He went out. Don't know. Some woman called and he just took off."

We all stood around laughing, especially me.

"Who cares if he's here or not? This is just between you and me . . . sure, it's important. That's why I'm calling. Can you come over? Are you afraid that Fang Yan . . . you're not? Right, why should you be? I'm glad you're not . . . now, come on over now, good, I'll be waiting."

Gao Yang put down the phone and said with a laugh, "She'll be right over."

Everyone lit up, except for me. I couldn't get a match to light, or if I did, it went right out. Xu Xun dragged like crazy on his cigarette to keep it from going out. "What are you shaking for?" he asked me. "How come?"

"I'm not, it's an earthquake." I laughed and tried another match.

"When she gets here, you stay out of sight," Gao Yang said without taking his cigarette from his mouth. "Give me your room key. I'll take her over there."

I fished a key with the hotel tag from my pocket and handed it to Gao Yang, then smiled as I dragged on my cigarette. Xu Xun, who was watching the street from the window, turned and said, "Here she comes. She just walked into the building."

"Don't any of you go over there," Gao Yang warned as he frantically grabbed a striped shirt. "You're only permitted to listen." He opened the door and walked out, trailing a laugh.

A moment later, Gao Yang's voice came to us from the hall: "That was fast. I thought you might be a little hesitant."

"What's so important it couldn't wait?" There was a hint of laughter in Baishan's voice. "Did Fang Yan really go with some woman? I don't believe it."

"Neither did I. What woman would come looking for him?"

Footsteps passed our door and stopped nearby. The door of the adjoining room opened and human sounds entered. *Slam* went the door, and silence returned to the hall. The intermittent sounds of a man's voice and a woman's giggles emerged from next door.

Qiao Qiao woke up and lay there looking up at us. Xia Hong slept on. Trees rustling, cars whizzing past, people on the street, the sounds merged. Water dripped from the bathroom faucet; a white cloud drifting over in the blue sky quickly dissipated in the searing rays of sunlight.

"Cards anyone?" Wang Ruohai asked as he sat on the sofa, picked up the deck, and shuffled it. Xu Xun and I sat down as he deftly dealt the cards. We played liar's poker. I picked my opponents' bluff cards every time.

There were no more sounds from next door, and even with the fan on high, I was sweating so heavily that the cards stuck to my fingers.

Qiao Qiao sat up and smiled sweetly in the direction of the door. We looked up. Gao Jin, fully dressed, walked in, followed by a younger Li Jiangyun, also fully dressed. Xu Xun and Wang Ruohai greeted them, but I kept my head down, seemingly absorbed by the cards in my hand. Li Jiangyun, who reeked of face

powder and sweat, walked up and studied my hand. I looked up
and said to Xu Xun, "Pick a card."

"Where's Gao Yang?" Gao Jin sat down, took out a cigarette, lit it, and tossed away the match. "Where'd he go?"

"Next door," Xu Xun said with a laugh.

"What for?" Gao Jin wondered aloud. "Did Feng Xiaogang
come over?"

"No," Xu Xun replied, looking at me with a grin. "He's
scrubbing Fang Yan's wok."

"Who's that? What's going on?" Gao Jin looked at me
guardedly.

"Fang Yan handed him Ling Yu. They're next door right
now."

"Is that right?" Gao Jin asked me.

"That's right," I said with a laugh, keeping my eyes glued to
my cards. "I handed him Ling Yu."

"You guys are terrible, a bunch of losers," Qiao Qiao exclaimed from the bed. "Isn't that right, Liu Yan?"

A younger Li Jiangyun just smiled.

"Cards, let's play cards." I realized that everyone was looking at
me. "What's the big deal? Everything serves its purpose. Women!"

They all laughed. "When did you finally see the light?" Gao
Jin asked me.

"He who laughs last, laughs loudest. You whack yours, and
I'll whack mine." I grinned broadly. "I used to be pretty dumb,
but we don't have any rule against that, do we? From now on, I
smarten up."

"I'm going to go knock at their door." Gao Jin stood up.
"We can't let things get out of hand. True feelings ought to stand
for something."

"Don't, don't go over there. I'll be pissed off if you do." I smiled at Gao Jin. "Whose true feelings are you talking about? I've never had any of those, not for anybody."

The toilet next door flushed. Then a man's voice, and a woman's. The window opened, and the voices were much louder.

Then the door, and the sounds moved into the hall, laughter mixed with conversation. A moment later our door swung open, and there stood Gao Yang, fully dressed, and Baishan, also fully dressed.

"You're here!" Baishan walked up to me as soon as she saw me. "Gao Yang lied to me, he said you were out." Her face was radiant cheeks red not a hair out of place, soft, silver-gray Naugahyde handbag draped over her shoulder.

"He asked me over on business, someone wants some Hong Kong currency, and I can make a little money on the deal. He made it sound so urgent, I thought it was something really important. But that was it. I can get my hands on some Hong Kong money. The question is, do I want to? Is it worth it? How much can I make? I told him I couldn't give him an answer right away, that I'd have to think it over. What do you think, should I do it?"

"Worth it or not, do it or not, that's up to you. That's between you two. I wouldn't worry about whether it's worth it or not."

"Are you saying I should do it?"

"Go ahead. It's no big deal." I smiled at Gao Yang.

"If you were here all the time, how come you didn't make a peep when you knew I was right next door?" Baishan looked me right in the eye. "Did you know or didn't you?"

I just smiled.

"What are you guys trying to pull?" Baishan took a look around. "What do you want to exchange currency for? How come they didn't get you to talk to me?"

"Go on home," I said. "Your uncle just phoned to say some relative showed up from the countryside and wants to see you. Whoever it is is taking you to dinner, so you have to be home by five o'clock."

"What the hell is going on?" Instead of leaving, Baishan looked at me stubbornly.

"Nothing, honest. I'll walk you downstairs." I put on a striped shirt and nudged Baishan out the door.

She turned to look at the others, all of whom smiled.

"How come you guys are all so sneaky?" Baishan asked when we reached the stairs. "I don't like your friends."

"No one's forcing you to like them. Stay away from them if you don't like them."

"I don't want to do business with Gao Yang."

"Go ahead, do it. You already said you would, so do it."

"What are you doing tonight?" Baishan asked at the hotel entrance.

"What could I be doing?" I stood there with my hands on my hips, looking out at the street. "I've got no place to go."

"Then I'll come over after dinner."

"No no, don't come over. Who knows, we might be going out, so don't come over."

"Then when will I see you?"

"Later. I'll phone you tomorrow, or you can phone me. So long."

"That Ling Yu, how did you train her, anyway?" The minute I stepped into the room, Gao Yang greeted me with a laugh. "I sweet-talked her, I did everything but beat the hell out of her, but she stood her ground. What sort of spell did you use to turn her into an impregnable statue? I got nothing, for the first time in my life, I got nothing. Couldn't budge her. We started talking, like you did that time, and the conversation just took off, way the hell out there."

"Look, if you did it, you did it." I laughed. "Trying to cover it up just makes it worse. You got what you wanted. Wang Ruo-hai, you're next."

"I'm not interested in steeping your tea leaves," Wang Ruo-hai said. "You won't catch me going out of my way to make it with someone like that."

"Yeah, she's not so hot," I said. "In fact, she's not much at all. Add water, and she's still too salty." I smiled, I gave them all a diabolical smile.

The sky turned overcast, the sunlight faded, clouds blocked out the sky; the canopy of trees beyond the window shook and swayed before strong winds that made the windows rattle. The summery heat was chased away by black rainclouds that dragged their shadows toward us, turning the streets dark and gloomy. Qiao Qiao closed the window just in time to keep raindrops the size of beans out of the room; they banged against the window and slithered down the glass. Under the cloudy sky, everything got blurry and misty; the people in the room, whether standing or sitting, were transformed into dark statues.

"Who are we supposed to be polite to? Who are we supposed to treat like human beings?"

Day Eight

The downpour knocked branches and leaves to the ground; torrents of muddy water ran down the street and trickled into sewer grates, which were quickly clogged by twigs and leaves converging from all directions. The muddy water then ran over the curbs and puddled around trees and flower beds before gurgling across footpaths and shimmering off into the distance. In buildings on both sides of the street, backlit figures rocked and swayed behind closed windows, as in shadow theaters.

I watched Qiao Qiao, Wang Ruohai, and Xu Xun emerge into the narrow, cramped hallway; Xu Xun stuck his head back inside to say with a laugh, "Hurry up. Everything's in readiness. Remember, once you're inside, not a word. Just cram it in."

He closed the door and walked off laughing with Qiao Qiao and Wang Ruohai, disappearing at the staircase. A moment later, the door opened again. I stepped into the corridor, closed the door behind me, and walked up to the room across the way, where I raised my hand, hesitated momentarily, then knocked loudly. When the door opened, a woman's hazy face appeared in the opening. I stepped inside with a mocking grin; the door closed behind me.

Downstairs by the entrance Qiao Qiao, Xu Xun, and Wang

Ruohai laughingly braved the pouring rain to squeeze into the backseat of a taxi at the curb. The door closed behind them and they sped off, spraying water in their wake.

It was coming down in buckets as another taxi sped up and came to a watery stop at the hotel entrance. A woman climbed out, dashed into the hotel lobby, and headed straight for the brightly lit mezzanine stairs.

The dimly lit narrow cramped corridor was musty yellow. Baishan knocked at the door of the room Xu Xun and the others had just left, but there was no answer; she tried the door across the way, the one I had just entered, but no answer there either. So she moved on to the next door and the one after that, but still no answer. After that she started trying doorknobs, but the rooms were all locked. When a man stepped out of his room up ahead and walked to the stairs, she looked up briefly, then lowered her eyes and headed toward the stairs.

Broad-leafed orchids in blue glazed ceramic vases by golden pillars carved with coiling dragons radiated life in the ornate lobby, where nattily dressed patrons trod on lush scarlet carpets, bathed in the light of crystal chandeliers reflecting off spotless mirrors hanging on the walls. Qiao Qiao, Xu Xun, and Wang Ruohai were playing video games on the mezzanine floor, firing at targets that flew across the screen to the accompaniment of computerized sound effects. They had an unobstructed view of the first-floor coffee shop where Gao Yang, highly animated, sat surrounded by nattily dressed Hong Kong Chinese, a smiling Xia Hong at his side. Puffing a cigarette, sipping his soft drink, and flashing smiles all around, Gao Yang was very animated. He passed something among his guests, pointing at it proudly with his cigarette hand and commenting solemnly:

"That's no run-of-the-mill gemstone, it's got quite a history." A closer look revealed that the object being passed around was a red, multifaceted object the size of a large melon seed. Gao Yang gave his pitch: "It's a gem *and* a relic, a witness to the historical vicissitudes of the past hundred years, a repository of the humiliations of the Chinese race. Mounted on the shoe of the Pearl Concubine, it traveled throughout the palace halls of the Forbidden City, and entered the imperial rooms and boudoirs, and trod upon the white marble steps of the throne room. It was witness to love between the Guangxu Emperor and the Pearl Concubine, to the stern countenance of the Old Buddha, and to the powerful looks of chief eunuch Li Lianying. It experienced the winds and fires of the Hundred Days Reform and the ups and downs of the Wuxu reform movement, then accompanied its mistress during her endless days in the little-known confines of the cold palace to which disfavored consorts were exiled to shed a lifetime of tears. When the Eight-Power Allied Forces entered Beijing, it went with the Pearl Concubine to the edge of the well and heard every filthy word she uttered against the Empress Dowager, and it was ground into the dirt by my grandfather the eunuch, leaving shoe prints that would last into the Republican era, but eventually disappear. When the Pearl Concubine went down into the well, it remained above ground. I'm not lying, gentlemen, when I say that it was my grandfather who stuffed the Pearl Concubine down the well. At the time he and Li Lianying were very close. Before going through with the deed, he ripped off her shoes and stuffed them up his sleeve. Though it is not generally known, thanks to my grandfather, the Pearl Concubine went to the bottom of the well barefoot. Whenever I reach this point in my study of modern history, my face turns red and my ears throb over the shame caused by my own grandfather. But on the other hand, if he hadn't kept his wits about him, you gentlemen would not be sitting here feasting your eyes on this treasure, which means he rendered quite a service."

"Yes, quite a service. Why destroy what the dead leave behind?"

"Right, my grandfather came from humble beginnings and couldn't stand seeing heaven's bounty wasted. Future generations need to be fed, after all."

"From what I'm hearing, this happened around 1900, so your grandfather must have been quite old."

"Very old," Gao Yang replied earnestly. "He lived to be a hundred but not long enough to witness the nation's liberation. Thus he died with a besmirched name."

"Tell me if I'm wrong, but you say your grandfather was a eunuch, and my understanding is . . ."

"I know what you're getting at. But this eunuch was unique. You simply don't understand anything, you're disgraceful. How little you people in your tiny backwater know about what goes on in the heart of the country. A eunuch can take a wife, whether he uses her or not, and can keep her around just for her looks. Besides, pretty soon it was the Republican era, and my grandfather was driven off by Lu Zhonglin's soldiers. Lucky for him, over the years he had not neglected to store up certain things the emperor wasn't using, so getting by would not be a problem. He bought a house and some land, and he married my grandmother, but just for show, since what he was really interested in was my father, who happened to be inside her belly at the time. My grandmother was pretty famous herself, one of Beijing's true flowers, the goddess of Brothel Lane, on intimate terms with the sons and grandsons of royalty and the very rich. So, you see, they were not a pair of lowborns, and in fact, must be considered members of the elite class. At the time my grandmother had just been seduced by one of Cai Yue's henchmen and was an emotional wreck. All she wanted was to find someone to be with, anyone as long as he was an honorable man. Someone like my grandfather, who never did anything but look at her and touch her here and there, without ever doing you know what. So they fell in love."

"Well, you sure didn't come by this gem easily."

"No way. At one time my family had lots of nice things, more money than any of you. Even our chamber pots were made of fine agate, but it all went up in my father's opium smoke. All that pot-smoking in the West, big deal. We Chinese were into that way before they were. By rights we should have been peddling dope to them. So, do you want it or not? I wish you'd stop rubbing it and gawking at it and smiling like that. Say something before you rub half of it away."

"You say this stone was inlaid in a shoe, so I'm guessing it must be one of a pair. Now if you had its mate, we'd be a lot more inclined to do business."

"I never said it wasn't one of a pair. Two eunuchs, each got one shoe, and the other guy took off with his. But if you're looking for a set, well, I've got the Pearl Concubine's actual shoe, but it's worth its weight in gold. A famous historical person's shoe is worth a lot more than any rock. I'm just worried the price might be too steep for you."

"Let's see it. With the shoe, we've got a deal. Ah, the top is velvet."

Gao Yang had taken an old woman's boat-shaped shoe out of his jacket. Qiao Qiao laughed and said to Wang Ruohai:

"He's showing them one of your grannie's stinky shoes. Apparently he's not worried that they might wonder how the Pearl Concubine happened to wear a size forty-two."

"Let me see." Wang Ruohai looked over the railing. "Wow, that asshole must think they're a bunch of fucking idiots," he said with a laugh.

"Is Gao Jin finished?" Xu Xun asked as he walked up. "How come he's not coming down? Qiao Qiao, go upstairs and take a look. We don't want him to get busted."

"OK." Qiao Qiao left the video game and walked to the elevator.

"That guy's really something," Xu Xun said with a laugh as he gazed downstairs at Gao Yang, whose head was shaking and swaying as he kept up his endless monologue. "Who'd have thought he could manage so much bullshit for just one bunch of dopes."

The Hong Kong Chinese were sitting there laughing loudly.

When Qiao Qiao stepped out on the top floor, she saw Gao Jin emerging from one of the rooms with a suitcase. He stopped in his tracks at the sight of her, then walked past and down the stairs. She continued on, past the service desk to another stairway, and headed downstairs.

Gao Jin, suitcase in hand, crossed the crowded lobby and exited through the automatic door.

Xu Xun and Wang Ruohai walked away from their video games.

Xia Hong glanced up at the mezzanine, only to discover that Xu Xun and Wang Ruohai were no longer there. She took out a cigarette and began smoking.

"Miss Chen, you smoke too?" one of the Hong Kong Chinese asked with a patronizing laugh.

She smiled and nodded.

Gao Yang glanced at Xia Hong, then banged his empty soft drink can on the table. "I'll take that treasure back," he said. "I can see you don't have the money to buy it, since you won't even make an offer. Quite a loss of face for us Chinese. Now I'll go sell it to the Japanese. They know the value of Asian relics. Yes, it looks like I'm going to have to let this national treasure fall into foreign hands."

Qiao Qiao rushed across the lobby, out the door, and disappeared into the darkness of night.

The rain was still coming down fiercely, turning leaves and bushes and grass soggy. Chilled winds came in through open windows, raising goosebumps on exposed skin. Smoky, sweaty air and foul bedding odors were swept away, the cleansed room filled up with musty yellow lamplight. Outside, the rainfall sounded like sand pouring through a sieve.

A younger Li Jiangyun was sobbing, keeping her head down as she gazed tearfully into a white handkerchief, which she folded first into the shape of a crane, then a mouse. With a wispy smile on her face, she spun her tale, as drops of clear snivel formed on the tip of her nose no matter how often she wiped it.

"My very first man was my teacher. I was in the fifth grade, he taught music. He was tall, good-looking, young, and had a booming, lovely voice that set your heart dancing. Most of the time during class he played the organ and sang sentimental Soviet songs, turning often to smile at us. The captivating, irresistible look in his eyes filled the hearts of every kid in the room. I can see his rounded mouth and swaying body and smiling eyes as if it were yesterday. I liked him a lot, all the girls did, and he liked us. I was one of his pets. All the teachers had them—boys for the women and girls for the men. He said I had a nice voice, and I believed him, since I probably did sing more sweetly than the other kids. But whether I did or not, it was reason enough to be invited to his dormitory after school, in order to keep others from talking. It was summertime, a scorching midday. I was in his room. I forget how he got me there, but it wouldn't have taken much. I worshipped him absolutely trusted him absolutely obeyed him absolutely did absolutely anything he told me to do, not to mention that in my eyes whatever he did was beautiful and noble and fulfilled other people's fantasies and intoxicated them. I wanted our relationship to be more intimate and more exclusive than his relationships with other people, though I didn't understand what that could lead to. His face drew close and grew large. I could see the acne on his forehead, even the pores in his skin. He was smiling and prattling away all friendly-like, almost fawning. And that's when I felt a sweaty hand fondling me. He smiled tenderly, and I hurt. He stroked my face like a loving father, and the pain grew worse. He smiled bewitchingly sweat dripped his mouth twitched a trickle of slobber oozed from the corner the look of crazed excitement in his eyes nearly blinded me, then he moaned as if suffering unbearable torment and his eyes closed, his face scrunched up like someone being whipped and he forced back the fear welling up inside him before shouting in a muted voice when he could hold it back no longer. After that he calmed down and the color returned to his cheeks. Slowly he opened his eyes, which were filled with joy and contentment. He smiled at me, as he had the whole time, except for that one brief moment. My pulse was throbbing and I started to cry, like an abused child, so he helped me tidy up, the way a doctor consoles his patient. While he helped me get dressed he talked to me all nice and friendly-like. I smiled when I saw the contented look on his face, smiled through my tears, and he smiled as he had the whole time, except for that one brief moment."

"Then what? What happened between you after that?"

"After that, everything was the same as before. He came

twice a week to class, sat in the sunlit classroom playing the organ and singing sentimental Soviet songs, and smiling and gazing at us as he swayed to the music and formed a circle with his lips. And we stood there with our hands behind our backs loudly singing along with him and the organ: 'When pear trees bloom in the fields . . .' 'We dip our oars in the water . . .' 'After a day's lessons . . .' Early on in the Cultural Revolution he was dragged away from his organ, his body was covered with paste, his face turned sticky with spittle, and a wooden placard was hung around his neck. Then along with the principal and student adviser and other teachers, he was paraded around the athletic field in a sort of stumbling chorus line. Eventually he killed himself, jumped out of a classroom window into a lime pit put there for an air raid shelter that was being dug, and the lime just ate up that beautiful face of his. He was rehabilitated posthumously some time later."

"You never denounced him?"

"No, but other girls did. He admitted what he did to me on his own. I felt sorry for him, and since I'd graduated and was already in middle school, I never went public with it."

"Oh."

"My father was the second man. I was in my second year of middle school, so I boarded in, and only went home on Saturdays. It was just my father, my mother, a brother much younger than me, and a nanny. In other words, three elderly people and a child. Our normally cold and cheerless home livened up a bit when I was home. My father was already an old man. I was his first child, and I didn't come along until he was over fifty. I remember him as a kindly old man with lots of poise, who always wore a gentle smile and spoke softly no matter who he was talking to. He doted on me. During my childhood, whenever we went out on a family excursion or just went visiting, he held my hand, while Mama carried my brother. He was always reading or writing something in his book-lined study. He knew several languages, and was treated with respect by all who came to see him. When I was a kid, he had me memorize famous poems from all around the world, and I can still recite them in the original languages, with all the right intonation and rhythm, though I've forgotten what they mean. Like students today, we used to copy sayings by famous people into little notebooks and treasure them as words to live by. Since my father knew so many languages, I had a lot more of those sayings in my notebook than my classmates, who never got anything but some quotes from Marx or Engels or Lenin or Stalin, plus a couple of other famous Russians, a far cry from what I had in my notebook. And theirs were all pretty much the same, while I could add ten or twenty wise sayings or maxims from around the world every week. I was the envy of my classmates, and proud of it. In my eyes my father was the embodiment of these maxims, because no matter what the issue, like my relationship with schoolmates or certain school activities, even my kid brother's bad behavior, he could always say the right and reasonable thing. I adored him I revered him as if he were a beacon lighting up my existence, which was joyful and free of cares and worries. It was summertime, summer again, and I was back home. One night, very late, after Mother and my brother were fast asleep, Father and I were in our own rooms reading in bed. I still remember what I was reading that night, it was *The Gadfly*,* and I was agonizing over the fate of Arthur and Gemma when Father came into my room, smiling and genial as always. He stood behind me and began massaging me, all very

*A novel by Ethel L. Voynich (1897), a socialist classic that, until recently, was very popular in Maoist China.

fatherly at first, which was soothing and satisfying and warm. But when his hands slid down off my head onto my shoulders and he started stroking my neck, then my chin, then moved down even farther, I knew something was wrong. Experience told me that this sort of touching went too far, and I couldn't believe a father capable of doing that to his own daughter, especially a man who seemed to be in touch with the wisdom of the world. I still couldn't believe it even when his hand touched a spot a father should never touch. I shivered and curled up into a ball, scared to death, and when I tried to resist, he grabbed me and pinned me down, then looked me in the eye and said, 'I'm your father!' That comment was as heavy with the same ironclad logic and philosophical wisdom and clear understanding of the nature of relationships as everything he said. I'm your father, the voice of authority, the person who gave you life; so, confronted by that single utterance and the possessed look in his eyes, I submitted, lowering my eyes in weak surrender to his gaze. In the way of older men, he took me skillfully and with great enjoyment, from start to finish retaining his dignity and poise, even when it was clear there was more he wanted to do if only his bloated, clumsy body had been up to the task. But his intelligence made up for that, and from start to finish he retained his poise and dignity.

"The old bastard!"

"Now that we'd crossed the line, Father came to my room every Saturday to exact payment for all he had given me. I was like his books or manuscripts, to be written or rewritten however he saw fit, all the way up to the beginning of the Cultural Revolution, when others took over, and people who had given him everything now exercised their authority over him."

"Was he ever rehabilitated?"

"Yes. My thinking was that as long as he was alive he could

supply me with maxims like 'People need to be their own masters.' That and expound upon the dialectical relationship between
big dogs and little dogs."

The rainfall outside had softened, grown quieter, become
gentle. Passing cars sent water flying, a pedestrian out there somewhere shouted. Clouds of steam rose from the ground, cottony
white as they floated skyward. The rain stopped, but water kept
dripping from the eaves of houses and sluicing onto the road from
between gaps in sheet metal rooftops; the moon appeared and
disappeared amid the cloud cover as it crossed the heavens and
sent icy moonbeams to light up a shifting panorama of shapes.

"The third man was a schoolmate, a leader of our school's
Red Guard faction who later went to the countryside, where he
became a company commander in a production and construction
corps. He was the first man I ever actually loved. In school he
was a brilliant student and a top athlete, but during the Cultural
Revolution his real talent surfaced when he emerged as a powerful and widely recognized factional leader whose words flowed
like a cataract, who cited all the right texts when he spoke, and who
was in the vanguard holding high the banner when it was time
to fight. After joining the corps, he did everything—chopped
wood on the mountain, hauled fish from the river, erected buildings, dug ditches, and plowed fields as far as the eye could see,
driving his tractor from sunup to sundown. He worked hard all
day long, then at night was never without a book, poring over
great works by Marx Engels Lenin Stalin, and filling pages with
brilliant insightful reading notes. He was one of those enlightened
intellectuals and faithful disciples of communism who thought
only of his country and its people. Convinced that the fate of the
Chinese nation and its people rested on his shoulders, he fretted
over what went on in towns and villages all over China. Like

Mao Zedong, he unearthed revisionists and opportunists of every stripe and hue, plus schools of thought that presented a threat to orthodox Marxism and confused the people, and even though Liu Shaoqi and Deng Xiaoping had already been ferreted out, he knew that a time bomb was ticking next to Mao Zedong, of which the Chairman himself was unaware. My schoolmate considered it his duty to alert Mao to the fact that only he could protect the Chairman from plots against him—the scoundrel he had unearthed was Jiang Qing, Madame Mao herself. He had noted in her words and deeds signs of disloyalty, public compliance but private opposition, dark designs. Devoting all his time and energy to writing one fervent denunciation letter after another to Mao, he poured out his heart and laid bare his soul, even wetting the pages with tears of anguish and swearing undying allegiance. Every other month or so he even sent the Chairman lengthy disquisitions on the cardinal principles of Marxism, boldly stating opinions that varied from those of Mao himself. In my eyes, he seemed made of different stuff than the rest of us, a god that needed no mortal sustenance. I fell in love with a god, but that god took no notice of me, blithely accepting everything I did for him—washing his clothes stitching his quilt bringing him water cooking his meals—without a word of thanks. It was summertime when I stopped him next to a haystack and revealed to him my feelings. Without a word he looked around to make sure we were alone, then laid me down on the bed of hay and began pawing and biting me. He had no experience, didn't know where to start, and was going nowhere fast, so I took the lead, and we managed somehow to take care of business before he got up without a word and bolted in a panic. The next day he publicly denounced me in a letter to the corps' political section, resulting in my being labeled a temptress slithering among the uprooted

youth from the cities. I was dragged to a public meeting and denounced by the entire complement of workers and uprooted
youth. He then reverted to taking no notice of me, except if we
were alone on the road or out in the field, when he would bolt
in a panic, like he had that summer night, as if fleeing from a pack
of wolves. My anger turned to disdain, and from then on I made
it a point to pop up unexpectedly whenever he was alone, until
one day he greeted me with an angry barrage of old-fashioned,
bookish curses. Before long the brass sent someone for him, and
he was taken away by jeep to the provincial prison. Sometime
later he was driven back to corps headquarters and sentenced to
death for counterrevolutionary activities. At the public reading of
the warrant, where he was cuffed and shackled, people say he
showed his mettle by holding up his newly shaved head, ashen-
faced, and just before they shot him, shouting 'Long live Chairman Mao' and 'Long live the Chinese Communist Party.' By
now, of course, he's been rehabilitated and declared a 'revolutionary martyr.'

"The fourth man I met after I returned to the city. The trou-
bled times had just ended, and people everywhere were ecstatic.
Citizens who had been stripped of status and authority and reputation were gradually regaining that status and authority and reputation, reclaiming living quarters from which they had been
evicted, riding new bicycles, and retrieving property that had
been confiscated. The living returned to their rightful places, the
dead were given back their good names, and everyone was making up for lost time. Wanting more than a return to the life they
once knew, they were determined to live better, happier lives. I
had plenty of time on my hands, since there was nothing for me
to take back and nothing to look forward to, except getting married and raising a family as soon as possible. He and I met in an

auditorium during a movie; he was a coarse man who impressed me as guileless and reliable. In no time at all we were living together, since I had to live somewhere and might as well be with a man I liked instead of with relatives who had become strangers. Why not give something of myself and avoid taking charity? He was an honest man, just right for me, except he wasn't very trusting. Probably he'd been treated unfairly in the past—most people like him had somewhere along the line—and it had taken its toll. Everyone took advantage of him, he thought, people were always plotting against him. If I went anywhere without him, he'd grill me as soon as I got home, gently at first, but later on he'd be more direct and much rougher. He even started shadowing me, which I found extremely repugnant, and though he never caught me at anything, he doggedly kept at it. Maybe he figured I harbored some deep dark secret precisely *because* he never caught me. He couldn't understand why I enjoyed a simple walk alone; maybe it would have been easier if I *had* taken a lover. Finally one day after I came home, he beat me. Now for me a beating is no great humiliation. What made me decide to leave was that I caught *him*. All of a sudden this common man craved personal distinction and status; he would have done anything to climb the social ladder, as if he sought to regain things he had lost, when in fact he'd never had them in the first place. Like someone who has suffered untold oppression and subjugation, he yearned to make up for his deprivations tenfold. When he met the no longer young but long-suffering daughter of a certain individual who he thought could boost him into a social class to which he could never otherwise aspire, he strove to win her heart. That's when he told me he loved me, even weeping to prove his sincerity. He wanted me to say I loved him, which I did for his benefit. Why not? It was no big deal. Then he said that with our abiding affection there was no need to worry about formalities, that we'd be lifelong friends, unbound by convention in a pure and undying love, that marriage was merely a means of consolidating something external to that love. Such innocence. It was all very touching. I understand what you're saying, I told him, and I don't have a problem with it. We'll do it your way, that seems best. He was so hyped he actually cried and said he'd love me forever, just like a husband would, that I'd know the joys of a woman who was blessed with an honest-to-goodness husband all my life and never be lonely, that 'my heart and yours are linked forever.' That night we were true lovebirds, and he told me I could 'call this your home till I get married.' I said OK. I moved out the very next day. Not to embarrass him, or appear resentful. I just didn't think there was any reason I should help him achieve his dream of having both a wife *and* a concubine. Now if I'd already had a husband who supplied the security I needed, I might have considered taking a lover. But not him. He was capable only of being a husband, a mediocre one at that, and was ill-equipped for the role of lover. He had no charm, no sex appeal; he was someone only a woman eagerly seeking the legal guarantees of marriage would consider sleeping with.

"After him I stopped counting. The majority were guys like you, who care only about yourselves, passing us around like melon seeds, eating the meat and spitting out the husks. None of you ever treated me like a real person, and I responded in kind. Then Feng Xiaogang came along. During the campaign to wipe out the Boy Scouts, Wang Kuanglin invited me over to the block of flats where he lived, and that's where we met. Xiaogang had just gotten out of the army and was still wearing plastic sandals that made his feet stink something awful in that heat. His baggy army pants were hitched up with one of those phony Sam Browne belts, and the armpits and back of his army shirt were sweat-stained. He was easygoing and laughed easily, although there was no mistaking his army background. As a foot soldier in the border war with Vietnam, he'd hidden in the jungle for a week; his arms were still scarred by Vietnamese mosquito bites that had gotten infected from being scratched. In his pants pocket he kept a third-class commendation medal, a key, and some fingernail clippers, all of which rubbed against each other until the commendation medal was scratched and pitted. When I asked about the war he talked about bombed-out tanks and burned-out villages and pon-toon bridges across rushing rivers and the lush green jungle and machine-gun shells flying overhead. The others laughed and asked him what Vietnamese soldiers looked like. He just mum-bled and turned red. Later on I learned that he had seen as many Vietnamese soldiers as the rest of us—exactly none. After crossing the border, his company had slogged across mountains to their designated position, where they were then ordered to proceed to another assembly area. The whole time they were marching they were harassed by snipers. In lush, seemingly safe valleys they'd come under withering fire and break ranks, returning the fire from the protection of ditches, shooting wildly in all directions, until the sounds of battle had died down, and they'd fall in again and move out, only to come under attack once more, break ranks, and hit the dirt to return the fire, repeating the process over and over as they passed through the Liangshan mountain region. He earned that third-degree commendation medal by not getting separated from his company at any time and by carrying one end of a stretcher all night in full battle gear, taking the company po-litical instructor, who'd been hit in the ass by a stray bullet, to the nearest field medic station. He kept saying how mortified he was, a real wimp, serving in a war and never laying eyes on an enemy soldier, dead or alive, not even a prisoner, as if it all had been some big joke. Before heading out, he'd even bitten the tip of his finger to write in blood, 'The damned Vietnamese are such sneaks, no wonder the Americans hated fighting them.' That's what he told me. I said no sweat, as far as I'm concerned you're a hero whether you killed any of the enemy or not. You're better off than guys who got all shot up. At least you came back without a scratch. I didn't shoot you, you didn't shoot me, and I got a free tour of your country. I really liked the guy. You don't often find people with a sense of honor these days, just a bunch of mean assholes whose only capital is their cruelty. I told him, You don't have to be embarrassed or feel you owe me anything. You can take off when we're finished. These days it's hard to find anyone away from the front lines who thinks they owe anybody anything; they think everybody owes them. You're no worse than anyone else. Well I left him the next morning and didn't give it another thought. But a few days later I ran into him again, and he wouldn't let me go, saying he'd been searching for me from one end of town to the other. He didn't care about other people, and he wasn't going to let it end like that, not with his moral code. I'd taken his virginity, so now I was stuck with him. Marry a chicken and love that chicken, marry a dog and love that dog. I laughed. You don't know what kind of woman I am, I said. He said he knew. He told me he was a member of the Naxi minority. 'My people believe that the best women in the clan have the most lovers.' Maybe you don't have a problem with this, I told him, but I do. I'm not going to marry you. You'd make a good lover, but not much of a husband. Different obligations. Gushing emotions just won't cut it. You also have to provide material benefits to create a comfortable environment for your wife. Given your age and financial situation, you're stuck with being a kept man. I told him to go have some flings with younger girls until he'd saved up enough money to seriously consider marriage. He said I was immoral, called me a seductress. Then he laughed and said it wasn't just about money, that'd be too easy. I said go out and see if it's as easy as it sounds. I'm getting on in years and I'm still broke. That's why I'm shopping around for someone with money. That someone, he said, was him. He was going to start working on it that very day, and all he asked was that I promise not to run off with someone else who got there first. I said Don't worry, any man who's well heeled won't want me for a wife. So I'm perfect for you, he said. I'll be well heeled someday, and I'm already in love with you. I don't doubt your feelings, I told him. I hope you have the will to take on the two roles and the talent to be successful and happy at both. Not long after that he came to say that he was on to something, that some army buddies of his, meaning you guys, were working a deal with some priceless ruby that could be the mother lode. He said he could buy into this deal, which would make them all rich. He was going around borrowing from everyone he knew, and asked me to help borrow more, which would be repaid with interest within three months. So I took him to see some old schoolmates, and he acted like a big shot, bragging about how shrewd he was and how he had life all figured out. Those schoolmates, who lived pretty austere lives, stared bug-eyed. Anyone that ruthless and that savvy was destined for big things, as they saw it. Sure to become a successful business-man, he was their man of the hour. Only someone that confident would stop at nothing to achieve his goal. The truth was, he'd picked this all up a few days earlier from me and some other people. That stuff about a ruby was all bullshit, some crap you guys dreamed up over a glass bauble you took from the stinky shoe of Wang Ruohai's grannie, a modern-day *Arabian Nights* scam. And

Feng Xiaogang was the only one dumb enough to fall for it. Like a swarm of locusts, the seven or eight of you feasted for days on the money we brought you. Like being back in the Vietnam jungle, where he tried to fight a conventional war against an army of snipers, Feng Xiaogang dreamed of glory. But I realized that he was a guileless blockhead, a weak, doltish person who trusted to luck that someone would always be around to make things happen for him. You guys made sure he always got the short end of the stick. If there was anything good to be had, his turn never came. I told him he was lucky to have that Vietnam war experience, especially coming home without a scratch, since he could brag all he wanted about heroic deeds to people who hadn't gone. All of you have that same talent: As long as there are no witnesses, you can make it sound like the sky is raining flowers, make out as if your life has been one death-defying escapade after another. The fact that none of you has ever become a writer puzzles me. That would be the perfect career for your kind."

The young Li Jiangyun, or Liu Yan, was crying, tears slipping down both cheeks.

"I'm really sorry I didn't meet Feng Xiaogang earlier, when we were about ten years younger, then he and I wouldn't be hanging out with you guys and spending all our time bullshitting. You'd never see us. We'd lie low in some out of the way corner living the contented lives of average citizens. But how am I supposed to snuggle up to my dreamboat like a lovestruck teenager and live with my head in the clouds now? Sure, I could pretend nothing ever happened, that I was some innocent little girl, but it would be an act. And even if I could pull it off, he couldn't, because he knows too much. I taught him. It's over, I know that. There's no way back, the road ahead is no road at all. All I can do is pretend everything's fine, that hope lies ahead, then close my eyes and keep on walking. I love him, I do, and he still loves me. But we have to let go and strike out on our own. At some point we became such heavy burdens to each other that it was time to look after ourselves. To keep on sacrificing now is not only pointless, it's futile. If today is all I have to show for it, I'm sorry any of this ever happened. Being more experienced than him, I should have known that fine-sounding words and protestations of love, no matter who says them, are pure bullshit!"

Liu Yan unfolded her handkerchief to blow her nose, and had no sooner dried her eyes than tears were running down her cheeks again.

"You've still got a chance," I said. "If it were me, I could pretend that nothing had ever happened."

"Maybe you could, but I can't." Liu Yan smiled. "And how long could you keep it up? There's no way out. At most we can put off the inevitable for a while. If you guys hadn't sweet-talked us with that cock-and-bull story, somebody else would have done it with a different twist. We weren't meant to live together in peace."

The door opened and Qiao Qiao stuck her head in. "Oh!" she exclaimed, quickly backing out.

I got up and walked to the door to peek outside. The hallway was deserted. Hearing Gao Yang, Gao Jin, and the others talking loudly in the room across the way, I went over and knocked on the door. When Xia Hong saw who it was, she let me in. They were digging through a suitcase: panty hose and nylon blouses were strewn all over the bed. Gao Jin, obviously dejected, looked at the pile of cheap clothing and said:

"We claw and we scrape to play for thrills, and still we wind up with a Hong Kong working stiff."

I went back to my room, where Liu Yan was standing at the

mirror putting on lipstick. With her handbag slung over her shoulder and an umbrella in her hand, she said:

"The rain has stopped, so I'm going home. I'm sure Feng Xiaogang is still up. Sorry I'm not in the mood tonight. Maybe next time."

"That's all right," I said as I stepped back to let her by. "I felt like talking anyway." I smiled. "What you said made me . . . I don't know, it left a sour taste in my mouth."

"Don't say anything to your pals," she said light-heartedly. "They'll laugh at you."

"I won't," I said. "I won't say anything to anybody."

"And don't feel bad for me. It's all behind me now, it doesn't mean a thing." She laughed and headed for the door.

"Hey!"

"What?" She stopped in the doorway and turned back.

I laughed. "Don't come around here anymore. It's a bad crowd."

"I know. Thanks." She gazed into my eyes and smiled.

"It's not easy to find a good man."

"I'll keep that in mind." She nodded, opened the door, and was gone.

"It's not easy having a good man," I muttered. "A good man, not easy."

That night I went out for a stroll through the dark, rain-soaked, quiet city streets. I didn't meet another soul. The air was cold and damp, my mind uncommonly clear. I was in a childish mood, crying one minute and laughing excitedly the next, without a trace of embarrassment. I couldn't turn and head back. I didn't have the heart to face my friends.

The city turned blurry through my tears, until I couldn't tell you which streets I walked down or which buildings I saw. What

I do recall are the orange moon above and the orange streetlights around me, that and the way they merged to cover one identical street after another with a pale halo. My eyes opened wide in the darkness, but they might as well have been shut tight.

I could feel the passions boiling, but knew I'd have to let my thoughts moulder away in my heart. I'd be a laughingstock if I said anything to anyone.

It occurred to me that I was being absurd. Knowing how foolish I must look in this day and age, I told myself this was something nobody needed, especially me. It was time to calm down and head back as if nothing were wrong, revealing nothing.

I hated what I'd become. I was no child, after all. By the time I showed up at the hotel around dawn, I was my old self again, like someone coming home after a night of partying.

Day Six

Heavy traffic passed up and down the street under a blazing sun. Wherever you looked you saw ice cream vendors under white canopies. I spotted my friends on the grass under a betel palm, talking, laughing, eating ice cream cones, and verbally sizing up passersby.

"If you want to lead someone to the slaughter, there's the type. A fat cat if I ever saw one."

A portly, balding old guy with a shapely young woman on his arm walked by. Xu Xun pointed at the man: "Look how that son of a bitch walks, two thirds belly, the other third legs. He fattens up on the flesh and blood of the people, then saunters along with some girl on his arm."

"That pisses me off." Gao Yang, who had finished his ice cream cone, wiped his mouth. "The old bastard doesn't know he's supposed to devote his golden years to wholesome activities. He's just asking for a beating. Shall we give it to him?"

"Sure, why not?" Wang Ruohai stood with his hands on his hips, his head cocked. "Gao Yang and Xu Xun, you two trip the old fart up, then keep him down and make sure he doesn't get up. Feng Xiaogang, you and Gao Jin go through his pockets and take whatever he's got. I'll carry off the girl."

"You won't get much carrying her off," Gao Jin objected.

"What do you want with a rotten piece of goods like that? Aren't you afraid her crabs will migrate to your crotch? No, we tell the guy that one of us is the girl's brother, and lay into him, her too. Beat them both senseless. Then we threaten to drag the old fart to the police station, either that or back to our place."

"Right, that's what we do, we have the old fart write a statement of repentance," Gao Yang said. "That's like money in the bank. As for the girl, find a toilet somewhere and stuff her down it. Either that or stick an eight-*fen* postage stamp on her forehead and mail her to Heilongjiang. How does that sound? But first we'd better find out what she is to that old fart. We don't want to mess with any father and daughter."

By then the old man and the girl were way down the street.

"So what if they are? We'll just say we're busting them for incest."

A well-dressed middle-aged man walked by.

"What about this one?" Xu Xun squinted.

The others turned to look at the man. "We can take him too," said Gao Yang.

"For this one we need Qiao Qiao or Xia Hong," Xu Xun said. "Let them cozy up to him and see if he'll take the bait. If he does, we go up and claim to be family who hasn't eaten all day, then get the asshole to treat us to a decent meal for starters."

"Let him off the hook for one lousy meal?" Gao Yang said. "If we're going to take him, let's go all the way. Qiao Qiao works her magic, then we enter the picture. After he cops a feel or something like that, we go to his place and have a chat with the little woman. Wang Ruohai pretends he's the abused husband and asks the wife what she thinks ought to be done. Your husband has seduced my wife, he says, and if you don't make things right with some cash, I'll do the same to you."

"Be sure to take the cash anyway, even after you do it. And if she doesn't come across, the four of you will make one happy family. You'll give their kid a second mommy and daddy." Gao Yang laughed and turned to Qiao Qiao. "What do you say, Qiao Qiao? You up for it? It could be your meal ticket. I guarantee you they eat well at that jerk's house."

"Sure," Qiao Qiao replied from her seat on the grass, where she was nibbling melon seeds. "Food's food, who cares where you get it."

"Can you handle him?"

"No problem," Qiao Qiao said confidently as she watched the middle-aged man's retreating back. "A snap."

"Hey, here comes another," Gao Yang said softly. "How does she stack up?" They turned to watch a decked-out baby-faced girl coming their way.

"She's right up your alley," Qiao Qiao laughed.

"Here's how I see it with this one," Gao Yang said. "Gao Jin, you and Xu Xun go up and harass her like a couple of thugs, then I'll come to the rescue and you guys take off."

"No, you and Gao Jin be the thugs, and *I'll* come to the rescue."

"I'm not taking off for anybody," Gao Jin complained. "I'll be the hero and make you guys take off. In fact, let's just see who can really make the others take off."

"That sucks," Gao Yang said. "If we turn on one another, I mean. Because while we're doing that, the girl takes off. Someone like her, the minute you approach her, she's off and running, leaving you *and* the thugs behind. I've got my reasons for letting you guys be the thugs. I'm more tactful than you. Do you think you're up to saying what she wants to hear about the ideal life? Think you can do a better job than me? First we elevate her consciousness by convincing her that material objects and money are dirty and vulgar, then we retrieve whatever she tosses away, looking as hypocritical as possible, which will disgust her. She won't know what's what, and money will no longer mean anything to her. She'll be contemptuous of us for the rest of her life, and if we ever run into her again she'll pretend she doesn't know us."

Everyone laughed. "What do you say? Make sense?" Gao Yang asked.

They laughed harder. The girl turned to see what was so funny. Gao Yang, who was laughing loudest of all, saw her turn. "Uh-oh, she's seen me hobnobbing with the thugs."

"Quit dreaming," Gao Jin said. "That scam's so old it won't fool anybody these days. Only poor people will talk to you about ideals. Anyone who's got it knows that money talks."

"But don't forget that people with money to burn are always looking for ways to save their souls."

"Look, you guys, here comes another one. We'll happily be the thugs and let you rush up to save the day. Would you look at that gold ring!"

An old lady in a black gauze dress limped toward them. Her wrinkled face looked like a peach pit. She knew they were laughing at her, but when she showed the whites of her eyes in disgust, that just made things worse.

"You shouldn't be having fun at her expense," Gao Yang said reproachfully. "Not a kindly old lady who looks like the immortal matriarch herself, someone who never hurt anybody. Take your time, old mother, don't worry!"

When the old lady saw that Gao Yang was shouting at her, she showed the whites of her eyes again, though she had no idea what he was saying.

They laughed so hard they looked like they were on rocking

horses. A country boy in shorts and sandals walked by with a carrying pole over his shoulder and immediately fell under their scrutiny. "How about this one?" Xu Xun asked Gao Yang.

"Nothing doing," he said. "He's worse off than we are."

"That shows how much you know," Xu Xun said. "Yokels have all the money these days. Don't be fooled by his dirty face. He's probably got stacks of money under his mattress at home."

"Then let's hand Qiao Qiao over to him." Gao Yang turned and waved to her. "Give the yokel what he wants for a few days, then put rat poison in his food. Everything he owns will be yours."

"Up yours," she said as she sucked a melon seed out of its husk. "Why not ask your precious Xia Hong to poison the yokel?"

Gao Yang turned and smiled at Xia Hong, who was sitting off to the side. "Xia Hong isn't right for this job. She's not his type. They like their women chunky. When they take a wife, they put her on the scales and figure the dowry by her weight."

"Then you go do it, since you beat us all where pounds and ounces are concerned."

"What are you afraid of? You don't think you're too good for our peasant brothers, do you? Yokels are people too, so what's the big deal? Take brother Feng here, who went to Vietnam and came back with a third-class commendation medal after seeing neither hide nor hair of the enemy. He made out OK."

Everyone turned and smiled at Feng Xiaogang, who was sitting on the grass; he returned the smile, sheepishly.

"You guys suck. Talk, talk, talk, and now it comes around to me."

"Dear brother Feng," Gao Yang said after walking over and sitting on the grass by him, "if I'd been you in Vietnam, I'd have found some deserted spot and put a bullet in me someplace, then pretended I was wounded in battle. You'd have come home with a lot more than a third-class commendation medal. They might have called you a hero, and you wouldn't have to be putting up with all these vile characters and their taunts. This way it's almost like your going to Vietnam was all talk and no action."

"You're the only man of action, is that it?" complained Liu Yan, who was sitting up against the betel palm. "While you've been wagging your tongues, waves of people have passed by, and they've all escaped unharmed."

"What would people think if we actually did all these things we've been talking about?"

"They'd think a company of paratroopers had appeared out of the sky," Feng Xiaogang said.

Baishan and I, laughing and talking, and sharing a parasol, made our way down the crowded sidewalk toward them. Heavy traffic passed up and down the street under a blazing sun. Wherever you looked you saw ice cream vendors under white canopies; shaded sidewalks were alive with jostling pedestrians. I spotted my friends at a tiny, run-down ice cream shop; they were eating plain old ice cream and watching people pass up and down the sidewalk in front of them.

"If I had an assault rifle in my hands right now, I'd step outside and *brrrp* spray the area. What do you think people would do?" Gao Yang fired his imaginary weapon for Feng Xiaogang.

"More of them would be trampled to death than killed by your bullets," Feng Xiaogang said.

"What if we all had weapons?"

"Then the city would be under our military control. We'd shoot our way into the municipal government to bring back the commune, where we'd form a revolutionary council and take turns holding the reins of power."

"I don't need the reins of power," Xu Xun interjected. "Put me in charge of literary and artistic activities, and I'll be happy."

"I'll take trade and tourism," Wang Ruohai said. "From now on, when you guys come to my restaurant, I'll pay you to eat there."

"Gao Jin gets public security, taxes, and customs. And Fang Yan, he can have family planning and patriotic hygienic campaigns."

"All banks and industries will be nationalized," Gao Jin said. "Small businesses and peddlers will be heavily taxed."

"A Northern Expedition?"* Gao Yang asked.

"No, why have another one of those?" Gao Jin replied. "We've gained our independence. If we can't set up a central government, we go for regional autonomy. The distaff members can be our permanent representatives to the central government."

"Oh, great, send us into the mouth of the tiger. We suffer so they can hold the reins of power, is that it?" Qiao Qiao laughed. "Well, if we can't contend for the lucrative posts, how about mass organizations like women's federations or labor unions?"

"No way," Gao Yang said. "You know too much. We can't keep you around. Your mouths must be sealed. I'll have to do the same with them too, one at a time. No witnesses. I have to kill them when I take power, don't I, Gao Jin? All prominent individuals, old fogies and young diehards, must face the firing squad."

*A joint expedition (1926–1928) by Nationalist and Communist forces against northern warlords.

"You can't start executing people right off," Gao Jin said. "You have to use them as hostages and lock them up first. Then, whenever trouble breaks out, you shoot one of the leaders from that locale as a warning. Hitler's way."

"Right, we can't repeat the mistakes of the Paris Commune," Gao Yang announced with a laugh. "I need to use an iron fist, that's the only way to consolidate power. Burning some books and burying a few Confucians alive, big deal.* When we start the killing, there will be rivers of blood. If you guys want to go on living in the new society, you'd better start treating me a little better. For instance, if one of you has some money on him, now would be a good time to buy me a decent meal. Once I'm in power, past friendships count for nothing. You could come crawling on your knees, and the best you could hope for was being sent to a concentration camp."

"What if the rest of us joined forces to kill you?" Xu Xun laughed. "Because by then we'd all have fiefdoms and troops under our command."

"Then we'll launch a cultural revolution," Gao Yang replied. "You'll be criticized and ostracized and trampled under the feet of the proletariat."

They loved every minute of it. Xia Hong was laughing so hard she accidentally knocked a plate off the table and sent it crashing to the floor. Gao Yang told the waiter who came up when he heard the sound of splintering dinnerware, "We'll pay for it, put it on our bill." After he paid the check, he stuffed the well-worn wallet back into his pocket, shook his head and sighed. "A fallen hero," he said, "a fallen hero."

---

*A reference to Qin Shihuang, the "First Emperor," who burned Confucian classics and buried Confucian scholars alive in 213 B.C.

"Let's take the fucking fallen hero while he's down," Xu Xun said to the others. "After all, what's good for him isn't necessarily good for the rest of us."

He reached over and gave Gao Yang's arm a hard twist, and the two of them were at each other.

Liu Yan glanced over at Feng Xiaogang. They exchanged perplexed smiles.

Heavy traffic passed up and down the street under a blazing sun. Wherever you looked you saw ice cream vendors under white canopies. Baishan and I, sharing a parasol, made our way down the crowded sidewalk toward them; my friends emerged from an ice cream shop and stood in the sun shouting at me, laughing and making a scene. Baishan and I smiled from under our parasol, waved at them, and continued on our way. Shaded sidewalks were alive with jostling pedestrians. Everywhere you looked you saw ice cream vendors under white canopies; heavy traffic passed up and down the street under a blazing sun.

Day Four, Day Three . . .

Everyone seemed to be on the move in the noisy, cavernous airport terminal: Loaded-down baggage carts threaded their way through the crowds, the feminine, cottony voice of a public-address announcer reverberated beneath the ceiling; people at service counters talked on the telephone, others stood in clusters engaged in genial conversation, still others dozed on sofas under massive sunlit windows. Sleek, silvery airplanes glided along the tarmac, and beyond them, open fields, irrigation ditches, and the hazy outline of a mountain chain were mantled by the sun's rays. The blue sky seemed washed clean. An airplane, contrails in its wake, climbed into the sky like a big bird, head up and wings outstretched, never veering out of the field of vision as it grew smaller and smaller.

There in the crowd I spotted Wang Kuanglin, the cripple, dressed in a Western suit and sitting stiffly on a sofa near the window, his face haloed in bright sunlight. I only saw him clearly from the neck down; he was wearing a fancy striped shirt under a dark suitcoat. He held a lit king-sized cigarette in his long, thin, ring-adorned fingers; his highly polished platform leather shoes glinted. A row of ticket counters stood opposite him. Gao Yang and I, who were standing alongside a luggage scale shooting the breeze with a female lounge attendant, were cut off from the streams of passengers. Gao Yang all but disappeared among the men and women queuing up for boarding passes, but I moved to the side, away from traffic. Then out of the crowd appeared Liu Yan and Feng Xiaogang, happily rolling their luggage down the ramp. Liu Yan, dressed in a gaudy white dress and heavily made up, stood out in the crowd. Feng Xiaogang stopped in a dim corner and was quickly separated from her by the mass of humanity. As I looked up, my gaze bored through the crowd to meet that of Liu Yan, who flashed me a radiant smile. Gao Yang turned when I nudged him, took a quick glance, then sprawled back over the counter to continue his conversation. I took off, but before I reached Liu Yan, Gao Yang ran up behind me, just as a Japanese tour group, farmers from Yamaguchi Prefecture in identical white sun visors and paddling along behind a flag-waving guide, crossed the terminal like athletes entering a stadium, momentarily swallowing us up in their midst. Once they had passed, and the crush of passengers with boarding passes had thinned out, she and I sat on a sofa in back of a terrazzo column, talking with our voices and with our eyes. Gao Yang and Feng Xiaogang were standing behind a tall ash receptacle with a China Airlines logo alongside the column. Liu Yan and I were alone. She said something that made me laugh. Another tour group, this one made up of larger Americans—gray-haired, pasty-faced, hairy men and women, breasts and paunches thrust out ahead of them—passed in front of us, carrying and dragging their luggage along.

A red taxicab appeared intermittently in the traffic up ahead.

The city was swathed in blazing sunlight; upscale boutiques and elegant hotels whizzed past the windows of our taxi, the crowds of shoppers a feast for the eyes. In this busy section of town, billboards and neon signs vied for attention; street after street was lined with shops; crowds of people jostled each other, bumper-to-bumper traffic filled the streets, combining to create a colorful lively dazzling human tableau in the bright light of day.

Windows on tall buildings and ground-floor shop windows reflected the sunlight like mirrors.

On a shaded street a low, wavy wall topped by green tiles and bamboo offered views of a park, with lakes and hills and flower beds, through uniquely shaped openings every few paces.

A river of dark green, seemingly stagnant water, on which clumps of duckweed floated, appeared by the roadside. On the opposite bank, lush green, long-stemmed, fan-leafed trees danced and swayed.

The red taxi drove past a tall white building and pulled up in front of a fancy arched entrance with raised red lanterns. I watched the bunch of us climb out of a taxi and walk single file under that fancy arch.

The interior was as resplendent as a palace setting in one of those old-fashioned plays. Dazzling light flooded the place with color. Sexy waitresses in satin cheongsams embroidered with dragons and phoenixes strutted like fashion models on a runway. Four or five hundred men and women, dressed to kill, sat at tables enjoying their food and drink. We were at an oval sourwood table inlaid with mirrors, reflecting another, perfectly identical group of diners. Exchanging smiles all around, we spread out our napkins and poured tea; the overhead light froze the smiles on our waxen faces.

In front of us, in an array of gorgeous silver serving bowls, lay a sumptuous spread.

Gao Yang, pasty-faced, his lips reddened, said, "If you've got the guts to do it, the money will come pouring in."

"If you've got the guts to think it, I've got the guts to do it," said Feng Xiaogang, pasty-faced, his lips reddened. "With my steely heart, I'm not afraid to kill."

"If you've got the heart to eat a child,* anything's possible." Gao Yang, pasty-faced, his lips reddened, pointed to each of us at the table. "Men of action, every one of them," he said. "We've turned this place upside down. If you join us, we can have some real fun."

The rest of us, male and female, pasty-faced, our lips reddened, laughed and looked at Feng Xiaogang.

"We've got to do it, that's all there is to it. Others are doing it. Greedy, bumbling people are getting rich, damn it."

"We held back because we're such good citizens. What's going to stop us from doing it now? You mean to say we can't kick ass like they can? The Vietnamese, they weren't hard enough to handle? The Americans weren't up to it, and had to call us in."

"We do it right or we don't do it at all, big-time, till heaven and earth tremble, till ghosts wail. We're a bunch of guys whose bellies are filled with bad water. Things the Blueshirts† never imagined, we're out there doing. Nothing in heaven or on earth, whether it flies in the air or runs on the ground, can escape our clutches. We embody the spirit of the nation."

"Let's do it, guys. It's not every day you find a bunch of guys in total agreement like this. We can't limp through life. Let's show them what we're made of. We're models in everything, from production to street fighting."

---

*The obvious reference is to the story "A Madman's Diary" (1918) by Lu Xun, a near-canonical attack on China's cannibalistic society. It may also be a sardonic allusion to the famous statement attributed to Mengzi (Mencius) about having "the heart of a child."
†A military and secret police organization formed by Chiang Kai-shek in the 1930s.

"I despise people who only talk a good fight. Either you keep your mouth shut, or you back up your words with thunderclaps."

"Take me, for example. I'm like a sleeping leopard. I'm hard to arouse, but once I begin to stir, I'm a liver-crushing, gall-draining force. Is there a man alive I'm afraid of? Get me started, and I'll snare the wind and carry thunderbolts. You can run but you can't hide. I'll take other people on the same way I took on the Vietnamese!"

"We're all like that. We may look stupid, but that's just an illusion."

Feng Xiaogang laughed as he raised his glass. "Anybody who runs into us from tomorrow on will wish they hadn't."

"Bring 'em on. They'll get what's coming to them!" Gao Yang said truculently.

Faces in the mirrors, male and female, were smiling. Liu Yan, pasty-faced, her lips reddened, looked at me; I returned the look. Dazzling light flooded the place with color. Sexy waitresses in satin cheongsams embroidered with dragons and phoenixes strutted like fashion models on a runway. Lovely figures radiant smiles blurred images reflected in mirrors shimmering in window glass.

Lights in the resplendent nightclub dimmed. A white taxi turned the corner and sped down the tree-dappled street. The moon was clear and bright, people jostled one another; the street ran parallel to a murmuring stream hidden in the dark; tropical fan-leafed foliage rustled in the breeze; a low wall under bamboo cover rolled like a petrified wave into the darkness.

A row of bright storefront windows shone like a hall of mirrors. People streamed past like schooling fish in an aquarium.

I saw tree-lined streets, some light, some dark, neon-reflecting leaves turned from red to green; I saw public squares, some actually round, crowded with people and sculptures.

The taxi pulled up to the gray hotel on a dark, deserted street, and stopped. Ling Yu and I stepped out of the taxi, which pulled away from the curb. She looked up at the hotel windows, light reflected in her smiling eyes. "This is where you're staying?"

"Not bad, hmm?" I said with a smile. "Come on up, the rooms are classy."

A yellow haze from overhead lights filled the corridor.

Flickering television glare emerged from the rooms. Muffled dialog and background music swirled in the narrow corridor: the shouts of men in battle, the rumble of tanks, the *brrrp brrrp* of assault rifles, the *whoosh* of rockets, the swell of a grand symphony, men's voices raised in glorious song, jet bombers shrieking across the sky, followed by the thud of exploding bombs.

My stomach was killing me—stabbing pains like a bladder about to burst. My mouth was filled with a sweet, fermented taste.

The room was pitch black, except for moonlight filtering in through the window shade. Figures flickered as in a shadow play. A moist mouth breathed warmly on my face. I detected the heavy perfume of violets, reminding me of the disagreeable yet intoxicating musk smell that seeps out of cages at the zoo.

She descended out of thin air, like a child slipping down a slide cross-legged. Ripples of contentment washed over me.

I grabbed a meaty handful of taut, quivering flesh. It was real, all right.

Someone was dialing a telephone in the next room. I heard the clicking sound of the dial on its return. That's all, no one saying anything, just the clicking sound, over and over and over—click click click.

The window curtain fluttered, moonbeams like frost, she was murmuring: "I love you I love you." The words lingered in the air. Warm skin and soft strands of hair brushed my cheek unbridled passions creaking bed springs like oars in their locks her body arching like a proud steed.

Down deep, I was aroused, enlivened; a wave descending from the distant heavens, ever clearer, ever more powerful, like ten thousand pounding hooves.

A sound, a single utterance, repeated itself in the room, like something I was saying to her but also like something she was saying to me, and getting louder all the time, as if an enormous face were speaking into a microphone, or a phonograph record were spinning round and round under a stationary needle: I love you I love you.

The plug was yanked out of the drain, sending a tubful of hot water spurting onto the tile floor, slippery, gurgling lightly, glisteningly transparent; the soles of my feet were hot, gusts of cool wind blew in.

Late that night, limpid moonbeams seeped into the room, the starry sky twinkled like a glazed bowl suspended upside down; the furnishings were all a blur. Beside me, a recumbent body like that of a white lamb, as if lying under the stars in a wakeful sleep.

The telephone rang, seemingly just as I dozed off. The noise seemed to come from an empty room, a rhythmic ringing followed by a pause, then another series of rings; no one answered.

The sun was out. Cars drove up and down the street, pedestrians strolled the sidewalks; a morning fog eddied atop the grass over which tropical foliage grew. Glistening beads of water dripped from leaf tips; a sunbeam poked a hole in the fog, then made more room for itself by expanding, boring through the mist and burning it off, sending steam skyward. Buildings and roadways came into view; the outlines of cars and pedestrians sharpened. Next to the road, hidden beneath the fanned leaves of French umbrella trees I saw a little river whose dark green water seemed frozen in place. Down a mossy path I walked, smiling broadly and heading straight for a girl coming my way. With a face like an open fan, gentle and tranquil, a soft, silver-gray Naugahyde handbag slung over the shoulder of her elegantly simple dress, she turned heads as she passed. Next to a heart-shaped opening in the low, wavy wall I blocked her way, flashed a smile, and said, "Haven't we met somewhere before?"

The girl gazed at me innocently without saying a word.

Another smile. "I just came to town yesterday," I said, "but I can't help feeling I've run into you here before, and more than once, that we often come here to take walks. What is this place? When was it that we met? Do you remember me?"

She nodded, then shook her head.

"Are we strangers or were we fated to be together? Why do we meet so often but have never spoken? You look at me and I look at you, but are we no different from these other people?"

She was like a necklace of dewdrops, transparent, fresh, seemingly about to roll off the tip of a leaf and merge with the moss on the slippery ground.

"I'd like to remember you," I said tenderly. "Tell me, what's your name? Where are you from? Where are you going? Where do you live? What do you do? Say something, why don't you?"

"It wouldn't do any good," the girl said softly. "You'd just forget."

"This is a dream, isn't it?" I asked with a smile. "This is all a dream. Who are you, anyway? And what are you doing in my dream? Are you real?"

"I'd like to know who you are, and what you're doing in *my* dream." She smiled, her face reddened.

"My name is Fang Yan, and I'm a bad person. I live in a city far away to the north."

"My name is Ling Yu, and I'm a good person."

"Good person bad person, since this is a dream, it makes no difference." I took her arm and we walked alongside the long, low, wavy wall. "No need to be afraid, or to worry that the bad person will take advantage of the good one, since we'll wake up sooner or later and both be in our own beds miles apart. We'll forget all this. At worst, it will have been a tearful nightmare, then you'll wake up and realize that none of it ever happened. Dreams have nothing to do with real life."

"Why won't you take me along and make it a good dream? Don't we decide what happens in our dreams?"

"If that's what you want," I said with a laugh and a long look. "Let's work to make this a good dream."

"Just the two of us. We won't let anyone else into our dream."

"No, we won't," I assured her. "We have the right to control our own dreams."

Day One

It was a large, polygon-shaped public square, bordered on all sides by tiers of tall buildings, old and new, in a variety of architectural styles: tapered roofs, flat roofs, one seemingly on top of the other, some poking holes in the sky, others stretching the length of avenues. In the sunlight the windows, from the top floors all the way to the ground, looked like neat rows of eyes looking down from all sides. One end of the square was occupied by a reviewing stand not unlike the bleacher section of a soccer stadium, complete with railings and concrete steps. On festivals and other important occasions, party leaders, both civil and military, stood on this spot, at different levels like choir boys, to view minor military parades or processions of local residents and to deliver important speeches or exhort the people on. At the moment the stand was deserted but for some young mothers climbing on it with toddlers in tow. The square had its flagpole, and on festivals and other important occasions, or when eminent people have passed on, the Chinese flag fluttered or drooped from its heights. At that moment, the flagpole was bare. All the way across the square, opposite the flagpole, was a large, newly built pool. On festivals and other important occasions, its fountain spewed columns of water, set off by bright lights and music. At that moment it was dry, a repository for ice cream wrappers and soft-drink cans. I saw Fang Yan and his friends sitting on colored stones around the edge of the pool; everyone was holding a candy bar in one hand and a cigarette in the other, legs dangling over the side, all crew-cut and dressed in baggy army pants, so young they could be high school kids playing hooky. Somber-faced adults walked around them with young children, stopping every now and then to take a picture of one or another tall building. Hordes of taxis sped down the tree-shaded streets on two sides of the square, pulled up in front of the luxury hotels, nightclubs, and office buildings, then sped off again. At the far end of the square, where the field of vision narrowed, they crossed a mammoth black suspension bridge with thick steel cables that fed into a tight network of avenues. A wide river flowed sluggishly under the bridge; steamships, tugboats, and barges churned the yellow river as they sailed past, whistles bouncing dully off the water's edge and drifting weakly over to the square.

The pavement baked in the sun; people were stifled by the steamy air; their thin shirts and blouses and shorts and skirts fluttered in the occasional breeze. Fang Yan and his friends squinted into the blinding sun and smiled.

"I like it here," Fang Yan said happily as he took in the view around the square. "I really take to the sun-drenched southern cities. I enjoy seeing elegant homes and handsome, well-dressed people."

"We want only the finest accommodations and the best food," Xu Xun said. "Before I came here I promised myself I'd sample every delicacy there was. A little extravagance is in order."

"I second that," Wang Ruohai said. "After all our sacrifices over the years, we've earned the right to enjoy ourselves for a change."

"Would you look at yourselves, a bunch of yokels from up

north." Gao Yang laughed as he sized up his friends, who had just been discharged from the army. "What makes you think you deserve to enjoy yourself here?"

"We've got money," Fang Yan said with a laugh. "Our mustering-out pay, several hundred RMB apiece. At least a thousand if we put it all together."

"A thousand isn't worth shit!* And a few hundred? Balls! All the money you earned for those years as a soldier won't buy you one decent meal. You talk about all the food you're going to put away. Hell, I could sell the lot of you and still not have enough. When Gao Jin and I first came here, we spent as carefully as we could, and within three days we were reduced to eating fried rice noodles. I was in the army longer than any of you, so I got more mustering-out pay. If you plan to stick around, find a way to make some money or learn to do without."

"Hey, we're not going to settle down here. We'll play around for a few days, and when the money's gone, we'll leave."

"Then you'd better leave now, since the money you've got is probably just about enough for traveling expenses. If you want to stay a night or two, take it easy, and forget about hitting the hot spots. Settle for a bowl of stew."

"Why should we do without?" Xu Xun complained, his eyes wide. "Who are we, anyway? We've always been the cream of the crop. We're people who eat meat while others drink soup, and this is no time to change."

"I don't believe it," Wang Ruohai protested loudly. "How could a great place like this not hold anything for us? Who are the masters of the nation? I'll send my troops to level the place."

"What the fuck are you bragging about?" Gao Jin laughed.

---

*Literally, "thousand pieces of gold," a metaphor for a girl or daughter.

"All you can send are service personnel, a grand total of three men. If you really want to make it here, you'll do better selling knock-off digital watches than sending some army over."

"Me? Do that? I'd die first. You won't catch me sinking that low. That's no job for a man, especially someone groomed to be Chief of Naval Operations."

"Right," Fang Yan agreed. "Don't lump us together with those people. Let those fuckheads make their fortune, then when they've got enough, we come at them with a one-hit-and-three-anti's campaign,* and confiscate everything. We can manage as well without money as other people can with it. Don't they know where they are? Whose world is this? Capitalism is firmly in place."

"Then you guys just be patient and wait till the country comes to bail you out."

"Ignore them," Gao Yang said to Gao Jin. "They've got their heads in the clouds. Give them a couple of days here, and just watch them change. What good is money? Lots of good. There are two kinds of people who don't know the value of money: Those who are born with it and those who have never tasted its joys. Pretending you're high-principled nobility is stupid. Where will you find China's nobility? They're in power now, but thirty years ago they were a bunch of cowherds. Close down the national treasury, and they'll all be out on the streets begging."

Just then a building on the edge of the square caught fire. Flames licked out of the upper-floor windows, lapping at the shiny aluminum window frames and beige outer walls, tongues

*A Cultural Revolution campaign (1970) against corruption, embezzlement, and privateering.

of fire turning everything sooty black. Glass and metal softened and turned molten in the searing flames. Windows on the next floor down caught fire, and before long half the building was engaged, flames burning through the roof and leaping into the bright sky, now painted red. Clouds of black smoke billowed upward to foul the vast blue sky. Speeding fire engines dragged siren wails behind them as they converged on the square.

"I'm tired of all those people who have no capital but act like they're members of the nobility, the upper class," Gao Yang said ferociously. "The responsibility of our age is to bury people like that, eliminate their kind from the face of the earth before they spawn another generation. Of course, their demise won't match that of the descendants of the Manchu dynasty, who at least left behind treasures that could be pawned for cash. All these people have at home is ugly government-issue furniture."

The high-rise was now a towering inferno, an enormous pine-bright torch. In the radiant sunlight the flames were the reddest of reds. A crowd had formed in front of the building; fire crews threw up ladders; silvery jets of water arched toward the rooftop; firemen's helmets glinted in the sun. Water sprayed everywhere, glittery and crystalline, flames leaped into the red and black sky, burning fiercely, a wanton display of might high up; rooftops, some flat, others tapered, were bathed in serenely stupefying sunbeams.

Off in the distance, I saw palm trees sharing the square with shifting throngs of people; I watched taxis flock to and from the station like birds on the wing; I watched people stream into and out of the station like tiny black ants. I watched a train leave the vaulted platform at the rear of the station, weave through city streets and past suburban houses, then head out into open spaces, through villages, across rivers, and past factories that dotted the countryside like stars in the sky or men on a chessboard; the train was a squat black caterpillar wriggling between heaven and earth. Even farther off in the distance, whitecaps hit the serpentine sea-shore, rising and falling like a slithering python, coiling and un-coiling, looping this way and slipping that. The Eastern Sea flowed toward the Western Ocean; a naval fleet rode the winds and cut through the waves, leaving an oily film that spread across the blue, wave-tossed ocean. Weaving this way and that, the short train cut across rivers and streams that dissected the land, crossed long mountain ranges that rose and fell like ridges of bone, passed over blackened hills, cracked and dry, vast and un-populated. Like a bead from a broken strand, I rushed toward the boundless land, and in that urgent state, there, settling earthward in the distance, I saw another Fang Yan.

I am sitting beside a window aboard a rumbling train, reading a book, it seems. Open fields whiz past, off in the distance there are villages and chimney smoke. A tiny bird streaking through the air plummets as if shot out of the sky; white clouds follow the train's progress. The protagonist of my book is a compulsive gambler who never does an honest day's work. One day he finds himself suspected of murder. Forced to delve into his memories by calling on old friends, he produces a book of life that is missing seven of its pages. I read how he takes extraordinary measures to ferret out old ghosts, all the way back to his youth, but to no avail. How stupid he is, running back and forth without a clue as to how anything might turn out. A deadbeat too far gone, he looks smug in his navy blues on his return to a rusting warship. The author appears reluctant to lay down his pen, wanting to keep at his copious excesses and take this fellow all the way back to his mother's womb. I don't feel like reading any more, since I figure he'll end up a chubby little darling with laughing eyes who waves his hands and sucks on a baby bottle as he's pushed around town in his stroller, rocking back and forth, loved by all who see him.

I close the book after getting through about a third of it; the pages I've already read and those I'll never get to are as different as: black and white.